… for the series

'…ocative, original world-building and a wonderfully feisty heroine: …p marks to Lucy Hounsom'
KAREN MILLER

'I thought it was great, reminding me of Trudi Canavan; it had me turning pages way into the night . . . What a mix: immersive world-building, secret societies, a flawed and hugely likeable protagonist, and awesome magic . . . be warned, this book will seriously damage your sleep'
JOHN GWYNNE

'A brave heroine, a perilous destiny, and an intriguing world full of myth and mystery make for an enthralling read'
GAIL Z. MARTIN

'Has all the elements to become a modern classic of the genre. It's essentially a coming-of-age story that breaks out into a wide-screen fantasy extravaganza with huge stakes'   *Independent on Sunday*

'*Starborn* is a solidly crafted, accessible, big fat fantasy book that you can immerse yourself in. It is a tale that both comforts and surprises, and is pleasingly assured for a debut novel'
SFFWorld.com

'A genuinely impressive debut, and Lucy Hounsom is definitely one to watch'   *The Bookbag*

'Strong and engaging . . . Hounsom's use of characters is quite unique …   *SFBook*

'Highly …   …ook Review

BY LUCY HOUNSOM

The Worldmaker Trilogy
Starborn
Heartland
Firestorm

HEARTLAND

Lucy Hounsom works for Waterstones and has a BA in English and Creative Writing from Royal Holloway. She went on to complete an MA in Creative Writing under Andrew Motion in 2010. Her first novel in the Worldmaker trilogy, *Starborn*, was shortlisted for The Gemmell Morningstar Award for Best Debut.

lucyhounsom.co.uk

Lucy Hounsom

HEARTLAND

The Worldmaker Trilogy:
Book Two

*

Map artwork © Hannah Ayers

Typeset by Ellipsis, Glasgow
Printed and bound by CPI Group (UK) Ltd, Croydon, CR0 4YY

PAN BOOKS

First published 2017 by Pan Books
an imprint of Pan Macmillan
20 New Wharf Road, London N1 9RR
Associated companies throughout the world
www.panmacmillan.com

ISBN 978-1-4472-6862-8

Visit www.panmacmillan.com to read more about all our books
and to buy them. You will also find features, author interviews and
news of any author events, and you can sign up for e-newsletters
so that you're always first to hear about our new releases.

For Iris, grandmother and inspiration

ACKNOWLEDGEMENTS

A huge thank you to my editors, Bella Pagan and Julie Crisp, who helped me hone this rambling collection of ideas into a novel. Your comments have always been spot-on and I'm incredibly grateful for the support and encouragement you've shown a new author who is still very much in need of guidance.

Thanks to my agent, Veronique Baxter, for allaying my fears over many a coffee and looking after the details. You're endlessly supportive of me and my work and I am very lucky to have you.

To all of Team Tor and Pan Macmillan: wow. I give you my word document and you turn it into a beautiful book that (hopefully!) people will want to read. From copy-editing and design to PR, sales and marketing, thank you for all your hard work. Seeing my words in print will never cease to amaze me.

Thank you to all the booksellers who supported *Starborn* and special thanks to my Waterstones manager, Helen, who has done so much in-store to help promote my book. It's deeply appreciated.

I'm fortunate to have a family who fully endorses my decision to live outside reality. Much love always to the parents for being the best and for reading *Heartland* as it was written, and thanks to my sister for helping me straighten the kinks. In the months since *Starborn* was published, my aunt and uncle have bought the book, spread the word and helped me whenever I needed a place to stay. Thank you, Cheryl and Dave, for being so generous, for feeding me and letting me camp out in your house.

And to all the readers who've contacted me to say they enjoyed my book, or took the time to seek me out at conventions: *thank you*. Your encouragement means the world to me.

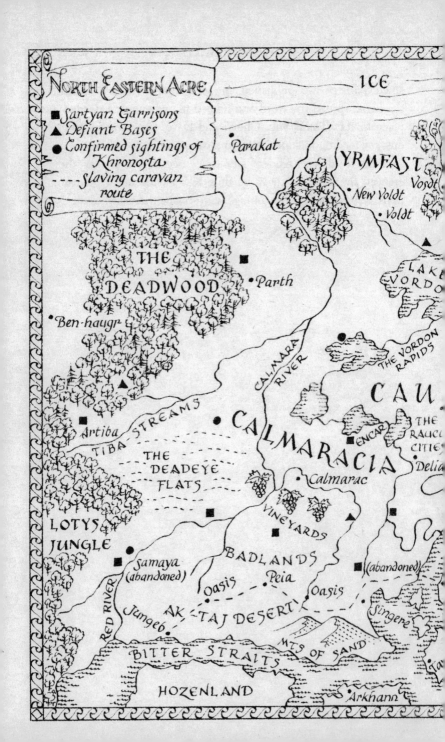

My stars shine darkly over me: the malignancy of my fate might perhaps distemper yours.

Twelfth Night
Shakespeare

A heavy weight of hours has chained and bowed
One too like thee: tameless, and swift, and proud.

'*Ode to the West Wind*'
Percy Bysshe Shelley

These are the Watchers, Noruri, Soruri, Austri and Vestri: the compass stars of North, South, East and West. As for the countless other stars, it is difficult to assign meaning, at least in human terms. The stars are ancient, everlasting and powerful beyond our comprehension. As their avatar, I can only offer a reader the simplest of labels – language is so unequal to the task.

Sigel – a ruinous star, its name roughly translates to fire and force.
Wynn – Sigel's sibling, the greater wind.
Lagus – another sibling of Sigel, it has power over all water.
Tyr – relentless, the warrior.
Hagal – the demon star, whose name means shadow.
Isa and Yeras – the bridges over the void.
Ansu – one that listens.
Pyrth – the preserver of secrets.
Thurn – a binding star, it holds, tangles, imprisons.
Fas – unseen, unheard, invisible.
Raad – to move swiftly.
Mannas – the star of finding.
Etoh – cleansing, ending.

*Page 3 of an incomplete compendium authored
by Kierik of Maeran, donated to the archives of Solinaris
and preserved after its fall by the Nerian, the people of the Saviour.*

PART ONE

I

The emperor's bedchamber was as lavish as the rest of the palace. Rare black ken – the little stones used as Acrean currency – gleamed from the walls where they had been used as common mosaic tiles. Most people preferred to keep their money in their purses, but the current Davaratch tended towards ostentation. Davaratch was the emperor who'd led Sartya to ascendancy centuries before; now every subsequent ruler took his name as royal title. *This* Davaratch was the twenty-first in his line and Hagdon found him reclining on top of the vast bed, surrounded by young men – all scions of noble houses. Their painted faces were careful, cautious.

General Hagdon of the Sartyan Fist looked away with a barely concealed grimace. The scene reminded him uncomfortably of his nephew; he couldn't help but picture the circumstances in which Tristan had died. When he made his report, however, his voice sounded flat and emotionless.

'Land to the east?' the emperor asked, sitting up.

'Uncharted,' Hagdon said. 'Our maps are useless.'

5

The Davaratch grunted and rose, shrugging into a robe. Standing, he towered well over six feet. An irritated flicker of fingers from his single hand sent the semi-clothed boys scurrying out of the door.

'Have them disposed of, Hagdon.' The emperor's dark eyes were chill. 'You ought to speak more carefully. I deplore the waste of young life.'

Cold gripped Hagdon's belly. 'Sire, nothing of import was said—'

'Was it not?' Those black eyes seemed to sink deeper into their sockets. 'I will not permit such news to reach Khronosta.'

'Our scouts report the land is in eastern Baior, sire,' Hagdon informed him quietly, 'on the other side of the hoarlands.'

'There is nothing on the other side of the hoarlands.'

Hagdon hesitated. 'You are of course right, sire, but—'

The Davaratch stopped him with a glare. 'Get Shune. We'll ask him.'

'At once.' Hagdon moved to the double doors, grasped a gilded handle. 'His Imperial Majesty wishes to see the Relator,' he barked at one of the red-mailed men standing guard outside. 'Inform him.'

The soldier smacked his fist to his shoulder and hurried away.

For such a large man, the Davaratch moved softly. He was already poring over the detailed relief of Acre set in a corner of the room. Hagdon joined him, following the curve of the Ak-Taj Desert further east to Baior. It was a poor region of rocky earth where crops regularly failed. Peasants' country. The hoarlands opened on to Baior's eastern frontier and Hagdon suppressed a shiver – people tended to vanish there. He'd lost an entire regiment several years ago.

The Davaratch wet the tip of his finger and brushed it lightly across the map. With a fitful flicker, the relief came to life. The grain of the wooden rivers seemed to flow, winds stirring the skeletal leaves of the Deadwood. Sartyan banners flew above cities, marking their allegiance. Hagdon blinked, surprised the map still functioned. The energy that powered it – ambertrix, the lifeblood of Sartya – was nearly spent. Even the palace was subject to rationing.

The eastern end of the hoarlands began to smoke, grey wood dissipating to reveal a rich red hue beneath. Hagdon stared at it, his skin prickling.

'Impossible,' the Davaratch breathed, fixing his eyes upon the glittering sands. 'No one's seen the Sundered Valley in five hundred years. Why should it appear now?'

'A question whose answer even *you* should learn to fear,' a voice said.

Belying his size, the Sartyan emperor spun round, a black-bladed knife flicking into his hand. Its point arced to rest against the neck of the old man suddenly standing there, scrawny with the years. 'Do not try your tricks on me, Shune,' the Davaratch growled. 'I wouldn't hesitate to cut the life from you.'

As soon as the knife retreated from Relator Shune's throat, the old man rubbed at the drop of blood it had drawn and frowned at the smudge on his fingers. 'Such reflexes stand you in good stead, Majesty, but alone they will not save you.' His pale, luminous eyes strayed to the map. 'You are unprepared.'

'For what?' the Davaratch asked, irritation tightening the muscles of his face.

'Change.'

A swift backhand sent Shune crashing to the floor. The

Davaratch stood over him, stormy-eyed. 'I won't suffer your rid-dling. You will tell me what you know of *this* –' he gestured at the Sundered Valley – 'or I will find another use for you.'

Hagdon saw a fleeting hatred contort Shune's face. The man had been Relator longer than he could remember. He'd served the current Davaratch and the one before him – and possibly even the one before that. Hagdon watched as the old man climbed unsteadily to his feet. Ignoring the trickle of blood that ran from his split lip, he said, 'It's Rairam.'

The room plunged into darkness. Hagdon's heart leapt until he realized it was only the ambertrix lights failing once more. The Davaratch let out a grunt of displeasure and Hagdon swiftly searched his pocket for the matches and taper he had taken to carrying around. Once he'd lit the candelabrum on the dresser, he picked it up, spilling its glow across the map. The Sundered Valley caught the flames, held them covetously like red-glass beads.

'Rairam,' the Davaratch said finally, his voice hushed.

Shune nodded and looked at the map. 'So, Kierik,' he whispered. 'You could not keep us out forever.'

The door crashed open and Hagdon whirled, a furious reprimand on his tongue, but it died when he saw who stood there, her red gauntleted fist on the handle.

'Majesty,' the woman spoke directly to the emperor, 'we've found them.'

Sparks leapt in the Davaratch's eyes. 'Have the unit keep a distance,' he said. 'Are they aware of you?'

'No, sire,' the woman answered. She was clad in the same mail as the guards outside, except that her pauldrons were black and embossed with three hooded greathawks. Stealth Captain

Iresonté. Her presence here could mean only one thing: Khronosta was found.

'The whole damn temple appeared near one of the outposts on the Baioran frontier,' Iresonté said. 'It's been two weeks and they're still sitting there plain as day.'

'Hagdon,' the Davaratch snapped and Hagdon stood up straighter. 'Choose your best men and accompany the captain into the field. I won't take any chances.' His lips thinned. 'The Baioran frontier. This is not coincidence.'

'The Defiant also have a base—'

'The Defiant are a ragtag band of outlaws and the captain here already has a man inside. I doubt they're foolish enough to meddle but if they do, take care of them.' The emperor swept them both with his black eyes and Hagdon saw Iresonté flinch. 'This could well be the day we have waited for. You have your orders.'

James, the Relator whispered in his head and Hagdon had to turn his startled jerk into a salute; he hated when Shune spoke to him this way without warning, *the emperor's obsession with Khronosta is blinding him to the real threat.*

And what is the real threat? he answered, uneasy at the mental intrusion.

Rairam, the old man replied. *We do not know the truth behind its return. It must be investigated.*

I don't take my orders from you.

No, Shune agreed in his hissing voice, *you take them from the man who murdered your kin.*

Get out of my head, Hagdon snarled silently, moving to join Iresonté at the door. He could feel the emperor's eyes like twin blades pressing into his back.

'General.'

He turned.

'This is our chance to end Khronosta. I want the floors of that temple to run red. They will know what it is to stand against me.'

General James Hagdon had commanded the Sartyan Fist for half a decade. His men called him the Hand of Sartya. His enemies – and he'd made many over the years – dubbed him the emperor's rabid dog. Today, he thought, as he trotted faithfully from the chamber, out to murder a people, the name given him by his enemies was the truer.

2

She stood on the black road that ran to the stars and watched him craft a world.

His skin was starlight, his dark blue eyes – so like hers – blazed with the power he bent to his will. He wasn't the madman here, weighed down with lost centuries, but young, handsome even, and filled with righteousness. She watched him tear at time, twist the dimensions of the earth to his liking, and she screamed at him to stop.

When he turned his head and saw her, she shuddered but didn't back away. Sigel was in his hands, a torrent of energy. Before she knew it, she reached for the star herself, tried to wrest its power from him. He snarled and fought her and she fought back, the world threatening to split apart under their struggle. She wouldn't let him win, not when the Breaking would destroy all of Mariar and its people, not when she knew the future.

He faltered and she seized her chance, tearing the power away from him. He cried out, clutched his head, and she used Sigel to incinerate the walls he'd raised between worlds. Acre had to be

11

whole. When he fell to his knees, screaming, she didn't pause, but tore viciously into his bindings until they snapped and the world sprang back into shape.

The moment she relaxed her will, the power rushing through her began to burn. She tried to hurl it away, but the stars crowded into her head, eroding everything she was. Constellations scored her palms and she gasped as the scars flamed up her arms, over her chest and neck and into her mouth so that it filled with their names. She choked them back, desperate to hide from them. But they were her. She could not fight herself.

Kierik crouched before her, hands fisted against his head, howling like the madman he was. The fire consumed her, rolled out of her, broke like a wave over the lands of Acre and Rairam, burning everything in its path until there was nothing left but ashes and death and darkness.

Kyndra opened her eyes . . . and the fire was real, hot, stellar white. She became aware of her cramped limbs, curled into a ball on the ground. She *was* the fire; it surged in sheets down her back, rippling out to either side. Voices called her name. Between each wall of flame, she caught sight of familiar faces, lit with fear, alarm, horror.

No.

Kyndra closed her eyes, concentrating, until she could pull herself back from the brink. In her mind, she slammed the dark doorway that led to the stars and their whispers quietened. The fire died, shrinking back into her skin as if it had never been. When she opened her eyes again, it took her a few seconds to remember where she was. Tentative, the faces crept closer. Kait's was suspicious; she watched Kyndra without blinking.

Medavle, the Yadin, was first to reach her side and then

Nediah, who – after the briefest hesitation – dropped down beside her. Worry vied with wariness in the shadows beneath his eyes.

There was a faint chime and Kyndra turned her head to see Irilin, her skin alight with Lunar energy. Filaments clung to the novice's hands; like cobwebs, they floated gently out to brighten the area. 'Shielded,' she said.

'Kyndra?' Nediah asked softly.

She sat as if sheathed in stone, staring at a patch of black-ness beyond Irilin's light. 'Fine,' she said, hearing her voice break over the lie. 'I'm fine.'

'This is the second time,' Kait said. 'Irilin can't shield us all night.'

'I'm sorry.' Irilin looked shamefaced. 'If I'd learned how to tie it off—'

Kait rounded on Medavle. 'Can't *you* help her?'

'Kyndra has to help herself,' the Yadin said coldly. 'She has to stop fighting them.'

'Never,' Kyndra growled from between clenched teeth. A headache was pounding behind her eyes. 'I don't want them. I didn't choose this.'

'Your stubbornness will kill us all,' Kait said and Nediah laid a reproving hand on her shoulder. She glanced at him irritably, but did not shake it off. 'We have no idea what we're walking into.'

'You're not in the Deep any more,' Shika spoke from the shadows. 'We're capable of handling trouble.'

Kait glared at the novice. 'What would you know of it, as well-fed and coddled as you are? Have you failed to notice that only one of us –' she nodded at Irilin – 'is a Lunar? And she can't even tie off a shield.' Irilin looked hurt. 'We're all but defenceless at night,' Kait continued. She jerked her head at Kyndra. 'And what help is a Starborn who refuses to use her power?'

'You don't understand,' Kyndra said quietly.

'Arguing will get us nowhere,' Nediah headed off Kait's retort. 'She does have a point though,' he said to Kyndra. 'You're making it difficult to keep our presence hidden.'

'I know, Nediah,' she said in a low voice. 'It won't happen again.'

Austri stirred beyond the dark door. *It will, if you persist in fighting.*

'It's not as if we've seen a lot of people,' Irilin said in an obvious attempt to smooth things over. Her Lunar aura limned her hair and skin in silver. 'I guess this place isn't popular with the locals.'

Shika shrugged. 'Would *you* choose to live out here?'

'Someone shut the children up,' Kait said. 'What did you bring them for, Starborn?'

'Don't call me that.' Kyndra allowed herself to meet each pair of eyes. Except for Medavle's. She felt his gaze, inscrutable, judging. 'I'll stand watch,' she said, ignoring the fact that she'd barely had any rest. 'You can go back to sleep.'

She turned away before they could argue and, from the corner of her eye, saw them dropping back into their bedrolls. Kait had dragged hers a little closer to Nediah's.

Kyndra stuffed her hands in the pockets of her coat. It was to keep them warm, she told herself, aware that it wasn't really. She didn't want to look at her palms. She didn't want to see the terrible patterns that marked her out as someone different . . . as someone dangerous.

She remembered the look of fear on her companions' faces.

To them a Starborn was a thing of horror; inhuman, implacable and uncontrollable. Kyndra thought of the frozen core buried in her chest, just beside her heart. Sometimes it felt larger, as if it would push the red muscle aside and take its place. Instead of blood pumping around her body, it would be power.

Kyndra shuddered. It was worse when she was alone. Then *their* voices would creep into her mind, echoing from an unimaginable distance. Some stars talked more than others and *Austri* was the worst. It was strongest at dawn, making it the first thing Kyndra heard upon waking. It called her out of dreams she didn't want to lose: of her home, Brenwym, before the Breaking, when it seemed her life was full of sunlight and summer.

They had left the Wielder city of Naris yesterday afternoon and instead of letting night catch them halfway across the red valley, they'd camped on its fringes. The valley's silence disturbed Kyndra. Even the birds were absent from the trees. No cricket chirped, no flies harried the horses. It was unnatural. *Where is everyone?* she wondered. A month had passed since Acre had returned. Surely Mariar — or Rairam, to give her land its Acrean name — could not have gone unnoticed this long?

Something was wrong. She just wished she knew what it was.

After an hour had dragged past, Kyndra glanced at the huddled forms of Irilin, Shika, Kait and Nediah lying behind her on the flinty ground; none stirred. The western sky was still and dark, but a pale light seeped in from the east. Under that watery glow, Medavle's open eyes looked all the blacker.

Kyndra started. The Yadin sat with his back against a scraggy tree and she wondered how long he'd been awake. 'Bad dream?' she asked.

Medavle did not answer. Perhaps this place was reawakening memories he'd rather forget. Choosing not to probe, she said, 'We'll reach the valley floor today. How come we haven't seen anyone?'

The Yadin regarded her silently for a moment before his eyes flickered beyond her to the valley. In the dim morning, the earth was the colour of old blood. 'I have not seen this place in five centuries,' he said softly. 'Its soil wasn't always red. So many died here. So many bled.'

A shiver passed across Kyndra's skin. 'You're saying the soil is red because of their blood?'

'I didn't say that.' Medavle paused. 'But the earth remembers.'

Kyndra looked into his stony face and decided it was safer to retreat to her previous question. 'Don't you think it's strange that no one from Acre has come to investigate?'

Medavle slowly shook his head. 'Perhaps they're unaware.'

Kyndra wasn't sure she believed him. She turned back to the valley. The sun's first rays spilled rubies across the earth and she found herself transfixed by the sight. *Austri*'s wordless whispering lessened.

The others were finally beginning to stir. When Kyndra glanced round, she saw Nediah sitting up, staring down at Kait, cat-curled beside him. The woman slept with one hand on the dagger in her belt, but despite the pose, her face was peaceful. Sleep softened the lines that cynicism had worn around her lips. Nediah watched her a moment longer and then he turned away, his face carefully blank.

Kyndra busied her hands with breakfast, avoiding the stares she could feel. Her lack of a plan gnawed at her. On the one hand, it was foolish to walk brazenly into the unknown, knowing nothing of Acre's powers or politics. But staying in Mariar was worse. What if Acre's idea of a greeting was to invade first and ask questions later? Hundreds of thousands of lives depended on what she did next.

'How are you feeling today?'

Nediah had come to stand over her, the Solar power glimmering in his eyes. He was dressed for travel, looking much like he had when they'd first met in Brenwym, when all she had to worry about was the coming-of-age ceremony. Kyndra stared at the familiar shape of his face and some of the knots in her stomach loosened. 'Fine.' She smiled.

Nediah did not look convinced. 'You stayed awake most of the night,' he said reprovingly.

She tried to ignore the tired prickle in her eyes. 'I don't know what I'm doing, Nediah,' she confessed, keeping her voice low. 'Everyone's looking at me to decide, but I don't know the first thing about leading a mission, about armies or politics, or any of that.' She shook her head. 'I'm an innkeeper's daughter, not a strategist.'

Nediah studied her a while before answering. 'You don't give yourself enough credit, Kyndra. You worked out how to stop the Madness from killing every Wielder in the citadel. You saved Mariar from the Breaking.'

'The Madness was my fault,' she reminded him bitterly. 'If there hadn't been two Starborn in the world . . .'

It was Nediah's turn to shake his head. 'Don't blame yourself for existing. You could just as easily blame Medavle for having meddled in your birth. And the Breaking was getting worse anyway. Brégenne and I saw –' He faltered, as if her name had stolen his words. After a moment he said quietly, 'It wasn't your fault.'

'Heads up, Ned!'

Nediah stiffened and only just turned in time to catch the bread Kait threw at him. He stared at her unreadably, and the hand holding the bread fell to his side. Kyndra looked at them both, feeling how tense the air had become. Finally, Nediah folded himself up to sit on the ground and Kyndra hastily passed him a tin mug full of tea.

Irilin was up and staring out at the valley. She shuddered once and turned away. 'There's . . . something down there,' she said hesitantly. 'Something doesn't feel right.'

Kyndra gazed across the red strip of land. Not wide, but long, it tapered to a forested ridge at its western end. Perhaps they could cover it in half a day. She held herself still, blocked out the others' conversation and listened.

Only eerie silence answered.

Shika came to stand beside them. 'What do you think Gareth's doing right now?'

'It's barely been a day, Shika.' Irilin raised an eyebrow. 'You missing him already?'

Shika flushed. 'No. Just wondering. I hope Master Brégenne finds a way to remove the gauntlet. Before we left, Gareth said it felt different.'

'I can't believe you two were stupid enough to steal it from the archives,' Irilin said. 'Didn't you think it was locked away for a reason?'

'So we made a mistake,' Shika retorted. 'Gareth shouldn't have to suffer for it.'

'Kyndra,' Nediah called and she turned. The others were staring at her expectantly, Kait with her arms crossed, Medavle his dark eyes distant. He seemed changed from the person of a month ago, as if the fire of vengeance that had sustained him for five centuries had died with Kierik. Kyndra didn't like the way he looked at her now, as if she were a constant reminder that the last Starborn had killed the woman Medavle loved – a Yadin like him. *I'm only here because of you*, Kyndra thought, *I'm here because you wanted Kierik dead.*

'If we're to construct a picture of Acre's infrastructure,' Nediah said, jerking her back to the present, 'the first thing we need is maps. We have to get an idea of Acrean geography, its major cities. Medavle says his memory won't suffice.'

Maps. It was the sort of thing she'd have mentioned sooner, if she'd been any real kind of leader. Kyndra felt her cheeks warm. 'Of course,' she said.

'Many of the cities I remember will no doubt be gone,' the Yadin said, 'but the region beyond the valley was called Baior. It's mostly farmland, no large settlements.'

'We need to know who's in charge,' Nediah continued, 'whether it's Sartya, or some other power. Do they have use of the technology Medavle remembers? What about Wielders and their role here?' The Wielder ticked the questions off on his fingers and then spread his hands. 'We don't know whether we even speak the same language. If our ultimate goal is to protect Mariar's interests, we need to know what to bring to a possible alliance.'

Kyndra blinked at him, feeling more stupid by the second. *She* should be the one asking these questions. It was obvious Nediah would make a better leader; she could see it in the others' faces. Anger flared in her. Why had they dumped this role on her shoulders?

When it became apparent that they were waiting for her to speak, Kyndra swallowed her feelings and said, 'Then that's what we need to do. As long as we can understand each other, the first people we find should be able to answer a lot of our questions.'

'What will we say when they ask us who we are?' Irilin said from behind her. 'If it turns out we don't speak the same language, they'll never believe we're from Acre.'

Kyndra saw Nediah open his mouth and quickly forestalled him. She had to contribute something. 'Let's tackle that hurdle when we get to it. Any town or village near here can't have failed to notice Mariar.' As she said it, she felt another flutter of disquiet. It *was* odd that nobody had come to investigate. She wished she knew why.

'Let's get started, then,' Kait said decisively and went to ready her horse.

Before she saw to her own, Kyndra moved to speak with Nediah. 'Thanks,' she said, too softly for the others to hear. She stared at Uncle's flank instead of the Wielder. 'I'm not very good at this.'

Nediah didn't ask her what she meant. 'You're doing fine,' he said and Kyndra looked up at him. The morning sun brought out the gold flecks in his eyes and a memory came to her of sitting beside him and Brégenne as he used the Solar power to cook them breakfast. Brégenne, she recalled, had strongly disapproved.

'I'm sorry for taking you away from Brégenne,' she said impulsively and then regretted it when Nediah's expression hardened.

'Leaving Naris was my decision,' he said.

There was a lump in Kyndra's throat. 'Thank you for coming with me.'

Nediah patted her shoulder, but his answering smile seemed in danger of slipping. 'You certainly keep life interesting.'

Kait was watching them. She watched Nediah a lot and Kyndra felt a wave of protectiveness. She hadn't forgotten her promise to Brégenne, the promise she'd made the night she and Nediah had accompanied Kait into the Deep. *I will look out for him.* And she would, Kyndra vowed, darting an inimical look at Kait before going to her horse.

It took her two attempts to mount, and not for the first time she wondered why Medavle had chosen such a tall horse. The black stallion danced restlessly beneath her. *He ought to have a name*, Kyndra thought. Perhaps something out of the old stories.

As she led the way down into the valley, talk struck up behind her, lightening the mood. Her companions seemed to have forgotten their near-roasting last night. Kyndra wasn't sure whether to be grateful or annoyed. What if it happened again, without warning? What if she burned everyone while they slept?

Better you do.

Sigel was a sudden furnace in her head. Kyndra tried to mute the star, but she couldn't block it out altogether. *Shut up*, she snapped at it, clenching her fists. *Leave me alone.*

The trail was wide enough for two to ride abreast and she found herself next to Irilin. The novice's dappled mare was much better suited to her size. This morning, Irilin's long blond hair spilled over a leather jerkin and shirt with its sleeves rolled up to her elbows. The glow coming off the earth rouged her pale cheeks.

I should stop thinking of her as a novice. By choosing to leave Naris, both Irilin and Shika had sacrificed the opportunity to complete their training as Wielders. They would never be masters in the eyes of the citadel. *Choose carefully*, Alandred

21

had said to them upon hearing of their wish to accompany Kyndra into Acre.

Kyndra looked sidelong at her friend. She wasn't at all sure the novices *had* chosen carefully, but she couldn't deny that she was glad of their company.

The sun was fully up by the time they reached the valley floor. Kyndra stared at the forbidding place, Irilin beside her. 'I don't like it,' the young woman said, tugging her sleeves down as if she were cold.

'Makes my skin crawl,' Shika agreed and Kyndra tried not to voice her own misgiving. She wondered what Medavle had meant about the earth remembering. From here, the valley's many small mounds looked like blood-drenched cairns. Kyndra shook her head, trying to dislodge the image.

Kait snorted at their apprehension, urging her mare on. The horse whinnied as its hooves kicked up the red dirt. Kyndra studied the woman's back, wondering at her reasons for coming. Was it to forge a new purpose after her master's death? She'd been Kierik's protector for fifteen years, ever since she'd sworn an oath to the rebel Wielders, to the Nerian. Now that an uncomfortable peace existed between the two factions, perhaps Kait felt she needed another purpose. Kyndra glanced at Nediah. He was looking at Kait too, his brow deeply furrowed.

They moved further into the valley and conversation gradually died. Something about the place discouraged talk. *Like not speaking at burial rites*, Kyndra thought with a slight shudder. No wind blew, no animal called. Preceded by the creak and jingle of harness, their little group was the only thing that moved. Clouds seemed nailed to the sky and the sun hung over their heads with a dim, ponderous weight.

Despite their unease, they encountered nothing but the

sick, stunted bushes that grew between the mounds. Two hours later, just short of the valley's lip, Kyndra let out a breath she hadn't realized she'd been holding. Irilin seemed relieved too and gave Kyndra a weak smile.

Then, up ahead, Kait burst into flame.

Nediah yelled and pushed his horse after her, but when he reached her side, the air around him ignited too. Kait's mare reared and, as she made a desperate grab for the reins, the animal bucked and threw her. Still burning, Kait rolled away from the dancing hooves, lurched to her feet and snatched at her mount's bridle before she could bolt.

Shika was the third to become a human torch. He almost fell off his horse in his hurry to dismount and Kyndra saw in his panicked face the same confusion that troubled Kait and Nediah. 'What's going on?' he cried.

If someone were to see them now – three figures wreathed in fire – they could be forgiven for believing that they'd walked into a nightmare, but Kyndra was used to the golden glare of Solar energy. The question was – 'Why are you drawing power?' she called.

'Can't help it,' Kait grunted, her face creased. 'It . . . won't . . . shut . . . off.'

Nediah's look changed from confusion to horror. 'Something's taking it,' he said, his green eyes sweeping the empty landscape. 'I can feel it using me. Like a conduit.'

Irilin sat tensed on her mare, but nothing happened to the slight girl as far as Kyndra could see. 'I feel something,' Irilin said. 'Like hands in my head.' She shuddered, her eyes widening. 'I think it knows I can channel the Lunar, but it can't reach it, not while the sun's up.'

It was then that Kyndra saw the skull, half hidden by the

thorny branches that pushed through eye sockets worn smooth by time. She stared, her gaze raking the ground. After that, it was impossible not to see the others.

They were in the middle of a charnel yard. Half buried and bleached, the flesh long stripped, there were fingers reaching through the sand, tibias, femurs and scapulas strewn about with no sense or order. Kyndra followed the arch of a human spine as it surfaced, curved and dived back into the earth like a sand snake. Cold sweat trickled down her neck.

'There are bones,' she said grimly, but Medavle had already seen them.

'Get out of here,' he said. 'Move.' Kyndra couldn't miss the warning in his voice. Kait and Shika tried desperately to calm their horses, but the brighter the Wielders burned, the more terrified their mounts became.

'We'll have to lead them,' Kait said from between clenched teeth, as she struggled to hold her horse in check. 'Perhaps it will stop once we get out of the valley.'

Kyndra's stallion seemed unfazed by the three burning fig-ures. She patted him gratefully and he broke into a walk without prompting. They managed another half-hour, but their pace was slow and the terrain difficult. They were on the slopes now, pathless and steep. Shika's breathing grew strained and Kyndra heard him drawing great gulps of the thick air, his face visibly paling. Kait and Nediah were holding up better, but both looked haggard.

'I can't take much more of this,' Nediah rasped after another ten minutes. 'I've never drawn this much power for so long.'

'Master . . . Master Rush told us we could burn ourselves out by . . . drawing too much,' Shika panted. 'That's not true, is it?' For the first time, he looked genuinely frightened.

Nediah shook his head. 'I don't know.'

Kyndra felt helpless. She glanced at Irilin and saw that her friend's knuckles were white on her reins. Medavle's gaze raked the landscape, searching for their invisible assailant.

Then, as if snuffed by a vast hand, the flames died and the three Wielders drooped like cut puppets.

The air burst open.

3

The Baioran Frontier, Acre
Hagdon

Remarkable, Hagdon mused, gazing at the distant temple that was Khronosta, its domes and towers looking as fragile as spun sugar. The structure was unfortified, without moat, drawbridge or battlements. In theory, it was a besieging army's dream. In reality, it had never been captured. There was no point to a moat or reinforced walls when the temple and all its inhabitants could simply move elsewhere at the slightest threat. Or else-*when*, Hagdon corrected himself.

'They need time to prepare their ritual,' Iresonté said, as if reading his thoughts. 'I don't intend to give it to them.'

'Time is their greatest weapon,' he replied, his eyes still on the temple, wondering what was going on inside. The Khronostians weren't usually so bold; they never stayed in one place longer than a week. 'Perhaps they don't intend to flee,' he murmured.

'When has Khronosta ever done otherwise?'

Hagdon heard the sneer in Iresonté's voice and finally turned to look at her. She was a striking woman, dark-haired with the pale skin and paler eyes common in the north. A cruel woman, too, and not one he wished to make an enemy of, but she seemed to take offence at every word out of his mouth.

'I wouldn't be much of an officer if I didn't consider the possibility.' He touched the scar on his lip, an uncomfortable reminder of the last time he'd engaged the *du-alakat*, the assassin-warriors of Khronosta. 'Perhaps they feel the time has come to fight.'

Iresonté gave a reluctant grunt of agreement and turned away.

'General.' Carn, his bondsman and friend, staggered over, balancing a clattering stack of armour.

Hagdon reached out to steady the pile before it fell. 'Why do you insist on carrying it all at once?'

Carn grinned and might have shrugged save for his precarious burden. He had a pleasing, open face that was just beginning to crease at the corners. His cropped hair was grey; Hagdon couldn't remember it being otherwise. Carn had served as vassal to his father and was the only person Hagdon could bring himself to trust.

'Are you sure about this, James?' Carn asked as he fitted the red plate Hagdon had come to see as a second skin. 'An assault on Khronosta?' He glanced darkly in the temple's direction. 'It may be a trap.'

Hagdon grimaced, shrugged the left pauldron into a better position. The armour seemed to weigh more every day. 'It's possible,' he said. 'But orders are orders and they've been out in the open for weeks now. We may not get another chance. The emperor believes they're behind the ambertrix shortage.'

'How so? Where does ambertrix come from?'

Hagdon shook his head. 'The best-kept secret in the empire.

Only the emperor and his Thabarat technicians know and he's worked hard to keep it that way.'

Carn secured the cloak to Hagdon's shoulders and passed him the Sartyan general's monstrous helm. Hagdon held it between his hands, staring into the eye holes. How many people had he killed while wearing it? Its bloody snarl would have been the last thing they saw in this world. Once, that had meant something to him. Now he felt nothing.

'Just . . . be careful, James.'

'Will you ever stop worrying over me?'

'If you'd only manage to find yourself a partner, I wouldn't have to.'

Hagdon shook his head. He tucked the helm under his arm and went to brief his officers.

It was a force of five hundred, chosen from the best of the Fist, that he led to the temple after sunset. The terrain favoured them, the rocky Baioran landscape offering cover almost to the foot of the low bluff on which the temple stood, looking incongruous amidst the arid landscape. His soldiers were ranged around the bluff, awaiting his signal, while Iresonté's agents prepared to scale the walls, using the delicate carvings on the exterior as footholds. Hagdon traced a serpent with his eyes, following its body as it twined around a great wheel. The spokes were numbers, he saw, and each was part of a further wheel and further spokes until he lost sight of where he'd begun.

Once Iresonté's agents were inside, they would open the gates for the rest of them. It would be quick and clean. In and out. Supposedly. But Hagdon hated to rely on stealth. More particularly, he hated to rely on men and women who weren't his own. The temple's obvious lack of defences disturbed him. It was almost too obvious.

No matter his disquiet, the attack would go ahead. If it didn't, if they failed . . . he remembered the emperor's eyes and suppressed a shiver.

'There's no need for you to risk yourself, General,' Captain Analia whispered, as they awaited the signal. 'We have our orders and Stealth Captain Iresonté's agents are the best in the empire. She's taking the field herself.'

Hagdon stiffened. 'She is?' It wasn't what they'd agreed.

'Captain Dyen saw her leading the group who'll scale the walls from the west.'

The unease swirling around Hagdon's belly grew stronger. While it was common military sense to realize no plan ever survived first contact with the enemy, he always ensured he went into battle with full knowledge of his troop placements, his own strengths and weaknesses – and the enemy's. There was already too much they didn't know about Khronosta. He'd have preferred to wait, to gather more intelligence, but the Davaratch was not known for his patience. Khronostian assassins had taken out too many key players in court, not to mention how close they'd come to infiltrating Thabarat, the ambertrix college of research. Hagdon should be relishing this opportunity to even the score. Instead he felt cold all over. This was *wrong*. And he never ignored his instincts.

'Captain,' he said quietly. 'When we move on the gates, I want you to take half your company round to the south. The other half charges with me.'

Analia gave a single sharp nod. If she wondered why the plan was changing at the last minute, she kept it to herself. 'Stay out of Iresonté's sight,' Hagdon added. 'If I have need of you, I'll send up a flare.'

As if to punctuate his statement, a green shower of sparks

blazed overhead, burning brightly for a second before fading. 'Iresonté's agents are in,' Hagdon said, nodding at the signal. See you on the other side.' Analia saluted and turned to pass on his orders.

Hagdon's troop broke cover, converging on the carved wooden gates just as they began to swing open. The courtyard beyond was more of an open-air passage which circled the inner temple. Pillars marched down its centre and around both corners, adding to the feeling of confinement. Although it looked deserted, the *du-alakat* were known to strike suddenly and from the shadows. *This could be suicide*, he thought. Iresonté had estimated their numbers at less than fifty, but one *du-alakat* was worth five of his elite.

Where was the stealth force? They were supposed to join him here. 'Spread out.' Hagdon passed the signal to Lieutenant Tara and in a few moments the passage was filled with red-armoured soldiers. The inner temple was a circular tower, domed, with two spires soaring up on either side. Grains of white sand rasped softly beneath Hagdon's boots. The orange stone seemed exotic, every inch of it carved with arcane symbols. They pressed in on him, stealing his breath; he had an acute feeling of trespassing in a sacred place.

The soldiers' mail was muffled; they made hardly a sound as they spread to cover the whole of the open area. Hagdon watched Tara complete a circuit. 'Nothing,' her hands said.

The gates banged shut behind them.

Heart pounding, Hagdon whipped round. Those he'd left to guard them lay sprawled, their blood soaking into the porous stone. A bell began to ring somewhere inside the temple and the flash of a yellow flare lit the sky – a signal and not one of his. Moments later, grey-bandaged figures stepped seemingly out of the air itself and into the courtyard, kali sticks held ready in their hands. Each wooden stick measured about two-thirds the length of Hagdon's sword. They were far lighter, however, and the speed at which the Khronostians swung them was deadly.

Hagdon caught movement atop the gates and saw someone crouched there like a cat. Their face was covered, but they wore the black of the stealth force. He signalled them furiously – 'Reopen the gates, secure an exit' – but they slipped down the far side and out of sight. For a moment Hagdon felt only disbelief. Then he had to counter as a kali stick swept towards his neck, too fast for him to block with his shield.

He caught the blow on his sword instead and used the shield to force the Khronostian away from him. Tonight every one of his soldiers fought with a shield. No Sartyan could compete with the speed of the *du-alakat*. It was far better to focus on defences – heavy armour, tower shields, long swords to keep the Khronostians at a distance. If they got in close, you were dead.

For several frenzied moments, it was all Hagdon could do to hold the warrior off. The bandages were wound thickly, their grey ends blowing free in the Khronostian's wake as they ducked and wove, making the fight a dance. Hagdon's attacks felt crude and clumsy by comparison. Eyes gleamed at him from between the face wrappings; the only other part not covered were the soles of the warrior's feet.

The Khronostian's speed increased and the figure began to blur. The *du-alakat* weren't only superb fighters; their power allowed them to slow time, making it seem as if they moved impossibly fast. Hagdon felt a sudden blow to his calf that staggered him and sent him to one knee. But luck must be smiling on him – another of his soldiers, fighting his own *du-alakat*, lost his shield. It skidded spike-up across the stone towards Hagdon just as the Khronostian solidified to deal him the final blow. The warrior's bare foot came down and the sharp point skewered it.

Hagdon moved fast. A thrust and two shield bashes sent the Khronostian tottering backwards, blood streaming from its injured foot. A low moan came from behind the bandages as the figure fell to one knee. Now that their positions were reversed, Hagdon didn't hesitate – to hesitate with the *du-alakat* was to die. He plunged his sword into the warrior's chest.

Those eyes blinked once at the blade as Hagdon pulled it free. Blood swiftly turned the grey bandages arterial red; it bubbled from the Khronostian's hidden mouth, which seemed to be trying to shape words. Despite himself, Hagdon bent down to hear. 'Khronos,' the warrior breathed. 'Once the Kala is found . . . our people will . . . return from the shadows.'

The head lolled to one side, rasping breath stilled. On a strange impulse, Hagdon reached down and tugged free the bandages around his opponent's face.

A woman looked up at him blankly, her green eyes fixed. One of her cheeks was liver-spotted with age; the other as smooth and unmarked as an infant's. Hagdon backed away, stung by the dead gaze, the shocking patchwork of flesh. He scanned the courtyard and saw more red-mailed bodies prone than standing.

'Tara!' he yelled and the lieutenant – about to help a fellow soldier – turned instead towards him. 'Get these gates open,' Hagdon said, 'and get our soldiers out. As many as we can save.'

'The stealth force—'

'Abandoned us,' Hagdon snarled, thinking of the black-clad figure perched on the gates. 'They let us in and left us to die.'

Blood flecked one of Tara's paling cheeks. 'What? Why?'

'I will know,' Hagdon vowed, 'but now we get our soldiers out.'

While Lieutenant Tara sounded a retreat, Hagdon made for the gates, lashing out at those *du-alakat* battling his forces. A couple he caught off guard with his charge, knocking one unconscious. His intervention was enough to turn one small fight in his soldiers' favour. Three-on-one, they dispatched the Khronostian with chill efficiency and Hagdon swept them up on his way to the gates.

They wouldn't open. A simple bar was all that secured them from this side, but it wasn't lowered. Something on the outside, then – Iresonté had locked them in. Hagdon cursed, thumping his mailed fist on the wood. When he turned to look back at the courtyard, he saw a massacre. A few grey-wrapped bodies lay among the dead, but otherwise the ground was a sea of red. Perhaps thirty Sartyans remained standing – the same number as there were Khronostians. Had the *du-alakat* routed them with so few?

'Open these gates!' Hagdon thudded his fist into the wood again. He wouldn't die here, wouldn't let Iresonté get away with treason. She'd planned this out, she must have, and the stealth force she'd brought along tonight would all be implicated in it. The scale of her betrayal was staggering.

'There's a bar and chain through the handles of the gates, sir.'

'Dyen!' Hagdon called. The captain was one of those he'd left to hold the gates.

'I'm working to get them free, sir, but . . . I think my arm's broken. Someone attacked us – from behind. The *du-alakat* must have had warning.'

Hagdon ground his teeth. His soldiers would not have expected an attack from the rear, not when they knew the stealth force supposedly guarded them.

Analia, he remembered, cursing the panic that fogged his mind. He groped for the flare, but it was gone, ripped from his belt in the melee. 'Dyen,' it emerged as a gasp, 'do you still have your flare? Captain Analia has men to the south.' *If Iresonté hasn't also ambushed them*, he thought.

He heard Dyen's hiss of pain as he was forced to use both hands to light the flare. Red streaked the sky and, slightly more hopeful, Hagdon turned his attention back to the battle.

Exhausted by the unrelenting speed of the *du-alakat*, his soldiers were barely holding their own. Hagdon rushed to one group's aid, laying about him with a fury fuelled by the bitterness of Iresonté's betrayal. The emperor would hear of this, he vowed, as soon as he returned to camp. The ambertrix receiver had enough power left for one conversation.

He slashed at a grey body, but the Khronostian leapt back, agile amongst the corpses that littered the courtyard. The orange stone seemed thirsty for blood – only stains remained as a patina on its surface. Shouts reached Hagdon and he gave silent thanks when he heard Analia's voice barking an order. After another second of fierce fighting, hammering began on the gates, the regular thunder and fall of axes biting into wood.

The gates weren't built to keep out an army – or even fifty soldiers with axes. With a crack, they splintered, shards spraying those closest. Captain Analia's half-company poured inside, kicking bits of wood out of their way. 'Injured,' Hagdon called, 'get the injured out!'

'Sir,' Analia said, 'you must go. We'll hold them.'

Hagdon found himself shaking his head, feeling a tickle as

blood seeped from one nostril. He wiped it, but the metal of his gauntlet merely smeared it across his skin. 'Get the injured out,' he repeated before turning to stalk through the field of his own dead. With a cry, he fell on the *du-alakat* battling Lieutenant Tara, sweeping his spiked shield down and out to catch the warrior across the hip as they disengaged. The Khronostian staggered and Tara took the chance to stab the bandaged figure through the eye. A moment later, she doubled over, hand to her ribs and Hagdon seized hold of her, draping one of her arms over his shoulder. 'Cracked,' she breathed. 'Damn greyface.'

When he reached the gates and looked back, it was to see Analia's force making a last stand. Whittled down to twenty, they stood shoulder to shoulder, their shields slotted together to form a wall. 'Captain!' Hagdon shouted. 'Get your men out of there.' Analia glanced over her shoulder and spared him a grim nod before calling retreat.

Bloodied, beaten, they pulled back from the orange-stoned temple, leaving their dead in the enemy's care. Hagdon's nose was still bleeding, but, clutching sword, shield and supporting Lieutenant Tara, he couldn't spare a hand to wipe it.

Were he the Khronostian commander, he would not have hesitated to send out warriors to nip and harry a defeated foe, but when he glanced back, the ranks of *du-alakat* merely stood there, stone-still in the splinters of their ruined gates. In their midst was a cowled, bent figure, leaning on a staff. 'Why?' Hagdon wondered. 'Why do they not finish us?'

'Because they know they *can*,' Tara said and he realized he'd spoken the question aloud. 'Their mercy is nothing more than a message of contempt to the emperor.'

Hagdon grimaced. The Khronostians didn't fear him; they didn't fear the might of Sartya and they didn't fear the emperor.

After years of running and hiding, striking, retreating to the shadows, they had come into the open and had held their ground. Something had changed. Again he saw the green eyes of the dead woman. What had she said? *Once the Kala is found* . . .

As Hagdon stumbled with his wounded comrade into the concealing darkness, a voice called out to them, carried on the hissing wind.

'Come, Sartya,' it said, 'throw your men at our walls. When Khronos, our Kala, arrives to lead us, your time in the light is ended.'

4

It seemed as though they were surrounded by people on horse-back. But there were no horses; the figures floated, bodiless and indistinct, as if seen through mist. A moment later, Kyndra realized it *was* mist.

Arms and heads coalesced, faded and coalesced. The figures writhed, unable to hold their forms for long, but more were appearing. They converged on the party from every side. Kyndra dismounted and urged her stallion closer to the others, the six of them backing into a defensive circle, holding tightly to their horses' reins.

'I can't touch the Solar,' Kait said. She whipped the knife from her belt and slashed at the nearest figure, whose ghostly hands hovered inches from her chest, but the blade passed right through. As she raised her fist again, Medavle caught it.

'It's no use,' he said, gazing at the spectral host.

One of the figures sharpened, leaving the others to fray almost to nothing. A face formed, featureless save for two eyes and a ragged slit of a mouth. The mist shrouded it in pale robes

37

and its voice hissed like wind over sand. The words made no sense to Kyndra, but Medavle's eyes widened. 'Acrean,' he said.

'Speak words we can all understand,' Kait growled.

You bring the sun. It is long since we felt it inside us.

Kyndra exchanged a look with the others. 'Not creepy at all,' Shika murmured. He was white-faced, as if the wraiths had drained him of blood as well as Solar energy.

'What do you want?' Nediah asked.

Life. Substance. Flesh. We want to live *again.*

Nediah frowned. 'Only humans can give life.'

A finger-like tendril of mist extended towards Irilin, who flinched away. *We are of the moon too.*

'Cosmosethic energy can't make flesh,' Nediah insisted. 'It can heal a body, but not create one from nothing.'

'It can.'

They all looked at Medavle. He hadn't stopped staring at the wraiths and now a terrible dread crept over his face. 'What are you called?' he asked them.

We are the Servants. We wish to live again. We wish to serve again.

'No,' Medavle whispered. His hand closed on the flute at his belt, though he seemed unaware of the fact.

'Medavle,' Nediah said sharply. 'What is it?'

'It isn't possible,' the Yadin said. 'I saw you die. All of you. The black wind –'

Ahhhh. A sigh ran through the wraiths. *The pain.*

Medavle staggered. 'No, this cannot be true. Not after all this time.'

Nediah moved to the Yadin's side, but didn't touch him. 'What are they?'

'My people.' Medavle looked up, eyes suddenly blazing.

'Isla!' he shouted and they all flinched at the agony in his voice. 'Isla, are you here?' His dark gaze swept the mist, but caught on nothing.

You are useless to us.

Medavle's face twisted. 'Don't you remember me? I am your brother.'

You are not human.

'You have to remember! We are the same.'

'These are the Yadin?' Kait asked. 'I thought you said Lord Kierik killed them.'

Medavle rounded on her with a snarl. 'He did worse. He doomed them to five centuries of . . . of *this*. They aren't alive or dead. They are lost.' His voice broke. 'I don't know how to help them.'

'I thought I rid the world of you.'

The words were so sudden, so shocking, that Kyndra clamped her hands over her mouth, but it was too late to call them back. Medavle slowly turned to look at her.

'I'm sorry,' she blurted, lowering her hands. 'I don't know where that came from.' But she did. Kierik's memories were massing like storm clouds behind her eyes. She felt his distaste for the Yadin as keenly as if it were her own. The Wielders had created them to act as servants in the golden age of Solinaris. *Playing at being gods.* The thought reached her like an echo and she tried to push Kierik's memories aside.

Her outburst had drawn the wraiths' attention. Kyndra felt their scrutiny as a prickling along her skin. Their response was instantaneous: malice, palpable as thunder, spread through their ranks. More wraiths took shape, their ill-formed faces no longer emotionless, but contorted in hatred.

If they *were* the Yadin, she wasn't the real target of their anger. Five hundred years ago, Kierik had stripped them of the energy that gave them form and used it to destroy the Sartyan army assaulting Solinaris. Only Anohin and Medavle had survived. 'I'm not him,' she said, taking an automatic step back. 'I've never done anything to you.'

You are a child of the stars.

Before Kyndra could snatch it away, a tendril of mist coiled around her right palm, stroking as a lover might.

You share his blood.

Their fury seemed to double. Kyndra felt it like a fistful of hailstones against her skin. 'He's dead,' she cried wildly. 'Kierik's dead!'

Then we must be content with you.

'It's not her fault,' Nediah said, but it was no use. Dreadful anger surged through the wraiths and a light took shape in their midst: a lance of Solar energy, the same energy they'd stolen from the three Wielders. Kyndra watched as more wraiths sacrificed their forms to feed the lance and although it looked insubstantial, she knew it could harm her.

Kait's panicked horse finally broke free of her hold. It reared, white-eyed with fear, and then dashed in front of the group, throwing itself down the slope and into the path of the Solar lance. The bolt took the horse in the chest. One moment it was there, outlined against the mist, the next it was gone and only an imprint remained.

There was silence as both sides stared at the place where the horse had been. Irilin gave a strangled whimper and Kait cursed. The wraiths began shaping another lance.

'Do something!' Irilin shouted at Kyndra, but Kyndra couldn't. Her feet felt heavy, rooted to the red earth, and dread lay like ash on her tongue, smothering any words.

Nediah took one look at her face and said, 'We have to run.' He seized Medavle's shoulder. 'Can't *you* do something? A shield at least?'

The Yadin stared back at him, eyes blank. He seemed in shock. Nediah swore under his breath and shook him. 'I don't have the strength,' he said, 'neither does Kait nor Shika. They'll kill us.'

Medavle seemed to revive at that. 'Split up,' he said. 'Do not give them such a large target. Each lance burns up more of the energy they took – they won't use it unless they are certain of a hit.'

'Reassuring,' Kyndra thought she heard Shika say as they spread out over the slope, heading for the relative safety of the treeline. She hoped the wraiths were confined to the valley, to the vicinity of Solinaris and the place of their deaths. Could they truly have lingered here for five hundred years, killing anyone unfortunate enough to stray into the valley? *Why didn't the wind destroy them utterly?* The last thought seemed to come from Kierik and she strove to push it down.

It was difficult going, what with her horse and the slope and having to look over her shoulder. The wraiths followed, but not swiftly; creating the Solar lance seemed to take all of their strength. When they released the second one, it was aimed at her.

Kyndra had known it and planned for it. There was an out-cropping of rock rising from the slope and just as she jerked herself and her horse behind it, she heard the lance shatter against the rock, sending out a spray of stone chips. Some grazed her neck, but she ignored the sting, took a firmer grip on her horse's reins and ran on up the slope. Little stones rolled beneath her stallion's hooves.

The six of them were strung out in a staggered line. Kait moved faster without a horse to lead and was almost under the shadow of the trees. Kyndra glanced behind and saw another lance glowing in the mist. None of the wraiths had form now; with any luck, they were nearing exhaustion. All Kyndra needed was a few more minutes. She wouldn't have to call on the stars, wouldn't have to speak their names or fear being changed by that terrible power.

You can't resist us forever, they whispered from the void.

She gritted her teeth, looking for another rock to deflect the lance she knew was coming for her. But this part of the slope was shale, dotted here and there with small boulders, and the trees were still out of reach. Kyndra glanced over her shoulder, breath coming hard in her chest, just in time to see the wraiths hurl the next lance.

It took her a second to realize that it wasn't aimed at her, another second to spot the wraiths' real target, and a third to watch the lance hit him.

Shika didn't even have time to scream. One moment he was there, outlined in fire, and then he was nothing. He was gone. His horse reared and plunged on up the slope.

Kyndra's heels sprayed up shale as she dug them in, bringing her run to a stumbling halt. Her horse whinnied a protest and she let him go. Irilin was screaming wordlessly, struggling against Nediah's grasp. The Wielder shouted Kyndra's name, but Kyndra didn't listen. She stood still, staring at the space where Shika had just been. Not even a body, not even bones. It was as if he'd never existed.

Dimly she felt her shoulders tighten up, her lips curl back from her teeth in a snarl. And then the surge of shock and guilt and rage carried her to the threshold of the void, where the stars shone coldly, temptingly.

She reached for *Hagal*, its whisper already in her ears. *Sigel* wouldn't do; after all, the wraiths absorbed power and she needed to strip it from them. She needed a force like the black wind – the spell from the Wielders' book which Kierik had used long ago.

Now that she'd stopped running, the wraiths slowed too. Their hatred washed over her, but it was nothing compared to the absolute ice of the void. She took *Hagal* into her veins, feeling the star's power like a thousand cold rivers flowing through her. Her skin had begun to glow with a dark radiance, the constellation of *Hagal* burning on her wrist.

She flexed her fingers and sent the star's power into the wraiths. It seeped like a foul oil across the living mist, dissolving it. Screams of agony reached her ears, but she didn't stop. *Hagal* left a gritty stain on her skin, but she didn't relent. Although she grimaced with the strain of holding on to the star, she wouldn't stop until every last wraith was gone, forms torn asunder. With a guttural growl she didn't recognize as her own, she drew on *Hagal* more deeply, reached out with its power and began to rip at the mist, grasping each wraith and pulling it apart.

'No!'

A horse whinnied and then Medavle leapt from its back to land in front of her. For a moment she thought he was one of the wraiths, his white robes snapping in the wind, dark eyes full of anger and the horror of a memory. 'Stop it,' he pleaded.

'There are more of them,' she said flatly.

He struck her.

Wreathed in *Hagal*, she barely felt the blow, but the shock

43

of it was enough to break her concentration and the star slipped from her control. Kyndra gasped as its fire flashed through her, whipping her insides like a lash. With a scream of effort, she tore herself away from the void before *Hagal*'s power could consume her. Choking back the pain, she seized Medavle by the throat. 'Never do that again,' she hissed. 'You could have killed me.'

He merely looked at her, eyes opaque, and the strength that held him up left her in a rush. Kyndra collapsed to the ground, clutching her stomach against a wave of nausea. The last few minutes were a blur; they felt unreal and she struggled to remember what had happened, what she'd done.

Shika.

Kyndra felt numb. She gazed at her hands, at the constellation dimming on her skin. It hadn't been enough. She hadn't done enough. It was her fault.

A voice reached her ears; Irilin was crying for Shika, her throat already raw with his name.

'Get up,' Medavle said harshly. He grabbed Kyndra's arm and she let herself be pulled to her feet. She thought she saw tear stains on his cheeks. 'What you've done –' He stopped, looked around at the empty landscape. There was no sign of the wraiths. 'How many did you kill?'

'I didn't kill them,' Kyndra said tonelessly. 'Just tore their forms apart.' She squeezed her eyes shut. If only she'd acted sooner, if only she hadn't been so afraid. But she knew the stars came with a terrible price. If she kept using their power, one day she wouldn't care if her friends were killed. She wouldn't be human any more.

She forced her eyes open, forced herself to look at Irilin's tear-streaked face. 'I'm so sorry,' she whispered. 'I'm so sorry, Irilin.'

The young woman gazed back at her and the look in her eyes said she didn't know Kyndra at all.

5

His first name wasn't Char. That was what the slavers called him. Neither was his second name Lesko: that was Ma's name. But Ma had raised him, so he had taken her name for his own. In a way, Ma was mother to the whole caravan. *We slavers are all Leskos*, he thought.

Technically, Ma was nobody's mother. She was a mercenary, perhaps the finest fighter in the Beaches. No slave escaped on her watch, and when she was present at negotiations, buyers paid the agreed sums and proper courtesies were observed. The slim kali sticks sheathed at her hips were a fierce deterrent to any who thought they could cheat the slaver master, Genge.

Still, if Ma Lesko was anyone's mother, she was his. She had found him as a baby, after all. And, for reasons known only to herself, instead of leaving him to die by the side of the road, she'd kept him and signed on as a guard with Genge's caravan. It wasn't a good life, but they had food and a tent over their heads. Ma had done her best. No matter that the slavers called him Char, saying his dark grey skin looked as if he'd been

46

pulled out of a fire. No matter that they shunned and spat at him when his back was turned. No matter that it was only his relationship to Ma that protected him from a coward's knife in the back. The slavers were yellow bastards at heart.

And that was why he was going to kill them.

Char eased the kali sticks into his palms. Ma had taught him that, when wielded right, they could break a neck in one strike. It was a quicker death than the slavers deserved and certainly too swift an end for their leader, Genge. But Char was no torturer. He'd settle for justice.

He moved through the camp, a shadow amongst shadows. The night came suddenly in the Beaches. If it caught you unaware on the dunes, you'd never see sunrise. There were worse things out here than slavers.

A voice moaned, loud in the quiet. Char jumped, silently cursing the slave. His fingers slipped on the sticks and he almost dropped them. *Concentrate.* He tightened his grip. One misstep and it would be *his* blood soaking the sand. He doubted even Ma could talk Genge down if the slave master discovered him out of bed with drawn weapons in the heart of the camp.

He tried to keep his breathing even, tried to find the calm centre Ma was always talking about. As usual, he couldn't sense it. He always felt so full of rage.

Char hissed through his teeth. *Concentrate, you idiot.* Too many thoughts. He was always thinking too many—

There was a sharp blow to his windpipe. Char choked and clapped a hand to his throat. His sticks tumbled to the sand as an arm encircled his neck and dragged him backwards. He hadn't even time to reach for the knife in his boot. Struggling to breathe, Char kicked back, hoping to catch his attacker on

47

the shin, but his foot met no resistance and the next moment, pain blazed across his knees. He crumpled.

'Stupid,' hissed a voice.

It took Char several seconds to recover his breath. 'Ma?'

'Shut up.'

He was dragged through the chilly night sand, back towards the safety of his tent, back towards the life he'd sworn to escape. Anger lent him strength. He felt that she hadn't used the full lock on his arms. Only one stick held them twisted behind his back. With a growl of effort, Char broke her hold and spun to a standing position.

Her full-armed slap sent him staggering back. He raised a hand to ward off another blow, forgetting too late that he'd dropped his kali sticks. Instead, Ma only looked at him. Her face was a chiselled shadow under the stars. He glanced at a dark smear on one of the elbow-length gloves she always wore. Blood. Char touched his stinging cheek and rubbed the wetness between finger and thumb. Ma's expression did not waver. In one smooth motion, she sheathed her sticks, seized his arm and hauled him bodily through the flap of his tent.

Char said nothing as she sat him down. He let her clean the cut on his face, ignoring the tincture's sting. Ma worked in silence. Only when she'd capped the bottle and cleaned her cloths did she reach for the two sticks tucked safely behind her belt.

Char took his weapons back. His throat still hurt from Ma's jab and he swallowed painfully.

'When you have surprise on your side, always go for the throat,' Ma said. 'With the right speed and pressure, you can close an opponent's windpipe for a few critical seconds.'

Char rubbed his throat and kept silent. For her, disarming

him had been no harder than taking an infant's toy. It rankled more than he wished to admit and he looked away.

Ma seized his chin, forcing him to meet her gaze. 'No,' she said softly and he knew what she saw: his eyes burned, black pupils narrowed to slits like a cat's. Char tried to breathe deeply, tried to force down the ever-present anger, but spiked with humiliation, it wouldn't leave.

'Boy,' she said. She never called him Char. 'Let it go.'

He shook her off. 'Why should I?' he snarled, as the untempered fury beat at his insides. Tonight it felt like vast, bound wings, straining to open. 'Why did you stop me?'

Ma faced him calmly. 'You know why.'

It was too much. Char felt walled in by years of unanswered questions, the same things asked over and over again. *Where did Ma come from? Why did they live like this? What stopped them from leaving?* Every way he turned, Ma was there with her inscrutable face and her refusal to answer. She was the only person he loved in this cursed world. He would never hurt her. But the rage boiled and writhed and lashed him, so that he almost cried out against the horror of what it could do if it ever got loose. 'Ma,' he breathed.

'I know,' she said in her husky voice, catching him in a rough hug. 'I know you hate them. But we must stay. We stay because it's safe.'

Char pulled away. 'I wouldn't call Genge *safe*.'

'No.' She shook her head, brown eyes opaque. 'But he's a different kind of dangerous.'

'How?'

Ma wrapped muscled arms around her midriff, though the tent was well insulated against the cold desert night. She gazed at him a while before answering, as if searching for the right words. 'Genge is a beast, but a beast we know how to handle. There are other beasts out there, ones I don't understand, ones I am afraid of meeting.'

Char shook his head. 'I wish you wouldn't talk like that.' His anger had begun to fade, a profound weariness taking its place. 'Can't you give me a simple answer for once?'

Ma dropped her arms. 'There are no simple answers, Boy.' Her dark face was hard. 'I've told you. I can't fight the beasts I don't know.'

'Then *I* will fight them,' Char said impulsively. He knew nothing of Ma's past, of the time before she rescued him. But it was obvious: she was hiding from something . . . or someone. He grabbed her gloved hands. 'You needn't be afraid, Ma. I'll kill whatever beasts you fear and then you and I will be free to go where we want.'

'No,' she said, and he recoiled from the fierceness in her voice. 'It is not your place.'

But Char had seen all that he needed to. Ma *was* hiding. And underneath her calm façade, she was terrified.

Char didn't sleep much that night. When dawn picked out the stitches in the stretched hide of the tent, he knew what he had to do.

He had reason enough to kill Genge, but his goal was manifold: he would do it for Ma. When Genge was dead, she'd have nowhere to hide. Years of running had blown her fear out of all proportion. She had broken her own rule: never turn your back on your demons. Now, when Ma glanced over her shoulder, her demons had become giants. *This* was the reason why she insisted they stay with Genge – always on the move.

Skin tingling with his decision, Char threw back the tent

flap . . . and got a face full of sand. The smoky black lenses he wore to cover his eyes blocked the worst of it. But the fine grains coated his lips and nostrils and stuck to the sweat on his face. Char retched and choked, guffaws ringing in his ears. Ren and Tunser. He spat his next mouthful at their boots.

Tunser let out a growl to match his girth. He was wide, unlike his brother, but with the same pale skin that blistered beneath the unforgiving sun of the Beaches. They hailed from the north, Char knew, up near the borders of Yrmfast, where they were still under bounty. Many of the men Genge hired were criminals in their own lands. But no matter what they'd done, the law wouldn't pursue them into the Beaches, not when the Beaches were themselves considered a death sentence.

Char straightened. 'Bastards.'

'Thought you'd like a blast,' Ren said, grinning. 'Scrub some of that dirt off you.'

Char shook the last of the sand from his clothes. 'Too stupid to think up anything new?'

Ren shrugged off the insult, but Tunser clenched his fists. Char laid a casual hand on the sticks behind his belt. 'Come on, then, Tun,' he said invitingly and rolled the night's stiffness out of his shoulders. 'Or you'll be thinking about me all day.'

Ren's grin disappeared. He grabbed his brother's wrist, a warning.

Char smiled. 'Just between you and me, Tunser,' he said, 'I think Ren's worried I'll hurt you.'

The big man shook off his brother and furiously lunged at Char.

He sidestepped the charge, spun the kali sticks into his hands and cracked one across Tunser's shoulder blades. That move wouldn't cause injury, but it would enrage him further.

Predictably, Tunser bellowed and swung a meaty fist at Char's head.

Char ducked it and punched the ends of both sticks into the man's diaphragm. Winded, Tunser staggered back and knocked over his brother. They tumbled to the sand in a tangle of limbs, and Char threw back his head and laughed.

Like a snake, Ren twisted free of his brother and sprang up, pulling a knife from his belt. He had none of Tunser's bulk, being spear-thin and half a head taller. Still, he was the more dangerous of the two, quick and vicious.

Darting forward, Char went for his wrist, using the first disarming form Ma had taught him. Ren parried and Char saw his error too late. The scuffle had carried him perilously close to one of the wagons. When Ren lunged back at him, he had nowhere to go. Char got one stick up to block, but the knife shivered along its length and sliced into his forearm.

Several things happened at once. Char gasped as Ren hooted in triumph. He watched as the wound on his arm opened, oozing blood. The pain came a moment later . . . and some restraint broke within him. Ren had only a moment to stare at the blood that ran in black rivulets down Char's arm before a wind hit him, a wind with all the force of the desert behind it.

Ren flew ten feet to smash against the door of an empty cage. The wind, which had come from nowhere on a windless day, held him there, splayed and defenceless, and his knife dropped from nerveless fingers. Char could see the whites of Ren's eyes, as the man stared at him, inaudible words forming on his lips.

Rage thundered in Char, boiling the black blood that welled from his slashed arm. The wind roared, filled his whole body with a whirl of air and sky.

'Lesko!'

Genge. And with his shout, the wind died. Char blinked. For the first time, he saw Tunser, contorted in a ball on the ground. Sand coated everything . . . everything except Char. He looked over his shoulder. The wind had come from the desert, but behind him, nothing was disturbed. Instead, a tumbled trail of debris spread in a rough cone from where he stood backed against the wagon.

Dazed, Char tugged off his headscarf to bind the wound. His grey hair, more the colour of true ash than the dark char he was named for, fell around his face. Hoping the slave master hadn't seen the blood, he wrapped his injury and pulled the scarf tight, biting off a curse.

Genge kicked a length of rope out of his way. Stepping over a spare wheel, he came to stand in front of the three men. Char felt light-headed. He rifled through the last few minutes, trying to make sense of them.

'What is this?'

The slave master filled his vision. Char stood, clutching his arm, and Genge's face darkened at his silence. It was a placid face with wide-set, not unpleasant features. It was a face few suspected and many came afterwards to hate. Char thought bitterly, *It is a face to hide behind*.

Out of the corner of his eye, he saw Ren uncurl from where the wind had dropped him in a heap on the sand. The brothers struggled to their feet, spitting out mouthfuls of desert sand. Char almost smiled.

'I said,' Genge breathed in a low voice, 'what is this?'

'He attacked Tun,' Ren said before Char could answer.

'It was self-defence.'

'He attacked him.' Ren spoke more loudly. 'He's wild, Genge. Like a dog. You ought to be rid of him.'

Genge's pale eyes flicked to the scarf wrapped around Char's arm and Char felt cold, standing there under the sweltering sun. Surely Ren had seen him bleed, had noticed the colour of his blood.

Then, cat-quick, Genge reached out and whipped the lenses off his eyes.

Panic shot through Char. But the slave master merely tossed the black lenses into the sand. 'You'll look at me when I talk to you.'

Char let go of his breath. 'Yessir.' If his pupils looked like a regular man's, then the rage truly had left him. For now. He had no illusion that this was anything but a temporary calm.

'I keep you on your Ma's word,' Genge said, grabbing a fistful of cloth at Char's neck. 'She says you're good. And she doesn't lie.'

How little you know her, Char thought.

With a glance at his bandaged arm, Genge shoved him away and turned to include the brothers. 'I pay you to fight bandits and mysha.' His eyes narrowed. 'Unless you want a night on the dunes, you'll keep your peace.'

Char grimaced and saw his expression echoed on the faces of Ren and Tunser. A night on the dunes meant death; there was no way to hide from the packs of sand dogs, the mysha, that hunted there. Although if it came to a choice between them and facing Ma's wrath if she found out he'd been fighting, he might opt for the mysha.

The caravan rolled on its slow course under the relentless sun. Char made sure to keep the slaves hydrated. Until they reached

Na Sung Aro and were sold at auction, their well-being was his responsibility. A dead slave meant a serious loss of profit for the crew.

They had several able-bodied slaves that Iarl Rogan would probably buy for his Causcan mines. And if they were lucky, Iarl Alder would take their girls, seeing as how he only ever staffed his smithies with women. Char grinned. Good stock sometimes meant a bonus and he wanted a new scabbard to hold his kali sticks. Na Sung Aro wasn't the best place to buy leather, but –

What am I thinking? Char snatched back the water skin from the slave girl he had passed it to, ignoring her pleading request for more. He jammed the stopper in savagely and hooked the skin onto his belt. *I need a plan to get out of here, not a bloody scabbard.* But it was difficult to think in this blinding sun, let alone to think logically.

The nameless girl slumped defeated against the bars of her cage, but her sister eyed him venomously, her blue eyes afire with hatred. She hawked and spat and her aim was unerringly true. Calmly, Char removed the black lenses he wore and wiped them clean. The girl should be grateful, he thought, as he turned away – at least she had shade and didn't have to trudge through the burning sands.

Blotting the sweat from his face with the trailing end of a fresh headscarf, he returned to his assigned place in the vanguard. Genge's caravan consisted of three covered slave wagons, pulled by a desert team of dune mules, a cart that carried whatever of the slaves' possessions Genge considered worth selling, and another that held the tents, weapons, water barrels and rations they'd need to survive in the desert.

Genge had been one of the first to capitalize on the empire's slackening grip on its territories. And its grip on the Beaches was the slackest of all. Stalked by the rabid mysha, baked by blistering sun during the day and frozen under clear skies at night, only the very brave or very stupid made a life here. The Beaches had seen off the last Sartyan patrol around three years ago and it seemed that the Davaratch was disinclined to lose another. It wasn't any surprise, then, that illicit trades had sprung up in and around the desert. Na Sung Aro had once been a ragtag straggle of huts sliding into the sand; now it was known as the Black Bazaar – a place that sold anything and anyone.

Char let his lip curl. Slavery was the cleanest trade out here in the desert, considering what else went on. He had no patience with those who dabbled in narcotics like ithum or the rare and dangerous lotys stems, worth ten times their weight in ken. But drugs were the lifeblood of Na Sung Aro and ensured that the Black Bazaar remained a haven for the empire's many enemies.

'Hey!'

The shout came from behind him. One of the slaves had managed to drag half the canvas covering off his cage in the front of the wagon and was standing as upright as the bars allowed. He was newly acquired from a ship unlucky enough to be wrecked on the barren coast of the Beaches. Most ship-wrecked died within days, either from injuries sustained in the wreck or at the jaws of a pack of mysha, but this man had suf-fered only bruises. Genge had considerately 'rescued' him and now intended to sell him in Na Sung Aro. Char didn't think he'd get much.

'Do you know who I am?'

Char sighed wearily. 'Don't waste your breath,' he muttered.

'My name is Iarl Blattley – of Calmarac!' the captive added, as if on sudden inspiration. 'My estate supplies wine to the Davaratch himself.'

Char glanced over his shoulder. The man's face was ruddy in the heat and his salt-stained tunic had shrunk to reveal a fat strip of belly beneath. 'Vintner to the Davaratch, eh?' he said. 'You must be good.'

'Yes – *yes*,' the portly man gasped, wiping his face on his sleeve. 'The secret of the golden grape has been preserved in my family for generations. No other estate can produce so rich a flavour.'

'A talent that brings in a tidy profit, no doubt.'

'Tidy, yes,' the man said eagerly. 'I knew you'd understand – you've a sharp look about you. I am a wealthy man, very wealthy indeed. And I could provide *significant* reparation were you to set me free.'

Char turned back to the desert to hide his smile. 'Exactly how significant?'

There was a pause in which he could almost hear the fat man struggling with his greed.

'I could stretch to, say, one hundred red ken.'

Char snorted. 'A hundred? I could make twice that from selling your hide in Na Sung Aro.'

'All right, two hundred,' the man said, a hint of desperation creeping into his voice.

Char turned to look at him again and the man visibly recoiled. 'Two hundred miserable red ken?' he asked him softly. 'You don't place much value on freedom, vintner to the Davaratch.'

'Three hundred, four hundred,' the man spluttered, but Char shook his head.

'You know what I think?' he said. 'I think you've never seen a bottle of Calmaracian wine in your life. Your tunic carries the signature of the Arkhann Weavers – fake, by the way – and your boots are made from green Stroc skin that only a local of the Hozen Swamps would be able to obtain. My guess is that you're a minor lord with a few debts in his saddlebags who decided to try his hand at smuggling. A storm blew up on the Cargarac – and if you were a genuine smuggler, you'd have known that it's currently storm season – wrecked your ship and destroyed your cargo of poteen, which is the only illegal substance that the people of the Hozen Swamps are any good at making.'

There was stunned silence from the man in the cage. Then – 'My tunic's a fake?'

'And a poor one at that,' Char answered. 'You can tell by the lack of double loops around the kingfisher's tail.'

'I'll kill Egger,' came the man's reply.

'So you see, my friend,' Char said, gazing out at the shimmering sands that hid Na Sung Aro, 'your knowledge of hooch-brew is worth more to us than your stingy offering of ken. Which, for the record, I don't believe exists.'

When he next looked round, the man had turned his back and small, smothered sobs shook his shoulders. 'In the desert,' Char informed him, 'tears are a waste of water.' He smiled without humour. 'I suspect you'll learn that the hard way.'

The walls of Na Sung Aro slowly shaped themselves out of the twilight and Char breathed a sigh of relief. He glanced at the surrounding desert, but nothing moved. Though mysha were shy around Na Sung Aro, their scavenger instinct was sometimes too powerful for them to ignore, particularly when the pack hadn't eaten well. So the people of the Black Bazaar were guarded by seven-foot walls of smooth adobe brick, which completely encircled the town. They might keep the mysha out, but they also kept people in and sand dogs were far from the only danger here.

Beyond the low, round-roofed buildings, a wind was blowing up in the east. Char felt it in his bones. He'd always been sensitive to the airy force that whipped up the dune tops in a frenzy of dust. He knew the direction the wind would come from; he knew how strong it would blow, as if something inside both of them was the same. As a boy, he'd mentioned the feeling to Ma, and hadn't forgotten the fleeting fear that had crossed her face. He'd kept quiet about it after that.

The wind tasted strange tonight. The familiar dry tang of the desert was there, but beneath it was something more, something he'd never felt. This wind was rich, as if it blew from a land far greater than the desert. Char thought he discerned pine trees, hot rock, frothing rivers and mountains – those fabled spires of stone he'd heard tell of but had never seen.

The only land east of Na Sung Aro was Baior . . . and the hoarlands. The Beaches might be famous for swallowing Sartyan patrols, but a whole division had once disappeared in the hoarlands. With Rairam gone, they marked the end of the world. The last Starborn had vanished five centuries before, taking the lost continent with him and thereby ending the Sartyan Conquest. Some people believed Rairam to be destroyed, gone forever, but Char wasn't so sure. Especially when the wind blew from the east.

'Lesko,' a voice snapped and Char realized he was standing as though frozen. He shook himself out of his daze and saw Genge. The slave master pulled a cloak over his leathers and shrugged up its hood to protect him from the whirling sands.

'Help Hake set up,' he said, 'and keep a watch on the girls.' His pale eyes narrowed. 'I don't want them spoiled before market.'

Char nodded and the slave master strode away towards the centre of town. He'd be back by midnight, his pockets bulging with ken – private viewings were reserved for top customers and accounted for nearly a quarter of the caravan's profit. They'd have tonight to prepare the slaves before potential buyers began arriving at dawn.

Several caravans had already set up camp in the space reserved for them just inside Na Sung Aro's walls. The makeshift paving didn't stretch to this apron of land where the sand was packed solid by the hard feet of the slave trade. Char took the water around again, letting the slaves drink their fill. Long practice had taught him to close his ears to the pleas and rages of people crying out for freedom. Although the harsh reality of the caravan was the only world he knew, he couldn't help wondering what his life might have been if his parents, whoever they were, had wanted him. It was a bitter poison that made him despise the caravan and his sordid existence all the more.

But Ma wouldn't leave, and if he belonged anywhere, it was at her side.

Tunser drew a whetstone in slow strokes up and down his blade; an empty threat. Char knew the big man wouldn't continue their quarrel. It was more than both their lives were worth if Genge returned and found them fighting. A quiet cough sounded behind him and Char turned to find Ma standing with bucket and sponge in hand.

'Time to see to the girls,' she said and then looked narrowly at his stained clothes. 'You could do with a bath yourself.'

He sighed. 'Do you ever think of a life outside the caravan, Ma?'

Her face darkened. 'We have spoken about this.'

'But there's a whole world beyond the Beaches,' Char pressed. The scent of the wind was still in his nostrils and it made him restless. 'You weren't born here. Don't you ever feel like going home?'

Ma's look was cold. 'I have no home.'

'So you keep saying.' The restlessness was creeping into Char's voice now, making it stronger. 'But you came from somewhere outside the desert. You had a family, a people. You *belonged*. I'm an orphan, so this is the only life I've known, but—'

'Enough,' she said, throwing her pail to the ground. 'I refuse to be judged by you – whom I rescued and raised instead of leaving to perish as I should have done.'

Char took a step closer, the strange wind at his back. It seemed to whisper in his ears, to blow shivering down his spine. 'You owe me the truth, Ma.'

To his surprise, she retreated, suddenly uneasy. 'I must see to the girls,' she repeated and snatched up her dropped bucket. As Char stared at her back, the east wind slackened and the resolute force that had driven him to confront Ma vanished.

Char helped Hake unpack the wagons and begin work erecting the tents. Genge's second was a sturdy man – not huge like Tunser, but equally muscled. Rumour had it he'd been born in Na Sung Aro itself, a true child of the Black Bazaar.

Char grunted with the effort of stretching the tight hide and tethering it to the metal pegs he'd hammered into the dirt. It was hot work, even in the cooling dusk, and sweat prickled his neck. When finally he rose to stow his tools, the unforgiving stars of the desert peppered the sky and lights bloomed in the town like fetid blossoms. The lamp-gas stank and the illumination it produced was yellowy-brown, a colour that suited the debauched streets of Na Sung Aro. Needing some space, Char flipped the gate guard a single white ken and stepped outside. The sounds of the town were muted here, the smooth sand untroubled by mysha prints. The dogs weren't haunting Na Sung Aro tonight, but he'd do well to stay alert. Char strolled a little way away from the walls, turning his face south to the sea. The Cargarac murmured in its restless sleep and turned over with a sigh. Waves lapped at sands still hot from the day and Char stood watching them, breathing in the salt-scent.

It might have happened between blinks, or in the still point at the end of an exhaled breath, but where before there was only empty beach, suddenly there was a figure standing a few feet away from him.

Char hissed and leapt back, his hands going for his kali sticks, but he'd switched his weapons belt for the one that held his tools and hadn't replaced it. Cursing, he took another step back, but the figure didn't follow. It just stood there with its arms held loosely at its sides, face shrouded in bandages.

'Who are you?' Char asked finally, his voice a whisper.

To his astonishment, the figure placed bandaged palms together and bowed. 'Kala,' it said in a male voice, 'we have searched long for you.'

'For me?' Char repeated, at a loss. More bandages wrapped the stranger's torso, arms and legs, leaving bare only the soles of his unshod feet.

'It is my honour to have found you,' the man continued, and he bowed even lower. 'It is my honour to serve the Kala.'

'What did you call me?'

The man spoke to the sand. 'My Kala, my master and teacher, guide and leader. The one who saw, sees and will see.'

'I've never heard of the Kala,' Char said, now thoroughly unnerved. The stranger must have mistaken him for someone else. 'How did you come here – how did you avoid the mysha?'

'All beasts are beneath notice, my Kala,' the man said, straightening.

Char stared. 'Few would agree with you.'

'You no longer need worry over others.' The bandaged stranger's voice was flat. 'You will come to us and we will be made rich.'

Something tightened in Char's stomach. 'I'm not going anywhere.'

'You belong with your people, who have searched through years and lands for the marks of your coming.'

The man was mad. Char swallowed and cursed himself yet again for shedding his weapons belt. Easing into a wider stance, he said, 'I think you have me confused with someone else. I'm a slaver, not a leader. I don't know who your people are.'

The man regarded him, his expression obscured in cloth. 'You will remember, Kala. Once we reach Khronosta, you will remember your people.'

Khronosta. The scions of time. This must be one of the *du-alakat*, the feared assassins bent on taking out Sartya's leaders one by one. Never seen, never heard, they left only corpses behind them. 'Shit,' Char said.

Before he could move, a figure loomed behind the man, darkening the stars: Ma. Her kali stick swept towards his neck, but the man dodged inhumanly fast and spun to face her, bringing a weapon into each hand.

Kali sticks.

Char's eyes widened. In all his life, he'd only ever seen himself and Ma wield the sticks. Most mercenaries considered them a child's weapons. Ma, of course, knew better, which was why she'd chosen to teach him. There were many ways to kill or disable a person and only a few of them required blades.

As Ma circled the stranger, her sticks gripped in gloved hands, Char saw his own shock mirrored in the man's eyes.

'Who are you?' the Khronostian asked Ma, whose face was grim and implacable. She did not answer, but continued to circle.

'How long have you—?'

His question ended in a gasp as Ma launched a flurry of strikes. Char stared – she was using her ironwood sticks and aiming to kill. The quick-footed stranger dodged and parried and Ma's attacks grew fiercer. If they'd been aimed at him, Char would be dead, his throat staved in, his skull cracked. But the stranger was a formidable opponent. He parried all but a handful of Ma's strikes and dodged the rest.

And then – Char blinked. For a moment, it seemed as if the man had vanished and reappeared just behind Ma. Somehow she sensed him there and turned to meet his attack, but she was a fraction too slow; one of the kali sticks slipped under her guard and smacked across her ribs.

Char made to rush forward, but she snarled at him, 'Stay back, Boy.'

'Why do you fight me?' the stranger asked, half lowering his weapons. 'You must be—'

Ma yelled and aimed a double blow at his kneecaps. The man dodged it, but only just. His face wrapping was loose and Char caught a glimpse of wrinkled cheek. It surprised him – the man's voice was surely that of someone years younger.

'You will not have him,' Ma growled and struck a vicious blow at the stranger's temple.

Under her onslaught, the man began to move impossibly fast – Char could not keep track of him. His heart was pounding and he found himself stumbling back. Was this the famed Khronostian power to manipulate time? If he hadn't seen it for himself, he'd have joked that such a thing was impossible. Surely Ma couldn't best the man, but it seemed that no matter which direction he attacked from, one of her sticks was always there to block him.

'You – who are you?' the stranger managed to gasp between strikes. Blood had soaked the bandages around his nose and his movements no longer flowed as they had at the start of the fight.

'I am Ma Lesko,' she said in a voice like death. The next moment, Char heard the sickening crunch of bone and saw blood pouring from the man's ruined eye. Ma's attack had come out of nowhere. The stranger staggered, equally shocked. With a gasp of disbelief, he fell to one knee and Ma was on him. Three blows split his skull, though she could have done it in one. The thirsty sand turned red.

Char stood, sickened and shaken, unable to meet her eyes. The whole episode had unfolded in less than five minutes. He looked at the corpse of the man who had bowed to him, his blood spilled out across the sands. He didn't even know his name.

'Help me.' Ma seized the stranger's bandaged legs and began to haul him away from the town. Char glanced back, but it seemed the fight had gone unnoticed. The gate was closed and the guard had disappeared. Ren and Tunser were probably dicing, as they always did before a night in the Black Bazaar.

Moving automatically, he grasped the corpse's arms and

helped manoeuvre it southwards. 'We can't go too far,' he said. 'What about the mysha?'

'What about them?' Ma said coldly. 'I mean for them to eat tonight.'

Char shuddered despite himself. When Ma considered them far enough away from the caravan, they dropped the corpse and lightly scattered it with sand. The mysha would do the rest of the work. By morning, there'd be nothing left. In silence they retraced their steps until they reached the site of the skirmish. Ma kicked at it savagely until the bloody sand became part of the desert once more.

'Who was that man?' Char asked as they approached the gate. 'He seemed to recognize you. And he used kali sticks.'

'Many people use kali sticks.'

'Then how have we never encountered anyone else using them in all the time we've travelled the Beaches?'

'They are not popular here. The sticks take years to master and against mysha, a blade is preferable.'

'He said he was from Khronosta.'

Ma's shoulders stiffened, but she didn't stop walking.

'He wanted me to come with him,' Char persisted. 'He seemed to know me.'

Ma moved so fast, her hand was at his collar before he knew what was happening. She pressed her face close to his, her teeth bared. 'He was *du-alakat*. If I hadn't turned up when I did, you would be *dead*.' She spat the last word and there was a terrible kind of rage in her eyes, only a shade away from fear.

'An assassin?' Char asked. 'Why would the Khronostians want me dead?'

Ma turned away from him and continued walking. Perplexed, Char hurried after her. 'Ma?'

'I don't know,' she said and Char didn't have to see her face to know she was lying.

'Why won't you tell me?' he asked, anger finally tempering the shock of the last few minutes. 'What are you hiding?'

Ma stopped just shy of the gate. 'More will come,' she said, 'especially when the first does not return.'

'Then we leave.'

Ma pressed her lips together, said nothing.

Char caught her arm. 'You *can't* think we should stay after this? You said they'll send more.'

She was silent for a long time. They returned to the caravan, now lit only by the oily light of torches spaced around the perimeter. Thick canvas draped the slaves' cages to keep out the desert night. There was no sign of Genge or the others.

Ma stopped when they reached her tent. She turned, hands resting on her weapons, staring into the darkness. 'Very well,' she said finally. 'We'll leave. Tomorrow night when the auction is done.'

Char stood stunned. After all these years, after all her refusals . . . Despite the threat of the *du-alakat*, he couldn't hold back his grin. 'You mean that? We're really going to leave? Forever?'

'Forever.'

The word dropped from Ma's lips with a finality that made Char shiver. He shrugged it off. 'We'll need supplies.'

'I will see to them. I can make back the ken at auction tomorrow.'

This really was happening. They were going to leave the caravan and the life he so detested. Char's heart had never felt lighter. The threats of assassins, his run-in with Ren, the rage that lit an uncontrollable fire in his chest . . . none of it could trouble him right now. 'Where will we go?'

'North out of the Beaches,' Ma said, keeping her voice low, 'and then west. We'll be safest in the Heartland.'

Char raised an eyebrow and held up his forearms. 'Your plan is to walk into the middle of Sartyan territory with tattoos that scream "slaver"?'

Ma looked unconcerned. 'They can be removed. The Heartland will be teeming with work for our kind.' She gently touched his face. 'We will disappear, Boy. No one will harm you, not as long as I breathe.'

A bit embarrassed at her vehemence, Char changed the subject. 'The way you moved tonight. I've never seen you fight so well.'

Ma's hand fell from his cheek. 'Merely long practice.'

'You were as fast as him. It was like he disappeared and then reappeared in another place. Can all Khronostians do that?'

'Only the *du-alakat* train in the art.' Her voice had turned peculiarly flat. 'They can slow time. To one watching, it looks as if they're moving unnaturally fast.'

'What about the rest of Khronosta?' Char pressed. 'Why are they called the scions of time?'

'They are the children of Khronos. He was their leader. He taught them to control time . . .' Ma looked away. 'But he died.'

'Control time?'

'Large groups can travel through time, but the power is limited. They must have an anchor – someone who was alive during that time. And they cannot interact with the world as it was.' Ma frowned. 'At least I hope they cannot.'

'What's the point of it, then?'

'The ability has kept them out of Sartyan reach for years. They have a ritual which lets them move their temple and everyone in it to . . . somewhere else.'

Char regarded her narrowly. 'How do you know all this?'

'I met a Khronostian once, long before you were born. Where do you think I learned the sticks?'

Another lie? Char wasn't sure. He wondered whether Ma had seen the Khronostian bow to him. If she had, why did she believe he was an assassin? Assassins didn't bow to their marks, they didn't call them 'Kala' and talk about taking them back to Khronosta. Unless that had merely been a trick to separate Char from the caravan, to put him off his guard.

One thing, however, was perfectly clear: the Khronostian had not reckoned on Ma. And that mistake had cost him his life.

6

Naris, Rairam
Brégenne

It was an hour past dawn and the passages of Naris were crowded. Wielders and novices hurried breathless about their business, but all made room for her. The silver robes she wore were trimmed with red, her hood lined with rich scarlet. As they passed her, each dipped their head respectfully. She was, after all, one of the three members of the Wielders' Council.

Brégenne doubted she'd ever grow used to it. The memory of her earlier disgrace was still too fresh and, looking back, she could hardly take credit for the events that had followed. But Acre was restored, the Nerian absolved, and it all lay at Kyndra's feet, the first new Starborn in centuries. She was barely eighteen and already she'd changed the face of the world.

Shaking her head at the wonder of it, Brégenne quickened her pace, telling herself it wasn't to escape the bows. The mere act of walking these corridors was a new experience after all the unsighted years of feeling her way or using her Lunar power as guide. It was a different world she inhabited now, a sharp world of colour and detail that she'd long thought lost. She'd need time to adjust.

I don't have time, she reminded herself. *Not with Acre on our doorstep and the citadel in disarray.* The mood in Naris was far from equitable. Wielders still shunned the Nerian and the surviving members of the rebel sect stubbornly kept to themselves. To make matters worse, Veeta and Gend, Brégenne's fellow Council members, took issue with every proposal she put before them, their chief disagreement being Kyndra.

'I know her,' Brégenne had told them when they'd met in her quarters two days ago, 'and I trust her. She's gone to broker peace for Mariar. For Rairam, I mean. We owe it to her to be doing the same here.'

'You formed your trust before the girl came into her power,' Gend replied. 'That makes a difference. She is not the same person, Brégenne.'

'She knows right from wrong,' Brégenne insisted. 'She's taken responsibility for her actions.'

'Brégenne,' Veeta said gently, 'forgive me for saying so, but you've always been a little short-sighted when it comes to this girl.'

'The Starborn is a liability.' Gend had become far more loquacious since the night he'd lost his erstwhile Council members, and clearly he hadn't forgotten that Kyndra had killed Helira. 'The last Starborn managed to shut away an entire world. That kind of power needs to be controlled.'

'You sound like Loricus,' Brégenne snapped. 'She's not Kierik.'

'She's his daughter.'

Brégenne took a deep breath and said as calmly as she could, 'We are not our parents. Kyndra is nothing like the man who fathered her. Until we brought her here, she'd had no contact with him and she worked to undo what he did. Without her, the Breaking would have torn our world apart.'

'Because she had no choice,' Gend said. 'We've already established that the only way to stop the Breaking was to rid Mariar of Kierik's influence.'

'Look at us.' Brégenne shook her head. 'We're reliving old history when we need to be devising a strategy for dealing with Acre.'

'What would you have us do?' Veeta asked mildly. 'Until we hear from the Starborn—'

'I meant here in Mariar. In Rairam.'

Veeta clasped her hands. 'Messengers were sent out with news of Acre's return.'

'An action I opposed, if you recall. News of this magnitude cannot be conveyed in a note.' Brégenne refrained from grinding her teeth. 'It will either be ignored, laughed off or cause wholesale panic.'

'Then what do you propose?' Gend asked.

'The first and most important thing is to send a deputation to the Trade Assembly in Market Primus. They alone have the power, coin and influence to unite Mariar. We must be prepared.'

'This is all conjecture, Brégenne.' Gend folded his arms. 'We've seen nothing so far from Acre that could be interpreted as a threat. Your talk of war is premature at best, unfounded at worst.'

His condescending tone only inflamed her temper. Brégenne took a deep breath. 'I admit,' she said, 'that I've no evidence to base my fears upon except the example of history, but we are trying to gauge the situation from a position of ignorance, not knowledge. *That's* why Kyndra, Nediah and the others volunteered to go to Acre. What I'm saying is, we can't sit idle here. It may be that it won't come to war – and let's hope it does not – but to waste what little time we might have is lunacy. We *must* involve the Trade Assembly.'

'What makes you think they would listen to us?' Veeta asked.

Brégenne matched her stare for stare. 'If you planted a Lunar spear in that great round table of theirs, they'd listen.'

The other two were silent. Brégenne thought she knew what they were thinking. How do you break five hundred years of anonymity? How do you reintroduce what ordinary people call magic to a world that functions without it?

'You would reveal us?' Gend said. 'You would break the rule put in place for our own safety?

'We are not homeless novices any more,' she replied. 'We have no need to hide from the world. We've rebuilt over the centuries, recovered from the war that started all of this. We are Wielders of Naris and we've a duty of care to the people of this world. It's high time we remembered it.'

It had gone downhill from there.

Now, as she strode along, her mind full of Veeta and Gend's arguments, Brégenne wondered why they found it so difficult to accept how desperately change was needed. She rubbed her temples in anticipation of the headache that was sure to return. *Not so long ago, you'd have made those same arguments*, she thought, grimacing at the truth of it. But Kyndra had not only altered their world, she'd altered Brégenne too. She affected all those she met. Perhaps that was an ability peculiar to Starborn, or simply Kyndra herself. Brégenne missed her.

And she missed Nediah. He was always in her thoughts. His

face was as familiar to her as her own, but these new eyes, the eyes he had given her, saw everything differently. When she'd first looked at him under a sun she hadn't seen for decades, she'd noticed all the things the moon couldn't possibly show her: the slight tan to his skin, the flush in his cheeks, the way his dark hair curled chestnut in places. But most vividly she recalled how very green his eyes were, like a forest at midday.

Stop it, she told herself. It wouldn't do for the whole of Naris to see her pining like a lovesick girl. She walked faster, as if she could leave the memory of his face behind. The constant ache of missing him would not go away, but she had plenty of problems to pile atop it.

There was one thing she, Veeta and Gend agreed on: the need to train all Wielders to fight. Only a few had learned to harness Solar or Lunar energy as a weapon and they needed to share their skills with their fellow masters – and novices too. Naris was woefully underprepared to face the potential threat of Acre.

A commotion pulled Brégenne from her thoughts. She'd just stepped through the doors to the atrium when a shining creature began trotting towards her. It was a wolf, its Solar paws turning the polished floor to gold. Some novices gasped delightedly and there were a few startled exclamations from the nearest Wielders.

Brégenne crouched down and the envoi put its front paws on her knees. She could feel the heat of it through her robes, as if a heart were beating inside it. She knew the wolf – its likeness stood on her dresser, a gift from Nediah. They looked at each other. The wolf's eyes were large and liquid, Solar-white, and Brégenne felt a lump in her throat.

Only a moment and then its shape dissolved. When she

pulled her hands from its fur, words covered them, written in the careless script she knew so well:

We are just about to cross the red valley. No sign of anyone yet, but Medavle says the region to the west is called Baior and that we should expect to find settlements there. Will be in touch when we learn more.

It wasn't the perfunctory tone that caused her eyes to prickle. She could feel the warmth in the message, the emotion he'd imprinted there. Though she berated herself for it, Brégenne couldn't stop her heart from pounding as the words faded, taking the sense of him away.

She stood up quickly, hoping that nothing showed on her face.

'From Nediah, I presume.'

Alandred pronounced Nediah's name with none of his usual scorn. In fact, his recent behaviour had been notably different. Gone was the boorish, arrogant Wielder who had once tried to force his attentions on her. Brégenne thought she could trace the change back to the Long Night, the eve of the Breaking. The Madness and the Nerian rebellion had claimed many lives, undoubtedly the greatest upheaval since the fall of Solinaris.

Now, to her astonishment, Brégenne found that she didn't actively dislike the new Alandred. 'Just an update,' she said. 'They haven't encountered anyone yet, but that will change once they cross the valley.'

Alandred sighed. 'I shouldn't have let the novices go.'

'They're both adults, Alandred. You did as much as you could. The decision was theirs in the end.'

He blinked. 'You're not concerned for them?'

'As much as I can afford to be,' Brégenne said evenly. 'But who's to say Naris is safer? The empire nearly wiped us out once before because we grew complacent. I don't intend to make the same mistake.'

Alandred seemed to find it difficult to look her in the eye, but finally he met her gaze. 'You're planning something.'

'Someone has to.'

'What about Veeta and Gend?'

'They're reluctant to act.' Brégenne regarded him closely. 'I could use your help, Alandred.'

'You have it.' The pitch of his voice dropped with his gaze. 'You've always had it.'

'I have to leave the citadel,' she said and held up a hand before he could interrupt. 'The Wielders can't sit at the edge of things any more. That time is past. We're part of this world and now that Acre is back – possibly the empire too – we need to show people we're first and foremost Wielders of Mariar. We can't afford to be seen as a threat when there's a far greater one on our doorstep.

'If it comes to war, Mariar isn't ready. We've been at peace for five hundred years. Our best hope is to do what we do best – make alliances. But that means talking to the Trade Assembly, most of whose members are daft, rich old fools who've never faced anything worse than a ruined cargo.' Brégenne let go an angry breath. 'Unless Kyndra brokers a truce, we could well be dealing with an imperial army trained to conquer. Not only our freedom, but our lives are at stake and Veeta and Gend can't see it.'

Alandred was staring at her, at the flush in her cheeks. How long had it been since she'd felt this much passion, Brégenne wondered?

'So you see,' she finished, 'I have to go. Like Kyndra, I have a responsibility. If there's to be a truce between our lands, I must work towards it here in Mariar. Right now, our lack of information on Acre is our greatest weakness, but I'm relying on Kyndra to correct that.' Brégenne caught sight of a sullen young man standing with a hand in the pocket of his robes. 'And Market Primus isn't my only destination. I've another journey planned, one I won't be making alone.'

'Look,' Gareth said, 'I'm not sure how much help I can be to you. Master Hanser took me away from home when I was this high.' He waved his gloved hand at the floor. 'I'm effectively an outcast.'

'You want to take *another* of my novices, Brégenne?' Aland-red sounded exasperated. 'Surely a full master would be more appropriate. I mean,' he hesitated, 'I could go with you.'

'And I don't even sound like I'm from the north any more,' Gareth continued obliviously. 'Been around Shika too long.'

Brégenne had borne their arguments in silence, but now she said irritably, 'It has to be Gareth – no one else here comes from Ümvast. If I'm to walk into a place famous for its hostility to foreigners, I'd prefer to do it with a local at my side.'

Gareth huffed. 'As far as they're concerned, I'm just as much of a foreigner as you are.'

'But you were born there. You must have family.'

A shadow passed over Gareth's face. 'Yes,' he said reluctantly.

'Your parents—'

'Sorry for saying so, Lady Brégenne, but you know nothing about Ümvast.'

That gave her pause, but only for a moment. 'They'll recognize you at the very least.'

'I wouldn't count on it,' Gareth said with a humourless smile. 'My father's dead and the last thing my mother said to me was: "Rot, then, you ungrateful bastard. If I see you again, I'll kill you." I was eight.'

Brégenne was temporarily speechless. There were stories about Ümvast – the one place in Mariar that was almost as much of a mystery as Acre. The grim folk were content to ignore the rest of the world. Not only did they refuse to trade, but they rarely strayed beyond their borders. No one knew anything about them save that they called the Great Northern Forest home – a forest as unchartable as it was inhospitable. She wondered how Master Hanser had managed to find and extract Gareth.

But there *were* stories. Where the rest of Mariar had grown soft-bellied and slow, it was rumoured that Ümvast alone maintained the skills of war. Brégenne had need of those skills. It could well be that the northerners were Mariar's only real military defence against Acre should diplomacy fail. She couldn't rely solely on her fellow Wielders. Not only were they too few, but many had little to no experience of fighting.

'I need to see Ümvast himself,' she said decisively, ignoring Gareth's splutter. 'Do you know him?'

'Know him?' Gareth looked at her in disbelief. 'When I was a child, he was like a legend to us.' His eyes grew distant. 'I saw him once. He was tall – taller than I am now – and he wore a great cloak across his shoulders that clattered when he moved, as if it were made of bones . . .' He shook his head. 'But that was years ago. There might be a new one now.'

Alandred frowned. 'You mean to say Ümvast is a title as well as the name of your land?'

Gareth nodded. 'The word means "chieftain".'

'How are new chieftains chosen?' Brégenne asked, interested.

'We have a kind of caste system. Families of old blood are referred to as *Kul*, but you can also earn the *Kul* through performing an important feat or service to the people.' Gareth shifted – uneasily, Brégenne thought. 'When the time comes to choose a new chieftain, they hold a great Melee. If you're entitled to bear the *Kul*, you can enter – there's no restriction on gender or even age. The last one standing is declared Ümvast.'

'Is this a fight to the death?' Alandred asked disapprovingly.

'Sometimes.' Gareth shrugged. 'It's not necessary, though. Most combatants leave with a few broken bones.' He smiled faintly. 'Shika would say it's uncivilized.'

Brégenne nodded to herself. Gareth's ties to his home were stronger than he liked to admit. 'So that's settled, then,' she said. 'Gareth will come with me.' When the young man began to protest, she added, 'He might find the experience quite *freeing*.'

Gareth shut his mouth and clutched his right arm guiltily. Brégenne was the only one in Naris who knew what lay beneath the glove he wore. There was something disturbing about the black gauntlet – beyond the fact that it wouldn't come loose.

The gauntlet might be a relic of Acre, but she was convinced that it would yield up its secrets with study. She just wasn't comfortable conducting that study right under Hebrin's nose. If he discovered Gareth's theft, the archivist would punish the novice severely and not even a Council member could overrule Hebrin in a matter concerning the archives.

As if he knew what she was thinking, Gareth looked at her, a silent question in his eyes.

Don't worry, she answered him just as silently. *We'll find a way.*

By the evening of the second day, she'd put her plans for the journey in place.

Brégenne had no intention of informing her fellow Council members of her scheme. Veeta and Gend had made their positions clear and the atmosphere in Naris was tense enough without an acrimonious confrontation between its leaders.

Everyone could see that the citadel's fragile peace hung by a thread. The Nerian were resentful and unaccustomed to taking orders and the rest of the Wielders did not appreciate sharing their space with fanatics. It was a poor situation in which to leave Naris, but Mariar had bigger problems, bigger than the holes Kyndra had torn in the citadel. Brégenne needed to be out in the world, amongst its people; she needed to see first-hand the damage that the Breaking had wrought in its last days.

The fervour that drove these thoughts died a hearty death when it met the reality of packing. To her great irritation, Brégenne discovered that crafting a sensible inventory was not one of her skills. The first pack she made for herself was too heavy to lift off the table. The second was just as bad. Swearing under her breath, she threw almost everything out so that the third looked more like a bag she'd take on a jaunt to Murta.

In a fit of pique, Brégenne flung it across the room and collapsed in a chair. Why was this so hard? How many times had she travelled across Mariar with Nediah?

But that was it, of course. Nediah had always assumed this duty and she had gladly let him. Brégenne cursed her past self. She should have made time to learn these things – what was necessary and what was not and how much of it was needed. The thought of how heavily she'd relied on Nediah made her uncomfortable.

Well, there was nothing for it. She'd shelve her pride and ask for Gareth's help.

She sent a messenger for him and then decided that at least she could get changed while she waited. Brégenne ran a hand down her council robes, feeling the smoothness of the silk, the heavy fall of silver. Colour was still so rich and strange, its vibrancy almost frightening. She stared at herself in the mirror, at the slashes of blood red and the long sleeves that fell impractically over her hands. Once, she had dreamed of wearing these robes. Once, power and influence was all she had thought she wanted.

Slowly, she began to strip the silken layers away from her body until she stood in her underclothes. Then she folded up the robes and laid them carefully on her pillow. Turning her back to the mirror, she reached for the garments she'd bought earlier in Murta and pulled them on instead.

When the knock came, Brégenne was dressed and she opened the door to find not only Gareth but Alandred too. 'I hope you don't mind me –' Alandred's words ended in strangled silence. His eyes were wide and Gareth was trying hard not to stare.

'What?' she said.

'You look . . . different, Lady Brégenne.' Gareth coughed and stepped into the room, looking about with interest. Brégenne guessed he'd never seen inside a council apartment.

'Are you coming in?' she asked Alandred, who hovered in the doorway.

'Yes, sorry.' He shook his head, scooted inside and then returned to staring at her outfit.

Brégenne shut the door. 'All right, what's wrong with it?'

'Nothing,' Alandred said and she was horrified to see he was blushing.

'I can't wear robes outside Naris,' she explained, a bit embarrassed, 'and my other clothes aren't fit to travel in.'

'Of course,' he said, finally moving his eyes to her face. 'It suits you.'

Brégenne glanced down at herself defensively. Her trousers were of soft brown leather and hugged her legs. A fitted tunic covered her shirt and her feet were snug in knee-high boots. She'd bound her hair into a loose plait that hung over her shoulder and a snide little voice in the back of her head told her she'd spent a bit too long looking at Kait. Brégenne ignored it.

Gareth grinned at her. 'You look like a bandit, Lady Brégenne.'

She glared. 'Would you have spoken to Lady Helira that way?'

'*She* wouldn't have dressed in leather.'

Brégenne smiled wryly at the thought, but sobered when she remembered how Helira had died.

'I could use your help,' she said to Gareth, gesturing at the pack on the polished table. 'I'm not sure how long we'll be away for and I need advice about what we should be taking.'

Gareth put his hands in his pockets in a gesture that reminded her painfully of Nediah. 'Of course,' he said.

Alandred sighed. 'You're set on this, aren't you?' When she nodded, he switched his gaze to Gareth. 'If you're going to rely on a half-trained novice as backup, Brégenne, you two should at least be Attuned.'

'We can't be,' Brégenne said.

'Why not?'

'Because I'm Attuned to Janus and he's still in a critical condition – Nediah couldn't bring him out of the coma. There's a chance that his link to me is keeping him alive. Breaking it could kill him.'

'This is not ideal,' Alandred said, clearly unhappy. 'And how are we supposed to keep in touch with you?'

'I can send you regular envois,' Brégenne said. 'If and when Janus wakes up, he'll be able to talk to me directly.'

'I don't like the idea of you going alone, even with Gareth. Revealing the existence of Naris won't be without its consequences – you have no idea how people will react.' He paused. 'And have you considered what Veeta and Gend will do when they realize you're gone? They'll be furious. They may even send a group to bring you back.'

'They can try,' Brégenne corrected grimly. She moved to stand right before Alandred, forcing him to look at her. 'I don't expect you to lie for me, but if there's any way you can hide my absence at least until I'm beyond the Murtan plain, I'd be grateful.'

He held her gaze. 'I'll do what I can, Brégenne.'

'Thank you.' After a moment, she extended a hand. 'We'll be leaving as soon as we're packed,' she said. 'Goodbye, Alandred.'

Alandred looked at the hand and then at her and seemed to be steeling himself. In the next moment, he hugged her and, reminded uncomfortably of that night in her quarters when he'd carried his intentions a little too far, Brégenne suffered it in stiff silence. 'I hope you know what you're doing,' Alandred murmured as he let her go.

'He didn't hug *me*,' Gareth said when Alandred had gone.

'But I enjoyed his "you'd better look after her" glare.' He grimaced and added hastily, 'I mean, as if you needed looking after, Lady Brégenne.'

'Just Brégenne from now on,' she said and beckoned him over. 'Can I look at the gauntlet?'

Clearly reluctant, Gareth pulled off the glove he'd taken to wearing to hide it and pushed up his sleeve. 'Does it feel any different?' she asked, peering closely at the black metal, careful not to touch it. It was a dark thing, more a bracer than a gauntlet, as it stopped short of Gareth's fingers. Spikes studded the knuckles and the part which covered his hand was embossed with a sigil or letters. Brégenne couldn't make them out. It encased Gareth's forearm almost to the elbow and she felt that chill again, as if the metal were solid ice.

'A bit tighter,' Gareth admitted. 'When I first put it on, it was too big. Now it fits.'

Disquiet raised the hairs on the back of her neck. There was a reason relics of Acre were locked away. She wasn't sure whether Gareth had taken the gauntlet to help Kyndra, or out of foolish curiosity, but it was clearly enchanted and the fact remained she knew next to nothing about its powers.

'I've done a bit of research,' she said, 'but I couldn't find any reference to it in the archives. It looks like we'll have to figure out a way to remove it on our own.'

Gareth just nodded and pulled his bulky glove back on.

'You *will* let me know if you feel at all strange?' she asked sternly.

He nodded again, but Brégenne wasn't sure she believed him. 'I've arranged to pick up some extra supplies in Murta,' she said, changing the subject. 'And Myst is already stabled there. They've prepared a horse for you too.'

Gareth perked up at this. 'Is it a Hrosst breed?'

'Very likely. I told the trader we'd need the best she had.'

'I've always wanted a horse,' Gareth said with something of a child's excitement at midwinterfest. 'But in Ümvast we hadn't a need for them.'

Taking Gareth with her had seemed like the perfect solution to both their problems. He could provide her with information on the north, acting as an ambassador of sorts, and on the way, she could work out how to remove the gauntlet.

'I wonder what Shika and the others are doing right now,' Gareth said and it was plain from his face that he wished he was with them.

'Probably something more useful than us.' Brégenne quashed her own speculations. She didn't like to think about Nediah and Kait together. She turned back to her inventory and snatched up a pen. 'Now, how much do you think horses eat?' she asked.

Dusk was starting to soften the sky when Brégenne and Gareth, cloaked and carrying packs, left the citadel through the main gate. It was easy to use the Lunar power to wrap them both in shadows and they moved swiftly across the rough new bridge and into the outskirts of Murta.

Brégenne headed for the trader's, where she'd stabled Myst and, when she saw the woman waiting there with a light, let her shadows fall away. The woman started violently and the lantern tumbled from her open hand, but Gareth caught it and held it out to her.

'Apologies,' Brégenne said politely with a snatched glance over her shoulder. 'We've come for our horses. Could you supply us with this, too?' She held out the list she'd made earlier.

The woman didn't take it, her gaze fixed on Brégenne's face.

Brégenne sighed. 'Don't be afraid,' she said, 'you know who I am. We spoke yesterday.'

'Your eyes are glowing,' Gareth said out of the corner of his mouth.

Chagrined, Brégenne dropped her Lunar vision, which had long been her only method of seeing. She'd barely noticed it, so instinctive had it become. Immediately, her surroundings changed. The light became warm and yellow, the basalt blocks of the stable pitted like the walls of Naris. So much detail in wood and stone, texture, colour – it was overwhelming.

'Sorry, Lady,' the woman said. 'You gave me a fright.'

'It's my fault.' Brégenne handed over her list.

'I can supply you with most of this,' the trader said, running a finger down the inked paper. 'You'll have to find horse blankets elsewhere, though. The airship is late with my usual deliveries.'

'That's fine. Did you find a suitable mount for my friend?'

The woman looked Gareth up and down, taking in his height, broad shoulders and barrel chest. 'I'm sure Rain will do,' she said as she turned and led them to a stall at the far end. Standing placidly inside was a horse with a flecked coat – Brégenne could see how he'd earned his name. The animal's mane was like a dark fall of water and his eyes were liquid and large. 'Oh he's quiet now,' the woman said, clearly more at ease among the horses, 'but once he's out in the open, even this lady's mare will have trouble catching him.' She gestured at the stall directly opposite and Brégenne moved to stroke Myst's neck.

'We doubt it,' she whispered and Myst nickered softly into her palm.

'Myst and Rain,' Gareth said thoughtfully. He held out his

left hand to Rain and the horse nipped him. Gareth cursed and snatched his hand back.

'Yes, he has a bit of a temper on him,' the woman said with a smile. 'But I'm sure you'll grow to love one another.'

Gareth looked at the horse darkly.

The real reason behind the trader's good humour became apparent when it was time to pay. Brégenne spotted Gareth's eyes watering at the number of gold pieces she counted into the woman's hand and she made a show of crumpling her near-empty purse. Once they'd readied the saddlebags, they led the horses out of the stable and onto the neat Murtan side street.

Their horses' hooves were loud on the stone and Brégenne winced as she swung into her saddle. The trader began to look a bit nervous the second time Rain shied away from Gareth, but then the novice placed his gauntleted hand on the horse's neck and the animal froze. Gareth climbed into the saddle. Rain shivered once and stood quietly, stiff-legged, head erect. Brégenne found her eyes straying to the gauntlet hidden under Gareth's glove and vowed to keep a close watch on him.

They took the streets at a walk, unwilling to make more noise than they had to. 'Did you just spend all of your gold at once?' Gareth asked, looking a little pained. 'I had no idea horses cost so much.'

'Most don't. Your Rain there is indeed Hrosst bred. Here.' Brégenne tossed him a purse and Gareth gave a grunt of surprise at its weight. 'You should hold on to some of our coin.'

He looked at her shrewdly. 'Just how much gold are you carrying, Lady Brégenne?'

'*Brégenne*. And as much as I could get my hands on at short notice.'

'Did you steal it?'

'Who do you think I am?'

'You *stole* it.' Gareth's face was alight.

Brégenne allowed a flicker of a smile. 'From the Council's private coffer. Did you know they were sitting on a good ten thousand?'

'You didn't—'

'Of course not. I'd need several large chests to cart it away. I took just enough to make us comfortable . . . and not to raise suspicion.'

Gareth's expression was slightly stunned. 'I don't think I know you very well, La—Brégenne.'

'Sometimes,' she said, 'I don't think I know myself.'

They travelled east.

It was strange, Brégenne thought, her eyes on the moonlit trail beyond Myst's ears. She'd taken this route dozens of times and always it had been Nediah who rode beside her. She had only to turn her head to see him there, or – in daylight – to listen for Uncle's hoof beats just in front. When evening fell and they began searching for a place to spend the night, she'd draw on the Lunar power and his tall silhouette would flicker into view, all greyscale, his face turned towards her, smiling at the glow in her eyes.

She clenched her fists.

'Are you all right?'

Brégenne looked across, almost startled to see Gareth there instead. 'Of course,' she said coolly, hating herself for daydreaming. But the swaying of the horse combined with the shadowy landscape was good for little else.

They reached the top of the pine-covered ridge just as the

sky was lightening. 'Right,' Brégenne said decisively, and she kicked Myst into a gallop. Gareth let out an exclamation as Myst's stride lengthened and his own horse leapt forward in response. The wind rushed at Brégenne, sweeping the plait of her hair out behind her. She leaned low over Myst's neck, relishing the breeze against her cheeks and the way it made her eyes water. Beside her, Gareth gave a whoop of excitement and she heard him shouting encouragement to Rain. The gelding drew apace.

'Show him, girl,' Brégenne called and Myst responded with another burst of speed. Gareth and Rain fell back. She heard him curse and grinned to herself. He'd have to do better than that to catch her. She raced for the dawn and the wind unravelled her plait so that her hair streamed like a banner behind her. But Myst couldn't run forever and reluctantly Brégenne let the horse slow.

She looked over her shoulder and was surprised to see Gareth so far behind. When he caught up with her, the novice's face was as wind-reddened as her own and he was muttering to his horse. '. . . let yourself be beaten by a girl,' she caught and smiled.

Her hair probably resembled a chaotic halo. Brégenne removed a stray lock from her mouth and, while Myst settled into a more sedate pace, she re-plaited it, letting the reins rest in her lap.

'You're not at all like I thought you were,' Gareth said abruptly.

She looked over at him. 'What did you think I was?'

He shifted awkwardly in his saddle. 'Like . . . I don't know. Like Master Alandred or Master Hebrin. The ones who only talk to you to tell you off for something.'

Like Alandred. Brégenne repressed a shudder. 'Maybe I was,' she conceded after a moment, surprising herself.

Gareth didn't reply and she was grateful he'd dropped the subject.

The morning brightened into what promised to be a glorious day. Now that the ridgeline lay between her and Naris, Brégenne breathed more easily and began to enjoy the warmth on her skin. A haze softened the desolate expanse, which was empty save for the great elevated chain that anchored the airships. Posts supported it at regular intervals and it hung heavily over their heads, clanking in the breeze. According to Captain Argat, the Trade Assembly still wouldn't permit the ships to fly solo. They claimed it wasn't safe, but Brégenne suspected the real reason: as long as the airships were tethered to the great chain, permitted to fly only where it went, they and their cargoes remained under Assembly control.

She and Argat hadn't parted on friendly terms and she wondered whether he was still upset about losing the red earth. If he only knew Kyndra had used it to restore a whole world . . .

They stopped early that night, primarily to catch up on the sleep they'd missed, but also because an idea had come to Brégenne as they rode. She sat Gareth down and asked him to roll up his sleeve to expose the gauntlet to the moon. Just looking at it made her shiver. There was something almost sentient in the coil of the sigils; she had the fleeting impression that they'd come alive if she stared at them too long.

When she'd tried to remove the gauntlet before, she'd found nothing for her power to latch on to. 'I'm going to look at your arm instead,' she told Gareth. 'It won't hurt — it's just healing energy.'

Gareth fidgeted nervously. 'Why?'

'Because we might need to change *you*, rather than the gauntlet.'

'I don't like the sound of that.'

'When I first examined it, the gauntlet didn't respond to the Lunar, but your body will,' Brégenne explained. 'I know it sounds strange, but there's a possibility we can . . . heal it off, I suppose you'd say.'

'It's worth a try,' Gareth muttered. He bit his lip, as if preparing to endure pain.

'I won't hurt you.'

He nodded, but didn't seem reassured. Brégenne took a deep breath, drew the Lunar into her veins and then, careful not to touch the gauntlet itself, laid her hands on Gareth's upper arm. The novice stiffened, but said nothing.

She closed her eyes, the better to concentrate, and sent her awareness into Gareth's body.

It was all wrong. The moment she saw what the gauntlet was doing to him, she wanted to flee, to run from the dark tendrils crawling through Gareth's wrist. They coiled up his arm like black ivy, offshoots branching out into his flesh. They were thickest on the back of his hand, under the sigils, and Brégenne felt a wave of nausea that almost broke her concentration.

Slowly, carefully, she reached out with the Lunar and touched one.

Gareth shrieked. Brégenne's eyes snapped open; she tried to pull her power back, but the black tendrils had hold of her, welding her hands to Gareth's arm. Inexorable as a spider, they drew her in, closer to their heart, and she struggled desperately against them.

Amidst Gareth's curdling screams, disjointed images assaulted Brégenne: a rearing horse; armoured men; a ruined city, its topless towers smoking against a forest backdrop; a trampled banner; a crater in the earth as if from a fallen sky-rock. Then she was elsewhere, in a dark place under the earth, and the pitch of Gareth's screaming changed. Entombed by the silence of death, a skeletal figure sat on a throne. As if it sensed her, its head snapped up, fire blooming in wasted eye sockets—

Brégenne gave a scream of her own and, summoning all her strength, hurled herself away from Gareth. Her breath came ragged, her hands were burning. 'Gareth!' she gasped as the novice toppled sideways. The gauntlet steamed cold in the mild night. Instead of removing it, she'd caused it to tighten further, so that it was beginning to look like a part of Gareth's arm. She drew a deep breath and almost gagged on the dank odour that lingered in the air.

'Gareth,' she said urgently, frightened by his rolling eyes, 'can you hear me? Are you all right?'

After a few moments, the novice recovered enough to nod. Brégenne could hear the breath rasping over his vocal cords, sore from screaming. A sheen of sweat glimmered on his face. 'I'm so sorry,' she said, 'I should have been more cautious. Are you hurt?'

'Think . . . fine now,' he whispered. 'But it . . . I was freezing. I'm cold.' He was shivering, despite the sweat on his face. Once he could sit unsupported, Brégenne passed him a water skin.

'I'm sorry,' she repeated as he sipped weakly. 'I won't try that again.'

'What . . . happened?'

Brégenne swallowed. She didn't want to lie, but the thought of the black tendrils and what they meant would terrify him. And the other images . . . Brégenne hugged herself against the

92

vision of the man on the throne, dead hands curled around its armrests. She could still see the flames in his eyes as they met hers. 'The gauntlet . . . it's attached to you, Gareth, on the inside. It tried to catch me too.'

When they met hers, Gareth's eyes were fearful. 'You mean it's alive?'

'It's sentient,' Brégenne said. 'And hostile.'

'But you'll try again. Won't you?'

It was the last thing she wanted to do. 'I'll think of something,' Brégenne said, putting a hand on his shoulder. She hoped he couldn't feel how much it trembled.

They refreshed their supplies in Jarra and briefly rested the horses. Summer was well underway now and the few stunted trees that dotted the outpost had all the leaves they were going to grow.

There was an airship docked for repair in one of the berths and Brégenne was grateful: the sight of it lifted Gareth's spirits for the first time since the night she'd tried to remove the gauntlet. He watched with fascinated eyes as workmen scurried over the half-dismantled deck, nails held between teeth, tools in hand. Several lounged against the deckhouse wall, wreathed in smoke from their pipes. Brégenne saw women too, dressed similarly in stained overalls. One with familiar dark skin and braided hair reminded Brégenne of Yara, Argat's first mate. She watched as the woman scurried up the mast that held the ship's braziers in position. The balloons themselves were absent, evidently down for patching. The woman shouted something to her colleague below and he tossed her up a small wrench which she caught deftly before applying it to one of the bolts.

Brégenne left Gareth to watch while she went in search of

news. Jarra had only one tavern and the paint on its door was peeling. She pushed it open and stepped inside. In the hour after lunch, the place was empty save for the barman, uninterestedly polishing a glass with a dish rag that had seen better days. 'What's a beautiful woman like you doing in a place like this?' he asked, but Brégenne could tell his heart wasn't in it. The glass he was supposed to be cleaning grew dirtier by the second.

'Seeking news,' she replied.

'Not much reaches us here,' the man said laconically, putting the smeared glass aside and picking up another.

'What about the airships?'

'The one out there docked a month ago. Only news it brought was bad. The damn Breaking hit the capital.'

Brégenne caught her breath. 'What?'

'You hadn't heard?' The barman frowned. 'Where you been?'

'Away. How much damage did the storm do?'

The man's ineffectual polishing slowed and stopped. 'Enough,' he grunted. 'The city was already full of refugees from towns got hit before.'

'And the Trade Assembly?'

'Recalled all ships. Trade's ground to a halt, I hear. And the dead number in the hundreds. City Guard'll have their work cut out – there's people sleeping in the streets.'

This was not good. She'd been counting on the Trade Assembly to spearhead Mariar's mobilization, but it looked as if they had enough to deal with without being told about the threat of Acre. Well, there was nothing for it. If it came to war, Acre wasn't likely to wait graciously for them to recover from the Breaking. Brégenne wished Nediah would send another message – she'd had nothing in the nine days since she'd left Naris.

'Thank you for telling me,' she said politely and turned to leave.

'Lady,' the man said just as she reached the door, and Brégenne glanced over her shoulder. 'If you're thinking of going to Market Primus, don't. Between the dead and the squatters, there'll be plague in the city 'fore long.' He gestured with the rag. 'Wait until the trouble passes.'

'I wish I could,' she replied fervently, 'but I fear the trouble's just beginning.'

7

Baior, Acre
Kyndra

They held a funeral for Shika in a wooded clearing, where the soil wasn't red and sunlight coaxed up little green shoots between the roots of dead trees.

There was no body to bury, or to mourn, but they built a cairn and laid Shika's few possessions among the stones. Irilin took his scarf, the one he'd always worn in Naris, and wound it about her neck. She'd stopped crying and her eyes were dry when Nediah spoke the words they used to lay a Wielder to rest. Nothing showed on her face but a terrible bleakness. Irilin looked exactly like Kyndra felt.

She hadn't asked Shika to come, but that was irrelevant; he'd been her responsibility. It was her duty to protect those who'd selflessly chosen to follow her and she had failed in it. When Irilin met her eyes over the little cairn, Kyndra knew she was thinking the same.

'We can't stay here.' Kait's voice was loud in the silence. They had stood for an hour, as the sun sank towards evening, none of them willing to turn their backs on Shika, to walk away.

It would mean saying goodbye; it would mean leaving the memory of him here alone in an alien world.

'Give them a moment,' Medavle said harshly. The anger in his dark eyes was tempered somewhat, but they still burned whenever they met Kyndra's. There was a judgement in them that she knew she deserved.

'No,' Irilin said suddenly, 'she's right.' She pulled Shika's scarf tighter around her neck. 'I don't want to be here any more.'

'Are you sure?' Nediah's eyes were red-rimmed. 'We can stay as long as you want.'

Irilin shook her head.

'There's a village not far from here.' Medavle had no need to point; they could all see the smoke that hung like a pall in the still air.

No one spoke of turning round, of going back to Naris. Perhaps they saw it as a betrayal, Kyndra thought. If they gave up their mission, Shika would have died for nothing. She moved to stand before the cairn, looking down at the pathetic tumble of stones that was all that was left of a life. She wondered where Shika's family were – the family he never talked about. They didn't know he was gone, how he'd died; it was likely they'd never know. And Gareth . . . how could she ever tell Gareth what had happened?

Kyndra made herself stop. She was supposed to be leading the others, supposed to be taking charge; if she let these thoughts consume her, she'd fail them too.

She closed her eyes briefly and then turned her back on the cairn. 'If we want to reach the village before nightfall, we had better be going.' The words sounded harsh and unfeeling.

They remounted, Kait riding Shika's horse, and left the little clearing behind.

The bare plain they travelled turned to fields, untidily dissected by drystone walls. Most lay fallow, the rocky soil dotted with weeds and tumble-down farm buildings. Kyndra found herself wondering whether war was responsible for this, or some other tragedy. There were no discarded weapons in the fields, no rusting armour or – thankfully – evidence of bodies. But as they drew closer to the village, strange, monstrous shapes began to appear, as dead as the land they lay on. Medavle reined in beside one and ran his hand over its blunted metal teeth.

'This is Sartyan technology,' he said. 'I think farmers used it to help bring in the harvest.' He tapped his knuckles on the metal hulk and it rang dully.

Nediah rode up to the great body of wheels and blades. 'How could horses pull that?' he asked, and Kyndra thought he seemed glad of the distraction the machine provided them.

'No horses.' The rusting metal had left smears on Medavle's white gloves. 'It is – or was – powered by ambertrix.'

'What's that?' Nediah circled the contraption; Kyndra could see him through the weeds that had sprung up to fill its interior.

'Ambertrix is the power that fuelled the Sartyan Conquest,' Medavle said. 'The emperor and his elite kept its origins a strict secret, but, like Solar and Lunar energy, it had hundreds of uses – from the domestic to the military. There was a college called Thabarat, founded solely to research ambertrix.' He smiled without humour. 'The Wielders of Solinaris and technicians of Thabarat were bitter enemies. They constantly tried to outdo each other.'

'To think that such a force existed,' Nediah said quietly, 'an energy available to all. If Mariar had had access to it, how different the last five hundred years might have been.'

'You should be thankful it didn't,' Kait said. 'If ordinary people had power like ours, what use would we be as Wielders?'

Nediah's eyes narrowed. 'How would we retain our superiority, you mean?'

'Don't sound so sanctimonious, Nediah. You were thinking the same.'

'Well, whatever this ambertrix was, it's gone now,' Kyndra said before the conversation turned into an argument. She glanced at Irilin; the young woman wasn't even looking at the machine. One hand rested on Shika's scarf; the other on the reins in her lap.

'Yes,' Medavle agreed, dusting down his white gloves. 'And perhaps that bodes well for us. If the empire has somehow lost the use of its technology, it can't pose the same threat it did five centuries ago.'

Glancing back at the machine as they rode away, Kyndra wanted to believe him, but she couldn't. Her naivety had killed Shika. If she'd been more careful, if she'd planned for every eventuality like a leader should . . . A voice in the back of her head told her she couldn't have predicted the wraiths. If they *were* the Yadin, it meant that the black wind hadn't destroyed them. Perhaps, if they'd never been truly alive, they couldn't truly die. She glanced at Medavle, at the harsh, ageless lines of his face, and knew she wouldn't be able to ask him.

The sun was setting by the time they reached the outskirts of the village. It was smaller than Sky Port East, Kyndra saw, and – like the Sartyan machine – it had seen better days. The houses were little more than huts roofed with straw, and there were gaps in the stone walls where the mortar had crumbled. Another dead Sartyan contraption sat in the centre of the village like an ugly totem. Broken ropes trailed from its spokes, as if the villagers had tried to move it and failed.

There was a large communal fire pit, blackened through years of use, the fatty remains of some animal clinging to a spit. They reined in beside it, staring around at the empty, dirt-paved square. The place smelled strongly of goat. 'This isn't exactly how I imagined Acre,' Kait said. Kyndra agreed with her. After all the stories she'd heard about the empire, after all the things she'd seen in Kierik's memories, a poverty-stricken village wasn't what she'd expected to encounter first.

With a wild cry, a group of men burst from behind the largest building and ran at them, brandishing a mismatched collection of farming tools. Before Kyndra had a chance to move, Kait leapt from her saddle in one smooth motion, twin daggers flashing in her hands. As the ten or so men closed on them, she spun into the nearest, deftly dodged the spade and planted a boot in his diaphragm. He staggered back with a gasp, bumped into his companion and tumbled them both into the dirt.

Kyndra blinked, amazed, as always, at Kait's dexterity. A man holding a pitchfork waited until the tall woman's back was turned before darting in to jab at her as if she were a pile of hay. Kait sensed him, jumped clear, and his momentum carried him into his fellows, who only narrowly missed being speared.

It was over in seconds. When every man lay groaning on the ground, winded and bruised, Kait said, 'Don't try that again.' She didn't sheathe her daggers, but held them poised at her sides.

'Who are you?' one man asked under a veneer of bravery. 'What do you want?'

Thankfully, he was speaking the common tongue, but his

accent was heavy and strange, unlike anything Kyndra had heard spoken in Mariar.

'We come from the east,' Medavle said. 'From Rairam.'

Muttering spread through the group; someone laughed. Medavle opened his mouth to say more, but a voice cut across him. 'If you keep your peace, I will speak with you, strangers.'

Kyndra turned her head to see an old woman, bent double from years of labour, standing in the doorway of a hut that looked slightly sturdier than its fellows. Other women were peering curiously from windows and doorways, their clothes rough and woollen, not wholly unlike those worn in Brenwym. The men had kirtles instead of trousers and their hair was short, cut close to the scalp. The women had short hair too and not a few of them were staring unabashedly at the length of Kait's.

'Please put away your weapons,' the old woman said wearily to Kait. 'We hardly have the means or the will to fight you.'

Kait reluctantly sheathed her daggers and Kyndra was glad she hadn't used them to draw blood – not from people who lived in such a wretched place as this.

The old woman exchanged a glance with one of the men before turning her back and disappearing into her hut. Medavle bent his head to Irilin. 'I think it best if you remain outside to watch our horses. I don't believe they'll try anything, but it's better to be cautious.' Glancing at the rapidly darkening sky, he added in an even quieter voice, 'Don't use your power unless you have to.'

Irilin only nodded. She hadn't spoken for hours. With a worried backward glance at her, Kyndra followed the others into the hut, pushing aside the ragged curtain that hung just inside the doorway. There was only one room – more like the inside of a tent than a permanent home. A bedroll lay on the hard-packed dirt, which was softened only by a scattering of rush mats. A few copper pots – well-used, by the look of them – hung from a frame above their heads. The old woman had few possessions and these were piled amongst earthenware jars and bundles of raw wool. A fire smoked in one corner beneath a rough chimney.

The woman poked it awake with a stick and then gestured them towards the mats. She threw several cones of what looked like incense on the flames and a moment later, a strong, but not unpleasant aroma filled the hut. It was an improvement on the stink of animal.

'I am Damesh,' the old woman said, one hand on her heart. 'Why have you come to Asha?' She spoke with the same thick accent as the men outside.

'This is the first village we've seen since we left Rairam,' Kyndra explained.

An unfriendly smile grew out of the wrinkles that ringed the old woman's mouth. 'If you wish to lie to me,' she said, 'you'd do better to choose words I'd have a hope of believing.'

Nediah shook his head, sober-faced. 'We thought you knew Rairam had returned – you live so close to the border. It happened over a month ago.'

'We don't venture east,' the old woman replied. 'The hoarlands are cursed. Only death is there.'

They looked at each other. Kyndra was glad Irilin had stayed outside.

'The hoarlands?' Nediah asked. 'Do you mean the red valley?'

The woman's face paled. 'You've . . . seen it?'

'We rode through it,' Kait said when Kyndra and the others didn't answer.

A pendant hung around the old woman's neck; she clasped it in gnarled, brown hands. 'The Sundered Valley,' she whispered. 'It was lost when the Starborn took Rairam away.'

Kyndra started. 'You know of the Starborn?' she said before she could stop herself.

'Everyone knows, child. The Starborn brought the war to an end, but Rairam was lost.'

'Lord Kierik's deeds were not forgotten here,' Kait murmured. Her eyes were shining. 'If only they were recalled so clearly at home.'

Medavle looked darkly at her. 'It is a mercy they weren't,' he said, his voice almost a growl.

I thought everyone would know about us, Kyndra thought. She'd half expected to find an army awaiting them, not a fearful bunch of farmers. 'We were hoping you could tell us about Acre,' she said, 'about the Sartyans.'

The old woman glanced once at the fire and hunched her shoulders. 'The empire has done much good. The Baioran villages are proud to live under his Imperial Majesty's rule.'

Kyndra exchanged incredulous looks with the others.

'But what about your contraptions like the one outside?' Nediah asked. 'It looks as if it hasn't worked for years.'

The old woman wouldn't meet his eyes. 'It's of no consequence.'

'Your fields, though. Most are lying fallow. How are you surviving here?'

Finally, she looked up to regard Nediah with a hostile glare. For the first time, Kyndra felt a wave of uneasiness. 'The Davaratch has more important issues to contend with than the problems of Asha.' The old woman paused. 'We are content with our lives.'

'Who is the Davaratch?' Medavle asked. 'That was the name of the emperor at the time of the Conquest.'

'Yes. Each new emperor takes his name as a royal title.'

'Why? Davaratch was a mons—' Medavle stopped. 'He was a powerful man,' he amended, 'but an oppressor. His methods were unnecessarily cruel. Lycorash was a tragedy.'

At the name, a memory came to Kyndra of standing in a burned-out husk of a city, a city whose majestic towers had once represented the hope of the Resistance, the rebels who had opposed the empire. The Sartyan Fist had offered them surrender and – after long negotiations – the people of Lycorash accepted. The gates opened, the Sartyans rode in and set to slaughtering every man, woman and child. These were Kierik's memories – if she closed her eyes, it was almost as if she were there. She looked at Medavle. As one of the ageless Yadin, he had seen first-hand how much of a monster Davaratch had been.

'And Baristogan,' Medavle said. 'Only a twisted mind could dream up something so repugnant.' He turned to the others. 'Davaratch contrived to send a group of children, orphaned by the very war he'd started, to the city gates. Of course the people of Baristogan took them in. But the children had been deliberately exposed to plague and it spread death through the city. All the Sartyans had to do was fire a few flaming arrows over the wall. They conquered Baristogan without even entering the city.'

Kyndra watched the horror of Medavle's story creep over the faces of her companions. She had a memory of Baristogan too, but it was foggy; she was beginning to feel a bit dizzy from the incense. She watched as the old woman shook her head. 'History has proven the Sartyans fair rulers,' she said, scowling. 'You are merely repeating rebel propaganda.'

'I was *there*,' Medavle growled. 'I saw the bodies, heard the screams. I smelled the fires that Sartya lit to hide its treachery. History is written by the victors.'

The old woman stared at Medavle, wide-eyed, and the Yadin seemed to realize he had said too much. The incense was becoming overpowering.

'Forgive me,' the old woman said then. 'One must be careful what one says. Sartyan spies are everywhere.'

'So the empire still rules.' Kyndra felt a leaden weight settle on her chest. Had anything changed at all in five hundred years?

'Sartya cannot be as powerful as it once was,' Medavle said before the old woman could answer. 'What about the ambertrix?'

'The army has use of it,' the elder said, her leathery face creased and sombre. 'And the Heartland. But we are far away. Ambertrix cannot be spared for us.'

Nediah placed a hand to his head. 'I need some air.'

Kyndra agreed. Her knees felt like jelly when she stood up. She swayed, the hut sliding sideways in her vision. Surprised, she grabbed at a shelf and pulled the whole thing over with a crash. 'Sorry,' she heard herself mumbling. Nausea struck her a physical blow and a part of her, the part that could reach out to the stars, knew something was very wrong.

Nediah and Kait were sprawled on the mats. 'You,' Kait snarled, trying to crawl towards the old woman. 'What have you done to me?'

Medavle had his flute in his hand. He gestured and silver chains bound the old woman. She gave a shriek and toppled to the floor. 'Too late,' she choked out at him. Beyond the door came the tramp of booted feet on dirt. *Irilin*, Kyndra thought muzzily. She tried to reach out to the stars, but the dark door was too far away and her head was full of the wretched incense.

'It is our duty,' she heard the old woman say, 'to report all strangers to the local garrison.' Her eyes narrowed, flicked to the flute in Medavle's hand. 'Especially rebel sympathizers such as you.'

Kyndra had a last glimpse of the Yadin as he ripped aside the curtain. A woman screamed. She thought she saw torches outside, the flare of flame on breastplates, but it was all a whirl of colour and she was slipping away.

It was dark.

A moment later, she realized her eyes were closed. They opened reluctantly, eyelashes stuck gummily together. She blinked until her vision cleared and she saw night. A fire burned nearby, its flames sending shadows careening wildly over a campsite. Awareness of her body came gradually. Her arms and legs tingled with pins and needles; they were tied. Shock drove away the fug in her head, but it still ached terribly.

Kyndra tried to remember. A hut. An old woman. An overpowering smell . . . it was still in her clothes. The incense had drugged her, drugged them all except Medavle. Memory came rushing back. The red valley, the wraiths, Shika, the village, the talk of Sartya. Where was she? Where were the others?

Her heartbeat thumped against hard-packed dirt. She lay on her front, head turned to one side. There was dust in her mouth; her tongue felt dry and hot and Kyndra thought longingly of water.

She flicked her eyes from side to side, trying to see as much of her surroundings as possible without moving and drawing attention to herself. She seemed to be in a corner of the camp, something hard – a rock? – at her back. With a sigh of relief, she spotted her companions nearby, each trussed up like slaughtered livestock. Except for Medavle. She wondered whether she'd ever see the Yadin again. The way he looked at her . . . she wouldn't be surprised if he took this chance to leave for good.

Nediah had a fan of blood across his forehead, but other than that, he seemed all right – at least he was breathing normally. Irilin and Kait lay on their sides, facing away, so she couldn't see whether they were injured too. When she glanced back at Nediah, his eyes were open. She gave him a small nod and he looked relieved. They lay a few metres apart – too far to exchange whispers over the noise of the camp. So Kyndra turned her attention to their captors, watching the activity through slitted eyes.

There was no doubt. Kyndra recognized the distinctive red plate from Kierik's memories: Sartyans, about fifty of them. A double guard was posted at the corner of the camp she could see, while the rest of the soldiers sat around cleaning armour, or moving busily from task to task while they waited for the spitted meat to cook.

Into the camp strode a heavy-shouldered man clad in the same red plate as the others, but from the way the soldiers suddenly scurried to attention, Kyndra guessed he was someone important. A cloak the colour of carnelian hung down to his spurred heels and the helmet tucked under his arm was hammered into a monstrous visage. There was a woman behind him, her pauldrons engraved with some kind of bird.

A female soldier hurried forward, bent her knee to both newcomers and thumped her fist to her shoulder. The two returned her salute and the soldier rose to her feet. She began to speak rapidly, pointing towards Kyndra and the others.

Immediately Kyndra shut her eyes. She lay there, tensed in her bonds, hearing their footfalls coming nearer and nearer.

The urge to look was overwhelming, but she couldn't reveal herself, not until she knew their intentions. A shadow blocked the firelight; she could see it through her closed eyelids. The footfalls stopped and Kyndra expected to be touched, but the shadow remained where it was and she could only imagine the three Sartyans staring down at her.

'Where did you find them?' the man asked. His accent was rounded, a little more precise than that of the villagers.

'Asha,' a woman's voice replied. 'The elder claimed they came from Rairam.' She laughed and the footfalls moved away as the Sartyans took their conversation elsewhere. Kyndra cursed silently. If only she could hear what was being said . . .

Ansu knows.

Kyndra went cold. Was the thought hers, or some vestige of Kierik, whose memories lurked in a distant corner of her mind? *He's dead,* she reminded herself, *he can't speak to me.* But sometimes it felt like he could, as if the madman were able to reach out from the past, to look through her eyes, to comment on the things she saw. Would it be the same for someone else one day? When she was dust and another Starborn walked the world, would Kyndra linger on in their head – an unwelcome shade of days long dead?

Ansu knows. Yes, *Ansu* would know, but it meant opening the dark door, crossing into the void, travelling its chill reaches until she found the star that could lend her the power to sharpen her hearing.

I don't want them. I didn't choose this. Kyndra remembered speaking those words a short time ago . . . and look where they had led her. Shika was dead and her friends were captured, likely about to be killed. She didn't have a choice. It wasn't just her life that hung in the balance.

Before her courage failed, she steeled herself, focusing as best she could. Every time it was a little easier, finding the black door buried in her mind.

As she opened herself to the void, awareness of her surroundings dissolved. Once more she stood on the black pathway under the chill regard of the stars. How could she find *Ansu*? She was never sure. Unlike the Wielders and their years of training, she relied on the stars to aid her. But they were oddly silent tonight – a challenge, she guessed. They would keep her in the void as long as they could, knowing that every moment she spent in this soulless waste meant she became a little more like them, a little less like the girl from Brenwym.

As it is supposed to be. One voice, numberless.

She cursed them, knowing they could hear her. *Very well.* Emotion was already fading, taking all thoughts of Brenwym with it. She was here for a reason.

Kyndra began walking. It was not really walking, but a series of seamless steps, as she searched countless constellations for *Ansu*. But there were hundreds of constellations, thousands. The sky was too vast, too full of itself. If she carried on this way, it would take an infinite number of years, and in that time, the world would wither around her.

She had to stop thinking like a human.

Call, Starborn, Kierik seemed to say. *Who serves whom?*

They will not serve me, she thought. *Why should they?*

I am their instrument. Without me, all their power is useless. She didn't know whether it was Kierik or her own subconscious that spoke. Perhaps now they were one and the same and it didn't matter. She understood.

The stars blazed all around her. The cold of the void pulsed in her bones. *Ansu*, she commanded, trusting to Kierik's knowledge that the star could not refuse the summons.

A light grew on one horizon, dimmer than *Austri* and paler than *Hagal*. *Ansu* was ancient and small. Unlike *Sigel*, it did not rave or clamour for ruin. It merely hung, burning, reaching out with long fingers of light for the Starborn's hand.

Kyndra took it and –

'The peasant believed it rebel rubbish.'

Kyndra was back in her body, peeping through narrowed eyes and holding fast to *Ansu*. The soldiers were still too far away for her to hear them naturally, but the star's power sharpened her hearing to the point where she heard other sounds too, all the scrapes and chirps of the night. She filtered them out, only half able to focus on what was being said. The other half of her had to concentrate on maintaining the connection to *Ansu* and it wasn't easy, not when she was trying to hold on to herself too.

'Sir?' asked the female soldier. 'What is it?'

The man had paled, noticeable even in the shadows that spilled out of the firelight. He turned and Kyndra shut her eyes again, imagining his intense gaze on her apparently unconscious form. He didn't scoff like the other soldiers. Did that mean he believed they *had* come from Rairam?

'General Hagdon?' the soldier said and Kyndra felt a thrill. A Sartyan general *here* – possibilities spilled into her mind, almost breaking her hold on *Ansu*. This was the man who would lead the Sartyan Fist into her home, should the emperor decide to invade. He had the emperor's ear. If Kyndra could convince him that Mariar was not a threat –

'Yes, excuse me,' she heard him say. Kyndra cracked open her eyes in time to see him turn to the woman with the birds

– hawks, she thought – on her armour. 'These prisoners could serve well, Iresonté. Perhaps they'll go some way to appeasing His Imperial Majesty when he hears what happened at Khron-osta.'

Iresonté wore unruffled arrogance like a mantle. 'We've spoken of this, Hagdon. You think he will excuse your failure so easily?'

'*My* failure?' The man clenched his fists, as furious as Iresonté was calm. 'You sabotaged the mission and killed five hundred of my men in the process. Do you want me dead so badly?'

'A wild story,' she answered, 'to cover your folly. I pulled the stealth force out of there before we shared your fate.'

'A fate you engineered.' Anger mottled Hagdon's cheeks. 'You betrayed us, Iresonté. You alerted the *du-alakat* to our presence and you left us to die.'

'A good general admits his mistakes, Hagdon.' She smiled coldly. 'And he learns from them.'

'I've learned never to place my trust in you again.'

'Ah,' Iresonté said. 'But you trust so easily, James. Even those who give you no reason to. Your nephew paid a heavy price for your trust.'

Hagdon's eyes darkened with a frightening kind of emptiness. For a moment, it seemed he would strike her. Perhaps Iresonté realized she had gone too far for she quickly turned to the other woman.

'His Imperial Majesty will not take this defeat well,' she said. 'Whatever Hagdon claims, the fact remains that we failed. The Davaratch is not a forgiving man.'

'Which is why I'll take your prisoners,' Hagdon said. 'If what they claim is true . . .'

'One got away,' the soldier informed him. 'An aberration.'

Kyndra lay quite still, closed her eyes and hoped they wouldn't notice the sweat beading her face. Holding on to *Ansu* was taking all of her strength and she could feel it ebbing. The memory of losing control of *Hagal* seized her and, suddenly afraid, Kyndra relinquished her grip on the star. It felt as if she fell from an impossible height to crash back into her aching body and pounding head. She gave an involuntary groan.

Although she now knew what the Sartyans planned to do with them, the knowledge was no comfort. Hagdon would take them to the Davaratch and Kyndra didn't need to hear the fear in the soldiers' voices to tell her that the emperor was a dangerous man. She couldn't afford to meet him as a prisoner. That would give altogether the wrong impression. And what did the female soldier mean when she referred to Medavle as an aberration?

One thing was clear to her: the Sartyans must not discover that Nediah and the others were anything out of the ordinary. If a group of Wielders could be subdued so easily, what did that say about Mariar? The emperor would see it as a country ripe for the taking.

The Sartyans' conversation grew even fainter. Kyndra opened her eyes again and saw them moving towards the fire. The aroma of roasting meat wafted to where she lay, starving and thirsty on the hard ground. Her stomach gave an angry rumble.

Nediah was awake. That was something. Irilin and Kait lay still, but even if they were just pretending to sleep, they'd be feeling as ill as she: none of them were in a position to fight their way free.

'Kyndra.'

The voice seemed to come from all around her, out of the

air, the ground, the night itself. So Medavle hadn't abandoned her after all.

'Can you hear me?' his voice asked.

Kyndra nodded her head a fraction, hoping he was close enough to catch the movement.

'About time you showed, Yadin.' That was Kait, and Kyndra suppressed a sigh of relief. She kept an eye on the Sartyans, hearing the small clatter of dislodged stones somewhere behind her. With a minute turn of her head, she spotted a Medavle-shaped shadow, as if the Yadin were cut out of darkness. He bent over her and the ropes binding her wrists and ankles fell away. Blood rushed into cramped limbs and Kyndra bit her lip at the pain. Slowly, carefully, she rose onto her hands and knees.

The leaping flames of the fire slapped Medavle's outline onto the flat rock behind him. If a soldier looked up now, they surely couldn't miss seeing the one shadow that didn't dance alongside the rest. 'Can you fight, if you have to?' he whispered and Kyndra realized he was speaking to Irilin.

The young woman nodded. Her eyes were bright, fever-bright. She didn't look well. Nediah was staring fixedly at her, his face whitening. 'No –' he began, but it was too late. Irilin jumped to her feet and strode plain as day towards the Sartyans gathered around the fire.

Medavle swore. 'I did not mean now.' Shadows ran off him like water until he stood fully visible, his pale garments a poor camouflage.

Kyndra could only gaze in horror as Irilin became a figure of moonlight, the Lunar turning her pale hair to glaring silver. She raised her hands, a ball of light burning in each.

The Sartyans' surprise was short-lived. In moments, they'd assumed a defensive formation that closed around Irilin, linked shields raised against her. There were no cries of dismay, no confused shouts. That told Kyndra two things. First, the Sartyans were familiar with a Wielder's power. Second, Irilin was in a lot of trouble.

Medavle digested the scene in one black-eyed glance and then swept the flute from his belt. 'Get to the picket line,' he said to Nediah and ran for the Sartyans.

Although Kyndra knew she had to move, she found herself staring. The flute grew longer in Medavle's hand until it resembled a metal staff, which he swung at the nearest soldier. The staff hit with a *thrum* of energy. Sparks in his eyes, the soldier stumbled back and Medavle's next swing took his feet out from under him. The Yadin dodged the sweep of a broadsword, reversed his grip on the staff and sent it into the groin of another Sartyan. He was fast, almost as fast as Kait, and Kyndra wondered why he hadn't used the ability before.

There came a shout as she and the others were spotted, and a squad of soldiers made for them. Kyndra turned and dashed with Kait and Nediah for the pickets. Their own horses were tethered in a group at the end of the line. Nediah pulled at the knots, while Kait searched for a weapon. Kyndra scanned the ground too, but the Sartyans weren't foolish enough to leave even a stray tool lying around.

Although it seemed to take forever, Nediah had the rope free in seconds, and Kait slapped the flanks of the nearest horses. The camp had become a chaos of light and noise, and the horses added their terror, breaking in all directions. Kyndra kept a firm hold on her stallion, afraid he would join them, but the black remained calm.

So did the Sartyans. Even amidst the tumult – amidst a battle they couldn't have foreseen – the soldiers were disciplined.

The group making for her split into three, some going to round up the horses, others bolstering the ranks of the soldiers around Irilin and Medavle. Kyndra could see the two would tire before their opponents. Irilin wore a fierce grin, almost a rictus. It turned her usually gentle face ghastly, so that Kyndra couldn't stand to look at her. Was she doing this for Shika?

Then, under Kyndra's horrified gaze, Hagdon rose up behind the young woman, his cloak bloody in the firelight. She sensed him at the last moment, and the smile froze on her lips. She leapt aside, but the Sartyan general caught the trailing length of her hair and pulled her up short. Irilin shrieked.

Kyndra couldn't spare her another glance. The soldiers were almost upon them. Nediah and Kait formed up around her, one at each shoulder, and Kyndra steeled herself. This was her duty; this was what she ought to have done for Shika. But her mind was bright and panicked as the Sartyans closed, their red plate looking impenetrable as a dragon's scales. Firelight licked along the length of drawn swords and the silence with which they charged was more frightening than a battle cry.

A voice screamed inside her, a voice that had witnessed this onslaught a hundred times before and seen the litter of bodies left in the Sartyans' wake. The hacked-off limbs of children, mingled with their parents'. The squires of the Kingswold Knights, who vowed to avenge their slain masters and were slain in turn. The killing didn't stop. Had his sacrifice been for naught in the end? It would all begin again, an endless cycle where the only victors were the ravens that pecked at the dead.

No. He wouldn't let it, not while he lived and had command of the void.

'Get out of my head!' Kyndra screamed, shoving Kierik's overbearing memories aside.

Burn them.

The star, *Sigel*, sang its furnace-song, as if it could sense the resolve fast replacing her fear. Why should she hold back? These were Sartyan soldiers, after all: the violent hand of the emperor. They had slaughtered their way through Acre –

But that was before. She couldn't hold these soldiers responsible for crimes five centuries old.

A sword swing interrupted her thoughts and Kyndra threw herself clear. Cold swept through her; were they aiming to kill? The next strike raked her shoulder. The pain hit a moment later and Kyndra pressed her hand to the wound. Hot wetness coated her fingers.

The wraiths hadn't cared that she was not Kierik. They would happily have forced her to answer for his crimes. She looked up at her assailant and saw a fierce-eyed woman, face stiff and dismissive. *I am nothing to them*, she thought. The Sartyan backhanded her and Kyndra felt her lip split as she was knocked sprawling. *And they are nothing to me.*

The fist swung again . . . and Kyndra caught it. She heard the woman gasp, as she tightened her grip. Armour crunched and the Sartyan hissed through her teeth. She tried to disengage, but it was too late.

Keeping a firm hold on the woman, Kyndra calmly raised her other hand. It wasn't *Sigel*'s power that clung like tarnished silver to her skin, but *Tyr*'s. She threw a punch at the woman's abdomen and noted, as if from a distance, how the red plate crumpled like paper and her fist passed right through the soldier's body. With no feeling apart from a cold interest in how easy it was, Kyndra wrapped her hand around the woman's spine and pulled. The Sartyan came apart in a spray of blood.

Gore coated Kyndra's arm to her shoulder. The bloody ruin slumped sideways and, dispassionate, she looked for another opponent.

Hagdon was shouting orders. His gaze was fixed on Kyndra, on the dead woman at her feet; so were the eyes of the Sartyans who'd planned to engage her. They were backing away, looking to Hagdon for instruction. Wrapped in *Tyr*'s hard embrace, Kyndra started after them, but a cry sounded behind her and she turned.

Figures leapt from concealment, dashing into the fray. The night was suddenly filled with battle cries, a stark contrast to the Sartyans' silent assault. The newcomers brandished miscellaneous weapons: swords and axes, morningstars, shortbows and spiked clubs. Torches flared and arrows were set afire. The strangers out of the night sent them streaking into the regrouping Sartyans, who raised hasty shields against them. But the arrows mostly struck tents and barrels, and the burning pitch spread swiftly.

Stunned by the sudden onslaught, perhaps, Hagdon's grip loosened, for Irilin seized her chance to escape. Kyndra watched as the young woman lashed out, her nails raking the Sartyan general's face. He yelled, clapped a hand to his cheek and Irilin disappeared in a cloak of shadows. As soon as she did, Medavle took her lead and vanished too. They left a dozen or so soldiers injured or dead in their wake.

Hagdon looked around for her before clearly conceding defeat and concentrating instead on this new foe. He barked a command and his soldiers formed into several close-knit diamonds, which spread out and systematically began to hunt down the strangers. Another squad of soldiers worked to bring the fires under control.

Close up, Kyndra realized the strangers' faces were obscured with mud or paint, the same stuff that caked their makeshift armour. Without the element of surprise, they were no match for the Sartyans and it seemed as if they knew it, for a voice cried out and the group tightened its ranks, preparing to break for safer ground.

Medavle and Irilin reappeared beside her just as Kyndra felt her hold on *Tyr* beginning to tremble. Where Kierik had spent an entire night with the stars, separating Rairam from Acre, creating his world, her control over them lasted scant minutes. The chill she had relished only moments ago was suddenly piercing, almost unbearable, and she practically threw *Tyr* from her mind.

Without the void's detachment, the chaos around her seemed magnified and Kyndra stood, dazed by the noise. A hand touched her shoulder: Nediah. 'We have to get out of here,' the Wielder said urgently. He pulled her, stumbling, around a burning tent and towards the motley group of rescuers.

'If you wish to live, come,' one said. The voice was female, but between the mud and the helm she wore, Kyndra couldn't see the woman's face. 'Aberrations are always welcome among us.'

There wasn't time to ask what she meant. Medavle was struggling to keep his horse under control; Irilin was looking behind him at the advancing Sartyans. She flung out her hands and something silvery and vast caught the edges of Kyndra's vision – a shield. 'I can't hold it long!' Irilin shouted.

Their rescuers took the use of magic in their stride; clearly, they were just as familiar with Lunar energy as the Sartyans. 'Move or die here,' the woman said, signalling. Archers hidden around the camp's fringes rose and began to drop back, firing as they went. 'Do not mount until we're clear of the camp.'

'Who are you?' Nediah asked, but the painted figure waved his question away.

'No time.'

'Until morning, we're outnumbered,' Medavle said to Nediah. 'My abilities are limited and Irilin is exhausted. If we stay, we'll be killed or recaptured.'

'Let Kyndra handle—' Kait began, but Nediah cut her off.

'No,' he said sharply. Was that suspicion in his face? Had he seen what she'd done to the soldier? Suddenly the blood that drenched Kyndra's clothes felt heavy and cold, weighing her down. She was glad of the darkness.

Without further argument, they broke and ran for the night, accompanied by the thump and clatter of feet and hooves on hard soil. Their unlooked-for rescuers ran beside them, bared teeth white in muddy faces. Thanks to Irilin's shield, the sound of pursuit swiftly faded, but Kyndra heard a furious shout as they fled and looked back to see Hagdon, standing at the edge of the burning camp, bloody scratches dark along one cheek. For just a moment it seemed as if they locked eyes and then the night swallowed him.

Once they'd left the chaos behind, they deemed it safe to mount and Kyndra scrambled gratefully into her saddle. She felt sick from a lack of food and water and the coppery stench of blood coating her clothes. Their mysterious companions didn't tire, but kept up an effortless lope. Kyndra looked sideways at Irilin whose face was grey and slack. Though she must be equally weary, she was still shielding the whole group.

'How much further until we stop?' Nediah called.

No one answered him. The sky was beginning to pale now,

bringing the cool of morning, and Kyndra shivered, thinking longingly of sleep. But she couldn't let her guard down, not yet, not until she knew who these people were and why they'd rescued them.

Irilin let out a sigh and slumped in her saddle, the shield winking out as the sun rose. 'Are you all right?' Kyndra asked her. She vividly recalled the young woman's face only hours before, with her fever-eyes and snarling mouth, fighting like a cornered beast. Now Irilin's eyes were shadowed; she was looking at Kyndra, at the blood that showed dark against the growing daylight.

Kyndra's face felt stiff with it. She looked down at herself, at her red hands gripping the reins, and swallowed, hoping she wasn't going to throw up. She'd been trying not to think of it, but the memory of what she'd done to the soldier, to a fellow human, returned to haunt her. Again she saw the spray of blood, felt the snap of the woman's spine, as if it were no stronger than a twig.

You did what you had to, she told herself, *she was going to kill you.* And yet . . . was that true? Hagdon had wanted them alive, bloodied perhaps, but alive. No matter how vicious the soldier had seemed, she wouldn't have taken Kyndra's life. But Kyndra had taken hers, as if she had a right to it. She closed her eyes against the horror, against the sight of the blood on her skin, but it was still there. What she had done would never go away.

Eventually, the terrain grew rugged and began to slope upwards, dark shapes rearing against the dawn. As they neared, Kyndra saw that the plain was broken by a tangled nest of cliffs and fissures – gullies that cut through a shattered mountain range.

When they passed into their shade, Kyndra shifted uneasily. It looked like someone had plunged a serrated knife into the land and then dragged it through as if it were flesh. 'What is this place?' she asked the mud-slicked man who jogged beside her.

'The teeth of the earth,' he answered, 'Skar.'

'Why have you brought us here?'

'It is our home,' was all he said.

They were deep into the gullies when the woman who led their group held up a hand for them to stop. The wind whistled as it navigated the rocky maze, stirring Kyndra's hair and causing the others to twist in their saddles, scanning the seemingly featureless sandstone. The sun had cleared the horizon now, but it would be hours until it shone directly into the gullies. Nediah and Kait looked more alert and not a little relieved at the return of their Solar powers. If their 'rescuers' tried anything, they'd likely get more than they'd bargained for.

The woman gave a loud clap and Kyndra winced at the reverberations that thundered through the surrounding rocks. When the echoes finally faded, she caught movement up on the sheer cliffs to either side and she tensed, hands clenched tight around her horse's reins. Figures melted seemingly out of the rock, camouflaged in clothes of the same colour. Some held drawn bows and Kyndra gave an involuntary shiver. For how long had she and her group been their unknowing targets? Kait hissed through her teeth when she saw the archers.

A small sound behind caused her to turn. More figures now blocked the way back, heavily armed, their lower faces masked. Kyndra suspected there were dozens of arrows trained on them from above. She was no tactician, but even she could see that the combination of narrow gullies and cliffs was highly defensible and perfect for ambushes. Who were these people? Why had they chosen to help them escape from the Sartyan camp?

As if she'd asked aloud, a man slipped out of a narrow defile and came to greet their group's leader. The woman removed her leather helm, shook out long hair, and Kyndra found herself pinned by hazel eyes, fierce amidst the face paint.

The man beside her was unpainted, his brow deeply furrowed, as if he carried the weight of a responsibility he was unable or unwilling to cast aside. 'Congratulations,' he said to Kyndra and the others, 'you've found the Defiant.'

8

The iarls arrived at dawn. As Char had guessed, Rogan and Alder were among them, accompanied by two more, dressed lavishly for the desert. 'New money,' Rogan said disdainfully in a voice he didn't bother to lower. He was a handsome man, as far as Char was any judge of it, swarthy-skinned and just approaching his middle years. He owed his wealth to a dozen mines situated north of the city of Cymenza. His friend, Iarl Alder, was perhaps ten years Rogan's senior and the two had a longstanding partnership. Rogan's mines supplied the ore for Alder's smiths. And it was Alder's practice of staffing his smith-ies exclusively with women that ensured Genge's caravan a regular income.

'Alder and I were talking shop,' Rogan said. He jerked his thumb at the overdressed strangers. 'Unfortunately, they heard. Wish we'd been more circumspect. I won't tolerate being outbid, of course, but they're a little too free with their ken.'

Char nodded absently, his mind still reeling with the events of last night and the plans he and Ma had made for this evening. He couldn't quite believe this would be his last ever auction.

'How goes it with you, Char?' Rogan asked as they watched Alder inspecting the two girls. The sisters stood beside their cages and it was only the chains on their wrists and ankles that gave them away as slaves. Dressed as they were in simple flax, they could have passed for townswomen out on some errand.

It took a moment for Rogan's question to register. 'All right, Iarl,' Char answered blandly. 'Looking forward to some time in 'Aro.'

'You men always are,' Rogan said. 'I spotted the brothers there last night.'

The Black Bazaar had left Ren and Tunser hollow-eyed and Char suspected they'd smoked a good deal of their wages away. Genge threw them dirty looks between the smiles he reserved for his customers.

'I'll be bidding, Master Genge,' Alder announced, his eyes flicking briefly to the two new iarls hovering off to one side. 'These are well up to your usual excellent standard.'

The blue-eyed girl opened her mouth as if to speak, but Ma was suddenly at her shoulder and she seemed to think better of it.

'How's Ma?' Rogan asked a bit too casually, his eyes lingering on her body. Ma wore her market-garb this morning – a pale, sleeveless top paired with airy trousers that narrowed at the ankle. She'd swapped her boots for sandals and a heavy gold torque ringed her neck, shining against the rich brown of her skin. Her hands were gloved as usual and leather thongs wrapped her forearms. A blue scarf covered her hair.

It was funny, Char thought, as he watched the lust on Rogan's face. Ma had barely changed in all the years he'd known her. Many men found her attractive . . . although most knew better than to try anything. 'Fine,' he answered shortly, hoping to kill the topic, but Rogan continued anyway.

'She, you know, had any offers of late?'

'No.'

Although the iarl shifted uncomfortably under Char's black-lensed stare, the one-word answers didn't deter him. 'So, speaking as someone who knows her well, do you think she'd be . . . *amenable* if I were to—'

'With respect, Rogan, I think she'd break your legs.'

'Ah yes, well. I thought it might be like that.' He sighed mournfully. 'What a woman.'

Char felt a reluctant smile pulling at the side of his mouth before Genge sauntered over and turned the conversation to business. 'Rogan, my friend. See anything you like?'

Rogan nodded and the two men moved apart from the others to converse in low voices. The fat man whom Genge had found in the shipwreck watched them, his face already beaded with sweat from the warming day – or perhaps from nerves. But he had little to fear if Rogan bought him. The iarl was not a cruel man, merely pragmatic. And despite his untiring pursuit of Ma, Char rather liked him.

Once Alder and Rogan were gone, the 'new-money' iarls who'd hovered on the sidelines approached Genge. Although Char was busy setting up for the auction, he didn't fail to notice Genge's look of interest, or the way both iarls glanced at the girls. It seemed Alder might have competition. When finally the men left too, Char found himself working to the tune of Genge's whistling. The slave master only whistled when in the very best of moods.

Ma had noticed too. 'I don't like those men,' she said to

Char as he unpacked the portable stage they used for auctions. 'I wouldn't be surprised if they're scouting for brothel girls. If they offer more than Alder, and I expect them to, then Genge will sell.'

'Well, why wouldn't he?' Char replied, securing one of the stage's struts. 'That's the point of an auction.'

He knew he'd angered her by her intake of breath and the way her shoulders hunched. 'I don't want the girls to go to them,' Ma said. 'Alder will work them hard but fairly. Smithing's a decent trade.' She paused. 'No woman should be forced to lie with a man.'

Char glanced round. 'It's still slavery, Ma. What difference does it make where the girls end up?'

'It makes a difference,' Ma said, her expression hardening. 'And I brought you up to realize it.'

The hypocrisy of the situation grated on Char. Anger prickled. He dropped the hammer in the sand and turned to face her. 'Those girls hate you,' he said. 'They hate me. Give them knives and they'd slit our throats . . . and they'd be right to do it.' He could hear the rage in his voice, bubbling, barely controlled. 'We are the monsters, Ma, not the iarls, not the pimps. It's us. We make this happen.' He swept an encompassing arm at the caravan. 'All of this. Who brought the girls here to be haggled over? Who takes their cut of ken after market? If the girls are sold into whoring, it's our fault. It's *your* fault.'

She hit him, a swift slap to the cheek. Char didn't flinch; he'd expected it. He bent and retrieved the hammer from the sand. 'Don't lie to yourself, Ma,' he said, his anger beginning to fade under the sting of his own words. 'This is the life you chose.'

Her sandalled feet moved off softly through the sand and Char returned to his work. There was much still to do. It was auction day.

'One hundred red ken. Do I have one fifty?'

'Look at the fat on him!' someone shouted.

Genge turned towards the voice. 'Which is why he's worth one fifty – for the next few months at least, he's his own food.'

There were snorts of laughter and – though his eyes were wide with fear – the pudgy man from the Hozen Swamps tried to tug his tunic further down his exposed belly. Char had positioned himself to the left of the auction stage, opposite Ren and Tunser who stood at evenly spaced intervals. He kept his weapons on full view, alongside a trio of knives stuck brazenly into his belt. The blades were only there for show since some didn't see his kali sticks as weapons. This part of his job was simple: discourage trouble.

'He's a hooch-brewer and a spiller of secrets. Tickle him with a knife and all sorts of information comes tumbling out. Information you'll find a use for, no doubt. He was a local of the Hozen Swamps, an area notoriously difficult to penetrate.' Genge made an aside to the audience, but his voice was loud enough to carry. 'And, once you've milked him dry, he's a houseboy in the making.'

More laughter. 'So do I have one fifty, sirs?' Genge shouted.

'One fifty!'

Genge graciously acknowledged the bid, his eyes raking the crowd. 'Two hundred?'

'Two hundred,' another voice echoed and Char was surprised to hear it was Rogan's.

'Two fifty?'

Silence. 'Do I have two fifty?' Genge asked again. His forehead wrinkled into an expression Char knew well: the slave master realized he'd get no more. 'Going once. Going twice . . .' He let the phrase hang in the air, holding out for a bid that wouldn't come.

'Sold,' Genge said with that wrinkle of disappointment creasing his brow. Char smiled to himself, recalling his words to the Hozener a couple of days back. So the man really was worth only two hundred red ken.

Ma wove through the crowd, ready to take Rogan's deposit, while Hake picked up the Hozener's chain and led him, whimpering, off the platform.

He returned with the two girls. Unlike the fat man, they fought tooth and nail to escape. Char noticed the extra and unnecessary chain that passed through the manacles on their wrists and ankles, linking them together. Each wore a slave collar, trailing more chain, which Hake secured to rings at the back of the stage.

The mood of the crowd changed as both girls struggled. Genge's manservant calmly finished tethering them and then retreated to stand at the edge of the platform. Gazing out at the gathered people, Char noticed the ugly shine in some men's eyes and narrowed his own. Auctions always drew a crowd. They came for the show and – by fighting – the girls were giving them one. The elder sister who'd spat at Char the other day was pretty with brown hair that tried to free itself of the tight plait Ma had secured it in. Although her teeth were bared in a snarl, her blue eyes were fearful and she kept darting worried glances at her younger sibling, whose cheeks were wet with tears. Char looked quickly away, their plight waking the anger he constantly strove to bury. *No*, he thought, trying to tamp down the rage before it became a torch. *Not here, not now.*

Genge's frown had disappeared and he practically beamed at the girls before turning to face his audience. Char loosened the sticks in their sheaths. This could get nasty.

'Sisters,' Genge said, 'the youngest no more than sixteen. Healthy, strong and – because I'm a kind-hearted bastard – selling as a pair.' There were leers and shouts from the crowd. Char caught Ma's eye. She'd moved back to get a clearer view of the audience. He spotted Alder and the two new iarls, their faces alight with the thrill of the auction.

'For such fine creatures, I'm opening the bidding at three hundred red ken,' Genge said and Char knew from the low starting bid that the slave master expected to make a lot of money.

On cue, Alder said, 'Three fifty.'

'Four hundred,' one of the new iarls countered.

'Four fifty.'

'Five.'

'Five fifty.'

Genge didn't have to say a word. Alder was glaring at the iarl bidding against him and the man smiled back serenely. The crowd had hushed to better hear the battle.

'Six hundred,' Alder said.

'Seven,' the other iarl countered and Alder's face tightened. Char saw Rogan put a hand on his arm.

'Seven hundred and twenty-five,' Alder said with more than a hint of sourness.

'Eight hundred.'

Genge was almost beside himself with glee. He looked at Alder. 'Do I have eight fifty?'

'You do,' Alder said fiercely, his face a thundercloud.

Genge gave him a gracious nod. 'Nine hundred?' the slave master asked with a glance at the other iarl. Char watched Ma's gloved hands curl into fists. Her eyes were fixed and steely. If looks were blows, the iarl would be pulp on the sand.

'One hundred,' the iarl said. Clearly confused, Genge opened his mouth, but before he could speak, the iarl added, 'black ken.'

The crowd gasped and Genge looked as if someone had struck him a blow to the head. 'Black?' he said stupidly. Char stared at the iarl, unable to believe his ears, and the distraction cost him his concentration. His grip on the rage that seemed to burn in his very soul slipped. He lunged for it, struggling to stay calm, but the fight was harder than it had ever been. Char stood stone still, but inside it felt as if he were being flung back and forth by a hurricane, a wind that tasted of fire. Sweat beaded his face.

'Black,' the iarl confirmed with a nasty glance at Alder, who stood aghast. Even the girls had ceased their struggles to watch.

Mutters stirred the crowd like a wind over loose sand. 'A bluff,' one man said loudly. 'No one has that kind of ken to spend on slaves.'

In answer, the iarl reached into a bag held by his companion and pulled out a small canvas sack. Untying the string that bound its neck, he tipped out a few small stones. Necks craned for a better look and there was a collective intake of breath. Through gritted teeth and watering eyes, Char stared at the little stones that lay like pieces of night on the iarl's palm.

Genge finally found his voice. 'Iarl Alder,' he called, 'do you stand by your bid?'

Alder's face had paled at the sight of the sack and he was

sweating. 'I do,' he declared after a moment. 'Eight hundred and fifty red ken is my final offer.'

'And you, sir?' Genge asked the other iarl.

'My bid stands,' the man answered, shifting the stones on his palm. 'One hundred black ken.'

'If you fail to produce the full hundred, the auction goes to Iarl Alder,' Genge said and the man acknowledged the words with a flippant gesture.

'Going once . . .'

Ma's face was as cold as the desert night. Char gazed at her dark, chiselled features, willing that serenity into himself. The iarl with the black ken licked his lips and Char couldn't help but glance at the girls again. They were both openly sobbing now and the rage was a red-hot fire inside him.

'Going twice . . .'

No one interrupted and Genge opened his mouth to declare the sale, but at that moment, the iarl's sack split, spilling its black bounty over the sand. The distraction punctured the growing tension like an overfull water skin and Char found the rage seeping out of him. As it went, it left his insides stinging like slapped flesh. Ma was no longer in his line of sight. After a few seconds of searching, he spotted her on the other side of the crowd, towards the back. How had she managed to get over there so quickly?

The slave master paused as the iarl bent down and hurriedly began scooping up handfuls of ken. One had rolled a little distance away from the others. As the iarl reached for it, the sun came out from behind the cloud, turning the sands white under its glare.

A hush fell over the scene. Half of the stray stone gleamed red.

The iarl ought to have used a better dye, Char thought, as furious shouts erupted from the crowd. 'A trick!' one man cried unnecessarily for they'd all seen the stone. The iarl straightened and began to back away, but the crowd closed up around him. Those who lived in the Black Bazaar might be the dregs of Acre, but they had their own kind of honour.

The iarl's companion was busy arranging his face into an expression of incredulity, but he needn't have bothered; the crowd only had eyes for the cheating iarl. As the atmosphere grew uglier, Char watched the man slip away. It seemed friendship only went so far.

When the screams began, Char averted his eyes. Na Sung Aro justice. His own silent fight had left him feeling weak and his hand trembled as he wiped the sweat from his face. A smiling Iarl Alder, he saw, was now counting out a deposit for the girls.

Ma had disappeared again. Char picked her out eventually, half-concealed in the shadow of the stage. She leaned against a supporting post, arms wrapped around her middle. Even from this distance, he could see the relief on her face. Or was it weariness?

As he watched, Ma pushed herself away from the wooden post and climbed the steps to the stage. She went to the two girls, who stood quietly now, perhaps stunned by the murder of the iarl, or the fact that they were now property, bought and paid for. Char had seen the same expression hundreds of times on hundreds of faces. It took a while for the truth to sink in and when it did, that shock would become anger, terror, uncertainty, even relief . . . Humans were strange creatures. From this distance, Char couldn't hear what Ma said to the girls as she unhooked their chains from the rings in the stage.

Genge had saved the sisters for the auction's finale and Char was glad it was over. His skin felt hot to the touch and a headache was building behind his eyes. He fiddled with the bracer that hid his bandaged forearm and the wound Ren had given him. It didn't seem to be healing well.

He would have to speak to Ma about the rage – how close it had come to sweeping everything he was aside. This time, she *had* to listen. Char took off his lenses and wiped the smears from the smoky glass. They were useful in the desert where sand and sun could blind a man, but that wasn't why he wore them. The force he thought of as the 'rage' had appeared three years ago, around the time he'd turned seventeen. At first he'd ignored it, but the volatile feeling had only grown stronger. It was like the wild northern reaches where fire rumbled beneath the earth, every so often roaring to the surface. At those times, he'd have to fight to push the rage back down, to control it. So far, he'd succeeded. For three years he'd held it in check and only his eyes betrayed the struggle. That was why he wore the lenses – to hide the rage that narrowed his pupils to slits and turned his yellow eyes fiery.

Ma avoided talking about it. Like her past, it was something she preferred to ignore. But Char could not ignore it. He knew that one day his will would fail and the rage would break through, and the thought of what it could do – what he could do – terrified him.

'Not a bad day for you boys.'

Rogan's voice made him jump. Char hurriedly pushed the lenses over his eyes and hid his shaking hands behind his back. 'If Master Genge's expression is anything to go by,' Rogan nudged him, 'you're in for a nice bonus.'

Char made a sound of agreement. He hoped Genge was in

a good enough mood to pay them their share upfront. He and Ma would need it.

'Are you all right, Char?'

Why couldn't Rogan leave him alone? Char forced politeness into his voice. 'A little too much sun, Iarl. And it's been . . . an interesting day.'

'Interesting,' Rogan barked a laugh. 'Yes. I'm sure our friend over there had no idea just how *interesting* today would turn out to be.'

Char followed his gaze to the torn lump of flesh that was all that was left of the iarl. His screams had long ceased and the blood-stained men and women around him began to disperse. A couple remained to dispose of the body in the usual way. Char watched as they each seized one of the iarl's legs and dragged him off through the sand, leaving a bloody trail. The iarl's face was a clawed ruin, unrecognizable, but the mysha wouldn't care. The men took the body outside the gate to the fringes of the desert, flung it down and then returned, chatting and laughing. It had been a good afternoon.

'I like 'Aro,' Rogan said mildly, watching the iarl's killers wandering unconcernedly back into town. 'Things are simpler here.' He raised an eyebrow at Char. 'Cymenza is still under the jurisdiction of the empire. Murder carries the death penalty there.'

'Imperial justice makes no sense,' Char said with a shake of his head. 'Punishing murder with murder? If the authorities are as guilty as the criminal, how is any sort of moral order maintained?'

'Exactly,' Rogan said. 'The Beaches might be full of utter shits – no offence, Char – but you all have a keener understanding of life.'

Char grinned humourlessly. 'Which is why you and Alder like to trot down here three times a year for a roll in the dirt and to spend what's left of your ken on slaves to do your jobs for you.'

While Rogan tried to work out whether he felt insulted or not, Ma called, 'Boy, come over here.' She stood with Genge and the rest of the slavers, poised for what looked like a post-sale discussion.

As Char turned to go, Rogan hissed, 'I'm not giving up on her. Put in a good word for me, won't you.'

Char ignored him and jogged over to where Ma and the others waited. The last of the spectators had returned to Na Sung Aro and now the stage needed dismantling and the cages cleaning before nightfall. Char felt weary at the thought. He and Ma hadn't planned on telling Genge they were leaving, which meant waiting until past midnight to make their move. They'd head into Na Sung Aro first; lose themselves in its serpentine streets until Genge gave up on them. Then they'd find a caravan heading north. It was too risky to travel the Beaches alone.

Genge, luckily, was celebrating. He clutched a bottle in one hand and even had a smile for Char. 'Well, what a day,' he said jovially. 'All the stock sold and not to mention that iarl and his black ken – I'm almost sorry he's dead.' He showed his teeth. 'Gave us quite a show.'

'The man was foolish,' Ma said coolly. 'He got what was coming to him.'

'That he did,' Genge agreed, 'but what luck, eh? That sack was decent leather – it's almost as if someone was on to him and sliced through it on the sly.'

Ren and Tunser grunted, but Ma's face remained inscrutable. Char looked at her suspiciously.

'Let's get this packed away and then we can celebrate in true 'Aro fashion.' Genge smiled beatifically at them all, turned, and made his way to his tent, leaving them to do the actual work. No doubt he wanted to count his new fortune, Char thought.

After he'd removed the pins that attached the struts to the small stage and packed the lot away in a wagon, he found himself working next to Ma as they both took sand and scrubbing brushes to the cages. 'Are you happy that the sisters went to Alder?' he asked her. An unwelcome image of the elder girl's blue eyes assailed him and he pushed it coldly away.

A few moments passed before she replied. 'Everything worked out as it was supposed to.'

'Only by luck,' he answered, using the abrasive sand to remove dirt from the floor of the cage. 'If the bag hadn't split—'

'But it did,' Ma said.

'I only meant to say it was a fortunate turn of events,' he replied.

'Fortunate.'

Ma was never very talkative, but the retorts were sharp even for her. *Something* was bothering her. 'What's the problem?' he asked.

'Nothing,' she said and Char sighed. Talking to Ma was exhausting.

He opened his mouth to tell her about his struggle with the rage when she threw down her brush abruptly. 'I should give you a lesson tonight,' she said.

'Can't it wait?' He stifled a yawn. 'It's been a long day and –' he lowered his voice – 'we've still got things to pack.'

'You should be able to fight at a moment's notice.'

Char was about to respond with a snipe, but paused. 'This is about the assassin,' he said.

Ma looked at him, her eyes glinting in the last of the light. 'I won't always be around to protect you.'

'He didn't hurt me,' Char said before he could stop himself. 'He only fought because you attacked him.'

'He would have,' Ma said with dark conviction. She straightened and shut the door of the empty cage. 'I'm going to change. Fetch your sticks. I want you ready in ten minutes.'

Char considered refusing, but some emotion in Ma's face kept him silent. It was like the fear he had seen on the night she'd stopped him from killing Genge. And it was like the panic in her eyes when the Khronostian had tried to talk to her. He watched her walk away, his brow furrowed.

After he'd swapped his tunic for a fresh one, Char strolled over to Ma's tent. No matter her secrets, they were leaving tonight. Finally, they'd be able to put these years behind them. He was about to push aside the flap when a sound came from within. Char went still, listening. He heard words – Ma, muttering under her breath. A chink of light shone through the opening where the tent's sides didn't quite meet and he put his eye to it.

Ma crouched on the floor, her back to him, a lamp shedding its oily glow over the leather tunic she wore. She was cradling something in her lap and one of her gloves lay on the floor beside her. Char stopped breathing. He'd never seen Ma without her gloves. They were leather, too, and skin tight, as if they were a part of her body. She fought in them, she ate in them and – when Char was small and they'd shared a tent – she'd slept in them. He stared at the discarded glove and his heart hammered in his ears. For the first time in years he thought of the question which he'd long ago given up on. Why did Ma wear the gloves and what did she want to hide?

As if Ma heard him, she snatched up the glove and, still with her back to him, drew it on. When she stood, the leather once again covered both hands and forearms. Char walked confidently into the tent, hoping it looked as if he'd only just arrived. He watched as Ma pulled on bracers and laced them tightly over her wrists.

'Ready?' she asked him.

He drew the kali sticks from his belt and made to go outside.

'No,' Ma said behind him. 'We'll practise in here.'

Char frowned. 'There's not enough space.'

'Enough to rehearse the forms.'

'What's the problem?'

'Tonight,' she answered after a pause, 'I'd prefer to have walls around me.'

Char thought of the way the assassin had simply stepped out of the air and found himself in agreement. He let himself fall into stance, standing with feet spread, one in front of the other, his knees slightly bent. Then he sought the calm, still centre of concentration that Ma so insisted upon. He thought he finally had it when his injured arm gave a throb of pain. His left hand opened convulsively and the kali stick tumbled to the mat.

Curse Ren and his dirty knife – the gash was probably infected. Char had wrapped the wound in a rag and concealed it beneath a bracer, hoping Ma wouldn't notice, but he couldn't deny that the pain was growing worse.

'What's wrong with your arm?' Ma said as he bent and scooped up the fallen stick.

'Ren cut me,' Char admitted. 'The other day.'

Ma hissed through her teeth. 'Stupid boy, why didn't you tell me?'

'I'm not a child,' he retorted. 'It was only small.'

'Let me see.' Without waiting for his response, Ma seized his arm, unlaced the bracer and peeled off the rag beneath. Char sucked in a breath at the sight of it. The wound oozed a thick, yellowish fluid and the flesh around it was swollen and red. He wrinkled his nose at the smell.

Ma stared at his arm, her face unreadable. 'This could kill you,' she said hollowly.

'It's nothing.' Char pulled his arm out of her grip. 'It'll heal.'

'Not without help.' Her eyes narrowed on his face. 'Do you feel well?'

'Yes.'

'No headache, fever?'

Char ignored the tightness behind his eyes. 'Everything's fine,' he said.

'Well, it needs cleansing.' Ma turned to fetch the pouch with her medicines and that was when the Khronostians walked in.

'Hold! We have no wish to fight you.'

The voice was an old man's. These two wore the same bandages as the Khronostian Ma had killed, so that only their eyes showed, glinting out at Char between the greyish wrappings. They were somehow more monstrous in the domestic yellow lamplight than their companion had seemed under the stars.

Ma's lips curled back like a wolf's; she gripped her kali

sticks and stepped between Char and the Khronostians. '*Du-alakat*,' she snarled. 'You shall not take him!' Ignoring the fact that the assassins hadn't drawn their weapons, she drove her kali stick with wicked speed into the nearest figure's head. The Khronostian ducked, but tripped over a crate and went down. Before Ma could finish it, the other leapt, kali sticks a lethal blur, and she was forced to counter a blow that would have shattered her kneecap had it hit her.

Again Char found himself standing frozen, stunned at the pace of the fight. The way the Khronostians moved wasn't human. The man on the ground regained his feet in one effortless twist and brought his stick around to strike Ma's forearm. She gasped, but didn't drop her weapon. Instead she jumped back, putting the large rattan chest between them.

'Run, Boy!' she screamed.

'No,' Char said and, though his arm throbbed a protest, he gripped his own kali sticks and raised them in readiness.

'Where is Rani?' the man asked. 'We came because we had not heard from him.'

'Be still,' his companion hissed and this voice was female. Who – or what – did the bandages conceal?

'I killed him,' Ma said. 'As I'll kill you and anyone else who tries to take the boy away.' She swung into action, kicking the rattan chest and leaping to the side as the female Khronostian aimed a blow at her.

The chest struck the bandaged man across the knees, but it was light and he kicked it aside. Ma was ready for him. She jabbed both sticks at his face in a move that echoed her fight the night before. The man blocked one stick, but Ma's second slipped through and cracked across his cheekbone. He leapt back, gasping, and the bandages came loose, falling about his neck.

The tent was suddenly still. Char gazed in horror at the Khronostian, revealed in the yellow light. His face was a patchwork of ages, as if someone had captured him at every decade of his life, sliced off a nose or an eye and then rearranged them in a gruesome collage. The old voice issued from a baby's fat lips above a bearded chin. Lines crept down over the forehead and around the eyes of a boy before fading into the shaggy cheeks of a man in his prime. It was a terrible face, a sad face, and Char couldn't stop staring and wondering how a person could look all ages and none.

Even Ma had paused at the sight, her lips pressed together as if to swallow a scream. The same fear was there again, heavy in her eyes. Her fists clenched inside her gloves, tightening around the sticks. Then – 'Go!' she yelled at Char and launched a flurry of blows at the female Khronostian, who parried them all.

'I can't leave you,' Char said, and as both Khronostians converged on Ma, he ran at the bandaged woman.

'No!' he heard Ma shriek, but he ignored her, swinging his stick at the Khronostian's neck. Quicker than he thought possible, she blocked him, smacked the stick out of his hand and shoved him backwards. Char staggered and, as he strove to keep his feet, his flailing left arm hit the tent's pole.

Pain exploded in the wound and he screamed, cradling the arm to his chest. The impact cracked the fragile scabbing and blood welled up.

Blood. His blood. Even in a mist of pain, Char knew what that meant and he put his other hand over the wound, hiding the black blood, feeling it slick on his palm. No one could see.

It was Ma's first and most important rule. Never let anyone see you bleed. Never let anyone see your eyes.

Ma looked over at his cry and took in his situation in one awful glance. Then she was moving, faster than even the Khronostians moved, until she'd placed herself in front of him, her sticks daring the assassins to strike.

And strike they did, in a sickening rush. Ma met their attacks head on, her own sticks a blur. When Char didn't think the battle could get any faster, the two Khronostians began to vanish and reappear, just like the assassin out on the dunes. They were slowing time, so that they could attack from several directions seemingly in the same moment.

Ma blocked every blow. Although she didn't vanish and reappear, still she seemed to know where each attack would come from before it did; always she had a stick ready to parry. Char could only clutch his arm and look on, helpless.

Finally, the two Khronostians stepped back, just as the other assassin had done when faced with Ma's prowess. 'Who are you?' the man demanded, chest heaving, his mismatched cheeks flushed with exertion. The woman tilted her head on one side, assessing.

Ma answered both question and gaze with silence.

'We do not wish to fight you,' the man said. 'We only came to take the Kala back to his people.'

The words dealt Ma a visible blow. Shock replaced the snarl she'd worn since the start of the fight. 'You . . . what?' she asked faintly.

'Now that the Kala is reborn,' the woman said, 'he must lead his people in the forging of a new world, as he himself foretold so many years ago.'

'That's why you're here?' Ma asked. 'You think *he* is the Kala?'

The way she said it was strange, Char thought, as if she'd heard the term before and was familiar with its use.

'We do not *think*, we *know*,' the man said. 'The marks of his presence are evident.' His fat lip curled briefly as he gestured at their surroundings. 'You may not be aware, but talk of this slaving caravan has spread far beyond the Beaches. Its fame is such that even we began to pay attention.'

'We shadowed you long enough to witness the Kala's influence for ourselves,' the woman said. 'It is surely thanks to the Kala's presence that this caravan has suffered so little misfortune. The sand dogs never attack you, even when you pass through the heart of their territory. You evade many an unscrupulous iarl's cut-throats, and you make more ken than you have a right to. You face the same threats as other slaving caravans and, where they fail, you continue to prosper.'

Both Khronostians turned to Char. 'Time and circumstance bend to your will, Kala,' the man told him and he bowed. 'You must return to your people. War is coming. The empire weakens and now is the time to strike. With you to lead us, Sartya will fall.'

'I . . .' Char shook his head. 'I didn't do any of those things. If we've done well, it's down to luck and skill. I don't have any power.'

Out of the corner of his eye, he saw Ma stiffen. Surely, *surely* she didn't believe this rubbish?

'You have had a potent guardian,' the woman said, 'one who has worked very hard to conceal the truth from you.' She looked at Ma through narrowed, speculative eyes. 'Hasn't he, Mariana?'

Ma's face blanched and she stepped back, closer to Char.

'It took me a while to remember,' the woman continued, 'the girl who turned traitor, who ran from our battle with the dragons. The prodigy – the one they said would be the greatest of the *du-alakat*. Does it sadden you to know we were victorious? The Lleu-yelin won't be bothering this world again.'

'You killed them?'

'As good as. They're shut away in a place where no one will find them, a prison they'll never escape.' Her eyes narrowed, flicked to Char. 'Such irony that it would be you who found the Kala. You won't be able to keep him hidden, Mariana. He grows more powerful every day.'

'I don't know what you mean,' Ma said, but her usual stoicism had cracked and fallen away.

'Why have you chosen to poison him against us, Mariana? Does your hatred run so deep?'

Char's breath caught. 'Ma?' he managed. Blood was beginning to drip through the gaps between his fingers and, though the pain made his eyes water, he tightened his hold on his arm. No one could see.

But perhaps it didn't matter any more. Perhaps the black blood meant he *was* this Kala, just as the Khronostians said. When his eyes flamed and the rage built – what if *that* was this power they spoke of? Char felt sick, remembering the fight with Ren and Tunser. The moment that Ren cut him, a wind had blown up, a wind out of a windless day.

'Gods,' he said. The slave auction this afternoon – what if *he* had somehow split the sack of ken? When the anger had flared up and he'd struggled with it . . . was this the reason Ma avoided talking about the rage, why she always told him to let it go? He looked over at her, a horrible desperation growing inside him. If the Khronostian woman was telling the truth, then . . .

'You're one of them,' he whispered, his throat burning, and Ma shook her head. But tears shone in her eyes and they told him all he needed to know. 'Why?' he asked, still hiding his blood from force of habit. 'Why didn't you tell me?'

'Because Mariana Leskovian is dead,' she said. 'I'm Ma. Your Ma. I *love* you.'

'Enough to lie to me,' he said viciously. 'Enough to imprison me in this forsaken pit of a life.'

'No,' she said, her face anguished. 'No, you don't understand.'

'I think I finally do,' Char said. His breathing sounded harsh in his ears and it wasn't the rage he battled against. This emotion was worse, sharper, as if his pounding heart had a razor edge and each successive beat cut him deeper until he couldn't keep his agony inside. 'Why shouldn't I go with them?'

'You mustn't,' Ma gasped. 'I saved you from them, I hid you. They want to kill you.'

'You are deluded, Mariana,' the woman said. 'Why would we harm our Kala?'

'Don't listen, Char,' Ma said and Char's surprise stopped him in his tracks. She never used that name, never. He stood confused, hurt and bleeding, looking between the three of them. They all wanted something from him, but no one had asked, had ever asked, what he wanted.

'I'm not your leader,' he said to the Khronostians. He looked at Ma and had to force the next words out. 'I'm not your son.'

For a moment it seemed Ma's face would crumple, but instead it hardened. 'You *owe* me,' she said. 'You have no idea what I sacrificed when I chose to save your life. I won't let you give it to *them*.'

Amidst the silence caused by her words, someone flung back the flap of the tent and stepped inside. 'I hate to break up this little scene,' Genge said, looking around at them all. Lamplight sparked along the drawn length of his sword as he turned a pale-eyed glare on the two Khronostians. 'But this is my caravan and these are my people. Now piss off.'

The female Khronostian moved . . .

. . . And Genge was dead.

It happened between breaths. Char had gasped at Genge's sudden entrance; by the time he exhaled, it was over and the slave master lay twisted on the ground, his neck broken.

Char couldn't stop staring at him. This was the man he'd been going to kill, the man whose death would free both himself and Ma from a life that had become a prison. *He* was the one to kill Genge, not some stranger. He'd planned this moment, imagined standing over Genge's sleeping form, gripping the knife that would spill out his blood. A coward's act for a coward.

But Genge was dead, murdered by someone who knew nothing of his crimes, or Char's own plan for revenge. With a furious cry, Char leapt at the Khronostian woman, whipping the knife he'd meant for Genge from his belt. But before he reached her, Ma caught him around the chest and knocked the blade from his hand. 'Don't let anyone see you bleed,' she growled and pushed him towards the tent entrance. 'If you *ever* loved me, then do as I say and run.'

Still stunned at the suddenness of Genge's death, Char stared at her. He *did* love her – like the mother he had never known. As the Khronostians moved towards him, he did as she asked and ran for the tent's entrance. They moved to stop him, but Ma was there, blocking them, giving him time to flee. As he threw himself into the night, towards the grimy lights of Na Sung Aro, Char knew his was a coward's run, a slaver's run. He didn't stop and he didn't look back.

Keeping his mind blank, fingers still clamped around his bloody arm, he burst through the gates of Na Sung Aro and made for the warren of sand-choked backstreets. His clumsy flight drew little attention. Someone was always running from something in the Black Bazaar – a trade that had soured, or a hooch-fuelled argument gone out of hand, or perhaps just an ithum-user chasing the visions. There were no guards to exact justice, as there were in the empire's cities. You were on your own in Na Sung Aro, and that was how most people liked it.

The wider streets were paved, but Char avoided those, preferring to lose himself in the darker alleyways where the desert still held sway. Sand drifts had piled up against the adobe bricks, making it seem as if the desert itself had birthed these buildings. None were tall, height being unwise on land frequently battered by sandstorms, and their windows were small and covered by mysha hide or canvas.

When he felt as if he'd put a safe distance between himself and the Khronostians, Char sank down on his haunches and put his back against a wall still warm from the day. The first thing he had to do was stop his wound bleeding – already he felt faint and the alleyway swam in his sight. But was that from the wound or from Ma's revelations? His whole world had shifted in a matter of moments with a few, significant words. For the first time, Char wondered – really wondered – who he was, with his umbra skin and his ashen hair and eyes that burned when the rage took him. Could he be the Khronostians' prophesied leader?

He began to laugh bitterly and found himself unable to stop. The ludicrousness of the situation – a slaver being the reincarnated leader of a band of disfigured magicians – was too much. Char laughed and laughed, clutching his stomach with the pain of it and he wasn't sure when the laughter turned to tears or who the tears were for.

Finally, his throat sore and his head pounding, he dragged off his headscarf, wiped his face with it and then tore it into strips to bind up his arm. He'd lost track of time. The black, starry sky told him nothing except what he already knew: he was alone and homeless without a single ken to his name. He wouldn't be able to return to the caravan – it was nothing without Genge. And the Khronostians would expect it. He tried not to think of Ma and where she was. Had the assassins overpowered her at last, or had she killed them with as little compunction as the first?

His brief fit of madness had left him sprawled like a drunk against the wall and now Char felt two hard objects digging into his hip. He looked down and was surprised to see the kali sticks he thought he'd dropped tucked behind his belt. Ma must have stuck them there when she pushed him from the tent. He slid both sticks from their sheath and closed his fists around them. Their smooth surface was cool and reassuring. He was glad to have them with him.

He ought to stay here, lie low until the Khronostians stopped searching. But they'd found him twice now and a chill and sudden certainty told him they'd never give up. He would need to leave Na Sung Aro, make for the nearest frontier – that would be Baior. Char tried not to think about what he'd do once there. Follow his and Ma's plan, he supposed, and head for the Heartland, hoping to meet up with her again. The only profession he'd ever known was slaving. Slaving and fighting, and the Khronostians had shown him quite painfully that he wasn't too good at the latter. Still, he knew enough to offer his services to a trade caravan – he'd fought off bandits before.

He needed food and water, supplies for the road. Char dismissed the option of asking Iarl Alder for help; he didn't know him well enough. Then he thought of going to Rogan, but the iarl would ask questions, too many questions, the first being why Ma wasn't with him. When it came down to it, did he even trust the man? Char grimaced to himself. Without the iarls' assistance, there was only one option left.

An hour later, as the fledgling thief ran through Na Sung Aro, a group of men hot on his heels, Char cursed himself for being a fool. Panting, he tightened his hold on his pilfered goods and swallowed profanities he didn't have breath to express. He was tired and injured. What had made him think stealing from *Walker* a good idea? The ithum parlour had seemed like the ideal target, peopled as it was with addled users lost in worlds only they could see. But he hadn't counted on the toughs paid to guard the parlour's customers, or just how ardent in their pursuit they'd be.

Stupid. His head was too full of fog to think straight. Thieving was rife in Na Sung Aro, even expected, but that didn't mean it went unchallenged. He urged his tired body faster, each gasped breath searing his lungs. A grim certainty dragged at him: he didn't have the strength to fight the thugs. And there was only one place to go where they wouldn't follow him.

Char swung a sharp left, narrowly missing an overturned crate. Leaping it, he dashed for the outskirts of the small town, scanning the walls for a likely spot to scale. With a heave, he tossed his sack up and over the wall and then launched himself at the bricks, scrabbling for purchase. A shout reached him. The men had entered the alleyway, but Char couldn't spare a glance. Boots slapped on sand, someone tried to grasp his ankle and he kicked out. He reached the wide top of the wall and crouched there against the sky, looking down at his pursuers.

Five men glared up at him. One made to climb, but another hauled him back with an oath. 'Enjoy that while you can,' he said. 'And give the mysha our regards.'

Char eyed the men. Their drawn blades glinted dully in the starlight. He could run along the top of the wall, certainly . . . and they would follow below, waiting for the moment his courage failed him and he slipped back into town. They'd likely beat him bloody then, perhaps they'd kill him. This was Na Sung Aro – no one would stop them. No one would care. His corpse would be feeding the mysha either way.

So Char gathered what little shreds of will he had left, turned his back on Na Sung Aro, and jumped.

9

Skar, Acre
Medavle

The atrium is a hazy banquet of sunlight, a colour of such start-
ling wonder, it brings tears. On clear days, it is always like this,
but he never wearies of it. He comes here to listen to the songs of
Solar birds. They fly overhead, golden wings filling the hall with
music. Fountains trill softly, as they trickle into basins. Trees share
their branches with tiny silver claws. The Lunar birds are statues
until night, glories of changeless metal.

Wielders drift around him. All is light and laughter and the
shadows of war are short. Their robes are silken, elaborate, but
there are others too, dressed simply and in white. Their faces turn
to acknowledge him and a few smile. These are his people and for
a moment, he feels sadness.

She chases it from him. He sees her across the hall. The sun
clings to her body, gilds each golden hair. She walks in beauty;
she is beauty itself. Like a lodestone, she draws him to her and she
smiles a smile that is his alone. Her lips are pale roses. Her eyes
are the sky.

'Isla . . .'

151

He cannot touch her, not here, not where the Wielders might see them. It is enough to be near her, to hear his name on her tongue. She lifts a hand to his face, briefly daring, and lets it drop. 'You're troubled,' she whispers. 'What is it?'

He woke, her voice in his ears, as clearly as if she were beside him. But she was ash and light, killed by a madman's dream.

Medavle raised shaking hands to his head – he had not dreamed of Isla in years. Perhaps now that Kierik was dead and Acre restored, she returned to show him how empty his vengeance was. It wouldn't bring her back. He remembered that awful day, the day Kierik had murdered all five hundred of his people, the Yadin, for the power in their bodies. All save himself and Anohin. Medavle had bound his own life force to the Starborn and so turned Kierik's spell back upon him. But whatever satisfaction he felt in breaking Kierik's mind was lost in the horror of running through doomed Solinaris, searching for any Yadin Kierik might have missed. *She* had to be all right, his Isla, the woman he'd loved the moment he saw her. No matter that it was forbidden for Yadin to love one another, no matter that their sole purpose was to serve their masters, the Wielders. What he and Isla shared was too powerful, too perfect, to give up.

So he'd run, the glass citadel crashing down around him, seeing pile after pile of empty Yadin robes. The ghosts of his people seemed to linger about the abandoned clothes, a fleeting impression of their presence, soon lost. He hadn't found her. Neither her robes, nor her ghost. It was as if she'd never existed.

Now he'd discovered his people again, only to lose them to another Starborn.

Medavle sat up, brushing a hand over his eyes. Kyndra lay

on her side, limbs curled in protectively, breathing the evenness of sleep: They were all here together, though the rebels had offered the women separate quarters. Kyndra had said firmly that they would stay as a group.

Although they lay under rock, he guessed it wasn't yet evening, and instead of returning to his troubled rest, he found himself watching Kyndra. Even in the dim torchlight, he could see the mark on her hand – a mark that was clearer since yesterday.

It wasn't the only one. Other constellations were sharper too, on her wrist, her neck. Medavle had seen what she'd done in the Sartyan camp . . . it had almost convinced him to take his knife and kill the young woman while she slept. She had shed her blood-stained clothes and burned them, perhaps thinking to destroy the memory in the fire too. But Medavle knew and the knowledge lay like an iron mantle across his shoulders.

He'd seen Kierik fight years before, on the fateful day the Sartyans marched on Solinaris. What he remembered most starkly of all was not the Starborn's speed or ferocity, but his face, absolutely devoid of emotion. Soldiers came and he'd killed them all, men and women, with blank indifference, as if the blood that soaked him meant nothing.

When Kyndra had driven her fist into the body of the Sartyan woman, Medavle recognized the same detachment. He had seen her arm, drenched in human gore, and he had seen her face, closed, distant. At that moment, she could have been Kierik – she had his eyes, dark blue and depthless.

On the night of her second test in Naris, he'd told her that she was his hope. She had proven him right, breaking Kierik's power, tearing down the walls between Rairam and Acre. But for Medavle to have his wish – for Kierik to die – there was a price to be paid.

Kyndra had paid it.

He still had hope for her. He knew she wasn't like Kierik, who had relished his power. Kyndra didn't want it, was terrified of using it, knowing what it would cost her. She was different; she had a good heart. After all she'd done for him, Medavle owed her his allegiance.

She lay very still, not even a twitch, her face terribly young in the fluttering torchlight. She'd only attacked the wraiths – the Yadin – because she'd had to; they'd killed the boy, Shika. If Medavle himself had been stronger, she wouldn't have needed to turn to the stars.

He rose and, moving softly, pulled the blanket around her, tucking it in. Was it his doom to be bound to Starborn? Medavle's smile was humourless. He returned to his own blanket, but couldn't sleep. Whatever happened, he wouldn't let history repeat itself. If one day Kyndra chose the same path as Kierik . . .

Medavle had created her. He could destroy her too.

10

Ségin, the leader of the Defiant, came to wake them himself, his wife, Magda, at his side. Magda had been the one to lead the rescue and, in the absence of camouflage paint, Kyndra saw an imposing woman in her middle years. She'd swapped her armour for softer leathers and wore her hair in a warrior's braid. A pitch-soaked torch burned brightly in her hand.

Nediah had thought it prudent that they remain awake in shifts, so Kyndra had taken the first watch herself, letting the exhausted Wielders sleep. Irilin had fallen into a death-like slumber, her face drawn and pale. Gone was the carefree novice who'd sneaked into Kyndra's room in Naris. Irilin's ready smile seemed to have died with Shika; she didn't look so young for her age any more, not wrapped in this terrible bleakness.

'Are you rested?' Ségin spoke with a roughened accent that reminded Kyndra a little of her stepfather, Jarand. She felt a pang of homesickness.

'You've been very kind,' Nediah said. 'We are in your debt.'

'Then I hope you'll share a meal with us. I'm interested to

hear how a group of aberrations attracted the personal attention of General Hagdon.'

The mention of Hagdon brought back the fight in a horrifying rush. Kyndra swallowed, remembering the wet weight of the soldier's blood on her clothes, the stickiness that coated her arm. Worst of all, she recalled the moment when she'd plunged her fist into the woman's body . . . and felt nothing at all. The death of another human being was meaningless to her, to the stars. The Sartyan had been an obstacle in her path and she'd removed it. What was she becoming? Was it already too late for her?

'We'd be honoured,' Nediah said, flashing his diplomatic smile; he'd used it to impressive effect several times on Kyndra's journey to Naris. She tried to pull herself together, to shut the thoughts away. They were deep in the heart of the rebels' territory and she couldn't afford to be distracted.

'If you would follow me.' Magda hoisted her torch. She led them deeper into the cave system and, as they walked, other rebels flanked them, so that their little group was surrounded on all sides. Kyndra darted nervous glances at the figures, but Kait, striding beside her, wore a look of supreme unconcern. The sense of déjà vu was overpowering among the honeycombed passages, and for Kait, who had spent so many years under Naris in the Deep, it must feel like home. Certainly the Wielder wasn't at all cowed by the labyrinthine trail and the rock hanging over her head.

'What time is it?' Kyndra asked Nediah out of the corner of her mouth.

'Still afternoon,' he said softly. 'About three hours after midday.'

Relieved, she smiled at him and Nediah returned it. She

didn't think the rebels meant them harm – they'd had every opportunity to strike while Kyndra's group slept – but she felt better knowing the Solar Wielders would be able to fight if they had to.

Finally, the twisting passage expanded into a bulb-shaped chamber. An underground stream bubbled on her right and the back wall was taken up with a stone oven, coals roasting in a shimmer of heat. 'Is there a chimney?' she asked in some surprise.

'Yes.' Ségin pointed. 'A shaft runs up behind the rock face. These caves were inhabited many hundreds of years ago by the ancestors of those who now live on the Baioran flats. We discovered them by chance and they've served as our eastern base ever since.'

The rest of the open space was taken up with rugs, crates and skins of water. 'This is where we gather to eat,' Ségin added, 'and to drink to the goddess of death when she takes a round of Sartyan lives.' His words drew appreciative grins from his followers, who arranged themselves about the chamber. Kyndra kept an eye on them.

'Sit please,' Magda said, gesturing to the rugs. While plates were fetched, Ségin passed around a carafe of wine. Kyndra looked gingerly into her full cup and noticed the others doing the same.

'Forgive our wariness,' Nediah said when Ségin raised an eyebrow at their reticence. 'We were foolish and accepted a villager's hospitality.' Kyndra shared a meaningful glance with Medavle, who seemed content to let Nediah do the talking. The Yadin's demeanour didn't seem so cold today and she wondered at it.

'All of us were drugged except Medavle here and we'd still

be prisoners if he hadn't freed us. Not forgetting your timely intervention too, of course.'

Ségin studied them. 'Any enemy of Sartya is a friend of ours,' he said finally and raised his cup and drank. 'To prove the wine is safe.'

His wife drank too and Kyndra and the others tentatively followed suit. She was glad for the water mixed with the bitter wine – she needed to keep her wits about her.

A dark stew was brought and ladled onto plates. Kyndra wasn't sure what kind of meat it was, but she ate it ravenously. After only a few mouthfuls, she started to feel better; when was the last time she'd eaten anything at all?

'So,' the rebel leader said once the plates were clean, 'your companion tells me you're aberrations.' He nodded at Medavle. 'It seems he tracked you, while we tracked the Sartyans. The Defiant don't take kindly to patrols camped on our doorstep.'

Kyndra eyed Medavle suspiciously. 'What's an aberration?' she asked.

'A person who can channel Solar or Lunar energy,' the Yadin said.

When Nediah looked aghast, Ségin held up reassuring hands. 'Do not fear. It is Sartya which persecutes aberrations. The Defiant are pledged to help them. No doubt you'd have been shipped to Parakat.'

Kyndra looked from Medavle to Nediah, uncertain what to say. She sensed that Ségin was a dangerous man to lie to and she simply didn't know enough about Acre to make a lie convincing. Perhaps the truth would serve her better.

'You asked why General Hagdon was interested in us,' she said. Beside her, Nediah opened his mouth to speak, a warning perhaps, but Kyndra couldn't let him make her decisions for her. This was an opportunity, she told herself. The rebels could give her the information she needed, that Mariar needed.

'It's because he believes we came from Mariar – from Rairam,' she amended quickly, meeting Ségin's eyes. 'We did.'

Silence. Kyndra felt hot under the rebels' stares. Her companions were looking at her too – maybe they thought she was mad for telling the truth, especially after the way the villagers in Asha had reacted. She glanced at Irilin and was surprised to see the young woman give her a slight nod.

Ségin broke the tension with a laugh. 'So it's true,' he said and Kyndra felt a knot loosen inside her. 'There were whispers that the Sundered Valley could be seen again. And I wondered at your accents – your speech is a little old-fashioned.' He studied them more closely. 'How did you get through the hoarlands unscathed?'

'Why are aberrations persecuted?' Kyndra countered. She didn't want to talk about the wraiths, not when the merest thought of them brought Shika's death vividly to mind.

Ségin frowned at her evasion. 'The Sartyans are frightened of their power. Lucky aberrations are killed. Those less fortunate go to Parakat, the prison built to hold them. There, they are kept weak, and tortured into serving the empire.'

He held up his hand before Kyndra could respond. 'Now it's my turn. Tell me of Rairam and how it has returned.'

'You call Rairam the lost continent,' Nediah said, 'but we call Acre the lost world. Many people believe it a myth.'

'Here, Rairam has never been a myth,' Magda said. 'To the oppressed, it is both proof and hope that Sartya can be defeated.'

Ségin gave each of them a searching look before settling on Medavle. 'We know our history,' he said with a new respect in his voice. 'We know *who* defeated Sartya, who took Rairam away. You must be he – the Starborn.'

In the shocked silence, Kyndra swallowed a hysterical laugh. Kait snorted and Medavle's face went absolutely cold. No one spoke.

'Am I mistaken?' Ségin asked. 'It's clear you know of him.'

'Kierik is dead,' Kyndra said, more harshly than she'd intended. She was glad of the low light. The marks on her face were still pale; she knew they'd be hard to pick out in the flickering glow of the fire. The tattoos only started to darken when she drew on the stars they were linked to.

'That is bad news,' Ségin said. 'I had hoped he would still be alive to lend us his aid.'

'What makes you think he'd have helped you?' Kyndra asked curiously.

Ségin considered her. 'He was ever an ally of the Rebellion,' he said, referring to the faction that had opposed Sartya's rise five centuries earlier. 'I had hoped that if the rumours were true and Rairam had indeed returned, he would have offered us the same terms.'

Kait sat strung like an over-taut harp string, almost vibrating with whatever emotion thrummed through her. Nediah touched her arm, a casual gesture but one that carried an obvious warning. Magda eyed the pair speculatively.

'If Kierik is no longer alive, how did Rairam return?' Ségin asked. 'The Davaratch will assume the Starborn is involved.'

'When Kierik died, the power that kept Acre and Rairam apart died too.' Kyndra felt the eyes of her companions upon her and strove to sound convincing. Ségin didn't need the whole truth, just enough to persuade him to help her. 'The six of us were tasked to come to Acre, to discover what we could.'

She paused. 'We don't want Rairam or its people to be seen as a threat.'

'Some of you look rather young to be undertaking such an important expedition.' Ségin's smile was cold. 'And in so small a number.'

Kyndra bit her lip, unused to bartering with the truth. Instinctively, she looked at Nediah. The Wielder was eyeing the room, taking note of the rebels, their hard faces, the stockpiled foodstuffs and bundles of newly fletched arrows. 'You've heard of Solinaris,' he said slowly.

Ségin and Magda and their people gazed back at him; for a moment the hollow chamber was silent with the union of shared memory. Their worlds might be as different as night and day, Kyndra thought, but everyone knew of Solinaris.

'The fortress of the sun.'

The voice was not Ségin's or Magda's. It came from a rough arch of stone that served as a doorway. A curtain hung there and a child stood hidden in its folds, the heavy material half concealing her from the room.

'Mura!' Magda shot to her feet. 'You were told to stay away.' The little girl ignored her. Still wrapped in the curtain, she said, 'Solinaris was made of glass and the people who lived there were Wielders.' The little girl's eyes were round and Kyndra was forcibly reminded of her younger self, caught in the wonder of old stories. 'But the emperor sent his army to destroy it.'

'Mura, I said—' but Ségin laid a hand on Magda's arm.

'Come here,' he told the girl.

'Yes, Father.' Mura untangled herself from the curtain and crossed to stand beside him. She could be no more than eight with a thin face and skin the colour of burned syrup. Her eyes were serious as they looked from Ségin to Nediah.

'You're right,' Nediah said. 'Solinaris was destroyed . . . but the Wielders were not.'

The leader of the Defiant closed a protective hand around his daughter's arm and pulled her back a step. 'You . . . you're Wielders?' The look he directed at Medavle was distinctly hostile. 'I thought you said they were aberrations.'

'There's a difference?' the Yadin asked a little too innocently.

'Aberrations aren't Wielders,' Magda said. 'They have power, yes, but the old ways have been forgotten.' There was a tremor in her voice that spoke of awe . . . and fear.

'Prove it,' Ségin said, rising to his feet. He pushed his daughter behind him. 'I want the truth.' Small sounds reached Kyndra from around the chamber, the rustle of fists closing on scabbards, the movement of leather-shod feet into better position. She realized her heart was pounding.

Nediah remained seated, radiating calm. 'I'm a healer,' he said. 'Was anyone injured last night?'

Silence.

'Owen,' a woman spoke up near the fire. 'My son. His arm is . . . very bad. He won't draw a bow again.'

'I will try my best,' Nediah said modestly.

'Send someone for him.' Ségin gestured at a man standing at the chamber entrance. 'If Owen agrees to it, we will see your healing.'

The waiting seemed interminable. Kyndra wished she felt as calm as Nediah looked. 'Are you sure about this?' Kait whispered. 'What if you can't help . . . or make it worse? They'll kill us.'

'I can help,' Nediah said firmly, as if the healing were already done.

When Owen arrived, Kyndra saw that his right arm was

swathed in bandages. He was being supported by the man who'd fetched him, his face pale and sweating. When he looked at Nediah, it was with little hope.

'Sit him here,' Nediah said, suddenly business-like. He rolled up his sleeves, gaze already travelling over the man's pallid skin and dull blue eyes clouded with pain. 'Can I take off these bandages?' Nediah asked him and Owen nodded listlessly. The rebels drew closer, the better to see.

Owen's mother hadn't exaggerated – the wound *was* bad. Kyndra felt a bit queasy looking at it. A sword slash had opened the man's arm from shoulder to wrist and torn a good deal of the flesh away. Nediah sighed when he saw it. He spent a few moments studying it before raising his hands. When they began to glow golden, there were sharp intakes of breath.

Kyndra leaned in. Although Nediah had healed her more than once, it was different watching him work on someone else. He laid his palms on the injured man, who grimaced, and then the Wielder closed his eyes.

Solar energy rippled out from Nediah, spreading up and down the man's arm, until a corona surrounded them both. Flesh grew seemingly out of the light, muscle knitting, skin smoothing, until the bloody lump began to resemble an arm again.

'A miracle,' someone whispered.

Kait wore a peculiar expression; one hand gripped her shoulder, as if it pained her, and there was a distance in her face like memory.

Slowly, the Solar light faded and Nediah opened his eyes to inspect his work. 'Bend your elbow,' he instructed the man, who could only gape at his arm. The pallor had left his face; with colour in his cheeks, he looked a different person. Slowly, as if frightened the wound would reopen, he bent and flexed his arm. Only the faintest of scars remained.

Tears stood beside the disbelief in Owen's eyes. 'I . . . don't know your name to thank you, stranger.'

Nediah held out his hand. 'Nediah, and no thanks are necessary.'

'I have nothing to give you in payment that could ever come close to matching the service you have done me, Master Nediah.'

Nediah looked a bit flustered. 'Please don't trouble yourself. This is what I do.'

The reverent hush that held the whole chamber in thrall broke like a summer storm. Everyone began talking at once and jostled to get a better look at Owen's arm. Nediah sat in the middle of it, still looking faintly embarrassed. Wondering what Ségin thought of the healing, Kyndra glanced at him. The rebel leader's expression was speculative and not a little bit calculating. It unnerved her.

Mura peered from behind Magda's waist, her face full of a child's fearless wonder. 'That was real magic,' she declared.

Nediah smiled at her. 'We call it Solar energy rather than magic. It's a way of life for Wielders.' He paused, seeing her face fall slightly. 'But I suppose it is a sort of magic, yes.'

'You have rendered us a great service,' Ségin said, 'and though you ask for no payment, you will have whatever is in my power to give.'

'Information on Sartya,' Kyndra said before Nediah could wave the offer away. 'Maps of Acre, if you have them. And if you'd be willing to answer some questions . . . ?'

'Agreed,' Ségin said. Looking again at Nediah, he shook his head. 'If Hagdon had only known what he had in his grasp.'

Kyndra felt another pulse of unease. Perhaps it was the mercenary way in which Ségin spoke, but she sensed something hungry in the words. Glancing around at the eager, firelit faces, she wondered whether they'd exchanged one kind of captivity for another.

11

The connection hissed so badly that it almost obscured the emperor's voice. General Hagdon doubted he'd be able to use the receiver again. As stores of ambertrix dwindled, the whole of the empire's carefully built infrastructure was falling apart. There was barely any power left in the little box and it had been one of the last remaining in New Sartya. The emperor had its twin. He flattened his palm harder against the glowing metal plate, striving to catch the Davaratch's words. 'Iresonté has informed me . . . tolerate another failure, General.'

Hagdon ground his teeth. 'May I know what she reported?'

'. . . this rivalry, Hagdon. Iresonté tells me . . . everything she could to warn you, but you refused to listen.'

'Sire,' Hagdon said, unable to keep his fury down, 'she's lying. She *betrayed* us, deliberately alerted the *du-alakat* to our presence. She locked the damn gates, penned us like cattle. I was relying on the aid of the stealth force. Without the element of surprise, we were slaughtered.'

'. . . did you not hear me? *You will put this rivalry aside.*'

166

Hagdon clenched his fists.

The emperor continued. 'Captain Iresonté . . . orders with regards to Khronosta. She informs . . . cannot be trusted not to interfere.' The connection momentarily improved. 'Now, report on the situation with the rebels.'

How had Iresonté convinced the Davaratch of her innocence? If only Dyen had seen his attacker, but the stealth force had covered their tracks well. Hagdon had no proof; even those of his men who'd survived attributed the failure of the mission to the *du-alakat*'s decision to fight instead of run, as they always had before.

'We've tracked them to Skar,' he said, trying to focus on the matter at hand. 'It appears the Defiant are sheltering the outlanders. I am still unsure of their motives.'

'But you're certain this group is from Rairam?'

'That's the story they told in Asha. They described the Sundered Valley accurately and claimed to have braved its dangers. And –' He hesitated. 'They seem unusually strong for aberrations, Your Majesty.'

He could almost feel his emperor's excitement. 'I want them extracted, Hagdon, and brought to me.'

'They may prove uncooperative, especially after days spent with the Defiant.'

'Iresonté has a man inside that base. Get her people to contact him. Find out what he knows.'

'Yes, sire.'

'If the outlanders refuse to surrender, threaten to destroy Skar. They owe a debt to the Defiant. It will be interesting to see whether they decide to pay it.'

'What if they don't?'

'You have artillery. Reduce the base to rubble.'

Hagdon swallowed. 'And if the outlanders surrender?'

'You know better than to leave an enemy behind you, General. It is high time the Defiant paid for the men they have slaughtered.'

'But there are—' He was going to say "women and children", but what was the point? The Defiant had made their ambitions clear. They were enemies of the empire, enemies who wouldn't hesitate to take Sartyan lives, be they military or civilian. Still, the order twisted Hagdon's insides like bad meat. He'd seen too much killing to want to order more.

'And, General—' The receiver pulsed, the pale blue of the ambertrix that powered it fading to grey. Hagdon watched it wisp out like smoke on the wind, taking the emperor's voice with it. He sighed, not a little relieved.

Iresonté herself was gone from camp, following up a Khronostian lead in the Beaches. Hagdon went in search of her second, a copper-skinned Azakander from lands south of the Red River. Fiercely loyal to Iresonté, the woman treated him to an unfriendly stare. No doubt she was under orders to report on his activity. 'How swiftly can you get a message to your contact in Skar?' he asked.

'How swiftly do you need a response?' Her tone, at least, was civil.

Hagdon straightened the scabbard at his hip. 'Immediately.'

'An hour,' she said.

'Give him our position. Tell him to meet me here.'

She raised an eyebrow. 'He would be exposing himself to discovery, General.'

'Iresonté chooses her agents with care.' He gave her a cold smile. 'I'm sure he'll find a way.' He watched as she moved off to converse with another member of the stealth force. They were a tight-knit, tight-lipped unit and no one save the Davaratch was fully informed of their members or their methods. Who knew what kind of people Iresonté had working for her.

It wasn't until long fingers of shadow crept out of the gullies that the agent arrived. Hagdon raised an eyebrow at his age – only a boy, perhaps fifteen, with amber eyes and a collared coat. The boy bent his head. 'Apologies, sir. I had to wait for my watch to begin before I could leave Skar.'

'I take it as a matter of course that you weren't seen?'

'I wasn't seen,' the boy said quietly.

'Tell me of the outlanders. I know Ségin took them in.'

He nodded. 'They say they're Wielders – like those in Solinaris.'

Hagdon stared at him. 'Wielders,' he said flatly.

'It's true, general,' the boy insisted. 'I saw one of them heal. Owen's arm was all but hanging off, then the Wielder touched it and the skin just sewed itself up.' There was a certain hunger in his face. 'He used golden light.'

'All right,' Hagdon said, slightly disquieted by the boy's expression. 'Did they talk of Rairam?'

'Yes, and they claimed the Wielders had survived the fall of Solinaris.'

Hagdon let go his breath in a long sigh. So Rairam had indeed returned. For a moment, all he could see was the emperor's black eyes, full of visions of the lost continent, the great prize stolen from his ancestor so long ago. There would be a reckoning. 'What do they want?' he asked heavily. 'Did they share their plans with Ségin?'

'They say they were tasked with coming to Acre, to find out what they could. Ambassadors of a sort.'

'Tasked by whom?'

'They didn't say, General. Rairam's leaders?'

Hagdon found himself plucking at the tunic he'd donned in lieu of his armour. It felt unaccountably tight across his shoulders. 'Ambassadors. In so small a number . . . perhaps that's the truth of it.'

'There's something else,' the boy said.

Hagdon left the tunic alone. The boy's amber eyes were darting over the ground, as if searching for a dropped trinket. 'Speak, then,' he said.

'One of the girls.'

Hagdon touched his scratched cheek ruefully. 'Did she have blond hair?'

'The redhead,' the boy clarified. 'She has markings she doesn't want anyone to see.'

'Oh?'

'I notice things. She pulls her sleeves over her hands so often that I don't think she knows she's doing it. I think it's to hide the marks. If you look at her face, you can see others. They're faint, but they're there.'

Hagdon frowned. 'Maybe they're scars.'

'All of them?'

'What else could they be?'

The boy shook his head. 'I don't know, general. I just thought it was worth mentioning. Despite the fact that she's young, the others sometimes treat her as if she's the one in charge.'

It could be nothing, but 'nothing' had a tendency to bite when you least expected. Hagdon stored the information away. 'You've done well,' he said. 'You'll supply me with the correct route through the gullies.'

For a moment, the boy's eyes blazed with some suppressed emotion, but he glanced at the red banner that snapped above the camp and the fire faded from them. 'I will draw it for you,' he said hollowly.

Hagdon signalled for Carn to bring him paper and ink and waited while the agent sketched out the means to destroy the Defiant. When he was done and the map was carefully folded in the pocket of Hagdon's tunic, the boy bowed. 'Permission to return, sir?'

'A battle is a hard place to distinguish friend from foe,' Hagdon said to him. 'I will not give the order to attack unless the outlanders refuse to surrender.'

It was a lie. The Davaratch wanted the Defiant gone and Hagdon had dedicated his life to carrying out his emperor's wishes. But he'd seen the fire in the boy's eyes and heard his hollow assent.

Any loyalty could be tested.

12

She woke, sweating and shaking, from a dream of blood.

It coated everything, slid down her naked body to collect at her ankles so that she stood in a growing red pool. And where it flowed over her skin, it ignited the marks with which the sky had branded her on the morning Kierik died – when she'd inherited the power of a Starborn. The stars were buried in her flesh, dark suns that whispered their chill advice. *Tyr* gloried in her bloody fists, in the way the soldier's body had broken open like overripe fruit.

'No!' she gasped and sat bolt upright. The fire was beginning to curl out of her pores, but she'd woken in time to stop it and no one had seen. No one except Irilin.

The young woman sat with her back to the rough wall, watching her warily.

Kyndra ran a clammy hand through her hair, flinching when she saw the constellation of *Tyr* glowing softly on her palm. She closed her fist and forced herself to breathe calmly.

'This place reminds me of home,' Irilin said, nodding at the rock walls, the low ceiling. 'The passages winding through stone . . .' She trailed off, but it was more than she'd said to Kyndra in days.

'Where's your real home?' Kyndra asked her tentatively.

Irilin's face was in shadow. 'Ilbara, the highlands.' She paused. 'I don't like to think about it.'

'Why not?'

'Because I left it behind.'

Kyndra took a deep breath. 'I know you blame me for Shika.' She forced herself to meet Irilin's eyes. 'I blame myself too.'

Irilin didn't say anything for a long time. 'I know,' she whispered finally. 'And I'm sorry . . . for what's happening to you.'

Kyndra wanted to look away, but she didn't, even though it hurt to hear someone else voice her fears aloud.

'I shouldn't have hesitated,' she said. 'It was selfish of me. If I'd acted as soon as the wraiths attacked, Shika—'

'Selfish to want to hold on to who you are?'

'It was my responsibility to protect him . . . to protect all of you.'

A little colour came into Irilin's face. 'No,' she said. 'Shika and I made the decision to come with you.' She looked away.

'Do you want to go back to Naris?'

Irilin shook her head. 'It's done now. There's nothing for me there, not any more.'

'What about Gareth?'

'Gareth was always able to look after himself.' A tear slid down Irilin's cheek; she brushed at it angrily. 'What will I say to him?'

There was a tightness in Kyndra's throat. No words seemed enough. They lapsed into silence and Kyndra wrapped her arms around her knees.

Selfish to want to hold on to who you are?

I'm still me, she thought fiercely. *I'm Kyndra Vale and my mother's name is Reena and my father's name is Jarand and I grew up in the best of places – Brenwym with its crooked streets and whitewashed houses. My friends are Jhren and Colta and they're getting married soon.*

And that was where it all unravelled.

Jhren and Colta weren't her friends any more, Brenwym had been destroyed and Jarand, despite her most fervent wishes, was not her father. Her real father was a madman who'd killed thousands, who had stopped a war and hidden a world. Her father was Kierik, the Starborn, and he lived on inside her head.

If Kyndra could have cried, she'd have buried her face in her knees and sobbed. Instead, her eyes were dry and her heart was harder. She wanted to tell Irilin that she would fight as long as she could, that she would hold on to all the thoughts and feelings that were Kyndra. But she feared that, eventually, a day would come when she wouldn't understand what having a friend meant. She wouldn't be able to fight it any longer.

Would that it were now, Austri whispered.

It was past midday when Kyndra woke again. She hadn't found sleep until dawn, and her eyes were sandy, her mood black. They'd been in the Defiant base for two days and still Ségin hadn't made good on his promises. She went in search of Nediah and discovered him with the others in the main chamber speaking with the rebel leader and a young man. Mura was there too. 'Some can throw fire,' the girl was saying. 'Not your fire –' she waved at Nediah – 'normal fire.'

'What Mura means is we cannot make fire from nothing,'

the young man said. 'We have to have a source.' He looked about fifteen or sixteen and was dark-haired, amber-eyed and slender. He wore a tunic that was almost a coat with a high collar and elbow-length sleeves. Black gloves covered his hands and wrists.

'Tava and his sister, Olial, are aberrations we rescued from a Sartyan wagon last year,' Ségin said. 'They were bound for Parakat, but thankfully we got to them in time.'

Tava looked at the floor. 'I won't forget it,' he said.

'Show the Wielder what you can do.'

The boy nodded and walked over to the fire banked against the baked stones of the oven. He reached in and swiftly palmed a coal, holding it for just a moment. Then he dropped it back and turned to face them. When he opened his hand, a flame danced there, crackling like a torch.

Mura let out a squeal and clapped happily. Tava smiled at her and then met Nediah's astonished gaze. The boy tossed the flame from hand to hand, split it in two and then three, juggling them all before letting them merge once more. He shrank it until Kyndra thought it had gone out, but then he spun and fire erupted from his boots as he went into a fluid series of kicks and jumps.

Finally, panting, Tava straightened and the fire flickered and died.

There was a burst of applause from the rebels gathered in the chamber and Kyndra found herself clapping along with them. Only Kait looked unimpressed, leaning against one wall, her arms folded. Irilin was watching too, unsmiling, but not as blank-faced as usual. She stood a little away from Kyndra, carelessly plaiting a lock of hair that hung over her shoulder.

'Amazing,' Nediah said. 'How long have you been able to do this?'

'A few years,' Tava answered. 'But I cannot do as you do.' His gaze was hungry. 'How do you make your fire?'

'The sun,' Nediah said simply. 'The source of all fire.'

Tava's eyes went round. 'You can touch the sun?'

'And I think you can too,' Nediah answered, 'with a little training.' He turned to look at Kyndra. 'These so-called aberrations might well be Wielders, but they've never been shown how to touch the Solar or Lunar powers. What else can you do?' he asked Tava. 'Is your sister the same?'

Tava shook his head. 'She doesn't need to use fire – she can make her own. But it only works at night.'

Irilin perked up at this; she even gave Tava a fleeting smile. 'Might we meet her too?' Nediah said.

'Olial is resting before her watch,' Ségin informed him. 'She'll be up in a few hours.'

'I can heat water,' Tava said, going back to Nediah's previous question. 'And I can do a few things with earth – move stone and stuff.'

'Impressive,' Kait remarked drily.

'So,' Ségin said with what Kyndra considered a poor attempt to hide his interest, 'you believe you could train the aberrations? Make them more powerful?'

'I would certainly like to meet the rest of them,' Nediah answered and then seemed to regret his enthusiasm when the rebel leader's smile widened. Kyndra mistrusted that smile. The same hunger she'd seen the other night was there again. She could guess what he was thinking. If Nediah *could* teach the aberrations to unlock their full potential, the Defiant would have the makings of a contingent of Wielders to fight for them.

'That's not the reason we're here,' she said loudly and winced as her words cut through the chamber's excited chatter. 'You promised us information, Ségin.'

'Of course,' Ségin said, turning his smile on her. 'And I mean to keep my promise. Lanan! Bring the maps here.' The named man hurried away, returning a few minutes later with a cylindrical leather case.

'Come.' Ségin gestured them over to a wide table covered with papers and ink. He shoved a bundle onto the floor and shook the maps out of their case. Tava passed him weights to pin down each corner and then went to stand quietly against the rock wall, amber eyes watchful in the gloom of the alcove.

As Kyndra peered at the unfamiliar territory, she felt a presence at her shoulder; Medavle had come seemingly from nowhere to stand behind her.

'This charts north-eastern Acre,' Ségin said. 'We're roughly here.' He jabbed his finger on the right-hand side of the map, over an illustration of twisting upright stones. 'You say you came through the hoarlands.' He moved his finger up and further east. 'These mountains mark the boundary where Rairam used to be.'

'The same mountains north and south of Naris,' Nediah said, leaning in to inspect them. 'Astonishing.'

'Where does the emperor live?' Kyndra asked and the temperature around the table dropped considerably.

Ségin's lean face turned hard. 'The city of New Sartya in the Heartland. A long way west of here.'

Kyndra studied the map, her gaze lingering on a city called Cymenza. She felt a little thrill at the name, recalling it from her book, *Acre: Tales of the Lost World*. And *there* was Calmarac. On the night she'd met Brégenne and Nediah, she'd told a bald lie about the inn's wine being Calmaracian. The memory brought Brenwym to mind . . . and Reena and Jarand. Kyndra felt her heart clench.

She hadn't seen her parents since the night of the Breaking when Brégenne had saved Jarand's life. Months had passed since then, months when they'd had no news of her. What if they thought she was dead? *Maybe it's better they do*, her own voice whispered coldly. *If they could see what you've become* . . .

Kyndra wrenched herself back to the present. From the little she'd seen of Acre, it was a chaotic place. Sartya, the Defiant, Khronosta . . . she didn't know enough about any of them, their goals or motivations.

'What do you know of Khronosta?' she asked Ségin now.

The rebel leader raised his eyebrows at the question. 'Very little. I'm surprised you've even heard the name.'

Kyndra remembered the conversation she'd eavesdropped on between General Hagdon and Iresonté. 'We heard it discussed in the Sartyan camp. An attack that failed . . .'

Ségin's eyes narrowed. 'That explains Hagdon's presence,' he said. 'If the Davaratch received reports of Khronosta in the area . . . well, he's far more determined to get rid of the Khronostians than he is us.'

'I saw the general talking to a woman,' Kyndra said, letting her curiosity win out. 'She had some kind of bird on her armour.'

'A greathawk. One of the stealth force,' Ségin said. 'It sounds like a raid. The emperor doesn't get many opportunities to attack the temple. The Khronostians are not like us – with permanent bases of operations. Whenever they're threatened, their power allows them to move the whole temple and all its people to a safer location. It makes them exceedingly hard to track.' He rubbed his chin. 'Hagdon must have received excellent information to plan a raid.'

'What power do these Khronostians have?' Nediah asked curiously.

Ségin gave him a narrow look. 'They can control time. At least to some extent. That's about all we know.'

Before Kyndra could voice her incredulity, Medavle glanced up sharply from the map. 'They travel through *time*? Is that how they move this temple of theirs?'

'Here my sources fail me,' Ségin admitted. 'We don't know the half of their abilities or exactly how they work, but they've evaded Sartya for two decades.' Kyndra saw frustration in the set of his shoulders. 'They would be our natural allies, if only they trusted us. In the last five years, the Davaratch has stepped up his campaign to hunt them down, but the Khronostians only seem to grow stronger.' He smiled thinly. 'They've assassinated many high-profile members of the emperor's court.'

'So they're warriors?' Medavle asked.

'There's a subsect in Khronosta called the *du-alakat*. Assassins might be a better name for them. They're swift as falcons and deceptive as a desert mirage. You won't know you're dead until you hit the ground.'

'And how many of them are there?'

Ségin raised an eyebrow. 'I doubt even the stealth force has such information. Just think what we could do with their aid,' he added passionately, clenching a fist. 'We have the numbers, the networks, and they have the means. Together we could crush Sartya.' He sighed. 'Or the dragons. They'd have made fearsome allies.'

Kyndra blinked. 'The Lleu-yelin?' All the stories came back to her, the wild people of the mountains, their dragon wings spread to catch the wind. She'd half thought them a myth. 'They're . . . real?'

'The Lleu-yelin are a children's story,' Kait said from her place against the wall.

'They might as well be,' Ségin agreed. 'No one's seen them for twenty years.'

'Why?' Kyndra asked, her heart beating faster with the thought. 'Where did they go?'

'No one knows. They were always aloof.' Ségin shrugged. 'They might not have helped us anyway.'

'Why does the emperor see Khronosta as a greater threat than the Defiant?' Medavle asked after a moment, that glitter of interest still in his eyes.

'I expect because he blames them for the empire's loss of ambertrix. It grows scarcer year by year.'

'What *is* ambertrix?' Kyndra said, frustrated at her ignorance. 'How could Sartya have kept it a secret?' She looked at Medavle. 'They used it to bring down Solinaris.'

'Because it's a secret that could destroy them,' Ségin said. 'I've spent enough lives trying to ferret it out. What goes on in Thabarat is a mystery to everyone but the emperor and his technicians. But when the last of the ambertrix is gone and the Sartyan Fist's weapons are useless, we will strike. Until then we recruit, we train, we grow strong, we *survive*.'

As if to punctuate his statement, a woman at the chamber entrance called, 'Ségin!' and the rebel leader turned on his heel. 'I am needed elsewhere,' he said firmly. 'We will talk again.' Ignoring Kyndra's attempt to speak, he shrugged his hide mantle up onto his shoulders and headed for the door, scooping up a trio of guards as he went.

Kyndra looked at Medavle and Nediah. 'What do you make of him?' she asked quietly.

'I think he's a man to seize opportunity with both hands,' the Yadin said, touching the flute on his belt. Kyndra eyed it with new respect, remembering the great staff Medavle had wielded against the Sartyans. 'Ségin may have sheltered us,' he added, 'but I doubt he made the decision out of charity.'

'He hasn't spoken of our leaving,' Nediah admitted with an uneasy glance at the rebels still in the chamber. Kyndra wondered if they had been deliberately posted there by Ségin. 'He hasn't asked after our plans at all.'

'I'm glad he hasn't,' Kyndra said, keeping her voice low, 'because –' she took a deep breath – 'we need to meet the emperor.'

They stared at her. Medavle's black eyes were as piercing as the day she'd first seen them watching her from the crowd in Brenwym. 'You don't think it's a good idea?' she asked, beginning to doubt it herself. What if *this* Davaratch was as bad as his namesake? The part of her that was Kierik – Kierik's memories, she corrected hurriedly – railed at her. *Sartya was birthed in war. It cannot understand peace.*

'You may be right,' Nediah said finally. 'We came to secure peace for Mariar. That must be our first priority. As long as the empire is in power, it's to them we must take our terms.'

Surprised, Kyndra's heart lifted. To know that Nediah agreed . . . suddenly her plan didn't seem so naive.

'You take a risk,' Medavle said in his deep voice. 'A crumbling empire can be far more dangerous than a secure one. It seems as if Sartya is the only thing stopping Acre from slipping into chaos. If the empire falls – a force that's kept control for more than five hundred years – the vacuum created might spark a whole new war.'

'You believe we should ally with Sartya's enemies instead?'

The Yadin hesitated then shook his head. 'I would like to know more about Khronosta. But in the meantime . . .' With a sweeping glance that took in the rough-hewn chamber and the rebels that were dotted around, he said, 'I don't trust Ségin. You'd be foolish to throw your lot in with his without greater assurance of his support. We have no idea of the Defiant's numbers.'

'The Defiant helped us,' Kait said, coming nearer. 'Their cause seems a just one to me.'

'A response I'd expect from one of the Nerian,' Medavle said with a curl of his lip. 'The Defiant are rebels, idealists holed up in the ground, fighting a war they're unlikely to win. It's no wonder you wish to join them.'

'Ségin,' Kyndra said firmly, hoping to head off the brewing scene, 'thinks that *this* Davaratch is as evil as the first. What if the emperor won't even consider a truce?'

'Our perspective of the empire is skewed in favour of the Defiant,' Nediah said, albeit a little grudgingly, 'and by the fact that our only experience of Sartya was as their prisoners. They thought they'd captured rebels, after all.' He always gave others the benefit of the doubt; right or wrong, it was one of the things Kyndra liked about him. 'We owe it to Naris – and Mariar – to at least make overtures before setting ourselves up as their enemy. It would be foolish to follow the pattern of the past unless Sartya gives us cause to do so.'

'What about the aberrations?' Kyndra asked, determined to consider the argument from every side. 'Ségin claims they're imprisoned. That doesn't exactly speak well of the empire.'

'Perhaps Sartya has never forgotten that Solinaris resisted imperial control,' Medavle said. 'If these aberrations exhibit the same powers as Wielders, they're unlikely to be given the chance to prove themselves as anything other than enemies.'

Nediah gave her a brief, reassuring smile. 'Don't doubt yourself, Kyndra. If Brégenne were here, she'd say we have to explore every avenue. And we don't have the authority to declare war on any power in Acre. If diplomacy fails . . .'

'Let's hope it doesn't,' Kyndra finished. If war came to Mariar, the blame would lie on her shoulders. She was the one who'd brought Acre back, who'd reunited the two lands. It was up to her to protect her home.

A small movement caught her eye: Tava. She'd forgotten him, standing obscured in the alcove. Dread raised the hairs on her arms. How much had he heard? He and his sister owed the Defiant their lives – if he knew Kyndra was entertaining the idea of a truce with the empire, he'd go straight to Ségin. She watched him carefully, but Tava didn't look alarmed or outraged. If anything, he looked like someone who had seen more of the world's ugliness than was right or fair. *That makes two of us*, she thought.

They spent the afternoon poring over the maps until Kyndra felt she had at least a basic grasp of Acrean geography. Kait kept up a steady stream of objections throughout, arguing for staying with the Defiant, helping to build a proper resistance with Wielder support. 'Lord Kierik gave his sanity in the battle against the empire,' she said. 'The Nerian would gladly join any rebel movement in his name.'

Nediah gave her a disgusted look. 'Why can't you see that

Kierik was a murderer? A man prepared to commit any crime, any atrocity to achieve his ends. He was mad long before the fall of Solinaris.' Medavle pressed his lips together; the only sign he gave of his agreement.

Kait advanced on Nediah and the two spots of colour that were always in her cheeks grew brighter. 'Lord Kierik was the only one strong enough to do what had to be done. I was glad to carry his banner; glad of the day we rose to show Naris the truth. We would have shown all of Mariar.'

'I watched you murder helpless people,' Nediah said in a low, hard voice. 'Don't pretend you and the Defiant share a common cause.'

'I waited fifteen years in the dark,' Kait said fiercely. 'I gave up fifteen years of my life to live as an outcast, reviled, forgotten.' She paused and then said in a softer voice, 'You could have come with me. I wanted you to come with me.'

Nediah's face was as pale as Kait's was flushed. For a moment it seemed he couldn't speak. 'You chose to give up those years, Kait. You exiled yourself.'

'I couldn't live under the Council any longer,' she replied, and Kyndra had seen that desperation in her eyes before. 'Not after they . . . I couldn't let them think they'd won.'

'They did win, Kait,' Nediah said quietly.

The flush in Kait's cheeks deepened. 'No,' she said in a small voice.

Nediah seemed older in the dim, flickering light of the torches. 'And you're wrong,' he murmured, turning away. 'You were never forgotten.'

Kait stared at him, tears standing in her eyes, but before she could speak, Ségin returned to the chamber in a whirl of leather, his face white and a dozen rebels at his back. 'He's here,' he said, a choked mixture of fear and rage in his voice. 'Hagdon. You've brought the Fist down on us.'

13

Out in the desert. Alone. Injured. Waiting to be picked off by mysha. It was a litany of the hopeless and it filled Char's mind with thoughts of death.

He'd put some distance between himself and the walls of Na Sung Aro – depending on how much they'd been paid, his pursuers might decide to check the spot where he'd jumped, thinking to find him huddled there, too frightened to venture onto the dunes. There'd be a bloodbath either way. *Beaten to death or eaten to death.* Char grinned humourlessly.

The wound on his arm kept him unwelcome company. It was a throbbing ache which his head soon began to echo, making it hard to think. The blood had finally stopped slowly seeping through the headscarf and had stained it black. A wave of faintness overcame him and he stopped walking, pulling in deep breaths. If he passed out now, chances were he wouldn't wake up again.

He was ill, he knew that. The fever would take him even if the mysha didn't. Perhaps he should have ignored Ma's warning

186

and gone with the Khronostians after all. Char pushed the doubts aside – he couldn't afford to be distracted out here. The gentle, starlit waves of the dunes were deceptively beautiful and the moon was shining upon the sands. Though a bright night wouldn't do him any favours, the mysha hunted by body heat and his raised temperature would look like a small sun to them.

For now, the desert remained silent and Char began to walk again. If he could make it until morning, he might stand a chance. But his feverish brain couldn't remember how far the Baioran frontier was. It could be several days away and although he had a bit of food and water, the mysha would surely find him before then. He shivered in the chill air, swivelling his head from side to side, convinced the sand dogs were watching him, yellow-eyed and hungry in the darkness.

Char opened his eyes. He was lying sprawled under the sun and he blinked, confused. Hadn't it just been night? His last memory was of trudging through moonlit sand and thinking about the mysha. But how did he come to be here? He felt a chill even as his body sweated in the heat. He must have passed out and lain here unconscious for hours. That he was still alive was beyond miraculous – perhaps the Khronostians were right and he *did* have some mysterious power.

The fever was worse today. His head throbbed, his limbs felt heavy, weak, and he found himself gulping down the water he'd brought from Na Sung Aro. Char knew he ought to ration it, but could not stop. There wasn't much left when he was done. He didn't have the strength to chastise himself, not when he was merely putting off the inevitable. He chewed on some tough pancake, but found it hard to swallow. Everything was an effort and the wound on his arm –

Char looked at it. The gash was still puffy and red, but for the moment it was closed. The crusted scarf was gone and so was the black blood that had dried on his skin. Someone had washed it off. Or something. Heart beating faster, he slowly turned his head to look around, but saw only empty sands and a haze to the south that could be the smoke of Na Sung Aro. As far as he knew, only mysha lived out here.

Standing up proved easier said than done. Char's legs trembled under his weight, his head spun and he fell back twice before succeeding. He needed shelter, another headscarf to keep out the sun. He had neither. The kali sticks hung at his hips, useless weight he would be better off without, but he couldn't bring himself to discard them. Ma had given them to him and though he barely had the strength to stand, he wouldn't throw his last relic of her away.

He hoped she'd escaped the *du-alakat*. She must have. Prodigy, they'd called her . . . did that mean she had grown up in Khronosta? *His* Ma? Once, Char might have scoffed at the idea, but he remembered Ma's face, the tears in her eyes, and knew them for truth. Khronosta was Ma's demon . . . the demon she'd been running from all these years. Why had she left? If he *was* the Kala, why had she chosen to hide him, to betray her people? None of it made sense. He wished he could talk to her.

Perhaps if he turned around, went back to Na Sung Aro, he'd find her. Perhaps she'd already be gone. Even in the Black Bazaar, questions would be asked about Genge's death. No, Char decided, he'd follow their original plan – escape to the border with Baior, head west to the Heartland. It couldn't be much further. But a terrible lethargy was spreading through him.

He was going to die out here.

Time must have passed, for the sun left a blazing trail as it crawled slug-like into the west. Dusk brought a welcome relief from the heat, but the temperature fell too quickly and Char began to shiver. His water was gone and although he knew he must eat, he couldn't summon the strength to gnaw at the toughened fare. His knees finally buckled just as the first star appeared in the sky.

This was it, then. He lay in the dim light, the sand still warm beneath him, and waited to die. The pain in his arm was spreading throughout his body and it was the only thing keeping him conscious. Char felt the sand of the desert against his cheek and thought of the life he had lived with Ma and Genge and the other slavers, turning a profit at the expense of another's freedom. Dying alone in this inhospitable place was a fitting end for him. Where were all those people whose own fragile lives had passed through his hands? He'd watched without mercy, without saying a thing, while Genge chained them up and sold them off like so much meat. He could have helped. He *should* have helped.

Freedom was an illusion, he'd always told himself. But out in this unprincipled wild, the cold words brought no comfort. They seemed arrogant – no, ignorant – spoken by a boy who hid behind his cowardice.

His parched throat managed a tiny gasp at the thought of the emptiness that awaited him, that sure oblivion he travelled to. His life might be worthless, but it was *his* and he wanted it. Using reserves he didn't know he had, Char pushed himself up onto his elbows.

That's when he saw the eyes – several pairs of eyes, yellow, unblinking, as they slunk towards him out of the gloom. There were perhaps six of them, more than enough to finish the job. *Dogs,* he thought almost hysterically, *they call them dogs.* The mysha were more like wolves, *big* wolves, all muscle and sinew. They'd come to well above waist height if he stood up. He could smell their sandy coats, all heat and dust, and their breath steamed gently as the temperature dropped. They padded up, near-silent, and they circled him and Char could only huddle there and wait for the teeth, which would show him no more mercy than he'd shown the slaves.

One was a little bigger than the rest: the pack leader, he supposed. It moved closer, its muzzle mere inches from his face. Char gritted his teeth. He wouldn't look away. But the mysha only sniffed him and then, as if in confirmation, drew back and sat on its haunches. The others followed suit.

The fear had burned away some of the fog in his mind. He gazed at the dogs, disbelieving. Why hadn't they attacked? He was a free meal. Char managed to sit back on his heels. It was a stiff, flinching movement – he fully expected to feel the crush of teeth – but the mysha sat quietly and their mood seemed one of curiosity rather than violence.

Char knew this strange truce was not down to any Khronostian power he might possess. Messing with time couldn't change animal nature. So what stopped the dogs attacking? A life lived in the Beaches had taught him that humans and mysha were enemies – a conclusion based on years of hearing about mysha attacks. Char had seen them often enough, tearing into a body thrown outside the walls of Na Sung Aro. These had the same razor teeth, the same malevolent yellow eyes . . .

His vision was clouding over, but Char thought the pack leader lowered its muzzle to the sand before him. Then he felt himself slump sideways, his body limp and heavy as a corpse's. As he lay beneath the chill stars, fighting to keep his eyes open, his last sight was of the mysha, finally moving in for the kill.

14

Tava flinched. He wasn't the only one. Panic avalanched through the chamber and Kyndra wasn't prepared for the terror she saw on every face.

'This is your fault,' Ségin snarled at her, at them all. 'Hagdon's here because of *you*.'

He was right, Kyndra thought, a sickening guilt churning in her stomach. Hagdon knew they were from Rairam. He wouldn't lose them to the Defiant, not if he had the means to take the rebels down.

'If it's us Hagdon wants, we'll ride out to meet him,' Nediah said, putting himself between Kyndra and Ségin. 'No one needs to die.'

Ségin hesitated. 'You would give yourselves up?'

'We would?' Kait said.

'*Yes*,' Nediah answered them both. He looked at Kyndra. 'We can't let the Defiant pay for sheltering us.'

'Didn't you say the route to Skar was a secret?' Kait asked, demonstrating her infallible ability to fan the flames. 'How did

Hagdon find his way here? There must be a traitor amongst you.'

Ségin's face flushed an ugly red. 'You accuse one of my people of selling secrets to *Sartya*?' Despite his anger, he swept a sharp gaze over all those in the chamber. Perhaps suspicion came naturally, a consequence of years of running and hiding.

'Show us Hagdon's army,' Kyndra said, unable to keep a tremor out of her voice. Ségin set his jaw and gestured them curtly to follow, snatching a torch from the wall. They passed out of the lighted areas onto paths winding and steep, which climbed unsteadily up through the rock. Wind gusted down from some opening above. It reminded Kyndra of that last mad hike through the innards of Naris, following in Anohin's wake. Perhaps Kait and Nediah were thinking the same; their faces were closed and distant.

They found evening at the top of the cliff, stars already showing in the dusty sky. *Starborn*, *Vestri* hailed her. Kyndra ignored the greeting, trying to remember a time when the stars were simply part of the night. Once, she'd thought them beautiful . . . cold, but beautiful. Now she knew what they really were; she'd walked among them, felt the burn of power – too much for any mortal to wield.

The lights of Hagdon's army mirrored the star-decked sky. In the growing darkness, they were a terrifying sight; the twisting gullies that led to Skar were like rivers of fire. Hundreds of torches burned, stretching all the way back to the distant plain where hundreds more waited. The Defiant had been betrayed, Kyndra thought, gazing at the force arrayed against them. The gullies were a maze with the widest, most promising paths often leading to dead ends. Someone had shown Hagdon the correct route. Looking down upon the might of the Fist, it seemed

Ségin had come to the same conclusion. His fists were clenched, arms stiff at his sides.

From her vantage high on the cliff, Kyndra saw the flames glinting off a dozen metal monstrosities and she wondered if these were the siege weapons Kierik remembered. The Starborn's memories told her that they spewed fire, that they could hurl flaming boulders a great distance. The walls of Solinaris had experienced their power first-hand and had eventually fallen to the ceaseless barrage. Watching two of them being trundled into position, pointing at the cliffs to ward off ambush, she knew she couldn't let it come to that here.

The sound of strenuous puffing behind her announced a man climbing out of the rock. 'Dispatch,' he said, handing Ségin a folded note. 'From Hagdon.'

The rebel leader frowned, cracked open the blood-red seal and read the few words printed there. Then he thrust the note at Nediah.

The Wielder tilted it so that Kyndra and the others could see. Irilin came to stand beside them, a faint Lunar light falling from her hand onto the parchment.

To Ségin, leader of the group that calls itself the Defiant: Release the Wielders into Sartyan custody. You have until midnight to comply.

There was no 'or else', Kyndra noted with another glance at the siege weapons. The threat was implicit enough.

'How does he know you're Wielders?' Ségin growled.

'Not only does he know we're Wielders,' Kait said, 'his timing makes me think he's aware that Nediah and I are Solars.

We can't use our power at night.' Her eyes narrowed. 'Someone has betrayed you, betrayed *us*.'

'We'll go, Ségin,' Kyndra said. 'No one is going to die because of us.'

'It's too late.' The rebel leader gave a hard shake of his head. 'I know Hagdon. He's not one to leave a thing unfinished. Once he has you, he'll still destroy us.'

Nediah's face was pale in the Lunar glow welling from Irilin's hand. 'He would go back on his word?'

'He has not given his word,' Ségin snarled. He snatched the paper and crumpled it in his fist. 'We are finished.'

'Not if I can help it,' Kyndra said. She tried to ignore the pounding of her heart, the guilt she felt on bringing this down upon the people who'd rescued them. 'There must be a way to get everyone out of these caves.'

'There was,' Ségin said, despair creeping into his voice, 'but the passage recently collapsed. I've had men shifting the rock, but it's a huge job. Olial isn't strong enough to help and Tava tires quickly.'

'Well,' Irilin said, 'Medavle and I can clear it.' She glanced at the dark-eyed Yadin. 'It's still four hours till midnight.'

'Once you have a way to get your people out, we'll go to Hagdon,' Kyndra said. 'We'll stall him as long as possible. If we can't convince him to call off the attack, you'll at least have the time you need to move everyone out of Skar.'

Ségin eyed her, half wary, half curious. 'You won't convince him,' he said. 'And you can't fight the whole army . . . unless you've some trick up your sleeve?' When Kyndra didn't reply, he let go an explosive breath. 'Very well. If you fail, we won't get far, but . . . I'll take whatever you can give me.'

'Show us the rockfall,' Irilin said, rolling up her sleeves. Her face was hard, but more alive than Kyndra had ever seen it. She seemed fearless. They followed Ségin back down the twisting natural staircase and into the main chamber, where the rebel leader stopped to issue orders. Men and women, outfitted for battle, hurried to and fro, collecting weapons and equipment while others – those who couldn't fight – gathered supplies. The atmosphere crackled with Hagdon's threat, the shock of the army camped on their doorstep. Although the fire had gone out, the room was hot and stank of sweat and grease.

Watching them prepare, Kyndra felt woefully under-armoured. If she found herself in a melee, the soft black leather of her clothes wasn't going to keep out any stray arrows or sword strokes. She could shield herself in *Tyr*, of course – its power was better than any mail, weightless, strong enough to turn the sharpest blade – but that meant letting the star inside her, where it would wreak its cold destruction.

Those men still labouring at the site of the rockfall turned grimy, hopeless faces towards Ségin and one called out, 'It's endless. We might as well be digging our way to the centre of the earth. Every time we think we're there, we find another bloody boulder.' He wiped a battered hand across his forehead, leaving smears behind. 'We won't have it clear in time.'

'Stand back,' Irilin said, not waiting for Ségin to speak. The men took one look at her glowing hands and scrambled aside. Irilin drew a complex pattern in the air, which hovered before her, pulsing silver-white. When it was done, she slapped a hand to the middle of the rune and sent it spinning into the tumbled rocks. There was a *boom* and the next moment they were showered with stone chips.

When the flash of silver light had faded, the men looked wonderingly at the cleared space. 'It was Master Tava who reported the cave-in,' one murmured, 'and even he had trouble shifting it.'

'Runic substantiation, eh?' Nediah said admiringly. 'I could never grasp it myself. Too fiddly.'

'And healing isn't?' Irilin said with a hint of her old humour.

'Don't use so much force,' Kait chided her. 'You're trying to clear the blockage, not bring down the rest of the ceiling.'

Irilin glowered, but took the point. Her next strike wasn't quite so powerful, but they were still showered with flying chips. 'It would have taken a week,' another rebel observed, 'and more rock behind.'

After Irilin's third rune, a tremor ran through the stone at their feet. Kyndra glanced down at it uneasily. 'I think I can see the path,' Irilin called. Before she could venture any further down the tunnel she'd cleared, Medavle said, 'Wait.' He moved to inspect the walls, which bore many small, ominous cracks, forked like snakes' tongues. 'These aren't safe. We'll need supports.'

'We don't have the wood to spare,' Ségin said.

'I was thinking something more temporary.' The Yadin retrieved the flute from his belt; Kyndra noticed it drew several perplexed glances.

'Is there anything you *can't* do with that flute?' Kait said. 'How did you come by it, anyway?'

'I made it,' Medavle said, 'long ago.' The flute stayed as a flute this time and he blew three chiming notes. Silver light grew about his left hand, gold about his right, brightening the sandstone tunnel as he moved along it, shoring up the stone. Kyndra had a fleeting impression of pillars, standing at even intervals, before the sight faded and the only clue that testified to their presence was a slight sheen on the walls.

'It will hold tonight and tomorrow,' Medavle said, 'no longer.'

Nediah shook his head. 'Solar energy at night . . . I'll never understand the Yadin.'

'I do not channel it,' Medavle said. 'Whenever I draw on Solar or Lunar energy, I take it from my own veins.'

'I remember Anohin saying the same,' Kait murmured.

Medavle's face darkened at the name and Kyndra wished Kait hadn't mentioned the other Yadin. Fanatically loyal to Kierik, Anohin had been a traitor to his people. And yet . . . the darkness in Medavle's face wasn't only anger, but grief for a brother lost.

'Start moving people out immediately,' Ségin ordered. 'We go north to Lake Vordon.'

'That's a five-week journey,' one of the rebels said. 'Surely the Calmaracian base is nearer.'

'The route leads too close to Cymenza,' Ségin countered. 'I don't want the children anywhere near that city.' His face flickered. 'I'll need to leave you for a time, but you follow Magda in my absence.'

The men nodded, picked up their tools and hurried away.

'Thank you,' Ségin said to Medavle and Irilin. 'You have given us a chance.' He placed his hand against the sandstone wall, ran his fingers over the coarse rock. 'Skar's been my home for five years, a safe house. I imagined it would be so for many more. How strange to leave it behind.'

'I'm sorry,' Kyndra said.

'Our cause endures. It is all that matters.'

Voices reached them as the first group of rebels arrived at the tunnel, Tava's sister, Olial, at their head. She was twin to her brother with the same bronzed skin and amber eyes. The glow of Lunar energy surrounded her. 'Ségin,' she said. 'I'll lead each group through and come back for more. We'll attract less attention that way. I can light the passage – it'll be too dangerous to carry torches. Hagdon will likely have scouts in the area.'

The rebel leader nodded. 'Thank you, Olial. Where's your brother?'

'I don't know,' the girl said. She bit her lip. 'He promised to help me get people moving, as soon as he fetched his crossbow. He hates it when he can't use his power.'

'We'll find him.'

Olial nodded and turned on her heel, calling to the group of people massing in the passage. 'Two at a time. Try to keep the children quiet.'

'She seems a lot older than fifteen,' Irilin muttered when Olial had led the first group into the tunnel.

'Her parents were killed in front of her by Sartyan soldiers,' Ségin said. 'They were trying to stop their children being taken to Parakat.'

Hearing that, seeing the fearful, uncertain faces that filed past her, Kyndra couldn't help but question her decision to seek a truce with Sartya. By aiding the rebels in their escape, she was setting herself up as Hagdon's enemy. But she had promised Ségin she'd go to the general, to do what she could to avoid bloodshed.

'I appreciate what you're doing for us,' Ségin said seriously. 'If you can stall Hagdon long enough to get away, head for Cymenza.' His cheeks were flushed, his hawk's eyes fierce. 'The Defiant have a friend there. If you wish to aid our cause, he will find you.' Before Kyndra could question him further, someone called his name. It was Magda, holding tightly to Mura's hand. 'Remember, Cymenza,' Ségin said. 'I hope we'll meet again.'

'We could go with the Defiant,' Kait said in a low voice when he'd moved away. 'What's to stop us?'

Nediah looked at Kyndra and again Kyndra felt the weight of unwanted, unlooked-for responsibility. 'We can't,' she said. 'I promised Ségin I'd go to Hagdon.' She hesitated. 'I want to speak to him.'

Kait threw up her hands. 'You want to speak to the man who's preparing to annihilate these people? They took us in, gave you your blasted maps – they *rescued* us!'

'Hagdon's here because of us, because of Rairam. If we go with the Defiant now, we automatically make ourselves his enemies.'

Kait shook her head. 'You're going to get us killed.'

Kyndra hardened her voice and said, 'I'm not defenceless, Kait. If Hagdon does mean to harm me, he'll soon wish otherwise. My power is not limited by the time of day.'

'You don't have to use it,' Nediah said awkwardly. 'That's why we came, why *I* came. To make sure you're safe. To watch over you.'

'*I* should be watching over *you*,' Kyndra replied, striving to keep her fear under control. Nediah thought he knew what touching the stars would do to her, but he didn't understand, none of them did, save Medavle perhaps. How could she say that each time she called on their power, she sacrificed a little more humanity – the feel of her mother's arms around her, the warm, woody scent of summer when the windows of The Nomos were flung wide, the bellyache she got after laughing too hard with Jhren. They were fading, these memories, the emotions they inspired. Not gone, but fading until they meant nothing to her.

'How long do we have?' she asked, hardening her voice.

Irilin glanced upwards, as if to stare at the moon hidden behind the layers of rock. 'Three hours.'

'I hope that's long enough for Ségin,' Kyndra said.

They rode out from a near-emptied Skar. The passage through the cliffs took an hour or more to traverse, Ségin said, but most of the Defiant and their families were now walking it. According to Olial, Tava was still missing, and Kyndra wondered whether the boy had already slipped down the secret way. He didn't seem the type to abandon his duty.

The guilt in Kyndra's stomach did not churn so much – she knew they'd done what they could to help the Defiant escape. The feel of Ségin's calloused palm in hers as he shook her hand stayed with her and she wondered whether – after this night – they'd ever cross paths again. Trying to take some reassurance from the warm weight of the horse beneath her, she gazed at the endless torches of the enemy.

Not the enemy, she thought, angry at Kierik's intrusion. The Starborn's memories told her the empire had committed terrible crimes in its journey to unify Acre. Someone had to answer for the thousands of men, women and children that lay dead, their homes burned, lives torn apart.

Kyndra forced down the memories before they could overwhelm her. *What's past is past*, she thought firmly. *These are not the same soldiers.*

Still, those memories curdled her blood as she urged her horse forward. A small contingent of soldiers awaited them, but Kyndra knew hundreds of other eyes were upon her and her friends. She felt the proximity of those fiery weapons as a prickling on her skin.

None of the Sartyans were mounted. There were ten in all

– officers, by the looks of the braid on their cloaks. Four other soldiers held torches; their combined light was overly bright after the gloom of Skar. Kyndra dismounted and the rest of her companions hesitantly followed suit.

One of the soldiers flipped back a cowl and stepped forward. Kyndra recognized General Hagdon. Now that she had leisure to look at him properly, she saw that he was younger than she'd thought, perhaps late thirties, his skin weathered through time spent outdoors. A scar barely missed his left eye, crept down his cheek and vanished into a short dark beard. It was a hard face, uncompromising. This was not a man to underestimate, she thought. The hilt of a sword stood up behind his shoulder, another hung at his side and his red plate glowed like embers.

General Hagdon greeted them with a stiff inclination of the head. 'The circumstances have changed somewhat since I saw you last,' he said. His voice was husky, roughened perhaps by years of shouted orders. 'I am General James Hagdon of the Sartyan Fist.'

'My name is Kyndra Vale,' she said and for a moment it seemed as if all this were some bizarre dream. *She* surely couldn't be here, in Acre, talking to the general of the greatest army history had ever seen. She'd barely had time to rehearse what she wanted to say. 'These are my companions, Nediah, Irilin, Kait and Medavle.' She paused. 'We know why you're here.'

If Hagdon was surprised to hear her do the talking, he didn't show it. His expression remained perfectly neutral, as he studied each of her friends in turn. His gaze lingered on Irilin, who returned it inimically. Hagdon's cheek still bore the scratches left by the young woman's nails.

'You claim to come from Rairam,' he said. 'Is it the truth?'

'It is,' Nediah answered. 'We wouldn't have been so forth-right with the villager if we'd known it would land us in chains.'

Hagdon's mouth twitched, just briefly. 'It's no surprise that the Defiant chose to shelter Wielders. They make it their business to keep as many aberrations out of Parakat as possible.'

'And that's a bad thing?' Irilin said.

Kyndra had tensed at his mention of Wielders. 'The only people who knew the truth were Ségin and those he most trusted,' she said. 'How do *you* know?'

'Sartya's arm is long,' a woman behind Hagdon said. She wore the same greathawk pauldrons as Iresonté: stealth force, then. 'Few things are hidden from us.'

'Except for Khronosta,' Medavle said.

It was as if he'd spat at their feet. Faces darkened and Kyndra silently cursed the Yadin. They were already on perilous ground. It still looked as if they were allied with the Defiant; the last thing they needed was for General Hagdon to believe they were also involved with Sartya's greatest enemy.

'How do you—?' the woman began, but stopped at a look from Hagdon.

'Ségin has clearly filled you in,' he said in a mild tone that raised the hairs on Kyndra's neck. Here was a man who felt entirely unthreatened, and she realized she was being allowed to talk on sufferance only. Everything from his posture to his choice of words told Kyndra that all he had to do was give the order and they'd be overpowered, trussed up and shipped to the emperor as gifts. That arrogance made her angry. It also made her feel small and terribly unprepared.

'The Defiant are gone,' Nediah said. 'Ségin's not foolish

enough to think he can win this fight. You wanted us and we're here, as requested.'

'You cleared the blocked passage, then,' Hagdon said, his eyes narrowing. 'Impressive. I was informed it was quite substantial.'

Kyndra stared at him. 'You . . . you knew about the cave-in. Did you arrange it?'

'Our little agent's quite resourceful,' the woman from the stealth force said. 'He's been doing our work for some time. Without your interference, Ségin would be holed up like the rat he is, nowhere to go but through us.'

'Only someone with Wielder abilities could have brought down that much rock,' Kait said shrewdly. She paused. 'It's a shame Tava disappeared so suddenly or we might have asked him.'

'Captain Iresonté casts her net wide,' the woman answered.

Tava . . . Surely that wasn't right. Kyndra felt sick at the thought. He and his sister hated Sartya. Soldiers had killed their parents, carted them off to a life of servitude. How could someone like Tava agree to work for the people who'd taken so much from him? Unless he'd had no choice.

'The Davaratch desires your presence in New Sartya,' General Hagdon said. 'With or without your consent.'

'I won't go before your emperor in chains,' Kyndra replied, her heart beginning to race. 'None of us will. We came to seek a truce, to broker peace for Rairam.'

There was silence. Then one of the officers began to laugh. '*Peace*?' he repeated. 'You think to broker peace? Your land is once again free for the taking. The Davaratch will stop at nothing to succeed where every emperor before him has failed. He will be the man who finally brings Rairam under the banner of Sartya.'

General Hagdon did not laugh. His expression was sober, almost sad, but he didn't refute the argument. Kyndra stared at the officer who'd mocked her, wondering whether she had her answer. Was a truce with Sartya so utterly unrealistic? Had she been a fool for even trying to make overtures?

The mood was changing. Hands were edging towards hilts, feet were shifting for better purchase on the rocky ground. Kyndra darted a look at Irilin and Medavle. She had no doubt that they'd take out dozens of soldiers before they tired, but Hagdon had thousands. She'd seen them stretching back to the plain. If they fought, they'd be overwhelmed. If they didn't fight, they'd be captured. Kyndra wasn't sure what Sartyans did to restrain aberrations . . . unless they had those like Tava working for them.

It left her one option, but the thought of using her power to kill again horrified her. 'Don't do this, General,' she said. 'If you think there's no chance of compromise, at least allow us to go free.'

'I am under orders,' Hagdon said.

'As am I,' she replied, thinking of Brégenne, of Naris and Mariar and the responsibility she had to them all. 'I can't allow you to capture me or my friends.'

Perhaps Hagdon heard the threat buried in her words because he hesitated, his eyes sweeping her face. And in that moment of uncertainty, before either of them had a chance to speak further, the air hummed and something white sped past her ear, so close that Kyndra felt the wind of its passage. The crossbow bolt struck Hagdon in the shoulder, missing his neck by inches. It punched through the red plate he wore and hurled him to the ground.

Kyndra and the Sartyans stared at the fallen general and then at each other. Kyndra read the intent in their faces, watched as they unsheathed weapons. 'No!' she cried, backing up a few steps. But the sight of Hagdon on the ground was like a spark to tinder and it roared back through the ranks of his army. The general moved feebly; he was still alive, though no doubt gravely injured and a dozen soldiers shielded him while their fellows bore him to safety.

It all happened in the space of a few heartbeats. Kyndra looked behind her and saw a shadow crouched on a low ledge. Metal glinted in moonlight: a weapon held in both hands. Another whistle and a second bolt hit the officer who'd laughed before he'd even fully drawn his blade. It was a good shot, taking him right through the eye. He toppled to earth and his comrades leapt over him, advancing on Kyndra's group.

More bolts flew from the darkness and more Sartyans fell, but then there came a cry from the ledge and a clatter as the would-be assassin dropped his weapon. Kyndra's group was surrounded now, though the Sartyans simply held them at sword-point. Another two dragged the figure into the light of the torches and Kyndra saw Tava, his face bloodless, hands clamped around the arrow embedded in his thigh.

'Shown your true colours, aberration,' the woman with the greathawks said, as he was dumped at her feet. 'Captain Iresonté will be disappointed. Especially after such sterling work.'

'I won't . . . I won't be your puppet any more,' Tava said through clenched teeth. 'Ségin is a good man, a better man.' He twisted round to look at Kyndra's group. 'I'm sorry,' he said and Kyndra thought he spoke to Nediah. 'I'm sorry.'

Nediah shook his head, his face pained and unable to speak.

'What Ségin does to inspire such loyalty, I'll never know,' the woman said and she casually slit Tava's throat.

For just a moment, the boy looked as shocked as Kyndra felt. Then the thin red line on his skin gaped open and blood spurted from the wound. Tava choked and spasmed, his blood pooling on the bare rock, running in rivulets into its dips and troughs.

'Take them,' the woman said.

It was different this time. Need drove her. There was no tentative feeling her way into the void, no calling out, no waiting to be granted power. As Tava's blood reached the rock on which Kyndra stood, flowing around her boots, she knew she had no time to summon *Sigel*; she had to be *Sigel*.

With that she *was* the star, a thing of terrible heat and force and light, unfeeling, uncompromising, resolute. Her body was gone, her flesh consumed instantly. *She* became *it* and threw out searing hands that retained their human shape only through long familiarity.

'Stand your ground, men,' one of the humans screamed – the female who'd killed the boy. 'You've seen aberration illusions before.' Her lips peeled back to show her teeth and *Sigel* saw itself reflected in her burnished armour: a figure of white heat with eyes as soulless and dark as the void. The human wielded a dagger in each fist, as if ordinary metal could stand to be thrust into the heart of a star. She attacked anyway, driving her blade into *Sigel*'s neck, as if hoping to find flesh beneath the flames. When the dagger melted without meeting resistance and ran in molten streams over her gauntlet, her eyes widened and she flung herself back, but *Sigel* caught her by the throat and squeezed until her face blistered and burned.

Throwing her corpse aside, it seized the nearest Sartyans

and incinerated them. The plate armour they wore was hardly less frail than their bodies, which crisped to nothing. Others came – foolishly – and *Sigel* destroyed those too, flames dripping from its arms.

A shout went up, as the humans began to retreat. *Sigel* gestured and the earth cracked at its command, opening a trench several metres wide. Another gesture and fire roared out of the chasm, climbing high over its lip. At least a hundred soldiers skidded to a halt, caught on this side of it, and *Sigel* set about them, revelling in the destruction, the clean chaos of death.

A growling reached it, even over the spit and crackle of fire. A moment later, a flaming boulder flew across the trench and struck *Sigel* in the chest. It was like tossing a white-hot coal into a sun. Other missiles came and the star absorbed them all until, with a wave of its hand, the trench-fire sank down to reveal the glowing siege engines on the other side. Little manipulations of metal, full of an unusual, blue energy, whose origin was not the sky. A volatile energy. *Sigel* heated them further until they exploded, catching the humans in the blast. Screams rose to join the fire's roar and the groans of shifting rock.

No more attacks. No more missiles. Already the humans were fleeing the field. But why stop now, *Sigel* thought. These soldiers would live to kill another day. Others would fight them and death would scythe through them all. If mortals desired an end to life, let them have it now.

Sigel lifted both arms and thrust them out, dragging up the ground into a wave. It towered higher and higher, rock dripping like foam from the crest, the soldiers beneath it mice under the shadow of a predator's wing. With a roar, the wave of earth crashed down, throwing up stone and tree and bodies.

It wasn't enough. This world was so fragile, it begged to be broken, so that all could return to the void. *Sigel* would burn the oceans, wither the forests, rip the mountains up by their roots. The earth was temporary, useless. Only the void was eternal. Nothing else had any meaning.

All will be ash. All will be ended.

As *Sigel* gathered its strength, a voice shouted and it looked down. Humans, hidden behind a Lunar shield. That its feeble sibling had power enough to shield them was surprising – reflected power too, for the moon still shone. One human edged forward, a male that *Sigel* recognized, an ally from another time.

'Kyndra, stop! Please listen to me.'

The man's companions were backing away. One, a female, tried to pull him away too, but the man shook her off and continued to call that name *Sigel* recognized: *Kyndra*.

But *Kyndra* wasn't *its* name, merely an avatar, an empty mortal shell it had once inhabited.

Something trembled within *Sigel* then, something that fought with all her tiny might. For a moment they were two, not one, and then she was one and she was pulling her atoms out of *Sigel*, reforming them into skin and blood and bone, until she stood naked and human once more.

Her eyes full of the devastation she had wrought, Kyndra took one faltering step towards Nediah. And then her legs crumpled beneath her and she fell.

PART TWO

PART TWO

15

Brégenne,
I don't know how long it will take this to reach you, but the Council knows of your absence and they've dispatched Wielders to bring you in. Veeta and Gend wish to keep your disappearance hidden, but I was one of those called to the meeting and it is commonly believed that you will be in Market Primus. If that is where this envoi finds you, get out while you can. They sent Barrar and Elois and two Solars – Yve and Magnus. If they catch you during the daytime when you've only Gareth to rely on, you would be wise to give yourself up. I urge you to reconsider your position. Send me word.
　Your friend,
　Alandred.

The envoi was dated almost two weeks ago and Brégenne cursed as she tried to work out how close the Wielders were behind her.

'From Alandred,' she said to Gareth, who was watching

curiously. 'Veeta and Gend have sent some Wielders to track me down.'

His eyes widened. 'What? How many?'

'Four – two Solars, two Lunars. I get the impression we'll be dragged back to Naris in chains.'

'That's only a couple at a time. We can take them.' Gareth gave her a grin and she stared at him, perturbed by its sharp edge.

'These are full masters, Gareth. If they find me in daylight . . .' She gestured to the knife in her belt. 'I have no idea how to use this. Even if I did, how would I fight off two Solar Wielders?'

'You forget – you've got me.' Gareth raised his arm. 'And this.' Where normal metal would glint in the rising sun, the gauntlet seemed to absorb the light and Gareth hastily slipped his glove back on, hiding it from view.

They'd stopped at the well-to-do town of Penion, not far from the capital, but found it in ruins, its streets clogged with debris. A few people sorted listlessly through the rubble of their homes, searching for anything of use. Although Kierik's death had ended the Breaking forever, it could not reverse the destruction the terrible storm had wrought. Brégenne had made their stop a brief one, unwilling to venture further into the town. They and their horses drew a few greedy-eyed gazes, but most of the displaced people had already left for the capital, hoping to find shelter behind its walls.

Now she frowned as they rode on, leaving the town behind. 'We don't know the extent of the gauntlet's power. It might be dangerous.'

'I don't think I'm a match for masters without it,' Gareth

admitted. 'Maybe they'll come at us in the night and you can fight them off.'

'They'd be foolish to do that and you've a great deal of confidence in my abilities. I haven't been in many fights.'

'I saw you that morning in the atrium,' Gareth replied, 'when you stopped the creature from killing Kyndra.'

'That was a defensive ward,' Brégenne said, remembering the effort it had cost her to keep the *Executis* at bay. 'It's not the same.'

'But you could use it to stop them while we escape.'

She was silent. Gareth was right – the last thing she wanted to do was harm her fellow Wielders when all hands might be needed to repel an invasion from Acre. Damn Nediah! Why hadn't he sent another envoi? She *had* to know what was going on. Anxiety squeezed her insides. What if something had happened to him – what if the six of them had been captured and separated?

No. Brégenne stopped the fear before it could run away with her. She needed to concentrate on the matter at hand. If Wielders were coming, she had to complete her business in the capital and get out quickly.

They reached Market Primus that afternoon, where signs of the Breaking were readily apparent. The city walls were cracked, their crenellated tops sliced off as if by a great knife. Gareth's eyes were wide as they approached and even Brégenne was shocked at the violence levelled at the city. The main gates were closed, their ivy stripped away. She could see the scuff marks where they had been forced over the cobbles. A few bleak-faced people were camped outside and one man looked at her beseechingly, a child curled up at his side, pinched and weary with hunger.

'State your business,' a voice called from above. Brégenne tore her eyes away from the child and looked up to see a guard perched on a makeshift lookout.

'There are people at your gates,' she called back. 'Why won't you let them in?'

'City's full.' An older guard joined the first. 'There isn't room.'

'You can't leave them here without shelter or food – they're starving.'

'They can starve just as well out there as in here, lady. There isn't any food to be had.'

Gareth wore a strange expression as he looked at the people slumped against the gates. Without taking his eyes off them, he reached into his saddlebag and pulled out the last of their bread. Before Brégenne could say anything, he'd slipped from Rain's back, divided the loaf into pieces and begun handing it out to the twenty or so refugees, making sure the children had food first. Wide-eyed, they snatched at it hungrily.

'Why has the Trade Assembly recalled the airships?' Brégenne shouted up at the guards. 'Surely they are the fastest means of bringing food and supplies to the city?'

The young guard opened his mouth to reply, but his colleague shot him a hard glance and he closed it. 'What the Assembly does is their business,' he said stolidly. 'But you and your generous friend are another matter. State your names and purpose here.'

'I am Brégenne of Naris and this is Gareth. We seek an audience with the Assembly.'

'The Trade Assembly are seeing no one.'

She felt a flash of irritation at his tone. 'We've come a long way to speak to them,' she said, attempting to keep a lid on her anger. It always seemed to be boiling over these days. 'We won't go until we have.'

'The city is in lockdown. No one enters or leaves without the say-so of the Assembly. I've had no orders to expect you.'

'I wouldn't assume you had. But I *will* see the Assembly, nevertheless.'

'I don't know who you think you are, lady, and I've never heard of this Naris you say you're from, but you are not setting foot inside these walls.'

Brégenne regarded him. 'Do you really believe you can stop me?'

'Stop you?' The guard laughed. 'What do you intend to do – break down the gates?'

'Gareth,' Brégenne said.

As Myst and Rain picked their way through the splinters, Gareth gave her a sheepish look. 'I didn't think they'd explode like that,' he said, guiding his horse around a larger chunk of gate. 'I only meant to set one of them alight.'

'Which hand did you use?' Brégenne asked him.

Gareth peered at the gauntlet. 'Oh.'

'If you're going to hurl fire around, I think you'd be wiser to use your left hand.'

'Remember, it was your idea.'

Brégenne grimaced at her own impatience. She and Gareth were now the focus of a host of terrified eyes. Ragged people kept their distance and she was ashamed to see some with minor injuries from the explosion. The lookout tower trembled, as if it might fall at any moment, and both guardsmen were hastily abandoning it. The racket had brought other guards to the scene and blades were quickly levelled at the two of them. Gareth held up his left hand and wreathed it in flame. 'Don't even *think* about it,' he said pleasantly.

Everyone except Brégenne stared aghast at the hand. Before Gareth started enjoying the attention a little too much, she said, 'I will see the Trade Assembly now. You can try to stop us, but I wouldn't recommend it. As you've just witnessed, I have little control over my friend here.'

Gareth let the fire climb up to his shoulder for emphasis and the crowd drew back amidst frightened mutterings of witchcraft. It reminded Brégenne of Brenwym. 'Not witches,' she said slowly and clearly, 'Wielders.'

The words made no difference to the apprehensive faces around her, but then the young guard who'd first challenged them stepped forward. 'Like in the stories?' he said, a little tremor in his voice.

Brégenne regarded him in some surprise. 'Like in the stories,' she agreed before adding, 'but Gareth and I aren't from a story. We're from Mariar, like you.'

'My grandfather said the Wielders died at the end of the war.'

'That was the rumour we spread,' Brégenne told him, 'to protect ourselves. But now we're here to protect you.'

The older guardsman grabbed his younger colleague by the shoulder and hauled him back. 'That's enough from you.' He gestured at the hole in the wall where the gates had been. '*Protect* us, is it? You could have killed us.'

'I'm sorry,' Brégenne said sincerely. 'Gareth still has a lot to learn.' She shot him a dark look and the novice had the grace to look abashed. 'But I *must* speak to the Assembly.' She switched her gaze to the guard. 'And if I have to use force to gain an audience, I will.'

The guardsman opened his mouth to respond with what looked like a retort, but the young soldier touched his arm. 'I know it sounds crazy, Sergeant, but if they really are Wielders, there's nothing we can do to stop them. My grandfather said—'

'Oh to the pit with your grandfather,' the sergeant snarled. 'I'm not letting a pair of witches into the city.' He eyed Brégenne and Gareth. 'If that's even what they are. All of this could be a trick.'

Brégenne's fragile hold on her temper began to slip. 'It was a trick that destroyed your gates, Sergeant?'

'There are powders that can do as much,' the man said. It hadn't taken him long to get over his initial fright, she noted sourly.

'But look at his hand.' The young guard pointed at Gareth. 'How can that be a trick?' His face firmed. 'I think they're telling the truth.'

The sergeant rounded on him. 'If I hear another word out of you—'

'You should listen to him,' Brégenne interrupted. 'He's the only one speaking sense.'

'Sense?' The man's face began to purple and she came to a conclusion. Words were no more use here.

'Gareth,' Brégenne said softly. 'How good are you at human *manipulation*?'

The novice's look was wary. 'I haven't practised it much. Why?'

'We're not getting anywhere here and I don't have time to mess around. The sergeant's going to take us to the Trade Assembly, whether he likes it or not.' She told Gareth what she wanted and then added, 'Try not to use more force than necessary. We don't want to come off as the enemy here.'

The flames around Gareth's hand died and the crowd gave an audible sigh of relief.

'There,' the sergeant said, as if the fire had indeed been a trick. He snapped an order. 'Restrain them.'

Gareth's expression turned introspective. He stared fixedly at the guard, tiny beads of sweat popping out on his forehead. The man opened his mouth . . . but nothing emerged. Instead, his eyes widened as his hand sheathed his drawn blade of its own accord and his feet swivelled to point him in the direction of the city proper.

'Your sergeant's had a change of heart,' Brégenne said to the rest of the guardsmen. 'No harm will come to him as long as he agrees to take us to the Assembly. But should you seek to impede us,' she spread her hands, 'I've heard there's a nice deep well in the market district.'

Slowly the blades lowered and the guards stepped back. When the sergeant again tried and failed to speak, pale fear stole the anger from his face. 'After you,' Gareth said politely and the man began a stiff walk like a marionette unused to motion.

It was safer to lead the horses through the city. Brégenne pulled up the hood of her cloak and the crowd parted for them. As they left the scene of wreckage behind, she glanced back to see the young soldier staring after them, an unreadable expression on his face.

Prompted by Gareth, the sergeant led them through the city streets. At first he made several attempts to escape, but the novice tightened his mental hold on the man's body and forced him forward. Brégenne was impressed. After the incident at the gates, she wasn't sure whether Gareth had the subtlety required for human *manipulation*. She'd heard some Wielders claim that *substantiation* was the higher and more difficult method of channelling energy, but Brégenne didn't agree. After all, conjuring Solar or Lunar fire came under that bracket and any Wielder over Initiated level could do it.

The sights and smells of the city began to intrude on her thoughts and she found herself staring. Gone were the clean, bustling streets she remembered. Now they were home to hundreds of displaced people, dirty and hopeless-faced. Women sat in the gutter so that their children didn't have to and men stood over them or sometimes sat beside them, dressed in clothes that might once have been fine.

She'd put the guard's claim about there being no room down to exaggeration, but he'd been telling the truth. Every lane and alleyway held its share of the dispossessed. Brégenne looked at the dreadful conditions – the clogged sewers, rubbish left strewn in the streets – and saw a disaster waiting to happen. Summer would breed disease as surely as sunny skies, and without adequate food or shelter these alleys would soon be filled with corpses. What was the Trade Assembly doing? Her anger grew apace as she moved deeper into the city, holding tightly to Myst's bridle.

A low rumbling reached them, coming from somewhere up ahead. The sergeant's face paled further and, after he cast Gareth a few imploring looks, the novice let him speak. 'We won't get through,' he said. 'When I told you that the Trade Assembly were seeing no one, I meant that they *can't* see anyone. They closed the inner circle for safety and now it's surrounded.'

The street they followed rounded a bend and Brégenne saw what he meant. A huge crowd was camped outside the white walls of the inner circle, now stained with hurled refuse.

Guards patrolled the top, armed with crossbows, shouting at the people who were trying to storm the doors.

'No closer,' the sergeant begged. 'If they see my uniform, they'll tear me apart.'

'A fate you believe you don't deserve?' Brégenne replied, narrowing her eyes. 'How long has this crowd been here?'

'Several days,' the man answered, sweating freely now, 'and growing all the time. When the first lot arrived threatening to take food from merchants' tables, the Assembly had no choice but to lock down the inner circle.'

'No choice? The Assembly could have given them what they wanted.'

'They'd have stormed the place,' the sergeant protested, 'and taken everything they could get their hands on.'

'I don't doubt it,' Brégenne said. 'But if the Assembly had acted with some humanity when the refugees began arriving in the city, all this –' she swept a hand at the angry crowd – 'could have been avoided.'

'I don't like the thought of going through them,' Gareth said to her in a low voice. 'I can't fight that many . . . and I'm not sure I'd want to.'

Brégenne shook her head. 'I wouldn't ask you to.' More people were arriving to swell the crowd and it was in danger of spilling down the side street where the three of them stood. She looked at the sergeant. 'Is there another way in?'

He shifted his feet, said nothing.

Brégenne went to stand in front of him, forcing him to meet her gaze. 'You have a choice. You can get us inside or we'll leave you out here with the mob.' She had to raise her voice over the volume of the crowd. 'At this stage, I'd say we're the better option.'

'It's a strict secret,' the sergeant protested. 'If anyone found out I'd shown you, it'd be more than my life's—'

'How much is your life worth to *them*?' Brégenne asked, gesturing at the angry group who had just rounded the corner and were coming their way. Every hand held a weapon.

The sergeant took one frightened look at them. 'In there,' he said, nodding at a dingy alley. It was little more than a gutter and they would have trouble getting the horses through it.

'Let him go, Gareth,' Brégenne said and all three of them hurried to the mouth of the alleyway, squeezing the horses in just in time to escape notice. The sergeant didn't pause but led them further into the narrow space where shadows lingered even under the late afternoon sun. The horses flattened their ears, skittish in the enclosed space, and Brégenne muttered soothing words to them.

'Urgh,' she said a moment later, having stepped in something that gave off a reek like rotting fish and excrement. Thankful for the high boots she wore, she covered her face with one hand. The gutter was wet despite the dry weather, the walls on either side pale-slicked with lichen and darker spots of mould.

Gareth kept close behind the sergeant, his bulky presence both an encouragement and a threat. Finally, they emerged into a street where the sounds of the mob were muted. The sergeant led them north-north-west until Brégenne found herself looking at the curve of the inner wall. A wide drain ran alongside it like a moat and the sergeant jumped in without preamble. 'This is the only way,' he said, not sounding especially sorry about it.

Brégenne jumped down after him. Her feet splashed into shallow water that smelled almost as bad as the alley and she chided herself for her squeamishness. She'd spent far too long surrounded by the comfort and wealth of Naris.

Once both horses had been coaxed into the water, they set off, following the curve of the wall. At a place where the stone joined a thicker section, the sergeant came to a stop. He snatched a glance over his shoulder to ensure they hadn't been followed and then knocked twice on what appeared to be solid stone. It sounded distinctly hollow. A few moments passed before the outline of a door appeared, opening towards them. Brégenne saw Gareth's eyes widen – the portal was wood, but cunningly disguised to blend with the dappled stone of the wall. A woman's helmet-framed face looked out at them, darkening when it saw the sergeant who stood there stiff and subdued.

Before Brégenne could speak, he blurted, 'Captain, get reinforcements. These two destroyed—' The rest of his sentence was muffled by Gareth, who slapped his gauntleted hand over the man's mouth. The sergeant's eyes rolled up in his head and he dropped.

Shocked, Gareth caught him, but Brégenne was already moving. Before the captain could reach for her short sword, Brégenne's knife was at her throat. 'Inside,' Brégenne hissed and the woman slowly backed up. 'Bring him, Gareth,' she said without looking around.

'Who are you?'

The woman's words were vibrations in the metal of the blade. 'I am Brégenne of Naris,' Brégenne said. 'And I *will* speak to the Trade Assembly if I have to hold every guard in this city at knifepoint to do it.'

Once both guards were trussed up, Brégenne and Gareth coaxed the horses into the high-ceilinged passage beyond. It led to a small courtyard with a well at its centre and from there into the streets of the inner circle. Brégenne was glad it hadn't come to actual blows because holding a blade to someone's throat was about all she could do with one. She'd picked the knife up in Jarra after her conversation with the barman. It was mostly for show – she had no idea how to use it in a fight and had even contemplated asking Gareth to demonstrate the basics. The novice wore a much nastier blade, which she was fairly sure *wasn't* for show. Gareth called it his only memento of home – his mother had thrown it at him along with her curses. 'I don't think she meant to hit me with it,' he'd said with a distance in his brown eyes. 'I'm pretty sure she meant for me to keep it . . . to use it. Although with my mother, you never know.'

Now Gareth placed his hand on the blade's worn scabbard. 'What're you planning?' he asked in a low voice as they attempted to blend in with the people strolling through the leafy avenues. Their lack of silk and fancy headwear was attracting a few stares. 'Sunset's coming on so don't spring any more *manipulation* on me.' Gareth huffed. 'Moving people is exhausting. Give me another go with the gates.'

'Not likely.' Brégenne slowed their pace a little and patted Myst's neck. 'When we get in there, let me do the talking. No surprises.' Brégenne nodded at his arm. 'Watch what you do with that gauntlet.'

Gareth tilted his hand. 'I didn't mean to knock the sergeant unconscious.'

'Just be careful.'

The contrast between the inner circle and the rest of the city was appalling. Sunset bathed the white buildings in a rosy glow; they seemed better suited to a town along the archipelagic coast where hot winds blew from the desert. There were no hopeless people in the gutters, no piles of rubble littering the streets. The more obvious effects of the Breaking had long since been cleared away while the rest of Market Primus rotted outside these pristine walls. The shops here all had grand awnings and signs that swung gently in the breeze. Although it wasn't dark yet, lights were being lit in lamps propped high on posts. They marched in neat formation down either side of the wide street, the middle of which was reserved for the elegant carriages of the merchant class.

The road branched off to the right where it wound up a small rise to a neighbourhood of pale stone mansions, glass windows sparkling in the last of the light. Gareth whistled. 'Nice place.'

'Yes,' Brégenne said darkly, glaring at their destination: a round building domed and palisaded with gates under guard. 'The Trade Assembly are very good at making money, but less so at spending it wisely.'

'The Assembly's in session,' one of the two guards said as they approached.

'Perfect,' Brégenne replied.

Unlike the more serviceable city guard, this pair wore decorative armour that suggested it would crumple at a blow. Their lances looked as if they'd never been intended for anything other than ceremony. The guards' eyes ranged over Brégenne and Gareth, their clothes, packs, the sewer-muck caking their boots and the legs of their horses. 'Who are you?' one asked. 'How did you get in here?'

'Oh, so you know about the mob at your gates?' Brégenne said coolly.

The guard's hold on his spear tightened. 'Answer the question.'

'My answer will likely make little difference.'

'You'll not sound so flippant after a night in the cells,' the other guard said. He was watching Gareth, his eyes on the sword sheathed at the novice's hip.

Brégenne glanced at the sky and smiled. 'At this moment in time, gentlemen, there is no power on Mariar that can stop me walking through those doors.'

Perhaps the guard who'd first spoken heard the warning in her words, or perhaps her smile unnerved him, for he didn't join in when his companion laughed. 'You going to take us both on with that little knife? At least your friend has a blade that might scratch my armour.' The grin he gave Gareth was more of a sneer.

Gareth shook his head. 'I'd stop talking now, if I were you.'

'Or what?'

The novice folded his arms and shrugged. 'Can't say I didn't warn you.'

Brégenne's hands began to glow. It was only a weak glow, being early in the evening, but it was enough to make the mouthy guard drop his spear in shock. 'Pick it up,' she said, crooking a finger and, his face blanching, the guard did as she commanded. The other man simply stared at her.

'What *are* you?'

'For the last time,' she replied, 'I am Brégenne, Wielder of Naris, and you are taking me to the Trade Assembly.' She mentally seized control of one guard's body and spun him around to face the building. 'You,' she snapped at the other man, 'will watch our horses.' White-faced, he nodded frantically and Brégenne turned her attention to his companion. 'Now walk,' she commanded and the mouthy guard stumbled forward, already flinching away from her.

Inside was a foyer, walls panelled in oak until they met the downward curve of the great dome. The translucent glass diffused what light there was left in the sky and bathed the place in an orange dusk. Lamps spaced evenly around the walls burned with a light that was harsh in comparison. The guard's mail-shod feet rang loudly on the marbled floor.

The double doors to the main chamber were closed and locked. 'Get out of my way,' Brégenne said, thrusting the guard aside. Then she lifted a hand, summoned a Lunar spear and hurled it at the barred doors.

The explosion was deafening. Someone screamed. As she and Gareth strode through, crushing splinters beneath their heels, the novice said, 'And you accuse me of overdoing it.'

Heart racing with the thrill of the Lunar running through her veins, Brégenne bared her teeth at him and then turned her attention to the chamber.

This was the seat of power in Mariar. She heard Gareth's intake of breath and, despite her anger, she couldn't hide her own awe. The grand hall of Mariar's ruling Trade Assembly made Naris's atrium look almost primitive. The walls were oak-panelled here too and hung with white and purple curtains. The stained-glass dome depicted various landscapes complete with an artist's impression of an airship with a rather fanciful figure-head. Two huge panes were given over to the heraldry of the Assembly: golden scales balanced on one end with weights, on the other with a handful of gems and little coins, each picked out in surpassing detail.

But the sight that dominated the chamber was a great round table, vaster than any Brégenne had seen, set with twenty high-backed chairs, each carved with a different family crest. Tonight all the chairs were occupied and paper littered the leathered tabletop, along with goblets, pens, jugs of wine and water. The session had evidently been a long one.

As she marched uninvited to the table, Brégenne couldn't help thinking of Kyndra, reminded of the time the young woman had interrupted the Council's hearing. Unlike the Council, however, the merchants were cowering in their chairs and she realized she held another Lunar spear ready to hurl. Planting it like a staff at her side, she said, 'Before you ask my name and we get to the tedious arguments over whether I am what I say I am, I have something very important to tell you.'

'Guards!' one merchant managed feebly and, when no help was forthcoming, he turned fearful eyes on Brégenne. 'What have you done to them?'

'Nothing lasting.' She let the spear vanish. 'I mean nobody harm.'

The merchants' eyes travelled from her to the ruined doors and back again. Clearly they disagreed.

When Brégenne simply continued to stand there, unthreatening, a woman plucked up enough courage to ask, 'Who are you?' After a pause she added, '*What* are you?'

'I am a Wielder,' Brégenne said, 'and so is Gareth.' She nodded to him. 'We come from Naris, far to the west in the mountains beyond Murta. We've been there since the end of the Acrean wars.'

There was utter silence.

'Children's tales,' one of the men said finally and against all evidence to the contrary.

Brégenne clenched her fists. 'You need more proof?' In the next second, another Lunar spear quivered in the centre of the great table. Curls of smoke rose from the blackened wood. The men and women of the Assembly leapt out of their chairs, stumbling over each other in their haste to get away from the glowing spear. Brégenne let it blaze there a moment longer and then it faded. The scorch mark it left behind did not, and those eyes that weren't fixed on her were drawn inexorably to it.

'It's time you started believing in children's tales,' she said.

Their answering expressions of horror reminded Brégenne that she hadn't come here to frighten them. She'd come to earn their trust. The smoking stain on the table told her plainly that she wasn't going the right way about it. Gareth made a sound in his throat; she thought he was trying not to laugh.

'How –' croaked the woman who'd spoken before, 'how do we not know of you?' She was dressed very finely in a shirt with puffed sleeves, ribbons looped across the bodice. It made Brégenne feel distinctly aware of her own workman-like garb.

'We suffered dreadful losses in the Deliverance,' she answered, letting her eyes range over everyone present. 'For better or worse, our ancestors chose to rebuild our numbers in secret.'

'And what makes you break your silence now?'

'War is coming,' Brégenne said and the hush in the room deepened, 'or at least the possibility of war. Acre has returned.'

'*Acre*?' a paunchy man repeated. 'It's a myth.'

'You might have noticed that the Breaking has ended,' Brégenne said testily. 'There have been no new reports of it in the last month.'

'A fact for which we're thankful,' the man replied. 'My business has suffered enough losses.'

She barely stopped herself from saying that it wasn't only his business which had suffered losses. 'Acre is the reason why the Breaking no longer plagues us. The lost world was never lost, merely hidden.'

230

'My sources would have informed me if a whole world had "returned",' another merchant said. The dark velvet of his clothes only emphasized his sallow skin, which looked as if it rarely saw sunlight. 'And returned from *where*? What devilry is this?'

'It's not devilry, Talmanier,' said an irascible voice, and everyone, including Brégenne and Gareth, looked around. One of the purple curtains moved and a figure stepped out from behind it. He was dressed in scruffy trousers at odds with the fine white shirt and long, rather piratical, waistcoat he wore over them. The waistcoat glinted, sewn as it was with myriad bronze buttons. Each bore a different crest like those on the back of the chairs. The man's leather boots were scuffed and creased from wear.

Talmanier stiffened at the sight of him. 'Argat! What are you doing here? How dare you? This is a private meeting.'

'I'm afraid Gunther's coin is a little better than yours,' Argat replied coolly and Talmanier switched his hostile gaze to the paunchy man. When Gunther began to splutter, Argat gave him a small smile. 'And my *current* employer's is a little better than his,' he added.

'Gunther, you scheming rat,' Talmanier spat, at the same moment another woman began shrilly accusing him of selling Assembly secrets. Brégenne kept her eyes on Argat and the captain returned her gaze, obviously pleased at the mayhem he'd caused.

'Enough!' said the woman who'd first spoken, her voice slicing through the babble. She addressed Argat. 'What do you know of this?'

Argat's look was unfriendly as he studied Brégenne. 'Your eyes,' he said. 'You've changed, woman. Where's your Islesman?'

'Busy,' Brégenne snapped, 'in Acre.'

'You've still a sharp tongue in your head. And your young friend . . . where is she?' Argat's dark eyes narrowed. 'Is she much changed too?'

'More than you could imagine.'

There was a hunger in Argat's face now. 'She has something of mine. I have not forgotten.'

'I doubt you'll get it back,' Brégenne said. 'The earth was used to break the power keeping Acre and Mariar apart.'

'Argat!' the woman repeated and the airship captain finally looked away from Brégenne. 'I take it you know this woman?'

'Aye, Astra Marahan. I carried her and two others as passengers aboard my airship.'

'And does she speak the truth concerning these . . . Wielders?'

Memory thinned Argat's lips. 'I believe she does,' he said. 'Her companion used some power against me and my crew.'

'It was necessary at the time,' Brégenne said, 'and I'm sorry for it. But I'm here to talk about Acre . . . and our future.' She swept her gaze over everyone in the chamber. 'If the powers in Acre seek war, the Wielders can't defend Mariar alone. We need to stand together.'

'We have more immediate issues,' Talmanier said, gesturing in the vicinity of the city. 'We're effectively trapped in here until that mob can be dispersed.' His eyes strayed to the scorch mark her Lunar spear had left on the table. 'If you are prepared to . . . resolve the situation, perhaps we can discuss this further.'

Brégenne felt a flash of anger. 'This isn't like one of your contracts. The whole of Mariar is in danger from a threat we know nothing about. Either we mobilize, or we risk invasion.'

'There – you've said it yourself. If we know nothing about this so-called threat, who's to say it's a threat at all?' The merchant folded beribboned arms. 'You're asking us to pour time and money into a hypothetical endeavour.'

'Five hundred years ago, the Sartyan Empire was unstoppable.' Brégenne chose her words with care, deciding not to mention Kierik or the term 'Starborn'. She didn't think the Assembly could take another revelation. 'We've sent a group into Acre to discover whether the empire still rules and what it intends. Until we know—'

'And who gave you authority to do so?' Talmanier interrupted, anger visible in the set of his velvet shoulders. 'The Trade Assembly is the ruling power in Mariar, not some group of . . . of magicians holed up in Murta. Once your story is corroborated, it is up to *us* to decide how and if to establish relations with a neighbouring kingdom.'

'This is not a kingdom,' Brégenne retorted. 'It's an empire with a bloody history, which controlled lands far larger than our own. While we can hope to "establish relations", as you optimistically put it, the fact remains that we've nothing in place to stop any power in Acre walking in and just taking what it wants.'

Talmanier made to reply, but Astra held up her hand to stop him. 'You clearly believe what you say,' she said to Brégenne, 'and if it's true, you've done right in bringing it to our attention. But Talmanier is correct. We have an immediate problem on our doorstep that must be taken care of. If you can come up with a solution, we will send scouts to verify your claims.'

'My *claims* need no verifying,' Brégenne said heatedly. '*If* I choose to help you, you will agree to lead the way in preparing Mariar's defence. And that means diverting sufficient funds.'

She paused. 'Need I remind you that you'd be protecting your interests? War is, after all, very bad for business.'

Throughout all of this, Argat had stood silently, his gaze rarely leaving Brégenne. Now he said, 'If the Assembly need proof of this woman's claims, I will take my airship and any Trader who feels it necessary to come with me and we will see Acre for ourselves.'

'That is . . . commendable, Argat,' Astra said. 'I myself will accompany you.'

'But,' Argat raised a finger, 'I have a condition.'

'Then speak it.'

'What you do with the other airships is your business, but I want the *Eastern Set* unhooked from the great chain. From now on, she'll be under my direct command and will fly where I order.' The captain's eyes glittered. 'I intend to make history.'

16

Foolish, the voice whispered. *Could have lost myself, destroyed my allies, destroyed the world.*

Whose voice was that? Whose thoughts? *Who am I?*

If I fear to accept what I am, I hand them power. And they are strong. They will *use me, if I let them.*

Kierik's words were light as a cat's whisker tickling her mind and that image brought her rushing back to herself. *I am Kyndra*, she thought with a snarl.

I risk the world, he said as he faded, *and that cannot happen again.*

The sun beat down on her eyelids, turning the darkness orange. She raised a hand to shield her face.

'She's awake.'

Shadows clustered, casting a cooling shade over her. Kyndra opened her eyes to find Nediah and Irilin staring down, each wearing a version of wary relief. Nediah's was more fervent. He helped her to sit while Irilin backed up to give her room.

They were camped in the striated lee of a rock which

235

protected them from the wind that must have blown up during the night. She could hear it sweeping across the bare expanse that surrounded them, whipping up the crests of dunes that rolled to the south.

Kyndra's mouth felt gritty and there was a tang in her throat that tasted like blood. 'Water?' she asked and her voice croaked as if she'd never used it before.

Nediah handed over a shrunken skin with a grimace. 'It's all we've got.'

The liquid went some way to washing the taste from her mouth. 'Where are we?'

'The fringes of the Ak-Taj Desert,' Medavle said grimly. 'They call this part of it the Beaches.' Kyndra looked at him and in his face she saw everything the others weren't prepared to say to her. That was fine; she wasn't prepared to reply. The memory of what she had done was razor sharp, so sharp she actually felt it as pain and she raised her hand to her cheek.

'Kyndra—'

'I want to see,' she said, cutting Nediah off. No one spoke while Irilin rummaged through a pack, finally coming up with a circle of polished glass. The mirror was tiny, clumsily set in wood, but it showed Kyndra what she feared. *Sigel* had always been clearer than the others, but still pale enough to seem a scar or a passing shadow on her cheek. Now the points that made up the constellation shone as if there really were stars buried in her flesh. The lines that linked them glowed softly, silver white. She felt strangely empty as she stared, wondering who was staring back.

She handed the mirror to Irilin. 'Are you all . . . all right?' she asked.

'No thanks to you,' Kait said. Despite her anger, she looked shaken. 'You could have killed us. It was only down to Irilin and Medavle that we weren't burned to a cinder.'

'What happened after I blacked out?'

'The fire disappeared,' Nediah said. His voice was very quiet. 'The landscape was . . . unrecognizable. We couldn't see anyone left alive.'

A wave of nausea swept through Kyndra. Her throat felt drier than ever. *What have I done?* But she knew very well what she, what *Sigel*, had done. Killing the humans – *Sartyans*, she thought quickly – hadn't been enough. She'd wanted to burn everything . . . she'd wanted to burn the world.

I came to Acre to seek peace.

'Do you think General Hagdon's still alive?' Irilin asked. 'Perhaps the soldiers got him away before –' She looked at Kyndra. 'I can't believe Tava betrayed the Defiant.'

'If Hagdon's dead, good riddance,' Kait said. 'He was going to hand us over to the emperor.'

'I'm not so sure,' Irilin said slowly. 'Didn't you see him hesitate? I think if any Sartyan was prepared to listen to us, he was.'

'And now I've killed him,' Kyndra said. 'I've killed them all.'

'Hardly,' Kait replied. 'Hagdon's army is thousands strong. When it comes to killing Sartyans, you barely made a dent.'

'We had no idea what we were walking into when we arrived in Acre,' Nediah said, shooting Kait a hard glance. 'If anything, we thought we'd only be dealing with the empire. Instead, we find a host of warring factions bent on annihilating each other.'

'If we cannot achieve a truce with Sartya,' Medavle said suddenly, 'why not pursue one with Khronosta?'

Kyndra studied the Yadin. 'It sounds like the Khronostians won't be found unless they choose to be,' she said. 'And we still don't know enough about them. Ségin said they're on their own side.'

'A wise side to take,' Medavle countered. 'They choose to avoid direct confrontation.'

'Some might call that cowardice—' Kait began.

'And others, tactics. Perhaps they wait for their moment.'

'If you didn't think siding with the Defiant was a good idea, why Khronosta?' Kyndra asked him.

Medavle had a certain habit of clenching and unclenching his gloved hands. She'd noticed it as a sign of his mind at work and it made her nervous. 'They have the potential to be a valuable ally,' the Yadin answered, 'now Sartya's out of the picture.'

Was Sartya out of the picture? Had the chance of peace with the empire died with the soldiers she'd killed? And what of General Hagdon? Irilin seemed to believe he'd been willing to listen and she had to consider the best course for Mariar. 'What now?' Kyndra asked despondently, addressing the question to Nediah. Surely he had to acknowledge the mess she'd made of things – how many of her decisions as leader had led to disaster. Shika's death lay at her feet, along with half a thousand soldiers. She'd broken the Defiant, forcing them to flee their stronghold. And she had nothing to show for any of it.

'We could follow Ségin's lead,' Nediah said. 'Go to Cymenza, look for this sympathetic friend of his.'

Kait gave him an approving nod. 'Sounds like a plan.'

'How far is it?' Kyndra asked.

'There's one of Ségin's maps in your saddlebag,' Medavle reminded her. 'But I estimate about two weeks' ride.'

Kyndra's legs felt a little weak as she moved to retrieve the map. She tried not to remember the terrible heat of *Sigel* as it consumed her body, or how she'd somehow remade it. That knowledge wasn't hers and she could no more remember how to do it than she could comprehend what had actually happened when she'd become the star.

She spread the map on the ground and they all peered at it. 'The terrain looks decent,' Nediah said. 'Fairly flat. If we can find the river marked here, at least we'll have water.'

'Hush,' Kait said suddenly. She wore a hood to protect her eyes from the bright sun and was squinting off to the west. 'I saw something.'

Kyndra turned to follow her pointing finger. Movement. It could be a mirage conjured out of the heated land, but she didn't think so. She took a few steps towards it, eyes narrowed against the haze.

'Kyndra,' Nediah cautioned. He and Kait both summoned Solar energy, so that their hands were lost in light. They advanced slowly towards the shapes outlined against a skyscape of dunes. Not people, Kyndra saw, the breath catching in her throat, but beasts, six of them on hulking paws, their hide a camouflage of desert yellow. Three had their heads close to the ground, teeth latched onto something that had left a rough trail in the sand. They'd come from the south, it seemed, from the heart of the arid country, dragging their burden.

The pack leader must have caught their scent, for it stopped abruptly and swung its blunt head towards them. It looked halfway between a cat and a dog, wolfish about the ears and tail, but with a low-slung body like a Dry Lands tiger – not that Kyndra had ever seen one in the flesh. A growl came from its throat, a low purring rumble which the others took up.

Kyndra eased back a step. 'What do we do?' she hissed.

'Nothing,' Nediah said tightly, 'just wait.'

It was hard, waiting. Kyndra's heart raced. She was convinced that the beasts would charge, that those hulking paws would hit her in the chest, knocking her sprawling. But the six creatures stood stock-still on legs that quivered with tension. Whatever they'd been dragging was hidden behind their bulky forms.

Then, at some silent sign, they melted back into the desert and lost themselves among the dunes. Their burden remained supine on the scrubby ground where sand met rock, a limp bundle of clothes and limbs.

Kyndra approached cautiously, but the body remained inert. It looked like a man, lying on his side in a tangle of greyish, matted hair. His clothes were unusual and torn in places, presumably by the beasts' teeth. She reached his side and squatted down. His skin was as strange as his clothes, dark like an archipelagan's, but lacking that rich brown hue. It was the grey colour of shadows, Kyndra thought, her fingers poised over the man's arm. He had a nasty-looking wound, puffy, badly healed. She listened to his breathing, ragged and almost imperceptible.

And then without warning, the man's other hand shot out and grabbed her wrist. Kyndra yelped in surprise and tried to jerk away, but she couldn't. He might be on the verge of death, but his grip was vicelike and his fingers tightened painfully, as if he sought to draw strength from her. He raised his head and even that small movement pulled a moan from his throat.

Yellow eyes met hers, already half-filmed with death, and despite the grey hair, Kyndra was surprised to find herself staring into the face of a young man. He could only be a few years older than her. Time seemed to stand still while they locked gazes and Kyndra felt a memory stir, a memory older than

Kierik's, older even than the Sartyan Empire, but when she reached for it, the details slid away and she grasped only air.

'We can help you,' she said to him, not knowing whether he could understand her.

'Don't touch me.'

'My friend is a healer,' Kyndra said slowly. 'He will make you better.' But privately she wondered whether he was too far gone for even someone of Nediah's talent to save. Instead of seeming reassured, the young man grew more agitated. Nediah came to kneel beside him, his gaze raking over the wound and the fever in the stranger's eyes.

'He is very ill,' the Wielder said softly. 'The wound looks like it has poisoned his blood, but I'll do what I can.'

The stranger flinched. 'Don't touch me!'

'You'll die if we don't,' Kyndra told him. He was still gripping her wrist, his skin hot and dry and dark against her own. 'Is that what you want?'

The stranger didn't reply, but he held her eyes with his odd yellow ones until his strength gave out and he sank to the ground.

Nediah and Medavle moved him into the shade of the large rock and laid him on several folded blankets. The others wore her own curiosity, Kyndra saw. 'If I'm to save him,' Nediah said, after placing his hands on the young man's body, 'we won't be going anywhere today. It's blood poisoning and very far gone. Most healers would give up on him.'

'But you're not most healers,' Kait said.

Nediah gave her a strange look before turning back to the dying man. 'To have made it this far,' he murmured. They watched the familiar Solar glow spring up around him. Nediah closed his eyes, but opened them a moment later with a little gasp.

'What?' Kait said, kneeling down beside him.

'He's . . .' Nediah shook his head. 'Later. I have to concentrate.'

The healing seemed to take forever, much longer than when he had healed Owen's arm. The sun dragged itself into the west and it still felt as hot as midday. Used to cool, Brenwym summers, Kyndra pushed sweaty hair out of her eyes and turned her face to catch the slackening breeze.

'The injury that caused this was made by a knife,' Nediah said abruptly, opening his eyes. He gestured at the now neat scar on the stranger's arm. 'This man had enemies.'

'Let's hope they're not about to catch up with him,' Irilin muttered.

Kait gave Nediah her hand. He hesitated before taking it and letting her pull him to his feet. Although he looked wrung out, his eyes were wary when they glanced down at his patient.

'Is he going to live?' Kyndra asked.

'Yes. He has some strength in him.' Nediah looked around at them all. 'Perhaps because he isn't human.'

'What?' Irilin took an involuntary step away from the stranger. 'What do you mean?'

'He's human enough to die from fever and he has the same internal workings as you or I. But his blood . . .' Nediah shook his head. 'There's something not quite right.'

That memory surfaced again, teasing, just out of Kyndra's reach. She sighed in frustration. 'I . . . something in me recognizes him,' she said. 'But I can't remember.'

'He has markings.' Kait crouched down beside the sleeping

stranger and pointed to his forearm. 'Here. They're hard to spot against his skin.'

'Let me see.' Medavle bent over the man. 'Slaver's tattoos,' he said after a moment, eyes travelling from one to the next, as if reading them like a book. 'This man comes from a slaving caravan in the Beaches. I think these —' he pointed at a cluster of inked pictures — 'are the names of towns along their route.'

Irilin made a noise of disgust. 'We rescued a slaver? Is slaving legal here?'

'It didn't used to be,' Medavle said. 'The empire outlawed the practice. But perhaps it's made a comeback if Sartya's hold is weakening.'

'What are we going to do with him?' Kait asked.

Kyndra's eyes kept straying back to the young man. A slaver? His dark face was peaceful, if pinched with thirst. 'He deserves a chance to explain,' she found herself saying.

'What's to explain?' Irilin snapped. 'He chained people up and sold them.'

'Nobody's perfect,' Kait murmured.

'Let's just leave him.' Irilin folded her arms. 'He's not in any danger now, is he?'

'But he's without food or water,' Nediah said, frowning. 'I didn't spend half the day healing him just so that he could die of thirst.'

Irilin looked at the sun. 'We can't afford to wait around, not if we want to reach Cymenza before our own supplies run out.'

'He's coming with us.'

They all turned to look at her and Kyndra was surprised at the strength of her own certainty. 'Those beasts brought him out of the desert,' she said. 'They saved his life. I want to know why.'

'Ned saved his life,' Kait said. 'It was just a very lucky coincidence that we happened on him.'

'Are you sure it's coincidence?' Kyndra spread her hands. 'I thought a lot of the things that happened in Naris were coincidence . . . before I realized they were all connected.'

'You're reading too much into this.'

'What if he knows something that could help us?'

'If he did, what makes you think he'd *tell* us?' Kait said.

Kyndra shrugged. 'He's in our debt.'

'Ned said he wasn't human.' The tall woman tilted her head on one side to regard her. 'That doesn't trouble you?'

Kyndra's mind filled with fire and death, memories of *Sigel* and the star's determination to destroy her world. 'What does it mean to be human?' she said softly.

She was thankful none of them chose to reply.

The sun set, the stranger slept on, and Kyndra found herself wandering away from the others to stand looking up at the bulbous Acrean moon. *The same moon,* she thought, watching it clamber up through the evening clouds. *We're all one now.* The wind had finally strengthened again, but too late. On the chill fringes of the night-time desert, it brought shivers instead of relief. Kyndra huddled deeper into her cloak and leaned against the side of a boulder taller than she was.

She caught an echo of Lunar song as Irilin set wards about their camp and the delicate chimes made her think of Brégenne. What was the Wielder doing even now, half a world away? Had she managed to convince the Trade Assembly of the threat Acre posed, as she'd hoped to? And what of Gareth and his gauntlet?

They owed Brégenne an envoi, but if Gareth was with her,

he'd see whatever Kyndra wrote about Shika. How could she put Shika's death into words? Gareth would never forgive her.

'You're looking serious, Nediah.'

Kyndra started. The clear night carried Kait's voice – the two Wielders must be standing on the other side of the rock. Perhaps Nediah had jumped too, for Kait laughed, a soft, throaty laugh that caused Kyndra to frown. She peered around the boulder and caught sight of Nediah standing stiffly, Kait quite close beside him.

Eavesdropping, her mother said, was not a nice habit, but Kyndra didn't move away.

There came a sigh. 'You're thinking of her, aren't you?' Kait said.

'What if I was?' There was silence and then Nediah sighed. 'I was wondering where all of this is leading.'

'You never cared before, when we were young. You never cared where each day would take us.'

'Perhaps I should have,' Nediah replied and Kyndra heard a heaviness in his voice. 'I'd have seen where our actions would lead. I could have stopped it.'

'Maybe, but I don't regret a moment. My years with you were the best of my life.'

Kyndra couldn't help it; she risked another glance. Nediah and Kait were of a height, standing eye to eye in the moonlight. 'Were they?' he asked, as soft as her laugh.

Kait held his gaze a little longer before sweeping the moment away. 'We were glorious,' she said and Kyndra ducked back behind her rock. 'Do you remember when we planted Councilman Everland's amulet on Alandred?'

'He wasn't a master back then,' Nediah said, some of the weight leaving his voice.

'And those love letters to Hebrin,' Kait continued. 'We made him think Master Markah was smitten.'

'I seem to recall he reciprocated it.'

'Yes – what was the likelihood? And then Hebrin confronted him.'

'In front of about a dozen witnesses. He must have been mad.'

'Or in love.'

'Hebrin didn't get over it for months,' Nediah said and Kyndra heard his amusement quite plainly. 'And Master Markah literally turned and ran whenever he saw Hebrin coming. One of our greatest triumphs by any account.'

There was silence and Kyndra cautiously peered around the rock again. 'You know, Nediah,' Kait said to the dark. 'The citadel hasn't seen our like since.'

'Oh I don't know. Kyndra and the novices were quite prepared to break into the seventh level of the archives.' The humour left Nediah's tone abruptly. 'They should never have been allowed to come here. I blame myself for what happened with the wraiths. If we'd been more vigilant—'

Kait laid a hand on his arm. 'There wasn't anything either of us could have done, Ned. Kyndra should have—'

Nediah pulled his arm away. 'You can't lay Shika's death at her feet.'

Kyndra's heart began to pound. She felt sick. *No good comes of eavesdropping*, her mother's voice chided, but still she couldn't leave. All she could do was cling to the rock, squinting at the shadows where Kait and Nediah stood.

'She's already laid it there herself,' Kait said.

'That doesn't mean she's right to.'

'She's a Starborn. She has all the power Lord Kierik lost and she could have used it to destroy the wraiths before they began shooting our own damn energy back at us.'

'It's more complicated than that,' Nediah said, putting some distance between himself and Kait. 'A Starborn's ability comes with a price.'

'Oh yes, the corrupting influence of the stars. Sacrificing a few feelings seems a small price to pay for the power to rip up the very earth.'

'Kyndra doesn't think so.'

'Then she's a fool,' Kait said bluntly. 'I wouldn't hesitate.'

Kyndra had finally heard enough. The sickness was climbing into her throat. She swallowed it back and turned, suddenly desperate to distance herself from the conversation.

'You *didn't* hesitate, as I recall,' she heard Nediah say in a hushed voice as she hurried away, her heart still pounding horribly. 'Not even for me. I loved you.'

'Some things', Kait replied, 'are more important than love.'

17

His hands tangle in her hair as he kisses her and both her own are pressed against his chest, one clutching his tunic, his heart beating beneath her fingertips. She is alive with the sensations that rush through her, a river sweeping her up in its current. She yields to the flow, letting herself feel every caress, every heated touch. There are no spaces between them and the air itself seems afire. He draws her down to him so that they both kneel and when he reaches for her bodice, she lets him and the material slides from her shoulders to pool at her waist. She meets his eyes and sees herself: a woman with a woman's body, her hair falling around her—

Brégenne opened her eyes. For a moment she was disorientated, blinking at the dark, unfamiliar room. Her heart was beating quickly. She pressed one hand against it and let herself savour the dream before wakefulness returned in a rush.

She sat up abruptly in the huge bed Trader Marahan had granted her for the night. She could feel the heat in her cheeks, though no one was there to see her blush. *I just miss him*, she tried to tell herself. It was natural to miss Nediah – they'd been together a long time. She'd become used to his presence, taken it for granted that when she turned around, he'd be there, ready with a smile or wry remark.

That didn't lessen the pain of his absence. Brégenne had to admit that what she felt was more, dangerously more, than the despondency of separated friends. It was a feeling that had crept up on her unawares, a feeling that had perhaps been years in the growing. Now that Nediah was gone . . .

She forced herself to focus on the day ahead. *First things first*, Brégenne thought as she dressed. The mob at the gates had to be dispersed. She was afraid that the peaceful solution she had in mind wouldn't find much favour with people who were half starved and maddened by grief at the loss of their homes and loved ones. She tugged on her boots fiercely, cursing the Trade Assembly. Charity and compassion were clearly not words with which the merchants were familiar.

Trader Astra Marahan greeted them in the breakfast room. The Marahans were one of the oldest merchant families and their affluence was gaudily apparent. Servants hovered by painted screens, waiting to spring into action at Astra's slightest gesture. Brégenne and Gareth sat in high-backed chairs, confronted by a veritable army of pastries. While Brégenne was impressed and faintly appalled at the surrounding luxury, she could tell by Gareth's frequent fidgeting that he was out of his depth. The first time he'd reached for a pastry – iced and arranged in a spiral – one of the servants had pursed his lips in unconcealed disapproval. There was an order to the eating of pastries and iced cinnamon spirals were among the last to be consumed. Gareth had dropped the thing as if burned, which caused the servant's lips to purse even more. Brégenne took pity and handed the novice an almond heart, which Gareth ate apprehensively.

Their host sat at the head of the table, her husband to her right and one of her sons to her left. Brégenne noticed that she hardly touched the food, but a servant – following some unspoken signal – frequently topped up her tea from an elegant silver pot. No one spoke and the room's silence was an uneasy one.

Brégenne decided to break it. 'Thank you for putting us up for the night, Astra. It's appreciated.'

If Astra didn't care to be called so informally, she didn't say so. 'You are welcome. If your news can be verified, the Assembly will be in your debt.' Her blue eyes were piercing and she placed an emphasis on the word *debt* that made it sound distinctly double-edged.

Brégenne swallowed the obvious retort and nodded graciously. 'When do you intend to leave with Argat?'

'I may not leave until the situation here is resolved.' Astra tucked her little finger through the cup's handle. 'Once it has been, I will give Acre my fullest attention.'

It was the best Brégenne was going to get, but it still made her want to jump up and shake some sense into the woman. The complacency that came with peace had taken root too deep. Even the terror of the Breaking hadn't been able to shake it.

'So Argat has been granted permission to unhook his ship from the great chain?' she asked.

Astra tilted her head. 'Temporarily. This will be made clear to those captains who seek the same. We take a risk in unhooking the *Eastern Set*. The ships are secured for their own safety and are far too valuable to hand over to their captains. Not all are as experienced as Argat.'

Brégenne frowned. 'Has Argat been informed that the situation's temporary?'

The tightening of Astra's lips told her that he hadn't been. It didn't bode well.

'Mother says you're a sorceress,' Astra's son piped up suddenly. He looked about thirteen. 'Is it true?'

'As true as Acre's return,' Brégenne replied with a pointed look at Astra.

'My tutor said Acre was just a story. Like magic.'

'Acre was never just a story, but if you'd asked me a few months ago, I'd have said it was a place none of us would ever see.' She met the boy's eyes squarely. 'And Wielders don't refer to their ability as magic. That's for the cardsharps in the street. We channel the energy of the cosmos itself, which is as real as you or I and all around us.'

'Could I learn to do it?'

'Tomas!' Astra barked before Brégenne could reply.

'Yes, Mother,' the boy mumbled to his plate. He didn't say anything else, but continued to shoot Brégenne and Gareth covert glances.

Brégenne raised her eyes to the window and froze. Outside, the sun waged war with rain clouds building in the west and their shadows passed over the white stone plaza that formed the centrepiece of the manor district. Four people were crossing the square. It wasn't their nondescript clothes that marked them out, but the way they moved – with a confidence born of power.

And the Solar envoi they followed.

Brégenne assumed they'd made it invisible to those around them, but it was like a beacon to her. A sharply indrawn breath from Gareth told her he'd seen it too. She watched the dog-shaped envoi lift its head, as if scenting the air. Then it turned and headed unerringly for Astra's mansion.

Brégenne pushed back her chair. 'I need some air,' she announced to the room, feeling her heart pounding. Her anger at the Assembly had pushed Alandred's warning out of her head, but now it came rushing back, along with the names of the Wielders sent to bring her in. Of course they'd chosen to come for her in the day. 'Gareth,' she said, 'if you'd accompany me?'

'I hope you're not ill, Lady,' Astra's husband said, also sliding his chair back and standing. He made to offer her an arm, but Brégenne waved him away.

'I didn't sleep well,' she said. 'I just need a walk to clear my head.'

All three Marahans looked surprised at her abrupt exit, but there was no help for it. The servants watched her go with the same suspicious eyes as their mistress.

When the two of them were out of the room, Brégenne began to stride down the corridor, hoping it was the one that led to the back of the house and the stables where Astra had housed their mounts. 'That's how they've found us,' she muttered. 'They're using an envoi to track us.'

Gareth frowned as he hurried after her. 'I didn't think that was possible.'

'Oh it is,' she said, as they turned a corner into a smaller, less grand passage. 'Especially if you know your quarry well or have something of theirs to scent.'

'We can't escape them, then.'

'No,' Brégenne agreed after a moment, 'but we can try to outrun them.'

'Or we can fight.'

She looked at him. 'Listen to me, Gareth. These are masters we're up against. You agreed to come with me and I know I haven't fulfilled my part of the deal—'

'Perhaps that's a good thing,' the young man said as they raced past a startled housemaid. There was a resolve in his face that bordered on eagerness.

'No,' she said again, more vehemently. 'If you're hurt, it'll be my fault.' She looked away. 'I made enough mistakes with Kyndra. I don't want to repeat them with you.'

'I'm not Kyndra,' Gareth said, wrenching open the next door before Brégenne could reach it. 'I'm a Wielder of Naris, if you hadn't noticed, and I can look after myself.'

They burst into a kitchen already bustling with the preparations for lunch and Brégenne knocked a hanging string of garlic to the floor as she hurtled past. 'Sorry,' she called without looking back. She fixed her eyes on the yard that sat between the outspread wings of the manor. There was a woodpile beside neat stacks of lamp oil and coal, and two gardeners were repositioning a tree in newly prepared earth. Beyond them the garden stretched away, dotted with patios and topiary. But no stables.

Brégenne cursed. They wouldn't get far without the horses. Perhaps the garden had a back gate they could use to circle around to the front of the house. They could pick up their mounts and –

She made her decision, tugging Gareth in the direction of a nest of manicured trees that offered cover of a sort. Although she strove to calm it, Brégenne's heart was pounding. It wasn't fear for herself, though she knew she was entirely defenceless. It was fear of what Gareth might do if the Wielders caught

253

them. She didn't want to be responsible for the injury or death of those just following orders.

They wove between the trees, making for the solid stone wall that circled the property. It was too high to climb, Brégenne saw now, and the clipped trees had no helpful branches to boost them up. She looked along the length of the wall for a gate, but there was none to be seen. She'd trapped them.

Gareth put his hand on the stone and she knew what he was thinking. 'They're close enough to feel it, if you channel energy,' she said.

'We might not have much choice, but I've never tried to punch through stone before.'

'There has to be a gate. They wouldn't take garden waste through the kitchens.'

But it was too late. Brégenne felt a prickling on the back of her neck and spun around. There they were, all four of them, striding across the grass as if they owned every blade of it. The dog-envoi at their side blazed brighter at the sight of her and Gareth standing penned against the wall and then it faded, its purpose spent.

'Well met, Councilwoman Brégenne,' Barrar said pleasantly. Being a fellow Lunar, he was not one she had to worry about. Instead Brégenne fixed her gaze on the Solars, Yve and Magnus.

'I doubt I'm still a councilwoman after what I've done,' she replied, striving for an air of her old serenity.

'That is up to Lord Gend and Lady Veeta,' Barrar said. 'Our only orders are to escort you to the citadel.'

'You and I both know I'm not going back to Naris.'

Barrar gave no sign that her words perturbed him – if anything, his tone became more conciliatory. 'Come now, Brégenne.

None of us wants to make this difficult. And you're currently in no position to resist.'

'She might not be, but I am.' Gareth widened his stance and planted his feet as if for a fight, but the only thing his declaration provoked was laughter.

'Be silent, novice,' Magnus said. He was a big man, though Gareth rivalled him in height. 'You'd do better to contemplate the punishment that awaits you on our return.'

'It's like Brégenne said.' Gareth matched Magnus stare for stare, despite a brief tremble in his shoulders. 'We aren't planning on returning.'

'Listen,' Brégenne said swiftly before the conversation grew any more out of hand, 'I'm doing what Veeta and Gend are too frightened to do. Surely you must see the threat that Acre poses. If it comes to it, do you want Naris to stand alone against an army that nearly annihilated our predecessors – predecessors whose numbers were far greater *and* who had greater powers at their disposal?'

'Whether *we* see it or not is irrelevant,' Yve spoke up. 'The Council decides our course.'

'And you're content to let them do so?' Brégenne asked the blonde woman. 'A situation that concerns not only the citadel, but the whole of Mariar?'

Yve regarded her with unfriendly eyes. 'That's why we have a Council.'

The statement was all the more ludicrous in light of their current stand-off. 'You have a member of the Council before you,' Brégenne said. 'But suddenly my opinion counts for nothing.'

'You were overruled, Lady Brégenne,' Magnus answered her. 'Council members Veeta and Gend have made it clear that the contempt with which you have treated our laws has put us all in danger.'

Brégenne opened her mouth to retort, but closed it before any more words spilled out. It was no use trying to reason with them – the hypocrisy of the situation told her that. Her stomach was boiling over with anger and frustration. She couldn't afford to go back to Naris – to lose what little time Mariar might have. But that meant fight or flight, and fight was clearly out of the question. Gareth couldn't defeat two Solar masters. That left flight, but even if they managed to escape the walled garden, where would they go that the Wielders wouldn't find them?

'The only way you're taking me back to Naris,' she said, 'is in chains.'

'If that's what you want, Brégenne,' Magnus said regretfully and she heard the familiar building roar of Solar energy.

Gareth stepped in front of her, glowing, adding his own note to the Solar chorus, and Brégenne grabbed his arm. 'No,' she said. 'I don't want you hurt for my sake.'

Gareth didn't look round, but kept his eyes on the two Solar Wielders. 'Who says I'm going to get hurt?'

'They're masters, Gareth.'

'You should listen to her, novice,' Magnus said darkly. 'Attacking us will only earn you a worse punishment.' His face twisted. 'Fighting an Inferiate novice is really no different from kicking a downed dog. I find it equally distasteful.' And, whip-fast, he sent a concentrated ball of light at Gareth's chest.

Brégenne threw herself aside as Yve's golden chain streaked for her ankle and so she missed the immediate aftermath of Magnus' strike. When she looked up, the Lunars were standing outside the battle with their arms folded and Gareth was picking himself up with a groan. An ill-formed Solar shield lay splintered at his feet and faded into light as she watched.

She gasped as the chain flew at her again and only just managed to avoid it with an awkward flip sideways. This couldn't go on. She'd have to give herself up before Gareth was hurt. Already Magnus was preparing another stunning strike.

Gareth's face was pale but hardened as he regained his feet. In one swift motion, he stripped off his right glove. The gauntlet was a fist of ebony gloom amidst the sunlight.

'What's that?' Magnus asked, squinting at it. The gauntlet looked less like a piece of armour and more like a part of Gareth's flesh. The novice clenched his fist inside it and turned a face to Magnus that abruptly looked nothing like his own. Foreboding seized Brégenne . . . and the chain found her wrist. Its links tightened as Yve pulled and a second chain flew at her ankle. She swung sideways in an attempt to avoid it, but it wrapped around the leather of her boot and brought her crashing down.

Perhaps it was the sight of her on the ground that caused Gareth to leap at Magnus, swinging his gauntleted fist at the Wielder's jaw. For a second it looked as though Magnus would laugh at the tavern tactic, but Gareth's fist connected and he staggered, blinking in surprise. His eyes widened as he raised a hand to his jaw. The flesh around the impact was darkening, shrivelling like a corpse's. Magnus screamed and Brégenne watched in horror as the Wielder's skin peeled back to show bone swiftly mottling with rot.

Yve's chain vanished as she ran to her companion, her hands already aglow with healing energy. Magnus' face was grotesque – his eyes bulging, open mouth lipless, the rot climbing his cheek towards his hairline.

Through all of it Gareth stood, his eyes dark. The expression

he wore was not his own; there was a malevolence in it that
spoke to Brégenne of some ancient wrong. But he roused at the
sight of the Wielder falling to the ground, or perhaps the stink
of putrefaction, for he took a step back and the alien look fell
from him, leaving horror in its place. He watched as Yve desperately tried to stem whatever force was pulling Magnus' face
apart. Eventually the Solar energy began to re-grow the damaged skin and the Wielder's cries eased to moans.

They wouldn't get another chance. Brégenne grabbed
Gareth and tugged him away. The Lunars made to give chase,
but perhaps their nerve failed; they were staring at the gauntlet
glowing sickly on Gareth's arm.

Brégenne ran for the house, Yve's shouts in her ears. She
yanked Gareth along until the novice came fully back to himself
and was able to run alone. There was an alley which they'd
missed when they'd come from the kitchens – it ran alongside
the mansion wall and led out into the plaza. The two of them
dashed along it, dodging bins and buckets, leaping a low gate,
until they found themselves in the sun once more. Brégenne
glanced at Gareth; his face was pale and he looked ready to
throw up, but they couldn't stop here, not this close to the
Wielders. As they crossed the plaza, their heaving chests attracting curious looks, the sound of running came from the alleyway.
Brégenne glanced over her shoulder to see Yve and the Lunar
Wielders. The woman looked shaken, but determined.

'I can't do it again,' Gareth gasped.

Magnus had come stumbling out of the passage. Yve's healing had restored part of his face, but the power of the gauntlet
was still visible in the shrunken skin. His other cheek was as
bloodless as Gareth's.

Yve advanced on them, another chain glowing between her

hands, uncaring of the shocked cries she elicited. The plaza was full of witnesses – not the quiet apprehension Veeta and Gend had in mind, Brégenne thought.

Gareth was in no state to fight. All he could do was throw himself aside as Yve's chain streaked for his ankle. It missed him by inches. The battle had drawn more observers from their homes and they stood gawking foolishly, unaware of the danger. 'Get away from here!' Brégenne screamed at them and in her momentary distraction was snagged by a chain. Magnus held the other end and, though his hands shook visibly, the Solar links were strong.

A familiar whirring reached her at the same moment that a shadow blocked the sun. Brégenne looked up, disbelieving. An airship was heading for the plaza.

Several moments passed before she recognized Argat's *Eastern Set*. Observers had begun to point at it, shocked by the sight of an untethered ship. The hull gleamed in the sun and the whine of the propellers changed as the craft began to slow. What was it doing here?

Brégenne strained against her bindings, Gareth backed up beside her, the Wielders closing in around them. She thought she glimpsed Astra, her face thunderous as she looked up at the rogue ship.

The craft dropped lower and there was the captain himself at the rail, his dark eyes taking in the scene, noting Brégenne's chain, the Wielders surrounding her. He must have made a swift decision for he shouted an order and two crewmen cast rope ladders over the side. They swung perilously as the airship approached.

'If he thinks we can catch hold of those, he's mad,' Gareth hissed at her. 'The airship's coming too fast.'

The Wielders weren't looking at the *Eastern Set*. Their gazes were fixed on Brégenne – and on Gareth's gauntlet. As it reached the far edge of the plaza, the airship dropped even lower until the bottom of the ladders swung around head height. Then it banked and made straight for them.

Gareth gave her a wild glance and Brégenne steeled herself, aware of the glowing chain on her wrist. And then the ladders were swinging towards them, passing the Wielders, and she and Gareth leapt.

She was almost shocked to feel the rope, rough beneath her curled fingers. Brégenne had only a moment to tighten her hold before the chain around her wrist pulled taut and almost yanked her off again. She held on with everything she had, feeling the resistance as the chain dragged Magnus along in the airship's wake. If it weren't for his injury, he'd surely have succeeded in ripping the knotted rope from her grasp, but whatever deathly power Gareth had used had taken its toll. Brégenne heard his scream of rage as the golden chain snapped.

Immediately, she climbed up the ladder until her feet were secure. The *Eastern Set* gained height just before Brégenne's boots scuffed the dome of the Assembly.

Gareth hung on the adjacent ladder, a little colour returned to his face by the breeze. He was shaking his head in relief – or perhaps in disbelief at their unlikely escape. Brégenne twisted to look back as they crossed the walls of Market Primus and saw the four Wielders reduced to tiny, impotent figures. Then the ladders were hauled up until she and Gareth could climb over the rail onto the airship's deck.

Argat stood there, impressive in his leather captain's coat, which flapped against the westerly wind. 'Well, then, woman,' he said to Brégenne. 'Consider my debt to you paid. In full.'

18

By the gods, it hurt.

He'd almost have preferred the tearing agony when the surgeons first wrenched the bolt from his flesh rather than this nagging, aching pain that kept him constant company. Already a poor sleeper, he was lucky now if he caught an hour's rest at a time.

'Stop worrying at it, James. It'll heal, but only if you leave it alone.'

General Hagdon glared. 'I'd like to see you in my place, Carn. That time when the dog bit you – I was tempted to issue an arrest warrant just so that I didn't have to listen to your moaning.'

'It was a wolf, not a dog,' Carn protested. 'And it got infected. If it wasn't for that surgeon, I'd be dead.'

'Clearly I paid him too much.'

Carn gave him a look of deepest hurt.

'I'm not cut out for this,' Hagdon said, dropping into a folding chair. Charts, maps and reports were piled haphazardly on the table in his spacious tent, an empty brandy bottle holding them down against the wind that occasionally gusted inside. 'What happened to the campaign days of clear objectives? We'd slaughter some rebels, secure the odd settlement.' He shook his head. 'I'm too old to get shot with crossbows.'

'You're thirty-six, James.'

Hagdon said nothing, grimacing at a spasm of pain in his shoulder.

'The youngest general in Sartyan history.'

'Don't give me that.'

Carn folded his arms. 'What I mean to say is you've done well for yourself. More than well.' He paused. 'If you asked His Majesty for leave, surely he'd allow it.'

'Asking for leave,' Hagdon said bitterly, 'is asking to lose my position. Perhaps even my head.'

Carn was silent and Hagdon looked up at him. 'If that comes as a surprise, Carn, perhaps you ought to reconsider your own position.'

'Don't be ridiculous,' the bondsman murmured. 'My loyalty is to you first and the empire second.'

Hagdon swallowed something that felt suspiciously like a lump in his throat. 'That's treasonous talk,' he said, his voice hard and hushed, 'and I don't want to hear it from you again.'

Silence descended. Without Carn's banter, Hagdon's thoughts turned back to the horror at hand. He glanced at the reports from a dozen sources laid out before him, though he'd read them enough times to make his eyeballs ache. *Fire*, they all said. *Hundreds dead.*

'"The very earth cracked open",' he recited, seizing one grubby sheet of paper. '"Flames roared out of the chasm. Men of the third division trapped. Burned to death."'

Carn came to stand behind his shoulder, leaning over to read the report. '"The siege engines melted like metal in a forge." That was our remaining artillery?'

'Most of it,' Hagdon said, massaging his forehead. 'A few remain in the garrison at Artiba.'

'A Starborn,' Carn whispered. 'After five hundred years.'

Hagdon clenched a fist, brought it down on the table. Papers jumped and scattered. 'The boy warned me,' he said. 'She had markings she didn't want seen. I should have put two and two together.'

'You can't blame yourself,' Carn answered. 'How could you ever have foreseen a Starborn?'

'An officer's job *is* to foresee such things. Every eventuality, no matter how unlikely, has to be considered.' Hagdon briefly closed his eyes. 'Those deaths hang around my neck.'

'It's a miracle you escaped,' Carn said. 'A few more moments and you'd have been killed with the third division.'

'In a just world, I ought to have been.'

'I don't care for this side of you,' Carn said, stepping away. 'Self-pity doesn't suit you, James.'

Hagdon didn't rise to the bait, not with duty weighing so heavily upon him.

'Does the emperor know?' the bondsman asked.

'He will by now. Locke's ravens are swift.'

Carn began to gather up the fallen reports. 'What will he do?'

It was a good question and one Hagdon feared the answer to. 'The Starborn made overtures of peace,' he said. 'Lieutenant Frexen laughed in her face.'

'He was among the dead, I take it?'

Hagdon nodded. 'I doubt she'll make the offer a second time.'

'So we've just made an enemy of a Starborn.'

'*I've* made an enemy of a Starborn.' He glanced up at Carn. 'You know what the last one did.'

'Halted the Conquest,' Carn answered unnecessarily. 'Took a whole continent and all its people away from the empire.'

'And that was in an age when Sartya was strong. We're weak now, and weakening further by the day.' Hagdon leaned back in his chair. 'Ambertrix was our best weapon. With it, we brought down Solinaris. Without it . . .' He shook his head.

'Why is she travelling with so few companions?' Carn asked. 'I'd have thought to see her at the head of an army.'

'If she genuinely wants peace, she wouldn't bring a significant military presence onto Acrean soil.' Hagdon picked up a map, stabbed a finger at the hoarlands. 'But who knows? Maybe she's strong enough not to need an army. Look what she's already done. Or she could have a force stationed just over the border, waiting to march on her word. I might've doomed us all.'

'We know nothing about Rairam,' Carn countered. 'Such a force might not exist, particularly if the Starborn's primary objective is to seek a truce.'

Carn might have a point. A vulnerable nation would indeed favour diplomacy. 'The Davaratch will want Rairam scouted out at the earliest opportunity,' Hagdon said. 'In a way I hope you're wrong. If it transpires that there *is* no force . . .'

'He'll march on Rairam,' the bondsman finished. 'The Starborn's homeland.'

Once, the prospect of a new conquest would have excited him. When he was young and brazen with zeal. Before the deaths of his nephew and sister, and the Davaratch's obsession with Khronosta. Now the thought of invading Rairam filled Hagdon with dread: the old war revived, the killing beginning anew and another Starborn on the loose. 'I hope you're wrong,' he repeated softly.

'General Hagdon.'

Lieutenant Malker was standing in the entrance to his tent, a small crowd of ranking soldiers gathered behind him. The sight raised Hagdon's hackles. He'd never really taken to the supercilious officer. And apart from Tara, whom Hagdon had fought beside, Malker was the only lieutenant to survive Khronosta. He'd been mysteriously absent from the fight. 'What is it?' Hagdon asked brusquely.

'The men wish to know how you'll answer the Starborn's crimes,' Malker said. His face was hard. He'd been a close friend of Frexen, Hagdon recalled. 'She killed hundreds of soldiers, a dozen officers among them. The Fist won't forget.' He curled his hand around the hilt of his long sword, glanced at those behind. 'We want her dead.'

Hagdon rose to his feet. 'The situation is complex, Lieutenant. The way in which we're seen to deal with the Starborn may have serious political consequences.'

'Politics be damned,' Malker snarled. 'She's a murderer. We demand justice.'

Hagdon narrowed his eyes. 'Watch your tone, Lieutenant. While I abhor the Starborn's actions, I will not move without the emperor's say so. More is at stake than justice for dead soldiers. Every one of them knew their duty.' He swept his gaze over the rest of the officers. Most wouldn't meet it. 'I expect you to know yours.'

Malker glanced at their downturned eyes and his anger seemed to double. 'I won't serve a coward,' he said.

Someone drew a sharp breath. A few officers at the rear of the group melted away, as if to distance themselves from Malker, though Hagdon had already committed their faces to memory. The tent was very quiet. 'Can someone remind me of the penalty for insubordination?' he asked.

The silence endured a few moments longer before a deep voice called, 'Fifteen lashes, General.' The younger officers parted to let Commandant Taske through. He was a man in his fifties, his shorn hair a grey fuzz over his scalp. His pale eyes were chill as they regarded Malker with contempt. 'At the very least. Such a statement is unbefitting a lieutenant.'

'Make it so,' Hagdon said and two officers who'd entered with Taske seized Malker's arms. To his credit, the lieutenant didn't protest as he was bundled roughly out of the tent. But his last baleful glare stayed with Hagdon. Like a parasite, it burrowed into the back of his mind and festered there. 'The rest of you are dismissed,' he said. 'The Starborn will answer for her crimes as the emperor sees fit.'

Taske remained behind. 'I apologize, General,' he said. 'Had I been more attentive, I'd never have permitted such a scene to occur. Malker needs watching.'

Hagdon sank into his chair. His shoulder grumbled at the movement, sending an angry pulse through his chest. He winced. 'Thank you, Commandant, but I should have expected it. In hundreds of years, there hasn't been such a bloodbath. It's no wonder the officers are upset.'

'How *do* you think His Majesty will respond?'

'A campaign to hunt her down, I expect. After that . . . I fear to say.'

The commandant nodded and took a few steps closer to Hagdon's desk. 'If you'll permit me, sir, I would consider the afternoon's events a warning. This business with the Starborn has stirred up the men. Rivalries abound and, without imperial direction, your position is not so strong as it might be.'

Hagdon looked up sharply. 'You're talking mutiny.'

'That's a strong word, General. Let's say . . . uncertainty.' Taske's gaze was oddly penetrating, as if he wished to convey something more than he said. 'The Fist has suffered an insult, which groups such as the Defiant will seek to exploit. As its general, you should move carefully.'

'That's the truth.' Hagdon gingerly prodded the wound in his shoulder. 'I appreciate the warning, Taske. Keep an eye on Malker and his little group.'

When the commandant had gone, Carn asked, 'What purpose would a coup serve?' He lowered his voice. 'And why now?'

Hagdon looked through the empty brandy bottle at the reports Carn had restacked neatly on his desk. The glass distorted them, turning the inked words into some spiky, unintelligible language. 'Because Relator Shune was right,' he said. 'Change is coming and we are not prepared.'

19

The Eastern Set
Brégenne

'I wasn't aware you were in my debt,' Brégenne said, looking around the familiar deck. She recognized some of the crew from when she had sailed with Captain Argat before, but there were a few new faces too. Yara was presumably below, tending to the airship's workings.

Argat grimaced. 'It was your timely arrival in the Assembly that led to this.' He swept out a hand. 'Whether your warnings of war are true or not, my ship is free at last.'

'I seem to recall that the situation was temporary.'

'Do you?' Argat's eyes glittered. 'Strange, because I don't recall that at all.'

'You didn't have to help us.' Despite Argat's talk of a debt repaid, Brégenne knew he wouldn't do something for nothing. 'Those were Wielders after us,' she said seriously. 'They won't forget this.'

'Good.' The captain's smile showed his teeth.

Brégenne shook her head. 'You have no idea. Gareth and I are wanted by Naris – they won't give up until we're caught.'

'Naris,' Argat said. 'That's where you and these other Wielders live?'

'Yes. Beyond Murta.'

'I see. And the people of Murta know about this?'

She nodded. 'Our ancestors founded Murta at the same time they rebuilt the citadel so that we had a means of contact with the outside world. The families living there go back generations. They provide us with food and services and in return they're well paid for their silence. There are some who aren't aware – visitors, passing tradesmen and the like – but we've worked hard to keep strangers away.' She gave him a searching look. 'Even you, Captain, have a healthy respect for superstition.'

'Astonishing,' Argat mused, 'to keep such a place secret.' His eyes narrowed. 'And more astonishing is why. With powers like yours, you could rule this world.'

'So thought one of our former councilmen,' Brégenne said, remembering Loricus and the plans he'd spoken of before he died. 'But none of us can forget that the Wielders were almost destroyed in the Acrean war, which, we discovered recently, was only ended because of a Starborn named Kierik.'

'Another myth.' Argat had that magpie glint in his eye again. 'It sounds as if you've a great deal to tell me. Preferably over dinner,' he added.

'I'd be happy to,' Brégenne replied, conscious of Gareth standing unusually silent beside her. 'But where are you planning on flying?'

'Wherever the wind blows,' Argat said. 'I admit I hadn't got as far as plotting a course. Yara would like to take her through a few manoeuvres.' He ran a fond hand along the rail. 'She's new to freedom. We don't know how she'll perform without an anchor.'

Brégenne raised an eyebrow. 'And us?'

'As soon as Yara works out how to land her, I'll set you down in a place of your choosing.'

'As soon as she works out how to land her,' Brégenne repeated flatly.

'That's right.' Argat paused to bark off an order. 'The *Set*'s never touched earth before. Lived all her life in the skies or in dock.'

Brégenne suppressed a groan. 'But Yara *can* land her, correct?'

The captain shrugged. 'Won't know until she tries.'

While dinner was being prepared in the galley, Brégenne went to talk to Gareth. She found him standing at the starboard rail, staring at the blur of landscape beneath. The novice did not look good; shadows ringed his brown eyes, making them appear darker than they were and his face seemed paler – or was that a trick of the light?

Brégenne stood beside him, waiting for him to speak first. In their flight from the Wielders, she hadn't had time to think about what Gareth had done to Magnus. Now the memory of the man's jaw rotting before her eyes returned all too vividly. If Gareth was remembering it too, she knew why he was quiet.

'What's happening to me?' the novice said finally in a softer voice than she'd ever heard him use. He took his gaze from the distant ground and looked at her. 'I don't feel . . . right, Brégenne.'

'What do you mean?' she asked cautiously.

'I feel not like *me*.' After a few moments, he added, 'And I'm cold all the time.'

He sounded very young all of a sudden and Brégenne gently touched his shoulder. 'We'll find a way, Gareth. I won't give up.'

'Why did it do that?' Gareth asked, returning his gaze to the wind. 'I only hit him. At least I think I did.' His face clouded. 'I'm not sure. And look.' He took off the glove, pulled back his sleeve and Brégenne suppressed an exclamation. Every time she saw it, the gauntlet looked less like a piece of armour. It clung tighter to Gareth's wrist as if it really were becoming a part of him.

'I don't like it,' Gareth said, his voice still small and uncertain. 'Please get it off, Brégenne.'

'I will,' she promised, but she remembered the black tendrils twisting beneath Gareth's skin and wasn't sure she could. She'd never encountered a type of magic that could rot flesh. Only death had that power. Brégenne looked at the circles around Gareth's eyes and fought down a shiver.

'It wasn't like this when I first used it,' Gareth said. 'When I helped fight the Nerian, all it did was throw people. And it wasn't that powerful. I remember each time I used it made it weaker. And it looked different then too.'

'Keep it hidden,' Brégenne advised, 'especially from Argat. He takes an interest in such things.'

'What are we going to do now?' A little life returned to Gareth's eyes. 'It's not that I won't enjoy riding on an airship, but what about the Trade Assembly? Argat's not going to turn about and pick up that Astra woman, is he? And she still has our horses.' He looked more pained at that than at anything else.

'I know.' Brégenne bit her lip. Being forced to leave Myst behind was a blow, but she couldn't see any alternative. She hoped the horses would be safe in Astra's stables. *What a mess*, she thought. Between the Trade Assembly's stupidity and Naris's interference, she'd achieved nothing. So far, this had been a wasted journey. *You knew it was going to be hard when you left Naris*, she reminded herself. But there were so many things she hadn't anticipated which she ought to have done – like the unrest in the capital. And she should have guessed it would take more than a show of power to convince the Trade Assembly that they didn't know as much about the world as they thought.

'Why haven't we heard from the others?' Gareth said, adding another worry to her plate. 'I wish I knew what Shika was doing. Irilin too.'

Brégenne wished she knew what Nediah was doing. *Could* something have happened to separate Kyndra's group? 'We're sticking to our original plan,' she said, putting her fear firmly aside. 'The Trade Assembly aren't the only power in Mariar.'

Gareth sighed. 'You still want to go to Ümvast.'

'Naris needs allies, Gareth, even if Veeta and Gend don't think so. And Ümvast should be warned. His lands border Acre in the west.'

Gareth shook his head. 'I don't think you'll find the welcome you hope for.'

His reluctance was half annoying, half intriguing. It was plain Gareth didn't want to go home. 'What happened?' she asked. 'When Master Hanser took you away?'

The novice turned to look towards the boundaries of the Great Forest, still many leagues north across hill and valley, beyond the frontier town of Svartas. 'I gave it up,' he said softly.

'Gave what up?'

Gareth returned his eyes to hers. 'Everything.'

*

'So you see,' Brégenne finished later over dinner, 'Kyndra needed the earth of Acre to help her reunite the two lands.'

'You tell an incredible story, woman, almost too incredible to be believed.' Captain Argat took a healthy swig of wine. 'And I consider myself among the more open-minded of folk.' He paused to put down his glass. 'Of course it explains why the girl was drawn to the earth in the first place. I'm not ashamed to say that the whole situation set my teeth on edge.'

Remembering Argat's mad pursuit of them across the wastes, Brégenne thought that a vast understatement. She regarded the captain with a certain amount of wariness – they hadn't exactly parted as friends. But Argat was a gambler, one of those men to whom the world owed its momentum, and he could be of use. The question was: how far should she trust him?

'Our business with the Trade Assembly did not go as planned,' Brégenne said carefully. 'I knew it would be difficult to convince them of the need to prepare for a potential invasion, but without your corroboration they wouldn't even have believed Wielders still existed.'

'They've never been confronted with a situation to match the one in Market Primus,' Argat replied. 'They're out of their depth and desperately treading water. No fewer than three different Traders approached me asking for help with various situations. My price, of course, was access to private Assembly meetings.'

Although she was curious, Brégenne stopped herself from asking what those situations entailed. 'I didn't plan to leave so suddenly,' she said. 'Perhaps I could have—'

'You've neglected to talk about your pursuers.' The captain speared a curl of ham, dipped it in mustard and raised it to his mouth. 'From where I was standing, they looked distinctly unfriendly.' The words were slightly muffled by chewing. Argat swallowed and said, 'Made some enemies, have you?'

'Not everyone in Naris agrees with me,' Brégenne admitted. 'I might have left the citadel precipitously. And I didn't exactly advertise my going.'

Argat gave her an appraising look. 'You surprise me. I didn't have you pegged as a rebel.'

'Few do,' Brégenne said, unable to keep the wryness out of her voice. 'Myself included. But someone had to act. Naris has a long tradition of hiding from the world and now we're reaping the rewards. It'll take time to earn people's trust – time we don't have.'

'Because of this impending war, you claim.'

She frowned. 'You're foolish to make light of it. If the powers in Acre decided to invade, who would you look to for defence? Mariar hasn't had a standing army since the Deliverance.'

'True.' Argat put down his fork. 'But why must it come to war? In my experience, everyone has a price.'

'We don't know anything about Acre. What's valuable here, they may have in abundance.'

'A good point. However, we'd be stupid not to play to our strengths. Peace has made Mariar very rich indeed.' He swept out a hand as if to include the airship's luxurious saloon in his meaning. 'We are masters of trade, of connections. What we lack militarily, we make up for in diplomatic skill. The Assembly may be a handful of arrogant fools, but they know business and they know people. And how best to combine the two.'

'That's why Kyndra went to Acre,' Brégenne said. 'We know we're best playing to our strengths.' She sat back, considering. 'But putting all our eggs in one basket is foolhardy. It was Mariar's – Rairam's – wealth as a continent that made it a target for the empire in the first place. And the Trade Assembly are too greedy for their own good. The situation in Market Primus is proof that they value their gold above the well-being of their city or indeed the rest of the world.'

'What do you think, Yara?' Argat asked his first mate, who had thus far been silent. The tall woman wore her hair in dozens of tiny braids and she'd swapped her grease-stained overalls for a plain shirt.

In response, Yara's eyes narrowed on Brégenne's face. Slowly she finished her mouthful of food and swallowed. 'You argue well, Captain. But she has it right.' Her accent carried the husky warmth of all Archipelagans. 'When faced with the unknown, it is better to keep your options open. This power in Acre you speak of, this empire . . . if it turns out they prefer the language of swords, we should try to learn it.'

'Truly a night of surprises,' the captain said. 'Since when did you become an advocate of war?'

'Not war, Argat, survival.' Yara hooked a chicken leg. 'I like my life, I like this ship. I have plans for both. If anything were to threaten them, well . . . I'd do what I had to.'

Gareth sat quietly, only picking at his food. His cheeks retained some of their earlier pallor and the dark circles around his eyes were undiminished. Argat was watching him too. 'You don't look well, boy,' he said suddenly.

Gareth's head jerked up. 'I'm fine.'

'When are you going to show me what you have on your wrist?'

Brégenne cursed. Did nothing slip past the man? Gareth was looking at Argat in horror.

'You've been tugging at that glove since we hauled you on

deck.' The captain pushed his empty plate aside and beckoned. 'Let's see it.'

Gareth looked at Brégenne. 'Go ahead,' she said with a sigh, and so the novice laid his right arm on the cleared space in front of Argat and pulled off the glove. An unnatural cold clung to the gauntlet. Even Argat must have felt it, for his brows drew together and he retracted his outstretched hand.

'Don't bother to ask Gareth to remove it,' Brégenne said a little caustically. 'It won't come off.'

'Fascinating,' the captain said, ignoring her. 'Look at the sigils.' His gaze moved from the metal to Gareth's face. 'Where did you find it?'

'The archives,' Gareth said. 'The Wielders' library in Naris. There're a lot of things left over from the war.' He glanced down. 'I was curious and . . . I might have borrowed it without asking.'

'I suspect we have a deal in common,' Argat said with a slight smile. 'Tell me – what does it do?'

'At first I used it to throw people aside. But not like a Wielder does.' Gareth glanced briefly at Brégenne. 'And although it was really powerful the first few times, it became weaker. Now I don't think it was made to do that at all.'

'Why?'

Gareth swallowed. 'This afternoon when we were trying to get away from the Wielders, I hit one of them. A man.' The fist inside the gauntlet clenched. 'I didn't mean to . . . I mean, it wasn't something I chose.' Gareth stuttered to a halt and Brégenne thought the memory of what he'd done to Magnus would stop him from continuing. But the novice took a deep breath and looked into Argat's face. 'The gauntlet made his skin rot,' he said quietly. 'It was like dying – I'm sure if I'd kept it up, the other Wielder wouldn't have been able to heal him. He would have rotted away to nothing.'

'The touch of death,' Argat mused with a dark smile. If Gareth's story had disturbed him, he gave no sign of it.

'And I felt cold,' Gareth said, 'like there was no life inside me. Magnus had life. I could take his . . . all that warmth. But I knew it wouldn't be enough, it would never be enough –' He stopped abruptly, dread in the lines of his face. 'I don't know why I said that. Sorry.'

The table was silent. Yara looked as if she wanted to edge her chair away from Gareth, and Brégenne understood how she felt. She remembered the dead king in his throne under the earth. Only Argat seemed unmoved. His face wore a stark and hungry fascination that made Brégenne's skin crawl almost as much as the image in her head. 'There's a tale –' the captain began and stopped.

'What?' Gareth said.

As they all waited, Argat splashed brandy into his glass, picked it up and leaned back. 'It was a story I heard a long time ago,' he began. 'When I was a young man, shipless, impover-ished, seeking to make my fortune . . .'

Yara gave a sigh of impatience.

'. . . Travelling Mariar in search of a future, one night a storm forced me to seek shelter at a small settlement just inside the borders of the Great Northern Forest.'

Gareth's expression sharpened and he shifted in his seat.

'Like many young men with a belly to fill and a thirst for ale, I made my way to the tavern. Mostly there were folk of Svartas, a few clansmen up from the plains, but in a corner sat a couple of men the like of which I'd never seen. Tall they were, wearing the clothes of the forest – skins and such – with claws for pauldrons and antlered helms. They spoke with a strange accent, but I recognize northerners when I hear them.'

Argat paused to give Gareth a narrow look. 'They were warriors from Ümvast and I asked if I might join them. The first had an unfriendly cast to his face and he told me in no uncertain terms that I wasn't welcome. Disappointed, but unwilling to provoke a fight, I was about to leave when his companion stepped in. "He looks like a man of the world," he said to the sour one. "What's the harm?" Then he looked at me and said, "Sit, traveller. Do you know this country well?"'

Brégenne conceded grudgingly that Argat was a born storyteller. He had them hanging on his every word.

'Now,' Argat said, 'the chance to see, let alone sit and share a drink with the folk of Ümvast doesn't come along very often. So I said that yes, I was a traveller, a man of the south, and I hoped to captain an airship one day. That got them warming to me – it seems as if the northerners are as curious about us as we are about them.'

'So where does the gauntlet come into all of this?' Yara asked, the snap of impatience still in her voice.

Argat ignored her. 'After a few rounds, which I bought, of course, they got down to business. They were looking for something, or some*things*. Pretty tight-lipped about why they wanted them, but they told me readily enough what they looked like.' Argat pinned Gareth with his eyes. 'Gauntlets. A pair of them. One as dark as the grave, the other bright as the sun. Together they bestowed huge power on the wearer, but only together. Wearing just one would bring down a curse upon whoever was foolish enough to be doing so.'

Gareth attempted to speak, but Argat raised a hand. 'They

asked if I'd ever heard of such a thing and I said no. But I was a collector of oddities – I'd already amassed my share of things too readily consigned to history – and I said I'd keep an ear out for rumours. They told me I'd be well compensated.'

'And were you?' Brégenne asked. 'Did you ever contact them?'

'Of course not – they never meant me to. The sour-faced one was waiting out back with a knife.'

Gareth nodded. 'Sounds like Ümvast.'

'Being perspicacious, I'd expected as much. Some men get a glint in their eye when they're contemplating murder. I slipped out with a caravan heading south. That was my first and last experience of northerners, but the impression they made ensured I never forgot the tale.'

The brief, respectful silence that accompanies the end of a story descended on the table. Argat nursed his brandy. Yara was looking at Gareth, her gaze darting between his face and the gauntlet. Brégenne couldn't quite believe their luck. On consideration, perhaps she'd been wrong to insist Gareth hide the gauntlet from Argat. The captain was a fount of knowledge, after all, an active seeker of mysteries. She eyed the gauntlet – could it really be the one out of the story?

'About this curse,' Gareth said, 'what does it do?'

'Can't help you there,' the captain answered. 'They didn't go into specifics. But I'm guessing that the only way to remove the gauntlet would be to unite the pair. Then both can be worn safely.'

'What if this is it, Brégenne?' Gareth said. He took his arm off the table and pulled down his sleeve. 'This is the dark gauntlet – for some reason it ended up in Naris.'

'We don't know for sure,' she said at the uncomfortable mingling of hope and fear in his voice. 'But it's definitely a start.'

'So the only way I'm going to get it off is to find its partner.' Gareth's face fell. 'It could be anywhere.'

'The men had a lead on it,' Argat said, his own countenance alight. 'If anyone knows where to find it, it's those in Ümvast.'

Brégenne and Gareth shared a look. She knew what the novice was thinking – it was eerie when purposes aligned. 'Then,' she said to Argat. 'I have a proposition for you.'

Hammering out the terms of the deal was no simple matter. Argat was the equal of any master trader and had fewer scruples.

'Acre is dangerous,' Brégenne said for the umpteenth time. 'You can't just fly casually over the border.' *Maybe he could,* she amended, looking at the determined lines of Argat's face, *but it's still a huge risk.* 'The balance of power might be delicate. Until I hear from Kyndra, I don't know what to expect. Who knows how people will react when they see a flying ship? It'll be all too easy for them to assume the worst.'

'From the little you tell me,' the captain retorted, 'Mariar's whole western frontier abuts Acre's – once word spreads, you'll not stop people from venturing across the border. And what about the rest of the continent? We've no idea what the geography looks like up north.'

'If you agree to fly us there, we'll see, won't we?'

Argat held a lethal-looking letter opener. 'There,' he said and jammed it into the map spread on his desk. It pierced a spot in the Infinite Hills. 'You tell me those mountains are gone. It won't take long for the clans of Hrosst to investigate – their lands lie due east. They could have men and horses over there as we speak.'

He was right. She'd already delayed too long. If only she could split herself into several bodies, Brégenne found herself thinking.

'You can't handle this yourself,' Argat said and she scowled at the truth of his words and at how closely they echoed her thoughts. 'And perhaps you oughtn't to. You saw how it was in the capital. The Trade Assembly are loath to act on anything that relies on someone else's evidence.' His eyes darkened. 'I suspect they wouldn't believe in war until an army was hammering on their gates.'

Although Brégenne grimaced at the image, it reminded her of another time – a time when the Wielders of Solinaris were too proud to acknowledge the threat of the empire. Kyndra had discussed her visions at length in an attempt to bring the Council up to date with their own history. Brégenne remembered her sitting at the table, trying to convince Veeta and Gend of the threat Sartya could still pose.

'You may be right,' she conceded now. 'And the unrest in the capital made my job harder.' Her gaze wandered across the map to the Great Northern Forest. 'If the Assembly can't spearhead Mariar's defence, I can think of only one people who could.'

'Ümvast.' Argat stroked his stubbled chin. 'It's risky. They've not had dealings with the rest of Mariar in generations. What makes you think they'd take up arms in its defence?'

'They'd be fighting for their own freedom as much as for Mariar's,' Brégenne countered. 'Surely they can't ignore a threat to their homeland.'

'It makes sense when you lay it out reasonably, but the practicalities of war rarely follow the course of reason.' Argat leaned both fists on the map. 'If you even manage to convince them you're telling the truth, the first thing they'll want is information – information you insist you don't have.'

'I will by the time we get there,' Brégenne said firmly, hoping it was true. She'd send another envoi to Nediah tonight. 'At the very least, they can be warned.'

'You're quiet, boy,' Argat shot at Gareth who hovered behind them. The novice looked a little queasy. 'Aren't you excited about a trip home?'

Gareth slowly turned his head to stare at the captain. 'I never expected to go back,' he said.

'Why not?'

Brégenne knew: once you joined Naris, you left your old life behind. But, watching the lamplight flicker across Gareth's face, she didn't think that was the real reason. He'd already mentioned his mother – with her sinister promise lingering in his ears, what did Gareth believe he was returning home to? Not a grand welcome, she guessed.

Gareth didn't answer and eventually Argat turned back to Brégenne. 'So,' he said, 'again you seek passage. This time to Ümvast.' His eyes narrowed. 'What are you prepared to pay?'

Brégenne reached for one of her coin purses, but Argat waved it away. 'I don't want your gold,' he said.

She stared at him, suspicion working its way into the space between her shoulders.

'I'll take you as far as the borders of the forest,' Argat said. 'From there, you'll have to make your way on foot. I'm not flying over Ümvast's territory – a couple of flaming arrows to the hull and I'd be finished.'

'Agreed,' Brégenne said.

'I'll supply you with whatever you need for your journey

north.' Argat counted out on his fingers. 'Food, water skins, tents, weapons, if you want them. In return – and bear in mind the costs involved at my expense – I want two things.'

Brégenne nodded, already sensing what would come next.

'First, everything you know about Acre.'

'You know most of it already, Captain,' she replied, 'and I strongly recommend you stay away. The other thing we know for certain about the empire is that it had access to a good deal of technology, including weapons of war.' She tilted her head. 'It could be they have airships of their own.'

'A risk I'm prepared to take,' Argat replied and the set of his jaw told her plainly that his mind was made up.

She sighed. 'What's your second request?'

Argat looked at Gareth. 'If I turn out to be right about that gauntlet and you manage to find its partner . . . I want the pair.'

'No,' Gareth said immediately. He clutched the gauntlet through his glove.

'Think about it.' Argat spread his hands. 'There are a lot of ifs. Who knows whether that old story is true or whether your gauntlet is even the one it describes? What if its partner is irrecoverable? You have scant chance of success – it's likely the curse will finish you off long before you find the partner.' He bared white teeth at Gareth. 'But, in the unlikely event that you *do* find it, you will willingly hand over the pair to me. That is my condition.'

Gareth's face had paled at the mention of the curse, but it firmed as he turned towards Brégenne. 'You *can't* agree to this. Why should Argat have the gauntlets?'

'We don't stand a chance on foot,' Brégenne replied. 'The Wielders will catch us and this time they'll be more wary of the gauntlet's power. They'll take us down from a distance.' She studied him. 'Are you so willing to unleash that power a second time?'

The question gave Gareth pause. 'Of course not,' he said unhappily. 'But I don't like the idea of *him* having them either.'

The captain folded his arms, said nothing.

'Gareth,' Brégenne said. 'We might never find the other gauntlet. That won't stop us searching for a way to remove this one,' she added hastily. 'The sooner we get to Ümvast, the sooner we can start our search. That's where the story originated.' She made herself say what she'd come to suspect, but never uttered. 'The longer you leave it on, the harder it might be to remove.'

'All right,' Gareth murmured. He didn't look at Argat.

'Excellent,' the captain said, giving a brief clap. 'Now that's sorted, we can set a course north. We've made a few adjustments since you last travelled with us.' He flattened his lips. 'Not quite the revolutionary developments Yara and I discussed, but we *have* managed to coax a little more speed out of her. Sailing as the crow flies and weather permitting, I estimate we'll reach the border of the forest in five or six days.' That crooked smile reappeared. 'A three-week journey by horse.'

Brégenne turned to Gareth. 'Are you ready to go home?'

20

The Edge of the Beaches, Acre
Kyndra

Kyndra awoke with a prickle of gooseflesh. The hairs on her arms stood on end, as if they were capable of sensing a presence her eyes could not. It was still dark, though a patch of lighter sky in the east told her dawn was not far off. She blinked and held herself taut, listening. The humped forms of her companions were huddled in sleep. A taller shadow sat nearby: Medavle. His white robes gleamed dully.

She moved to stand and a hand clamped over her mouth. Kyndra jerked and gasped a breath through her nose, trying to twist free. The skin against her lips was dry and rough. And now she could feel the body at her back, unyielding and unnaturally hot. When her sleep-addled mind finally caught up, she remembered the stranger from yesterday. A quick glance from the corner of her eye showed her his empty blankets.

He let her turn her head to look at him. He was crouched close behind, very still, his odd yellow eyes glowing slightly in the dark and she recalled Nediah saying he wasn't human.

Kyndra struggled more violently and his hold on her tightened. 'Quiet,' he hissed.

'What are you doing?'

'They are close,' the stranger said. 'I can hear them.'

'Who?' she breathed, but he didn't reply. They waited in the dark, tense and silent, and finally a voice drifted out of the gloom.

'Kala,' it said, soft and sibilant. Kyndra felt the stranger stiffen. 'Kala, come with us.'

Medavle leapt up, eyes scanning the darkness and, at the same time, the young man let Kyndra go. 'Too late,' he said. 'They've found me.' He stood, two slim sticks sliding into his hands and she scrambled to her feet as well.

'Kyndra?'

Nediah sat up and Kait shook Irilin awake. 'What?' the young woman said. Then she spotted the stranger, noting his stance and the odd sticks he held readied like weapons. 'What's going on?'

Four figures stepped calmly into their camp. They were wrapped head to toe in bandages, ragged ends blowing free in the wind. They brought to mind the Svartan custom Kyndra had heard tell of wherein the dead were wound with linen and lavender before being laid in the ground. The comparison only made the newcomers more sinister. Eyes glinted out at her between the grey wrappings.

'Who are you?' she asked.

One of the figures spared her a glance. 'We have no business with you,' it said. 'We are here for the Kala.' She couldn't place the voice as male or female.

'Kala?' Kyndra repeated, frowning.

'You were difficult to track, Kala, but it is time to stop running,' the second figure said, ignoring her. It was speaking to the young man, who gripped his sticks more tightly.

'I have no intention of going with you,' he said. 'And you will find me stronger than your companions did.' Indeed, he was straight-backed, his knees slightly bent as if poised to move on a moment's notice. Standing, he was a little shorter than Nediah and stockier, with broad shoulders. His tattooed arms were muscled like a fighter's. He wore a ragged shirt, the sleeves rolled back to expose his arms, and a long tunic that fell to cover trousers tucked into soft leather boots.

'We have no wish to harm the Kala,' the first figure said in its snake-like whisper. 'But you are not yourself, Master. Once we reach Khronosta, you will forget this life. You will remember your people.'

'You're mad,' the stranger said and he lifted his sticks higher. 'I am not your leader. I don't believe in reincarnation or prophecy. We only have one life.'

'This is true of all men save Khronos,' the third figure said. 'He alone mastered the cycle of ages. He died so that he could be reborn. Now you will pass on your learning to us, to the people who have held your faith, who look for your coming. Long years have passed since you left us. You will find we have grown wise.'

The young man shook his head. 'You aren't listening. I told you—'

The figures blurred. Kyndra couldn't think of any other word to describe it. One moment they were standing in front of her, the next they were either side of the stranger, who swept out his sticks as if he'd anticipated the attack. One stick hit ribs, the other missed and the young man jumped back before those bandaged hands could close on him.

287

'Khronostians,' Medavle said, watching them with something akin to hunger on his face.

The stranger moved well, but not as fluidly or as swiftly as the people trying to capture him. He stepped from one stance to the next, keeping the sticks always in play, but his opponents ducked and dodged, as if they knew where each blow would land before it did. It seemed they were serious about not harming him; they kept their weapons sheathed.

The one-sided battle continued as Kyndra stood immobile, unsure what to do. All of them were strangers – it seemed prudent to let them fight it out amongst themselves. But then a Khronostian knocked one of the young man's sticks out of his hand. Wide-eyed, he watched it clatter on the ground, rolling out of reach. The bandaged figures seized their chance. In the next moment, the man's hands were behind his back and he was struggling fiercely. Kyndra spotted sweat on his brow and heard his laboured breathing. For someone who had lain near death only hours before, it was remarkable he had stayed on his feet this long.

'Let me go,' he gasped. 'What have you done with Ma?'

The Khronostians shared a glance. 'There was no sign of Sul,' one said, 'but Chaka lived long enough to tell us about the actions of the traitor, Mariana.'

Kyndra watched a vicious smile curl the stranger's lips. 'She deserved death,' he said. 'Why couldn't you have left us alone?'

Although the Khronostians' faces were hidden, their bandaged hands visibly tightened around the young man's arms.

'Stop,' Kyndra said and all five turned to look at her. 'This man has said he doesn't want to go with you.' She swallowed. 'He's made it quite clear.'

'Stay out of this.'

'You are Khronostian?' Medavle asked. 'We've heard a lot about you. Will you give us your names?'

'Why should we reveal ourselves to you?' the second Khronostian said, still holding tight to the young man. 'Our only concern is the Kala.'

'By all means, take your Kala,' Medavle said. 'But we've come a long way to forge alliances—'

'Whoever you are, your alliances mean nothing.'

'We come from Rairam,' the Yadin persisted. 'You know of the lost continent?'

'We have seen the sun rising in the distant east,' one said.

Medavle clearly took it as confirmation. 'Then you understand we're not friends of Sartya.'

'If that is so, stand aside and let us bear the Kala away.'

The Yadin's conciliatory tone began to wear thin. 'We can help each other,' he said. 'I am Medavle of the Yadin. Do you know of my people?'

Kyndra watched the bandaged figures exchange another glance. Something passed between them. 'We thought your kind destroyed,' one said finally. 'How come you live when all others do not?'

For a moment Medavle's shoulders seemed to carry the weight of everything he had seen and done in more than five centuries of life. The little Kyndra knew of him was like the tip of an iceberg; not for the first time, she wondered what lay beneath his still, cold surface. The Yadin sighed and straightened. 'It's a long story,' he said. 'If we could come to trust one another, I'd be glad to tell it.'

His words gave them pause, but then one said, 'Our duty is clear. We will take the Kala back to his people.'

'You're wrong,' the stranger spat and he began to struggle

anew against the bandaged hands. 'I'm no one. I don't have any power.'

Kyndra took a long look at the man the Khronostians named Kala. His face was the colour of smoke on the wind, hard and unyielding. It was a face that had seen more of life's cruelty than she ever had. And yet she couldn't shift the sense that she was looking at someone who was more than he seemed.

He's not human.

'Maybe you *should* go with them,' she heard herself say. Her voice sounded hollow in her ears.

'Did I ask for your opinion?' the young man snarled at her. 'Did I ask for your help?'

Despite the retort, Kyndra saw fear in his face for the first time and she made up her mind. 'We can't let them take him,' she said. 'Nediah, Kait, are you with me?'

She felt the heat against her back as the Wielders drew on the power of the rising sun.

'No,' Medavle said sharply, but the Khronostians merely laughed.

'You expect us to cower from a power so constrained by the laws of time?' the first asked. 'A power so weak it is reliant on the common turning of day and night?'

'You won't sound so confident when I burn out your tongue,' Kait said, flexing her fingers. Her threat seemed only to fuel their contempt and before Medavle could stop her, she threw two fireballs at the Khronostian's head.

The world froze.

Kyndra blinked.

It didn't freeze, exactly, but it slowed. Everything was cast in grey, the rocks, stunted trees, the sands of the desert. The cerulean sky with its fresh morning sun had dulled to ashes. The only colour remained as a blueish tinge around the bodies of her companions, the young man and the Khronostians – who were looking at her, wide-eyed through their bandages.

Kait's fireballs hung in the air, creeping forward like snails, leaving sleek golden trails behind them. Her face was caught in a snarl of concentration, an expression slowly easing its way to anticipation. It was the strangest thing Kyndra had ever seen. And it took her a moment longer to realize that she was unaffected by it.

The same realization must have disrupted their focus, for time suddenly sped up and the Khronostians had half a second to hurl themselves and the young man aside. The fireballs roared over their heads and exploded harmlessly.

'You stand outside time,' one of the Khronostians said to Kyndra. The tumble had loosened the wrappings about its face and, as the figure climbed to its feet, they fell away to reveal a woman . . . or at least what Kyndra thought was a woman, for the Khronostian's skin hung in papery folds over one cheek, as if hundreds of years old. The other cheek was smooth and young, the skin the colour of new parchment, and the eyes were different again: one narrow, clouded with age, the other a bright green.

Irilin's gasp was audible. It was a dreadful sight, this grotesque jigsaw of a face.

'How?' Kyndra found herself asking. 'How did you come to look like that?'

The woman tried to hook the bandages back into place, but only succeeded in covering one cheek. When she spoke, her voice was harsh. 'We are *du-alakat*. It is the price we willingly pay for our power.'

One of the Khronostians hauled the young man to his feet

and Kyndra saw the stranger wincing. 'Don't, Aru,' the Khronos-tian said. 'They are not deserving of your words.'

'I wish to know what she is,' Aru replied, looking at Kyndra.

'*What* she is?' the stranger repeated, his dark face creased in a frown.

'She is Starborn,' Medavle said, stepping forward to stand at Kyndra's shoulder. The Khronostians drew in hissing breaths and the young man gazed at her with a mixture of horror and dread. Kyndra made herself look away from him, but her heart was pounding. Would it always be like this, she wondered? Would people judge her before they even got to know her?

'*You* are responsible for the lost continent's return,' the woman called Aru said and Kyndra nodded, not trusting to her voice. The young man was a stranger; why did she care what he thought?

She took a step forward. 'Let him go,' she said, 'and I won't harm you.' There seemed something very wrong about letting the Khronostians take him away.

The greyscale world returned without warning. This time, Kyndra saw how the Khronostians were doing it. There was a web of energy about each of them, which they fed with strands of light from their fingers, so that it grew ever more complex.

Although her companions were moving at half their normal speed, she found she could walk easily through the greyness. She seized the throats of the Khronostians who held the young man; their eyes went round and both their webs broke, fraying as colour rushed back into the space around them.

Kyndra threw them with the strength of *Tyr*. They landed badly some feet away and one cried out. Forgetting the young man, who was swiftly snatching his sticks off the ground, the Khronostian woman rushed to her companions, dropping to her knees. The one remaining backed away from Kyndra. It turned its bandaged face towards the other Khronostians and then called out, 'We will return, Kala, with the full force of the *dualakat*. You cannot hide behind the Starborn forever.'

The landscape seemed to bend around them, distorting the air. When it sprang back into shape, all four had vanished. Blood flecked the rock where the Khronostians she'd thrown had fallen.

Kyndra stared at the glowing tattoo on her palm and her shock was such that it ripped the star from her grasp. She couldn't even remember deciding to use *Tyr*. Struck with the horror of that thought, she watched her tattoo darken and didn't see the blow coming until it was too late.

Fortunately, Nediah did; Kyndra felt a shower of sparks and the young man's banded weapon glanced off the shield that protected her skull to smash her shoulder instead. Pain exploded and she staggered back. The young man made to run, but an invisible force knocked him down and golden chains bound his wrists and ankles. He let out a stream of curses.

Kyndra put a hand on her shoulder and uttered a few choice words herself. 'I should have let them take you,' she said.

'Why didn't you?'

She turned her back on him and walked painfully over to the others. 'What do we do with him?' Kait asked. She nudged Nediah, who was looking at the stranger with dislike. 'And after you went to all that trouble to heal him.'

'Did I ask you to?' the young man interjected from behind. Kyndra could hear him struggling vainly against whatever binding Kait had used.

'You would be dead if not for Nediah,' the woman told him. 'Ungrateful bastard.'

'Here,' Nediah said, beckoning to Kyndra. He placed a hand on her shoulder and almost immediately the pain eased. 'Cracked the bone,' the Wielder murmured with a surprised glance at the stranger's innocuous-looking sticks. Kyndra felt a hot shock in the wound and then Nediah took his hand away and she rolled the shoulder experimentally. It clicked in protest before settling down.

'Thanks, Nediah.'

The Wielder smiled at her. 'Healing you is a breeze.'

For the first time, it seemed, the young man looked at the faint scar on his arm that yesterday had been a festering gash and Kyndra heard him mutter something.

'I think that's the best you're going to get,' Kait told Nediah drily.

Forcing down the trepidation she felt on facing the stranger, Kyndra returned to stand over him. 'What's your name?'

For a moment she was convinced he wouldn't answer, but then he said, 'You might as well call me Char. Everyone else does.'

She frowned. 'Why would they call you that?'

'Why do you think?' The indignity of his forced sprawl on the ground was obviously getting to him.

'Let him up,' she said to Kait.

The woman raised an eyebrow. 'You sure?'

'There's more than enough of us to handle him.'

The young man said nothing as he climbed to his feet, except to glare at them venomously.

'What makes those Khronostians think you're their leader?' Kyndra asked him. 'Why is this Kala so important?'

'Why should you care?'

'Because saving you has likely made us their enemy,' Medavle said with a hard glance at Kyndra. She hadn't seen him so animated since the morning he'd confronted Kierik and Anohin. She frowned. Why was he so concerned about Khronosta?

'We couldn't just let them take him away,' she said.

Char rubbed a dusty hand over his forehead. 'I don't know why they think as they do,' he said, but a flicker in his face told Kyndra he was hiding something. 'The Kala is supposedly their leader Khronos reincarnated.'

Kyndra raised an eyebrow. 'Please don't say you actually *are*.'

He gave her a contemptuous look.

'The Khronostians seemed quite convinced,' she said.

'They're mad. You saw what they hide under all those bandages.'

Kyndra sighed. It was barely morning and she was already tired. 'Where did you come from? We found you on the edge of the desert. Some dog-things dragged you there, but they ran off when they saw us.'

For the first time, Char looked uncertain. 'Dog-things? You mean mysha? That's impossible. Mysha are carnivores – they hunt humans.'

But you're not human. Kyndra swallowed her first response. 'Well, maybe they weren't hungry.'

'I remember . . . I remember the pack looking down at me in the moonlight. Then nothing before I woke up here.' Char clenched his fists. 'It doesn't make sense.'

'Who's Ma?' Kyndra asked and then wished she hadn't; his look was a snarl.

'Don't you speak of her,' he spat.

She held up her hands. 'All right.'

'It's not the first time you've encountered these Khronostians,' Medavle said. His hand rested on the flute that hung at his waist. 'What can you tell us about them?'

'They control time. You saw, didn't you?'

The Yadin shook his head. 'I don't know what I saw. I've never encountered anything like it.'

'That Khronostian said you restored the lost continent,' Char said then, his yellow eyes travelling from face to face. 'Is it true?'

When Kyndra nodded, he seemed to take it in his stride and again she thought how differently Acre and Rairam regarded each other. She remembered Magda saying that Rairam had never been a myth, that its disappearance was an accepted part of Acrean history. That attitude put the powers in Acre at a distinct advantage, she thought uneasily. Unlike Rairam, no one here needed convincing that there was another land beyond their borders. *Or* that it was full of a power they would call magic.

She considered the young man called Char. He stood tensely, as if on the brink of exploding into action. 'Bind his wrists,' she said to Kait. 'He's coming with us.'

21

Causca, Acre
Medavle

'Meda,' she says and his name is a caress when she speaks it. 'Your face is always so serious.'

He looks at her white form, clad in the same robes he wears. He looks at her golden hair spilling like silk over her shoulders and finds that he cannot answer.

'What's the matter?' she asks and the catch in his throat finally loosens.

'Nothing,' he says, aware that his fingers are twitching at his sides – they long to run through her hair, to tilt her chin up, to trace the bud of her lips. He keeps them still with an effort. There were always eyes watching. 'I was thinking about us.' He blushes. 'I mean, all the Yadin too.'

A tiny frown creases her brow and he almost raises a hand to smooth it away. 'What about us?'

'I was thinking about our purpose,' he explains, unable to take his eyes from hers. How was it possible for anyone to own such eyes? They were the colour of ocean and sky and the mirrored *sunny surface of a forest pool. 'I was thinking that we could be so much more than we are.'*

'More?' She half smiles. 'We live in this beautiful place, surrounded by the light of brilliant minds. I am content to be with our people and to love our masters.'

Perhaps she sees how her words pain him, for she raises a daring hand to his face. He shudders under her touch and closes his eyes; the heat of her hand awakens the desire he works so hard to tamp down.

'What would you say if they were not listening, Isla?' he asks her. 'If we were alone?'

Her face hardens. 'This is forbidden,' she whispers, 'traitorous. We must be careful.'

'Is it traitorous to want a world where we can love one another freely? Where I can take you in my arms and nobody will stop me?'

She holds his gaze, almost sombre now. 'Where we may live as the Wielders do, serving only ourselves.'

'Yes. To be free to love whom we want. Live how we want . . .' They have drawn closer to one another, the better to whisper their dangerous ideals. He can smell her skin, fragrant with herbs. The temptation to give in is overwhelming, but he cannot. If the Wielders were to see them –

He pulls her out of the atrium into a corridor, a quiet passage whose marbled floor might give fair warning of approaching feet. He presses her against the pale wall, cups her face. His hand looks rough and dark against her cheek. His heart is pounding and he can hear her quick breaths, as they gaze at each other, closer than they've ever been.

And despite the danger, despite the Wielders, he finds himself kissing her, passionately, fiercely. Her lips are firm and soft. When they open beneath his, a rush of heat fills him, making his knees tremble, and he draws back. 'I have no control around you,' he breathes. 'I'm sorry.'

'Don't be,' she says, pushing dark hair away from his face. 'Kiss me again.'

But he can't — they can hear someone approaching. They spring apart just as the Wielder rounds the corner. The man regards them disapprovingly. 'What are you doing here, servants? Don't you have tasks to perform?'

A last glance as they move off in opposite directions. He goes with the hot memory of her body against his and with a simmering rage at the world — at the Wielders he is supposed to love and respect for giving him life.

A moment of vertigo, and Medavle lunged at the reins of his horse before he slid out of the saddle. He steadied himself with a curse. What was he doing, dozing on horseback like a child? He didn't remember closing his eyes.

She's dead, not even a ghost.

But now that Kierik was gone and everything he'd worked for achieved, Isla was always with him, as if she'd returned to share his flesh. Had she really been so perfect? he forced himself to ask. Had her eyes truly been the colour of water and sky and her hair like silk? He didn't know and that pained him more than the memories which kept him constant company.

Medavle shook his head and urged his horse into a trot until he drew alongside Kyndra's stallion. The young man who called himself Char was perched on the big horse, wrists tied, as far from Kyndra as he could get without falling off. It reminded Medavle of how he'd felt at seeing the terrible, flaming figure Kyndra had been at the Defiant base and, partly to his shame, the memory awoke the same feelings of disgust he'd had for Kierik. It wasn't fair, of course, especially since he'd been directly responsible for Kyndra's birth, but prejudices ran deep and Medavle knew better than anyone not to trust a Starborn.

'You come from the Beaches,' he said, hoping to stir Char into conversation.

The young man grunted. He wore a pair of black lenses he'd had hidden somewhere on his person and Medavle found it slightly disconcerting not to see his eyes. 'How long have you been a slaver?'

'Forever,' Char said shortly.

'I thought slavery was outlawed in the empire.'

'It is.'

'Then why—'

'Because we're small fry and no threat compared to Khronosta.'

Medavle studied him closely. 'Exactly what kind of threat does Khronosta pose?'

'You're not going to stop, are you?'

'We've little else to do while we ride.' Medavle nodded at the Solar cuffs that bound Char's wrists together. 'And it's not as if you're going anywhere.'

'Fine,' Char said irritably. 'Khronosta is the one faction Sartya has not been able to crush or control.'

'What about the Defiant?'

The slaver snorted. 'The rebels? They've no real power in Acre. Oh, they have sympathizers, certainly. But I doubt they could challenge the Fist.'

'What does the emperor fear Khronosta can do?' Medavle asked, unable to hide his interest in the question.

Char regarded him narrowly. 'No one's seen the extent of

their power. I didn't even know what they could do until recently. But time itself . . .' His gaze turned inward. 'They can time travel, but Ma said they need an anchor – one of their number has had to have lived during the era they intend to visit. She said she didn't think they could directly affect the past.' He paused. 'But what if they could? What if *that*'s why they want the Kala? They told me before that he's supposed to possess huge power – that he was going to lead them to victory against Sartya. Maybe they could rewrite history.'

An ember, long cold, flared to life inside Medavle. 'What would the Khronostians rewrite?'

'They'd probably do something to undermine Sartya, wouldn't they?' Char said. 'If they could weaken the empire in the past, the present would be different. They wouldn't have to keep running and hiding from the Fist.'

Medavle kept his face blank, as his mind roiled with possibilities. The Khronostians could slow time – as mad as that sounded, he'd witnessed it – but to reverse it? That went against every law in the cosmos.

'What can you tell us about Cymenza?' Kyndra asked abruptly. 'We need to pick up supplies there.'

'If you're angling for ken, I don't have any,' Char said. 'I left Na Sung Aro in a hurry.'

'Ken?'

'Stones, money, whatever you like.'

'We have our own gold, thank you.'

Char barked a laugh. 'Gold? Are you serious?'

'Surely someone would be willing to change our coins for yours—' Kyndra began.

'No they wouldn't,' Char said. 'Gold is as common as mule

shit. We use ken for currency – small precious stones of different colours.'

Kyndra stiffened in her saddle and twisted round to look at him. 'You're saying our gold is worthless?'

'Worthless?' Char smiled. 'Not entirely – it makes nice jewellery.'

'It won't buy us food?'

'You could try trading your coins as curiosities. Some might take them as payment.'

'I can't believe we didn't think of this,' Kyndra muttered. She shot a sidelong look at Medavle. 'You never mentioned it.'

'I didn't know.' And he hadn't. Gold had been the common currency in his time. Something huge must have happened to force Acre's economy to abandon it.

'I'm not a historian,' Char said when Medavle asked him whether he knew. 'It's always been ken.'

'Don't you have any questions about us?' Kyndra said, her gaze fixed on the scuffed, dusty trail ahead of them.

'I'm your prisoner.' Char hefted his Solar-bound wrists, which left him just enough room to hold on to the back of Kyndra's saddle. His weapons were stashed in Nediah's pack. 'That's all I need to know.'

'Does it make a difference, you being the one in chains, slaver?' Irilin asked bitterly.

Char pressed his lips together, said nothing.

'Slavery is evil,' Irilin continued. 'Chaining people up, trading their freedom for profit—'

'Freedom is an –' Char stopped, swallowing the rest of whatever he was going to say. There was a distance in his dark face.

'Freedom is not *yours* to take,' Irilin said.

Char twisted around to look at her. 'You know nothing of my

life, nothing of me, or what I've seen. And so I don't give a damn what you think.'

'You are not our prisoner,' Medavle said in an attempt to smooth things over, 'but you attacked Kyndra. Until you prove yourself a friend, the manacles stay on.'

'You wouldn't have done?' Char demanded. 'I had no idea what you were going to do to me.' He wavered. 'I still don't.'

'You could start by showing some gratitude,' Kait said acerbically. 'We saved your life *and* kept the Khronostians from taking you.'

Char was silent. 'Why don't you just let me go, then?' he said finally.

'What would you do?' Medavle asked him. 'You have no food and no supplies. You stand little chance of evading the Khronostians on your own.'

Char's lips thinned and Medavle knew the young man agreed, even if he didn't like it. 'What did they mean by the full force of the *du-alakat*?' he asked, remembering the Khronostians' parting threat. 'Are there many more?'

'The *du-alakat* are the assassin-warriors of Khronosta,' Char said sourly. Perhaps he was remembering how easily they'd overpowered him. 'And yes, I expect there are a whole lot more.'

Medavle smiled to himself. If Kyndra had done one thing by rescuing Char, it was to ensure another meeting with Khronosta. As long as they had the young man, the Khronostians would come to them.

He caught a pale flash and turned his head. There she was, not a hundred paces away, standing on a rock, her robes impervious to the hot wind that blew dust into his eyes. He blinked and Isla was gone, a mirage of his yearning. Medavle swallowed and looked away. Yes, the Khronostians would come for Char, as long as they believed him their leader reborn. The cogs of his mind began to turn. If what Char said about their ability to time travel was true, they needed someone to serve as anchor. What might the Khronostians do with a man who'd lived through the war, who had witnessed the rise of the empire and the fall of Solinaris?

The ember in his stomach became a spark, a spark that he'd thought Kierik's death had extinguished: *hope*.

22

Causca, Acre
Char

At least they'd removed his manacles. The golden bands had weakened as the day waned until they'd faded altogether. So this was what an aberration's power looked like. Char remembered how the Khronostian had dismissed it, mocking its reliance on the cycles of sun and moon. He wasn't ready to share that attitude just yet. These Wielders – as they called themselves – were dangerous opponents. He remembered the fireballs thrown by the tall woman; he remembered the stench of them like superheated metal. Had the Khronostian not pulled him aside, he'd be a charred husk now, and then he'd truly resemble his name. The thought brought an ironic smile to his lips.

They had made camp in the first grove of trees they'd come across, which meant they had finally reached the edge of the blasted waste that was Baior. Char knew they were now entering a region called Causca, home of the Raucus Cities. Except the Raucus Cities weren't actually there any more, not in the way they had been. Unlike Cymenza, they were shadows of their former selves, their famed towers torn down by Sartyan artillery. Cymenza had witnessed the fall of its siblings and surrendered before that same artillery toppled its own walls. Because of that, the old city was still standing, one of the only relics of pre-Sartyan Acre. Char had never seen it.

A pathetic stream dribbled through the grove, but it was enough to slake their thirst and refill skins of water. Char sipped from one, trying to put his thoughts in order. The Wielders from Rairam had saved him twice over and he resented being in anyone's debt.

Then there was the Starborn. Char grimaced at all the questions he was too proud to ask. Rairam and Starborn seemed to go hand in hand; it shouldn't surprise him that one had returned with the other. But why had she done it? The last Starborn had saved Rairam from the empire while the rest of Acre fell to Sartyan rule. What if the Davaratch began the conquest anew? Char remembered the wind he'd felt in Na Sung Aro, the wind from the east, the wind of Rairam. He had a sudden desire to see the lost continent for himself, remembering the scent of its mountains and forests. Maybe he would ask the Wielders some questions after all.

'Why do you hate Starborn?'

It was *her*, come to stand beside him on the edge of the grove. Char thought he could see the glimmering curve of the desert far to the south. Where was Ma? Would he ever see her again? At least now he knew she'd escaped from the Khronostians in 'Aro. 'I didn't want company,' he said flatly.

'I saw your expression when you looked at me earlier,' she continued, as if he hadn't spoken. 'You were horrified.'

'I know the stories. The last Starborn to walk Acre had the power to rend stone, to call fire from the deepest parts of the earth. He was like lightning in battle, walked into a fully manned Sartyan garrison and slaughtered them all with his bare hands.' He paused. 'The Sartyans did some bad things, but Kierik did worse. Starborn aren't human.'

Something he said raised a bitter smile from her, but she didn't go away. 'It's strange to hear his name spoken so openly,' she remarked. Char returned his eyes to the distant silver sands. He felt a rumble in his chest – the familiar uncoiling of the rage as it woke – and he took a deep breath. Not now.

'I don't want this power,' she said finally.

The declaration surprised him. 'Why not?'

'Because it's changing me.'

'You are what you are,' he said. 'And even if *you* don't want to use your power, there are others who would. If you let them, they'll make the decision for you.' Why was he talking to her? He wanted to be alone, needed to concentrate on not submitting to the force that only his skin was keeping in. 'You don't belong here,' he said harshly, turning away. 'You know nothing about this world.'

She was silent again and he thought his words had angered her – she seemed to be struggling with herself. 'Then show me what I don't know,' she said.

It was such an unexpected answer that he looked at her again. She had pushed back her hood and the moon brought out the glowing points of light on one of her cheeks. Other marks pulsed in her skin too, but none as bright. She was holding her hands rather stiffly at her sides and there was a stillness about her that he found both alien and appealing, perhaps because he was never still. The rage roiled and raved inside him so that he trembled slightly with the effort of holding it in. Tonight it felt like wind and fire and it wailed, as if desperate to escape the prison of his bones. He drew in a ragged breath and tightened his hold, but it always grew more difficult.

'What's the matter?'

He had no concentration spare to reply and he closed his eyes before she noticed the flames in them. And then there was a cool touch on his arm – no, a cold touch, so cold it was almost painful. Under her fingers, the force that flayed his insides subsided. Shocked, he opened his eyes, already feeling the rage dwindle, and he drew a few breaths, remembering Ma's lessons on finding the calm centre in which all great warriors fought.

'How did you do that?' he said without thinking.

She took her hand away, but the rage stayed curled up inside him, compliant now. 'I didn't do anything,' she said. 'I thought you were ill.' Her face flickered. 'But I felt something. You were fighting it.' The capricious moonlight showed him a flush in her cheeks.

'I don't know what you mean,' Char lied quickly, unwilling to discuss the rage and what he feared it could do. He dropped his eyes, staring at the sparse growth that carpeted the grove. He found the place disconcerting. The only trees in the desert belonged to the small, widely spaced oases that disturbed the dunes of the Beaches.

When he glanced up again, she seemed to be on the verge of saying something – her expression was like a decision half-made. Then she sighed. 'What's Cymenza like?'

'I don't know,' he said, grateful for the change in subject. 'I've never been there.'

'Anything at all?'

'It's the capital of the Raucus Cities,' he offered. 'Rich.'

She raised a hand to her forehead. 'That reminds me. This

gold problem could be the end of everything I'm trying to do. Without the possibility of trade . . .' She looked at him squarely. 'If I ask you a question, will you answer honestly?'

He shrugged. 'Depends on the question.'

'I came to Acre to forge alliances,' she said. 'I hoped we could forget the past, leave the war behind, but now that seems naive after everything we've been through. Do you believe the empire would ever agree to a truce with Rairam?'

Char was about to scoff at the idea, but he hesitated. Was it so outlandish? Khronosta was gaining in power; rumours spread of assassinations in the upper echelons of the emperor's court. Those same rumours attributed the killings to the *du-alakat*. Compared to Khronosta, the Defiant weren't a threat, but their reach *was* growing – Char had seen their propaganda in the streets of Na Sung Aro.

And then there was the ambertrix. The empire hadn't been able to hide its decline – it was too much a part of Sartyan infrastructure. No, he couldn't deny it. Sartya did not need another enemy, especially not one as potentially powerful as Rairam.

The Starborn saw his hesitation and some of the tension left her face. 'You *do* think it's possible, then?'

'Possible, not probable,' Char said. 'Conquest is in the empire's blood. But Sartya is weaker now than it's ever been. Territories it's held for hundreds of years are slipping back into old ways. Slavery in the Beaches is a case in point. And I've heard that the Lotys Jungle's been reclaimed by the natives.' He paused. 'That was a blow. Sartya's always monopolized the lotys trade.'

'Lotys trade?'

'Drugs,' he said bluntly. 'What do you have to offer the emperor to seal this truce?'

'Right now?' she said. 'Little except the goodwill of a Starborn.'

Char smiled wryly. 'I'd say that counts for a lot actually.'

'Does it?' She glanced over her shoulder at her companions. 'I'm no leader,' she confessed, turning back to him. I'm an innkeeper's daughter first and a Starborn second. My great plan was to come to Acre and scout out the lie of the land.' Her tone turned bitter. 'Well, I've done that, but instead of peace, all I've achieved is more killing.' She paused. 'I . . . I lost a friend in the red valley. It was my fault he died. Then the people in the first village we reached handed us straight to the Sartyans. The Defiant rescued us, but wanted to make us part of their rebellion. One of them shot General Hagdon before I really got a chance to speak to him properly. I don't know if he survived. Now Khronosta is going to hunt us down because of you.' She shook her head. 'It couldn't be worse.'

Char realized his mouth was slightly open. 'General Hagdon?' he repeated. 'As in *the* Hagdon of Sartyan Fist fame?'

She nodded miserably.

'Gods,' he muttered. 'And he might be dead. How did you get away?'

Her face closed up at the question. 'I . . . I'd rather not talk about it.' He noticed she looked down at her palms as she spoke, as if to trace the patterns emblazoned there.

'Sorry about your friend,' Char said a moment later.

She just nodded.

'So you're going to the Heartland?' he asked. *And thinking to take me along.*

'That was the plan. But I'm not sure it's a good one any more.'

It was his and Ma's destination, the place where, ironically, she thought they'd be safest. Now that he knew it was the Khronostians she feared, he realized why she'd chosen it: the power base of Sartya where Khronosta's reach was weakest. Was that where she'd go? Even now they were separated? Char didn't have any other leads.

He looked at the Starborn. Her name, he recalled, was Kyndra. 'All right,' he said. 'If you can keep the Khronostians off me, I think I'll stick with you.' Whatever mad road he followed now, it wasn't the slaver's and for that Char was thankful.

23

Brégenne was out of luck.

In a temper, she threw down her cards and tossed a handful of coins across the deck with enough force to make Yara yelp. The first mate scrambled around, picking up the rolling coins and stuffing them into a pouch at her belt. When she was done, she returned to smirk at Brégenne. 'No one likes a sore loser.'

'I *could* burn you to cinder,' Brégenne replied with a flicker of her fingers.

'Except you can't.' Yara glanced at the sky. 'I've a few minutes to hide before sunset. I'll come out in the morning.'

Brégenne smiled. The days she'd spent on the airship had done more to cement Wielder relations with the outside world than Naris had achieved in centuries. *Argat's airship is hardly the outside world*, she reminded herself. But it was a start. She had high hopes that one day Wielders would be as usual a sight in Mariar as the sun in the sky.

'Another game?' Yara asked, shuffling the cards. She wore a short coat this afternoon over her cut-off trousers, though her

312

feet were still bare and as grubby as usual. Flying north was a little like going forward in time. Where the southlands were still bathed in the sunny skies of late summer, here autumn's colourful decay had already set in and the country beneath the *Eastern Set*'s hull was a patchwork of fire, all yellows and reds.

Brégenne was about to accept when a flash caught her eye. She stood up, looking west, and saw it again: a golden streak swooping out of the light. Her stomach clenched; it was an envoi, racing the sun, which was fast sinking behind the mountains on their left. Yara stood and then had to duck with a curse as the bird narrowly missed her head. Brégenne held up her wrist and the envoi landed.

She sensed Nediah's signature in the Solar energy and there was another beside it, adding to the power of the envoi. But they were both still Solar. As the sun fell beyond the horizon, the words racing across her palm came to a sudden halt midsentence. Brégenne swore.

'What in the name of all things sacred was *that*?'

'A message,' Brégenne said, feverishly scanning the words before they faded. It seemed her run of bad luck wasn't just manifesting in the cards. The envoi had reached her at the worst possible time. A few moments earlier and she'd have had the whole message. A few moments later and the envoi would have dissolved, reformed with the dawn and delivered the message in full. Now it was lost.

'Who was it from?' Yara asked.

'You remember my companions – Nediah and Kyndra.'

Yara's lips quirked. 'Yes, of course. Nice-looking man, very gullible. And the young lady – captain liked her a lot.'

Brégenne frowned. 'The last time Argat saw her, he tried to

kill her. And me,' she added. 'I seem to remember you were involved.'

'Ah.' Yara bared her teeth. 'That's just our way of showing affection.'

'I'll take your word for it.' Brégenne shook her head and walked to the western rail. The mountains that had been the Infinite Hills now resembled foothills of rubble that stretched as far as the eye could see. It was lucky no settlements had been built in their shadow, lucky that they had spilled their bones across a nameless Acrean plain. Or perhaps it wasn't luck, but Kyndra. She had never told Brégenne exactly how she'd destroyed the last of Kierik's power, but the force that had torn down mountains seemed equally capable of protecting Mariar from the resulting backlash. Brégenne remembered a rumour she'd heard on the road to Market Primus, of a monstrous wave that would have swept the archipelago and the Eversea Isles into oblivion. It had vanished moments before it struck, prompting most to dismiss the tale as a drunken fisherman's dream.

Ironic, Brégenne thought, as she stared at the crumbled mountains. They were almost as much of a barrier in their fallen state as they had been in their original. She couldn't imagine an army attempting to cross those hellish ruins.

'Brégenne,' Yara said and she realized she was standing frozen, her hands clenched like vices on the ship's rail. 'What did the message say?'

'They've run into their fair share of trouble – captured by Sartyans, rescued by a rebel group, some of whom might be Wielders.' That gave her pause. To think the ability had survived in Acre . . . it could mean a whole new purpose for Naris, a purpose they'd lacked since the war. They could rebuild the citadel in a world from which they didn't have to hide.

'The Sartyan army caught up to them,' she continued, 'but not before they'd helped the rebels escape. Kyndra tried to reason with the general . . . that's where the message cut off.' She clenched her fists in frustration. 'I saw something more about the red valley and maybe a name – Cymenza? I don't know. The envoi couldn't have delivered the message at a worse time. It was constructed from Solar energy and can only function during the day. Once it finds its recipient, the power is spent.'

Brégenne realized she was speaking very quickly and she made herself stop. Yara had her head tilted on one side and was giving her an appraising look. 'You don't seem happy about something,' she said.

'Of course I'm not happy,' Brégenne snapped. 'It sounds as if they're lucky to be alive.' But that wasn't it and she hated that it wasn't. She could feel a flush in her cheeks. Why hadn't Nediah sent his own envoi? Surely it hadn't really been necessary for Kait to add her power too.

'You miss him,' Yara said. Brégenne looked at her in surprise and the first mate gave an unapologetic shrug. 'And there's someone with him, isn't there? Someone close to him, someone who isn't you.'

Brégenne narrowed her eyes. 'Why do you think that?'

'I know jealousy when I see it.'

She looked away, embarrassed and angry all at once. Was she so easy to read? All those years she'd spent schooling her expression to stillness, striving for serenity, for control. *That wasn't real*, she told herself. *And look where it got you.* Enclosed in that supposedly strong, uncaring shell, she hadn't been able to hear her own heart, not until it was too late.

'I'd tell you it isn't worth it,' Yara said to the wind as it rushed by their faces. 'But sometimes, perhaps it is. Then you shelve your pride and you fight.'

'I thought my pride was all I had,' Brégenne said so softly she hoped the ship and the sky would carry the words away.

But Yara heard them. 'And you found you were wrong.' She gave a crooked smile. 'Life is a hard mistress, Brégenne. We live her all the same.'

The next morning, as they approached the borders of the Great Northern Forest, Gareth began to wear his trepidation like a cloak. They could go no further; there was no guarantee they'd find a clearing to land in and holding the airship steady in the air while Brégenne and Gareth disembarked required a skill Yara wasn't sure she possessed. Brégenne kept a close eye on the young man – anxiety at returning home wasn't wholly responsible for his pallid face and diminished weight. The gauntlet was taking a toll on his health. What it was doing to his mind, she didn't like to guess.

Now Brégenne stood on deck, staring out at the inexhaustible bank of trees. This was as far north as she'd ever been and the map Argat had provided left a lot to be desired. No one had successfully charted the forest – explorers had an unfortunate habit of disappearing. Gareth's memories were a child's; he had only a vague knowledge of Ümvast's location. Their best bet was to head due north until they found a path. It wasn't much to go on.

'Do you have everything you need?' Yara asked, nudging one of the two packs with her toe.

'Probably not,' Brégenne admitted, 'but we'll manage. I wish we had our horses, though.'

'They are no loss.' Yara gestured at the forest. 'The trees are thick and the paths narrow. You will do better on foot.'

Brégenne nodded. She had come to trust the first mate's judgement and, with an unexpected pang, realized that she would miss her. She reached out and grasped Yara's hand. 'Thank you,' she said. 'Hopefully, it won't be too long before we meet again.'

Yara grinned and tossed her black braided hair over her shoulder. 'Look after yourself, Brégenne. You haven't lost nearly enough gold to me.'

'Ready her to land!' Argat called and Brégenne remembered that he'd never grounded the ship before. Yara gave her a wave and returned to her post in the boiler room. Brégenne's stomach clenched as the *Eastern Set* trembled and lost height and she wondered whether they would miss the grassy plain entirely and crash into the trees. But then the airship's descent slowed and began to level out. 'Grab on to something!' she heard Argat yell and she lunged for the rail just before the hull began to skim and bounce along the ground, almost jerking her hands free. The braziers had been doused, leaving the balloons hanging slack and the paddles at the ship's rear had dropped to a leisurely spin.

As they slid to a stop, Gareth emerged from the deckhouse, faintly green. 'I think I'm going to be sick,' he muttered, palm clamped over his mouth.

But Argat's eyes were shining. 'Did you see that?' he cried, dashing up to them. 'I knew she could do it.' He patted his ship affectionately. 'We're a team, her and me.'

317

'It's nice to be appreciated,' Yara said drily, as she emerged from below, wiping greasy hands on her trousers.

Argat clapped her on the shoulder. 'Your skill goes without saying.'

'My *skill* likes to be acknowledged, Argat.'

'I hope you can get the ship aloft again,' Brégenne said, eyeing the shrunken balloons.

Yara waved a hand. 'Don't doubt it for a second.'

Gareth had turned his gaze to the wall of trees ahead of them. The forest looked far more imposing from ground level. The open plain rolled right up to it and stopped like sea at the tideline. There was no overlap – between one step and the next, grass ended and trees began. 'Are you ready?' Brégenne asked him and Gareth nodded.

'Well,' Argat said, 'I've fulfilled my end of the bargain, woman. Now it's your turn.'

'If you're planning to scout out the borders of Acre – I know you, Argat – you need to be careful. The Sartyans have weapons that can knock your ship out of the sky.'

'They can try,' the captain said with his usual bravado, 'but my thanks for the warning.'

Brégenne sighed, scooped up her pack and shrugged into it, watching Gareth do the same. 'Remember, boy,' Argat said, 'should you find the gauntlet's partner—'

'They're yours,' Gareth muttered. He seemed cowed by the proximity of the forest.

'We have that settled,' Argat said. 'Should you have need of me or my ship, send word.' His leather coat flapped in the chill north wind and Brégenne was glad of the furred cloak secured on top of her pack. She had a feeling she'd need it before long.

'Fair skies,' Argat said as Brégenne and Gareth traversed the gangway his crew had lodged against the grass. 'Bring me back a tale or two, won't you?'

They stood on the dark lip of the forest watching the balloons reinflate and the paddles begin to turn. The *Eastern Set* lifted slowly from the ground, grass and mud clinging to her belly, leaving long grooves in the earth behind her.

Brégenne and Gareth watched the airship until it dwindled to a grey smudge and then they turned to face the forest, its reaches as strange and unknowable as Acre itself. Gareth's face was stony, but he squared his shoulders and took the first step and Brégenne followed on his heels. Trees swallowed them, the day dimming to false twilight beneath the canopy. The greenish air smelled strongly of earth and must.

'It will be hard to navigate in here,' she said with a glance at the thick net of leaves and branches overhead. 'We had better find a path and stick to it.'

'I know there's one leading north out of Svartas,' Gareth said, 'but we're far to the west of it. We'll have to cut our way through until we find another.'

They quickly discovered that was easier said than done. Although Gareth had his sword and Argat had lent them another, it was hot, hard work and Brégenne had to admit she didn't have the muscles for it. After several hours of cutting and sawing, pulling and cursing, they had covered less than a quarter-league and blunted their blades. At this rate, it would be midwinter before they reached even the outskirts of Ümvast's territory.

Gareth was sweating. 'Can't we do this the easy way?' he said as they leaned against a knot of trunks. 'We're getting nowhere.'

'Forest fires can quickly get out of control,' Brégenne said. They'd already had this conversation. 'And are you so keen to advertise our presence?'

Gareth dragged a sleeve across his forehead and then he slowly lowered his arm, staring at it. 'There might be another way,' he murmured.

'No,' Brégenne said sharply, seeing what he intended. 'Remember what happened before.'

'I remember,' Gareth said and there was an echo of fear in his eyes. 'But we can't continue like this, Brégenne.' He looked away. 'I don't know how much time I have.'

'Use the Solar, then,' she said, placing a hand on his shoulder. 'We'll be careful.'

Gareth shook his head. 'The smoke would give us away – you're right. And it's not only my people we have to worry about. This forest is home to things that wouldn't hesitate to attack us. Tree-cats and bears, snakes – wolves up near the Rib Wall. I know we're not defenceless, but this is their ground, not ours. We're at a disadvantage.'

He was right, but she didn't like the idea of using the gauntlet, not after seeing what it had done to Magnus. Gareth had looked ill for days. He *still* looked ill. 'It might not work,' the novice admitted. 'I acted out of instinct in that fight with the Wielders.'

'Can you control it, though?' Brégenne asked. 'Every time you've used it, it's surprised you. And I was watching you, Gareth. You didn't look like yourself.'

A shadow passed across his face, adding to those already gathered there. He swallowed. 'I know,' he said softly. 'But something changed that day. I've been able to . . . to feel the gauntlet in a way I couldn't before. Like it's not just a piece of armour any more.'

She frowned, disturbed. 'What do you mean?'

Gareth looked from his arm to her eyes. 'It has a will.'

'No,' Brégenne said. 'Gareth, you don't know what you're doing. If there's even a grain of truth to Argat's story, that thing is unbalanced. It's incomplete. Without the other one—'

'I don't need the other one. Not right now. Not for this.'

Brégenne looked at the resolute set of his face and realized that there was little she could say to dissuade him. Gareth took off his glove, turning to regard the tangle of branches blocking their path. He stretched out his hand and gripped one. Brégenne tensed, but nothing happened. Wrinkles spread down Gareth's brow as he frowned at the trees. After a minute or so, he sighed, lowering his arm. 'It's no good —'

Gareth stiffened, his body going rigid. Brégenne reached for him, but stopped abruptly, horrified by the black film covering his eyes. She took a step back. 'Gareth?' Oily shadows seemed to climb out of his skin, surrounding him in a miasma of dust and death. Gareth lifted his right arm, splayed his fingers and the branches in front of him shrank, withering to dead winter twigs. When he stepped forward, they crumbled and the grassy floor on which he trod turned brown, the fronds of ferns curling away from his boots. He began to walk, pushing his way through easily, leaving death in every footprint.

Brégenne followed at a distance, trying hard to control her fear. *It's Gareth*, she reminded herself, *he wouldn't hurt me*. But he wasn't *just* Gareth. There was something else within him – a will contained in the gauntlet that was coming close to consuming him. What was this power? So different from Solar and Lunar energy, it negated rather than added or changed. As if the inevitability of death, of ending, could be harnessed into a force.

Gareth stopped – they'd broken through to a surprisingly wide path which seemed to lead north-west. Under the heavy forest shade, the novice seemed larger. His shoulders bore a suggestion of massive, spiked armour and the same shadowy substance covered his head in a dark helm. When he turned, she let out an involuntary gasp. The shadows on his cheeks had bled together to form a faceguard, cruel-lipped and cold as a winter lake. The eyes that looked out at her were bottomless pits and, as she stared into them, a caul of hopelessness smothered her. She opened her mouth, but no words came out.

For just a moment, a gust of wind parted the canopy, allowing a brief ray of late-afternoon sun to touch the path. It caught Gareth full in its light. He blinked and doubled over as if to vomit, shuddering violently. The smallest spark of Solar energy condensed in his fingertips and she watched as it slowly grew to cover his hands. When it reached the gauntlet, Gareth cried out and fell to his knees. The shadowy armour dissipated with a hiss. Hands pressed against the scorched earth, Gareth shook as the two powers fought each other and Brégenne could only watch helplessly.

Eventually, the Solar light bathed the whole of Gareth's body and his flaming figure reminded her of Nediah on the day Argat had chased them into the west. The black drained from his eyes and he shuddered, pushing himself back onto his heels. Tentative, Brégenne crouched down beside him. 'Gareth, are you all right?'

The Solar power faded. Gareth's hands were balled into fists and there were tears on his cheek. 'So cold,' he whispered. 'I'm so cold.' He slumped sideways and lay unconscious on the path.

'Gareth,' Brégenne hissed, 'you need to wake up.' The novice had slept for hours and now the moon filtered weakly through the leaves. She had tried healing him, but found nothing to heal. His skin was unnaturally cold, dry like a snake's. She'd also tried to get some water into him, but he hadn't swallowed it, just lain comatose, as still as the dead. Several times, she'd had to reassure herself that he was still breathing.

'Please, Gareth,' she said. 'Someone's coming. I need you to wake up.' Because she'd heard voices, the tramp of feet, seen the flicker of torches through the trees, as if a significant number of people were heading their way. Gareth groaned. She wondered whether she could use Lunar energy to lift him without being noticed. Brégenne hooked her hands under his arms, attempting to drag him off the path, but she was a small woman and even with the weight Gareth had lost, it was like pulling a sack of stones. 'Gareth,' she hissed, half impatient, half anxious. She remembered him saying that the warriors of Ümvast had a tendency to attack first and ask questions later. Who else would be tramping the forest paths at night?

'Where am I?' Gareth muttered. 'Brégenne?'

'Yes, it's me,' she said, glancing over her shoulder. The packed earth shone yellow in the advancing torchlight. 'Can you get up? There are people coming, sounds like a lot of them. They might be from Ümvast.'

Gareth heaved himself onto hands and knees. 'I don't remember,' he said. 'How did we find a path?'

'I'll explain when we're safe,' Brégenne said, forcing down a surge of unease at his amnesia. She wedged herself under

Gareth's arm, helping him to his feet and wincing at the weight he leaned on her. 'This way,' she said, but it was too late – the torches had thrown their shadows into relief against the path and exclamations were followed by the ring of steel.

'Oh no,' Gareth said, his head swivelling at the unmistakable sound. There was little point in trying to run; Brégenne could feel his knees trembling. It was a miracle he was even standing upright. The naked silhouettes of swords preceded those of the newcomers as they rounded the final bend and halted at the strange sight of Brégenne supporting Gareth. There were perhaps fifteen of them, men and women all dressed alike in furs and leathers. They were heavily armed. Axes hung from belts and many carried bows with arrows half-nocked.

Perhaps their most striking feature was their resemblance to Gareth. All had the same dark hair, worn long, the same brown eyes and wide faces. Despite the unfriendly curl of their lips, the warriors studied Gareth with equal curiosity. Although his hair was shorter and his clothes cut in a southern style, the marks of his heritage were quite clear.

'Who are you?' one man asked finally. 'What do you do here?' He wore a wolf pelt across his shoulders and his accent was unfamiliar; the vowel-sounds harsher than Brégenne was used to. She realized Gareth had the same accent, but it was watered down from many years listening to the rounded brogue generally spoken in Naris.

'We are travelling to see Ümvast,' she said before Gareth could answer, and she felt him tense. 'I mean to speak with your leader.'

It was the wrong thing to say. Angry mutters rippled back through the group. 'Ümvast does not give welcome to strangers,'

Wolf-pelt said to her. 'Tell us why we should not cut you down as trespassers.'

'You'd harm one of your own?' Brégenne indicated Gareth, who pushed her gently away so that he could stand by himself. Even in the yellow light of the torches, his face was pale.

'I claim guest-right,' he said. He drew his sword and laid it across the palms of his hands.

'That's a Kul blade.' It was a woman who spoke. Her face was framed by the long-dead jaws of a white bear fashioned into a helm. Its fur hide covered her back so as to make her near-indistinguishable from the winter snows. She narrowed brown eyes at Gareth. 'Who are you? Why would someone with a Kul blade claim guest-right?'

The novice hesitated. 'My name is Gareth Hafgald,' he said. 'Guest-right is the only right I am worthy to claim.'

A hush spread back through the ranks of warriors. Brégenne tensed, ready to open a channel to the Lunar at a moment's notice. But whatever strange meaning hid in Gareth's words seemed to give them pause.

'Kul'Das can judge,' the man in the wolf pelt said finally. 'We will take them to her.'

Two other men came to strip the packs from Brégenne's and Gareth's backs. They were searched, their food and water removed and then the packs returned. The woman in the bear armour took the knife from Brégenne's belt, gave it a contemptuous look and tossed it to a comrade. Gareth's sword was another matter. When the woman tilted it, its shining blade caught the torchlight, igniting the symbol engraved there. Gareth watched, his face guarded. 'It will be kept safe,' she said, tucking it through her own belt. 'You shall have it back should Kul'Das find you worthy.'

Brégenne allowed her hands to be bound, wincing at the rough scrape of rope. She had no intention of using her power; the last thing she wanted was to frighten or threaten the warriors with a display of magic. The most important thing was reaching Ümvast – better that she and Gareth arrive as prisoners than be responsible for slaughtering his warriors. *Or be cut down by them*, she thought grimly, eyeing their weapons.

The novice's cheeks were still rather pale, but his colour was returning. He stumbled along in the centre of the group, staring at nothing, perhaps concentrating on staying upright. 'Who is Kul'Das?' Brégenne asked him softly.

'I don't know,' Gareth answered, 'but "Kul" before a name denotes authority. Whoever Das is, she's important. Maybe an old bloodline, or she's performed some great service to the people.'

Brégenne swallowed the obvious question about his sword, sensing that perhaps he'd tell her in his own time. 'Do you recognize anyone here?'

Gareth shook his head.

'How far is it to Ümvast?' Brégenne called and predictably was answered with silence. *Probably several days*, she thought. *We're on foot and not far from the forest's southern border. Still it could be worse* – although, looking at the pale-faced novice stumbling beside her, his hands bound like hers, and a mere glove hiding the gauntlet that had almost killed him, she doubted it.

In fact, it took almost a full week of travel before they began to see signs of human habitation. Brégenne had waged several silent battles – part of her longing to seize the Lunar and incinerate the rope around her wrists. *You can't*, she constantly reminded herself. If the warriors escorting them knew how dangerous she was, she'd never be granted leave to speak with the mysterious man who shared his name with his people.

'What do you think this group were doing so far south?' she'd asked Gareth one night.

The young man looked troubled. 'I've been wondering that too,' he said quietly. 'It's rare to find warriors so far from home. They must be returning from some mission.'

Their captors refused to speak to them, despite casting several assessing looks at Gareth when he wasn't aware of it. So Brégenne was none the wiser when they arrived at the first camp one late afternoon. The forest had grown deep and dark, enclosing them in a rustling world of green, but now they emerged into a clearing where several tents were pitched amid banked fire pits and stacks of supplies. A few people glanced up from their work when the warriors marched into the encampment. Gareth was looking around and frowning.

'Egil,' one man called, striding over to them. His gaze swept across Brégenne and Gareth, still tied and penned in the middle of the group. 'What news?'

Wolf-pelt went to greet him. They briefly clasped arms and then the two men walked away, out of earshot. 'What is this place?' Gareth asked the woman in the bear armour.

'Bor Tun,' she answered shortly. 'One of many encampments we were forced to build.'

'Forced? Why?'

But that was as much as she'd say. 'Something strange is going on,' Gareth murmured to Brégenne. 'I'm sure this didn't used to be here. I wonder what's happening in Stjórna.' When she raised a questioning eyebrow, he said, 'Ümvast's hall.'

'A *hall*?'

'It's a big hall,' Gareth offered with a weary grin and Brégenne was glad to see it. She hadn't seen him smile in days, not since he'd last used the gauntlet.

'We're moving on to Bor Sundyr immediately,' Egil announced as he strode back to them and there were mutters among the warriors at their lack of a rest. 'The situation in Stjórna worsens.'

That silenced the muttering. The woman Gareth had been talking to laid a reassuring hand on Egil's shoulder. 'Don't worry. We'll make it in time.' Egil opened his mouth to reply, but closed it when he noticed Brégenne and Gareth listening.

Over the next two days, they picked up the pace and Brégenne gritted her teeth against the pain of her aching calves as she lay curled beneath a blanket during their brief hours of rest. The following dawn, as Gareth was prodded to his feet with a groan, she was shocked anew at the amount of weight he'd lost since leaving Market Primus. His face was drawn, almost gaunt, his belly had shrunken and his shoulder blades stood out sharply before he swung his cloak over them.

Worried, Brégenne shrugged into her own cloak, glad of its fur lining. Although the heavy evergreen canopy kept much of it off, the odd snowflake found its way through. Brégenne caught one and watched it melt on her fingertip with an echo of a child's wonder. She hadn't seen snow in years.

The warriors did not share her pleasure, but regarded the snow darkly. 'Barely autumn,' a man muttered to his fellow, as each craned their necks upwards. 'It can only get worse.'

Bor Sundyr turned out to be another encampment, much like the first, but home to a greater number. Its wood-and-hide shelters – halfway between tent and hut – were more substantial and the fire pits had a permanent look about them. Gareth wore his consternation plainly. 'These camps are all new,' he said, pointing out a couple of men working on another structure. 'I don't understand what's going on here.'

Brégenne's unease deepened. Each makeshift settlement they visited had a charged atmosphere that spoke of some shadow stalking the northerners. She tried to crush the feelings of similarity it engendered, tried not to compare the situation in the capital with what seemed to be happening here. She had gone to the Trade Assembly for support only to find them besieged by problems of their own. These scanty camps and bleak-faced people told her the same story.

They passed through Bor Hurr and then Bor Vir and each camp was filled with displaced northerners, their fur cloaks and boots damp with melting snow. Wooded clearings were hidden under thick white blankets and the trees they passed beneath had an unsavoury habit of shedding their icy vestments when the wind blew.

Brégenne began to think longingly of fires, warm blankets and rich winter stews. She could use the Lunar power to warm herself, of course, but she and Gareth were constantly surrounded by Ümvast's warriors, who kept them under close watch, so she didn't dare.

'We *must* be near Stjórna now,' Gareth said one morning after they'd climbed painfully out of their blankets.

'I hope so.' Brégenne couldn't stop her teeth from chattering. 'I've never been so cold in my life.'

'Southerner,' Gareth said with a shrug, as if that explained everything.

'Oh?' She narrowed her eyes at him. 'And who was that shivering in his blankets last night?'

Gareth looked sour. 'All right,' he said, 'it's cold.' Weak

sunlight struggled to reach them through the evergreens. 'Colder than usual. As far as I remember, we never had snow this early in the year.'

'Do you think it's responsible for the camps?' Brégenne said quietly, darting a glance at the nearest warrior.

Gareth shook his head. 'I don't know what's happened to drive them so far from Ümvast's hall. It can't be anything good.'

By midday, the sunlight had lost its battle with the clouds and the scraps of sky above them were white – the flat grey-white that presaged snow. No sooner had the thought crossed her mind when Brégenne felt the first flake on her face. Even the warriors, who Gareth claimed were no strangers to it, hunched their shoulders miserably.

Another chilly few hours passed before Gareth drew a start-led breath and Brégenne looked up. Not a quarter-league away, the trees ended. Beyond them, through the swirling snow, she glimpsed a vast expanse of grey stone which barred the way ahead. As they approached the clear space, the warriors around her began to shift nervously. Weapons were loosened in sheaths, arrows retrieved from quivers and put to bows. They reached the end of the trees and the warriors slowed, their eyes scanning the swirling white to either side. Some looked upwards, Brégenne noted with disquiet, as if they expected an attack from the skies.

Their group was the only thing that moved as they crossed the icy ground. The building loomed ahead, its corners disappearing into the rising snowstorm. It had to be colossal. Sensing safety, the warriors picked up their pace, near-jogging the final distance, and soon they stood before a pair of gates that made the great portal of Naris look like a back door. The woman with the bear armour brought out a knife and sliced the ropes from Brégenne's and Gareth's wrists. Surprised, Brégenne gave her a grateful smile as she massaged life back into them.

Egil knocked thrice upon the gates, his armoured fist making no more than a whisper. Nevertheless, a voice answered him. 'Who seeks entry to Stjórna?'

'Egil Streth-Son' the warrior said loudly and clearly. 'We return from the south and our news is vital. May Vorgarde take me if I lie.'

'Vorgarde?' Brégenne whispered to Gareth.

'Death – the lightless land,' the novice replied with the slightest of shivers.

'Enter then and welcome.'

The gates began to creak and swing, ponderous on their hinges. Beyond them a second set were opening and then a third set beyond those. Brégenne couldn't tell if they were constructed of wood or metal; ice coated them in a thick glassy hide.

Before they could enter the fortress, a roar came from their left. A flash of movement as something huge streaked past and then Egil was on the ground, blood pouring from a slash across his face. It happened so fast that for a moment all Brégenne could do was stand there, gaping at the hot blood on the snow.

Then the warriors formed up, those with shields in front of their archers. Two more grabbed Egil's legs and dragged him towards the gates. Brégenne saw the third set closing, as shouts warned of the attack, and still she didn't know what they faced. Warriors spilled from the towers on either side of the gates, swords naked in their hands, bows angled at the sky.

Gareth was looking wildly about, trying to locate the source of the roaring, but the muffling nature of the snow made it seem as if it came from everywhere and nowhere. Brégenne couldn't reach the Lunar; it wasn't quite evening and the sun, though hidden, still held sway. Straining for it, she glanced automatically at the sky. It was the only thing that saved her. With a scream, she yanked Gareth aside just as the creature dived for them. Claws raked the place they'd been standing and the beast overshot, skidding across the icy ground. A spear whistled over their heads and struck the creature in its white flank. Dark blood spurted and the thing howled, scrabbling to tear the lance from its flesh.

They had no time to catch their breath. With a clap of leathery wings, another beast catapulted out of the sky. Gareth groped for his sword, but it hadn't yet been returned to him and his belt was empty. He looked at Brégenne, his eyes widening, and she ducked instinctively as he hurled a fireball at the creature rearing behind her. The force knocked the beast off its course; the great wings beat, carrying it up and away from the novice. Flames wreathed Gareth's hands, as he summoned more energy, but channelling the Solar was taking its toll. His face was white.

She couldn't tell how many beasts were attacking their group; blood flecked the ice. Some of the warriors were down, but most still fought in a tight ring. Brégenne strained for the Lunar and, though she felt the tiniest flicker, the Solar still bound her power. Gareth gave a scream of effort and hurled a blazing spear into the sky. His aim was off; the spear merely grazed the creature's hindquarters and – maddened – it threw itself towards them. The Solar shield he conjured at the last moment was too weak to withstand its charge; it shattered and they were sent flying. Brégenne tumbled across the slick ice, flailing for purchase. Bruised and bleeding, she picked herself up, searching for Gareth. He was on his hands and knees, his chest heaving. The creature stalked him, lizard-head lowered, scenting the blood that dripped from a gash on his brow.

Brégenne gave a cry of rage and, without thinking, she hurled herself between them. Teeth bared, woman and beast faced each other across the ice. Instinct drove her, the will to survive, and, as she lunged for the Lunar, the Solar cage that encased it cracked. Power flooded into her, though not as much as she wanted – the evening was young. She raised her hands, jabbed them at the creature and a hundred silver darts flew from her fingers, embedding themselves in its flesh. The beast's answering screech was terrible, but it wasn't enough. Its hide, half scales, half fur, was tough and the darts could not fell it.

Brégenne sent out a wave of force instead, which staggered the creature and then she turned, yanking Gareth to his feet. 'Back to back!' she cried, seeing other beasts closing in, their four-clawed feet scoring the ice. The novice was trembling with exhaustion. 'The sun's almost gone,' he gasped. 'I can't do much more.'

'Make for the gates,' she said, realizing their battle had carried them away from the only safety to be had. Still back to back, she and Gareth began inching their way towards the fortress. The beasts kept pace with them. Gareth burned one and Brégenne froze another, but the Solar fire worked better. They were creatures of the snow, resistant to cold, and they quickly shook off her binding. When two charged at once, one from each side, Brégenne sent out a circular wave of force that caught both and hurled them back. It didn't harm them, though. Even Gareth's Solar flames took a long time to burn through the creatures' hides. Brégenne used more darts and the combination of the two dropped one of the beasts. 'Again,' she said and Gareth groaned. His strikes were growing weaker as the sun waned. The window where both powers were active was narrow; soon she'd have to defend them against the creatures alone.

Egil's warriors charged with a cry, their swords biting into the beasts she and Gareth had weakened. More blood spattered the snow. Brégenne laid about her, using her darts, spears, all the offensive techniques she could remember. Eventually, a high, inhuman scream pierced the melee and the largest of the creatures lifted itself into the air, blood dripping from dozens of wounds. Those beasts still alive followed its lead, their white wings buffeting Brégenne with a strange, sharp scent like resin and seawater. They were near the gates now and Gareth collapsed to his knees in the snow.

The next thing she knew, the warriors surrounded them, bloodied swords pointing at their chests. 'What are you?' one man asked, his voice harsh with pain or fear. His left arm hung at an angle, useless at his side.

'They saved us, you fool,' the woman in the bear armour said, coming forward. She slapped the man's sword down.

Slowly the other warriors lowered their weapons too and Brégenne relinquished her hold on the Lunar. 'What *were* those things?' she asked.

'We call them wyverns,' the woman said, 'though no doubt they bear a different name wherever they come from.'

Acre, Brégenne thought to herself. *The Rib Wall is gone. They must have come over the ice.* One of the beasts lay at her feet. Even peppered with wounds, it was majestic, its snowy hide covering a body like a lion's. Its open eyes, filmed with death, were ruby and its flat head was a lizard's, black tongue lolling out between a double row of teeth. She felt almost sorry for it, lying lifeless in the snow, but the bodies of a dozen warriors were being borne across the shoulders of their comrades and she swallowed, realizing that she and Gareth hadn't helped them all.

Despite the woman's favourable words, Brégenne and Gareth were kept under guard as they walked through the gates of Stjórna. Brégenne supported the novice, uneasily entertaining the image of a monstrous gullet – the walls here were curved, smoky stone and the gates set into them almost circular. The *boom* they made as they closed behind did nothing to reassure her.

Another five warriors dragged a wyvern corpse inside and dumped their trophy in the dark vestibule. Brégenne looked up to see another of the creatures held by a dozen spears against the stone. It looked as if it had been there a good month, its white hide hanging slack and eyes shrunken in their huge sockets. A piece of stone adorned the wall beside it, carved with names. Its victims? Brégenne wondered.

They moved into a gloomy entrance hall, which became a corridor further along. A woman was striding down it. One of her hands held a staff, longer than she was tall, decorated with feathers and small bones. To her disgust, Brégenne saw a trio of shrivelled raven heads dangling from a strip of leather tied to the top. The woman was dressed in a combination of furs and leathers cut to resemble robes. Pauldrons lent her outfit a warrior's air, crafted from the tusks of some unfortunate animal.

'Take the injured to Gysalt's Chamber,' she said when she reached them. 'Make them as comfortable as you can. I will see to them on the morrow.'

'Your will, Kul'Das,' the woman in the bear armour answered, bowing her head. Before she moved off, she turned to Gareth, taking the sword from her belt. 'You have earned the right to reclaim your blade,' she said, handing it over. Gareth received it with a weary nod.

'These two claim guest-right,' the woman added to Kul'Das. 'It falls to you to judge them worthy, but without their aid, more would lie dead. They seek audience with Ümvast.'

Kul'Das studied Brégenne and Gareth, her eyes travelling over their battered forms. They were sharp and blue, distinctly out of place amongst all the brown. 'Stjórna welcomes you,' she said coldly. 'You will tell me your names and your reasons for coming here. If I find them satisfactory, I will take you to Ümvast.'

Brégenne didn't care for her tone, but she kept her own civil. 'I am Brégenne of Naris,' she said. 'My news is for Ümvast alone.'

Kul'Das pursed her lips. 'And you?' she said to Gareth.

The novice hesitated. 'Gareth Hafgald.'

'Why would a child of the north take a southerner's name?' Kul'Das tilted her head on one side to regard him. She wasn't a tall woman – not much taller than Brégenne, in fact – but her sheer presence more than made up for it.

Gareth shrank under her regard. 'Ilda-Son,' he muttered.

One of the warriors swore softly; others simply stared at Gareth.

'Ilda-Son?' Brégenne repeated, wondering why the novice would hide his real name. 'What does it mean?'

'That's how we're called in the north,' he said shortly. 'Ilda is my mother's name. I am her son.' He wouldn't meet her eyes.

Kul'Das's expression had turned, if possible, even colder. After a few more moments of scrutiny she said, 'Ümvast will see you. Come.' She began striding back down the shadow-draped corridor, as if she owned it.

Escorted by ten warriors, they followed Kul'Das through hall after hall, chamber after chamber, until Brégenne was sure they had to have reached the other side of the fortress. Although the grey walls were lined impressively with shields and crossed weapons, she didn't care for them. Compared to the warm, dark stone of Naris, which felt as if it had a life of its own, this was a soulless place. Dust layered the tapestries they passed, bright scenes lost beneath a thatch of cobwebs.

At last they reached their destination: two hammered-metal doors that depicted a battle scene. Gareth stared at the tableau of swords and axes, caught forever mid-swing above the muti-lated bodies of the fallen. At one end of the battlefield was a contingent of warriors – knights, by the look of their plumed helms and plate armour. The butts of their spears were firmly planted in the soil and their banner streamed behind them on the frozen, metal wind. Gareth seemed transfixed by the knights. One stood out in front, his visored face concealed. The figure was tall, his raised, gauntleted fist clenched in triumph. Shallow loops of writing stood proud from the carving and Gareth leaned in closer, trying to make it out.

Kul'Das pushed the doors open and the scene split in two. Gareth recoiled as if burned. The woman shot him a glance and then with a small, abrasive smile, she led the way into the chamber beyond.

Uneven flagstones made up the floor, the central ones worn smooth. Kul'Das struck them with the butt of her staff as she walked and the sound was overly loud in the near-empty space. A mere dozen people, mostly warriors, dotted the vast hall, which could have held a thousand. Draped in furs, a great chair took up the far end, its wide back almost a wall in itself, carved with more battle scenes, though none as riveting as the one sunk into the metal of the doors. Instead of the man Brégenne expected to see, a woman occupied the chair, clad in the same furs and leathers as the warriors escorting them. A mantle adorned her shoulders, sewn with beads, bones and bright bits of glass. When Gareth saw her, he gasped, his face a mixture of shock and dismay.

After an endless voyage across the stone floor, they reached the foot of her throne. Ümvast watched them come, her face utterly emotionless. She wore no helm and her hair was intricately plaited, silver streaks augmenting her air of authority. A scar puckered her cheek, starting at her nose and tapering off towards her left ear.

The ruler's gaze acknowledged Kul'Das and swept over Brégenne, finally coming to rest coldly on Gareth. The novice met her eyes for the briefest of seconds and then sought solace in the floor.

'Why, if it isn't Kul'Gareth,' Ümvast said, her voice glacial. 'Though you shame the Kul.'

Gareth swallowed, still studying his boots. 'Hello, Mother,' he said.

PART THREE

PART THREE

24

He woke from the dream of his sister's body hanging from the tree.

Hagdon sat up with a yell, groping for his sword, but what good was a blade against a memory? The drop hadn't killed her and the scarf around her neck wasn't tight enough to make it quick. Her purpled face told him how much she'd suffered as she twisted alone in her little garden. She'd once sat beneath the very same tree to read to her only son. His death had broken her – the child she'd longed for, the child she'd been denied so many years. Even Hagdon, with all his status, hadn't been able to protect him from the emperor. An accident, the Davaratch had lazily explained, when the young man's naked body, wrapped in a sheet, was returned to the family home.

It was his fault, Hagdon knew, for securing Tristan a position in court. Paasa had been so grateful – the tutelage her son would receive under Relator Shune would be second to none. But the Davaratch's dark eyes had been on the young man, watching, desiring. Hagdon felt sick.

341

I swear to uphold and defend Sartya, its lands and peoples, from all enemies. It was the vow of service he'd sworn upon joining the Fist as a junior officer. *I swear to obey my superiors, to place their requirements above my own.* Gusts battered the canvas walls of his tent, like a fist hammering on wood. 'I swear to serve the Davaratch,' he whispered aloud, 'in whose name the empire was founded, and to protect him from all harm.'

When he'd cut his sister's body down and laid it on the earth, smoothing a few dark hairs away from her cheek, a dreadful chasm had opened in his chest. He was glad that neither of his parents was alive to see her like this. His brother was in the south, hundreds of leagues away, and Hagdon was left alone in their grand house. He'd given it up, taken a room in the barracks with his soldiers, tried to bury himself in duty.

Despite the late hour, he redressed and donned his armour, as if it could defend him from the twisted world in which he continued to serve his nephew's murderer. There was a last swig of brandy left in the bottle. Hagdon downed it and then flung the empty bottle across the tent with a yell.

It narrowly missed Iresonté, in the process of blazing inside. She spared a glance for the smashed glass before turning her glare on him. 'You bastard. You did it deliberately. As revenge.'

'Did what?' Hagdon said shortly.

'Let Galla die!' Her blue eyes were aflame. 'You sent her against a Starborn.'

'I didn't know the girl was Starborn,' Hagdon replied coldly, 'and you forget – I lost soldiers of my own that night.'

'Sir.' Carn poked his head through the flap of the tent. 'Is everything well?'

'Get out,' Iresonté snarled.

'Carn is my man. You won't order him anywhere.'

'I'll be outside, General,' Carn said and disappeared. Hagdon wished he'd stayed.

Iresonté stood there a few moments, her chest heaving before she regained control. 'I thought to find you abed.' She nodded at his injured shoulder. 'The men talk of little else, you know. How their general fell to a Defiant dog.'

'I heard tell he was one of yours,' Hagdon said darkly.

'I regret losing little Tava.' It sounded as if she regretted nothing of the sort. 'Good aberrations are hard to come by these days, what with the continuing raids on the prison wagons.'

'Did you come here merely to irritate, Iresonté? Or was there something you wanted?'

'Ah, to business, then,' she said. 'Jed, Caleb, bring him in.'

Hagdon blinked as two of the stealth force entered his tent, dragging a ragged figure between them. They dropped him at Iresonté's feet and retreated with a hasty salute. Hagdon studied the prisoner. It was a man, dressed in trailing, grey tatters that left most of his flesh exposed. He was bound hand and foot and blood caked the side of his face.

In one vicious gesture, Iresonté seized his head and jerked it up.

Hagdon started violently. His shoulder gave an angry throb, but he couldn't dwell on the pain, instead transfixed by the prisoner's face. It was a horror, surely assembled by a blind man, for none of the features matched. One of his cheeks was wrinkled and his eye, though swollen shut, was sunken with age. But the rest of him was unlined, bits and pieces garnered from every stage of life.

Iresonté wore a smug smile. She had a right to: the man was Khronostian.

'How did you find him?' Hagdon breathed, quite unable to tear his eyes from the barely conscious prisoner.

'You know I travelled south,' she answered, 'following a lead I had from the Beaches.' She glanced at the Khronostian. 'We found another of them dead, but this one . . .' Her smile widened. 'He hadn't managed to crawl far. Someone did a good job of roughing him up. When I found him, he could barely lift his head.' She released her hold and the man dropped to lie prone on the floor. 'I'd give a lot to know who felled a couple of *dualakat*.'

'I hope he's not too far gone to talk,' Hagdon said, gazing down at the man at his feet.

'Oh, he talked.'

Hagdon's head snapped up. 'You interrogated him without informing me.'

'Interrogation of prisoners is my province, Hagdon.'

'Not when that prisoner's Khronostian.' Hagdon glowered. 'You had a duty to bring him to me.'

'You're in no position to reprimand me, *General*. I've achieved what you, in years, have not. His Majesty is pleased.' Her eyes narrowed. 'And grateful.'

Hagdon strove to hide his unease. 'You've heard from him?'

'Why, yes,' Iresonté said. 'A raven brought a message today. The prisoner has supplied us with an excellent means of leverage.'

'The Kala will . . . destroy you.'

They both looked down. The Khronostian coughed; blood flecked the thick mats spread over the tent's floor. 'He will bring ending. He will bring . . . beginning.'

'We got a lot of that,' Iresonté said easily. 'But reading between the drivel, the Khronostians are seeking a person they call "Kala". They're obsessed with this man, seem to think he's akin to some reincarnated god.'

'Khronos –' the prisoner choked, his every breath a wheeze now – 'has returned. The sun . . . sets . . . on your empire.' He gave a long sigh and his head lolled to one side.

'So much for your pet Khronostian,' Hagdon remarked.

Iresonté nudged him with her armoured toe. 'It's no matter. I got what I needed. A description of the Kala – he'll be hard to miss – and the next location of Khronosta itself.'

'Congratulations,' Hagdon said sourly. 'So what are His Majesty's orders?'

'Why don't you come and see?'

Hagdon frowned as she turned and left the tent. He strapped on his weapons, picked up his helm and followed her.

Something lay sprawled just outside. Hagdon tripped over it and, cursing, he looked down. He'd trodden on a pale hand, lying limp and bloody on the earth. Eyes widening, he followed it up an arm to a shoulder – a shoulder that bore his colours. His family's colours. A cry built in the back of his throat. 'Gods,' he gasped, crouching to turn the body. 'Carn, no.'

The bondsman's eyes were open, staring accusingly up at him. A ragged slash across his throat still oozed blood; blood soaked the front of his tunic. Sensing the silence, Hagdon looked around.

A circle of torches lit the space before his tent. Men and women stood there, grim-faced. He knew each and every officer by name. Lieutenants next to sergeants and corporals, even some recruits barely out of their training. Fists gripped blades. Hagdon gazed at them and they gazed back. A few seemed troubled, but most wore a hard determination. The smoking torches stung his eyes and he blinked, half convinced it was all a fever dream.

Iresonté stepped forward. A dark red cloak now hung from her shoulders. She plucked the helm from his unresisting fingers and then her expression was lost behind its snarling faceguard as she settled it on her head. 'Kill him.'

Lieutenant Malker saluted Iresonté; the movement was stiff – he'd still be smarting from his lashes. 'Yes, General.'

Hagdon knew it was over – there were too many of them. But he wasn't going down without a fight. Carn's dead eyes bored into his back as he drew his weapons. Long sword in right hand, short sword in left, he faced Malker across the naked earth. The two men circled each other. Malker bore a greatsword – powerful, but slow to swing.

Only long experience saved Hagdon from a blow that would have taken his head. Sensing a presence behind him, he threw himself aside and Malker's second overbalanced with the fierceness of his attack. Hagdon turned his lurch into a spin, came around and thrust his short sword up under the lip of the man's helmet and into his neck.

'A coward, Malker?' he said, pulling the bloodied blade free. His shoulder throbbed a warning at him. The lieutenant glanced at the dead man and then at the rest of the soldiers. His grip tightened on the hilt of his sword and he cut low, forcing Hagdon back. Hagdon kept his blades up, conscious of the greatsword's range. He parried the next strike and tried to get around Malker, but the lieutenant reversed his grip and drove the pommel of his sword at Hagdon's temple. Hagdon blocked it, but only just. His shoulder made him slow. A shout of warning went up from one side and he chanced a look. Two soldiers coming to aid Malker had fallen to their knees, wearing twin expressions of shock. They toppled forward and Hagdon caught the glint of metal protruding from their backs.

Chaos broke out as every fourth soldier present drew a blade and slashed it across his or her neighbour's throat. Iresonté was shouting; the black-pauldroned stealth force closed up around her protectively. Malker's triumphant snarl slid off his lips. He bared his teeth at Hagdon and brought up his blade, but his eyes kept darting from side to side, watching as more soldiers he'd thought loyal pulled blades on their fellows.

Counting on his distraction, Hagdon took a risk and lunged, trapping Malker's blade with his short sword. The lieutenant caught Hagdon's other sword in one hand as it came for him, but it sheered through gauntlet and mail to pierce his belly.

Malker fell back with a gasp, yanking Hagdon's arm down. The greatsword slid from his hand and Hagdon kicked it aside.

'General!'

He planted a foot on the corpse, hauled his blade free and turned in time to see Commandant Taske break a recruit's nose, sending him stumbling into one of the torches. The recruit knocked it over and the flames caught on a piece of sacking, consuming it hungrily before jumping to the young soldier's cloak. Hagdon looked away from his shrieks and saw Carn's body instead, discarded like an old tool, forgotten in the chaos.

'Taske,' Hagdon forced the name through a dry throat. 'Have you come to kill me too?'

'No,' the commandant said, 'but if you ask any more stupid questions . . .'

Somehow, terribly, Hagdon wanted to laugh. He blinked at the scene unfolding – Sartyans fighting Sartyans, soldiers killing soldiers – 'Such a waste,' he whispered.

'In war, there always is.' Taske took him by the arm. 'Our

numbers are not quite so great as the Fist's,' he said and the whole of it was surreal, another part of Hagdon's dark dream. 'We must go now if we're to get you out.'

A shrill whistle went up; a signal. Numbly, Hagdon followed the commandant through the camp, where more and more soldiers joined them, so that eventually Hagdon was surrounded by a human shield at least two hundred strong. Those on the fringes fell and were replaced and he couldn't see their faces, these nameless giving up their lives in the dark. It seemed to take forever, but eventually they broke free of the camp's perimeter. Hagdon caught the fresh, reedy scent of the lake and he breathed it in deeply, trying to rid himself of the taste of smoke and blood. 'A waste,' he whispered.

'Iresonté's scouts will track us,' Taske said.

'They can try,' answered a voice and Hagdon shook his head in amazement. The woman who spoke wore black pauldrons; so did another beside her. Whatever this was – whatever rebel faction splintered away from the Fist – even Iresonté's people were a part of it. Surely the emperor couldn't know.

'We'll double back, lay false trails,' the woman said. She gave a piercing cry – the greathawk call that the stealth force was known to use – and she and another ten companions melted off into the night.

'Most are double agents,' Taske said to Hagdon, 'working right under Iresonté's nose.' His smile was sharp. 'She trained them too well.'

'Who are you?' Hagdon asked, still haunted by the feel of Carn's hand under his boot. How casually Iresonté had pulled his life out from under him. After Khronosta, he should have seen it coming. But to think that the emperor . . .

Faces surrounded him, illumined now only by moonlight.

They were all ages and genders, some high ranking – with a little shock, he spotted captains Dyen and Analia, who nodded gravely to him – and scattered across all the corps of the Fist. They looked to Taske to answer.

'We', he said, 'are the Republic of Acre.' He put a hand on Hagdon's shoulder. 'And since you currently find yourself without one, we're here to offer you a job.'

25

Cymenza, Acre
Char

The streets of Cymenza were in uproar.

It was an elegant city, its pale stone buildings topped by colourful turrets. Roads ran off from sunburst-shaped inter-sections, their cobbles worn smooth. Merchants' stalls were shaded by elaborate awnings . . . or would have been, if those awnings weren't lying trampled in the gutter.

Char and the others had reached the gates of Cymenza to find them wide open, guardposts abandoned. A dull roaring came from deeper in the city, as if a dam had broken upriver, but he realized it was the sound of many raised voices. The street they were in did indeed look like a river had swept through; it was littered with bits of wood and shop fittings, all strewn at random across the cobbles. An old man huddled beneath an overturned cart. Char slid off the back of Kyndra's horse and crouched down. 'What happened here?' he asked.

'Riots.' The man shrank away from him. 'Tension's been building for weeks. Defiant work, no doubt. Then the Starborn rumour reached us and ignited the lot like a match dropped in oil.'

Char almost looked at Kyndra. 'What Starborn rumour?'

The old man blinked at him with rheumy eyes. 'You haven't heard?'

'I wouldn't be asking if I had.'

'They say a Starborn slaughtered a whole division of Sartyan soldiers.' His voice was hushed. 'Killed hundreds. They say General Hagdon was among the dead.'

This time Char did look at Kyndra. She'd closed her eyes, as if in pain. Did that mean it was true? Is this what she'd refused to discuss the other night? He swallowed, glanced back at the man. 'When did the rioting start?'

'Yesterday evening. It began in the docks and spread through mid-town and the trade quarter. Only the iarls' district's left untouched.'

'Where are the guards?'

'Trying to put it down, boy,' the old man said and spat. 'All this on the strength of a rumour. And of Starborn!'

'You don't believe it?' Kyndra asked quietly.

'It's a Defiant plot – a story spread to take advantage of the unrest.' He shook his head. 'Hot-tempered fools. They'll see us all dead.'

Char left him in his dubious hiding spot and turned to the others. 'What now?'

'We have to cross the city,' Medavle said, narrowing his dark eyes. There was something about the man that made Char nervous. 'We steer clear of the worst of the fighting.'

'Can we not do something to help?' Kyndra said. Her face was distraught as she looked around at all the wreckage.

'You can't blame yourself for this,' Nediah told her firmly.

'You heard what the man said. It sounds as if the riot's been brewing for weeks, long before we were ever here.'

The woman, Kait, seemed the only one not perturbed by the situation. Char watched her as they set off cautiously into the city, leading the horses and keeping to the smaller streets. Her eyes were bright; she seemed pleased at the half-constructed barricades they passed, the furniture thrown out of windows, heaped in haphazard piles. Nediah was looking at her too and Char didn't blame him: with her height, long legs and almond eyes, Kait was a beautiful woman. But there was a hard edge to her, a sliver of something unstable in her smile that he couldn't bring himself to trust.

The noise grew louder as they advanced through the city and the warm air stank of smoke. The horses grew twitchy, except for Kyndra's stallion. Perhaps it was a strange side effect of her presence, but the black remained quite calm under her hand. Grey plumes flowed into the sky, throwing flecks of soot to the wind. Irilin, who, Char guessed, would like nothing better than to stick a knife in his back, began to cough. People surrounded them now, jostling; one thrust a grubby white banner into Nediah's hand. Words scrawled across it read: CYMENZA STANDS.

'Isn't that the Defiant sign?' Kait said, tracing the crudely drawn clenched fist.

Irilin nodded. 'I saw one like it in Ségin's base.'

'You might do better to throw that away,' Medavle said. He scanned the jostling, shouting crowd. 'I see Sartyans.'

Char looked where he pointed and spotted the telltale red armour, as thirty soldiers, moving in a phalanx, thrust their way through the populace. Their drawn swords dripped with gore and blood spattered their faceguards. 'Well, that's one way to put down a rebellion,' he muttered.

'No,' Medavle said, seeing Nediah gazing at the carnage. 'We can't get involved. This is not our fight.'

Nediah's face was very pale as he watched the Sartyans cut the townspeople down. Even those that flung their weapons aside, who fell on their knees in surrender, were not spared. '*This* is the emperor we're trying to ally with,' the Wielder said almost to himself. He seemed unable to take his eyes from the slaughter. 'We're taking peace talks to *him*?'

'For Mariar's sake,' Kyndra said. She was pale-faced too, but her expression hardened, as she watched the Sartyans quelling the rioters. 'If we don't, then *this* could be Market Primus.' She looked at Nediah. 'I'll do whatever it takes to protect our people.'

Nediah shook his head. 'Is it worth the price?'

If Kyndra had an answer, she'd no time to voice it. 'Drop your weapons,' came an order from behind them and Char felt the point of something distinctly sharp pressing into his back. He slowly turned his head. A woman stood there, wearing the red plate of Sartya – it was *her* sword threatening his shoulder blades. 'Drop your weapons, slaver,' she repeated.

Damn it all. The incriminating tattoos crept from under his shirtsleeves and Char wanted to laugh. Here he stood in the middle of a full-blown riot beside the Starborn who'd sparked it all and the Sartyan was arresting him for *slavery*.

Hesitantly, as if terrified of the sword at his back, he slid his hands towards his kali sticks, drawing them into his palms. 'Drop them,' the woman barked.

Char had no intention of doing so. Tucking his head in, he dived, rolling clear of the blade's reach. Then he spun, bringing

353

his sticks up in front of him. Now that he had a good look at his opponent, he cursed. She wasn't alone, but flanked by a dozen soldiers.

Char darted a glance at Kyndra. The Starborn's eyes were fixed on the Sartyans and she looked haunted – perhaps she really had slaughtered as many soldiers as the rumour claimed. He saw her tremble and realized that she'd be no help at all. Kait, however, raised her fists and in each out-thrust hand there appeared a curving golden sword. Twin blades readied, Kait sank into the same preparatory stance as Char and he couldn't help but gape at the scimitars and the way her hands were curled unflinchingly around their fiery hilts.

Medavle drew the silver flute from his belt, flicked it once, and it lengthened into a metal stave. He spun it several times, whistling through the air, and suddenly the odds didn't seem so bad to Char. He grinned fiercely, feeling the blood pumping through his veins. Anticipation made his heart race . . . or was it the rage, uncurling from the depths of his stomach? For once, he almost didn't care.

Irilin darted out to snatch up the reins of the horses, pulling them away from the Sartyans. The soldiers hadn't reacted at the display of magic. In chilling silence, the woman who'd threatened Char advanced on him and began to circle, her blade flicking out to test his reflexes.

Char caught the blows on the edge of his sticks, maintaining a defensive stance, eyes narrowed. She was slower, in all that mail, and she couldn't swing her broadsword as fast as his sticks. But he was unarmoured; even a glancing blow could be fatal. Speed and agility were the only ways he'd win this fight.

The black lenses fell out of his tunic onto the cobbles and the soldier crushed them beneath her heel. With a growl, Char whipped a kali stick at her neck. She angled the sword high and horizontal and caught Char's blow on its edge, but she'd left herself open and she knew it. He drove his left stick into her side with all the force he could muster. The mail links were finer there and though they still cushioned the blow, he hoped he'd at least cracked a rib. The woman gasped and sprang back. Her teeth were bared; she wouldn't make the same mistake again.

They returned to circling each other and Char glimpsed the others, battling the Sartyan woman's companions. Kait fought three, her face fixed in a stiff snarl of concentration. She was fast, possibly faster than he, and, in his distraction, Char almost let the soldier's next strike through his guard. He ducked to one side and spun, aiming a kick at the back of her knee. It connected, but the blow was glancing and didn't seem to slow her.

The air around Medavle's staff pulsed with energy, invisible waves snapping out with each swing, knocking the soldiers back. Nediah guarded Irilin with a shimmering shield and Kyndra, to Char's chagrin, stood behind it, gazing at the battle with dark eyes. Her expression warred between fear and resolve; it was a helpless look and it made Char angry, fuelling the rage that pounded beneath his skin.

Their fight was just another part of the greater battle ringing through the streets, though the Wielders' display was starting to attract notice. Char dodged his opponent's lunge, feinted high and went low, aiming for the back of her knee again, but the soldier didn't go for it. She kicked out with her mail-shod foot and caught him in the hip. He gritted his teeth; if he lived through this, it would make a spectacular bruise. He circled, keeping his eyes on the deadly blade.

Kait cried out and Char risked a glance. There was blood on

her shoulder and one of her hands was red; she was having trouble gripping the flaming blade and it disappeared as he watched. Nediah yelled something and Kait jumped back, just as a sheet of flame sprang up between her and the soldiers.

His distraction cost him. The woman made a feint of her own and Char fell for it. His backward leap was more of a stumble, his heel slipping on the unfamiliar cobbles. The edge of her sword sliced across his chest and blood flowed like black ichor. The Sartyan froze, staring at the wound she'd delivered. Her eyes moved to her blade, to the sticky black blood that dripped from it. She took a step back.

Just as it had once before, on the day Ren had cut him, the rage exploded in Char. It raced up his throat, roared out of him, and a great force hit the soldier, hurling her back like a rag doll. She smashed into the front of a building and crumpled. Char turned to face the remaining soldiers, who looked from him to the broken body of their leader. The rage was building again, that roar of air and force, and he couldn't hold it in. It roiled in his belly, trying to melt his bones. Although Char fought, he knew he couldn't stop it. Part of him didn't want to. His whole body prickled; the skin on his arms rippling, as if there were a sea beneath it, or a wind.

Eyes fixed on him, the Sartyans edged backwards. The rippling beneath Char's skin became unbearable and he sank to his knees, fists clenched. A moment away from giving into it, he felt a touch on his bare arm and looked around. Kyndra crouched beside him, her fingers curled around his bicep, pressing them almost painfully into his flesh. Char shuddered; her touch was ice, colder than ice, and, just as it had last time, the force that battered his insides quailed beneath it. He gasped as it sank back into his belly, into the heart of him. Her hand was pale against his dark skin. Her eyes held his implacably; they were depthless, a blue that was almost black. 'You're not human,' she said with terrible conviction.

Char stared at her, confused. As soon as the rage dwindled, the pain of the sword slash rose up instead, and he had to grit his teeth. 'We need to get out of here,' Kyndra said. She let go of Char's arm and he tensed, half expecting the rage to come surging back, but it lay quiescent.

Rioters were closing in on the remaining soldiers, giving Char a wide berth. 'Leave them to it,' Kait said, clutching her injured hand. Char caught a glimpse of the soldier he'd killed. He didn't know what to think as he stared at her still, broken form. Her sword lay beside her; she'd held onto it even as she died. Char felt drained, wearier than he'd ever been in his life. But not weary enough to stave off a sharp stab of regret.

The tides of battle were turning in the rebels' favour. A group of people, masked like vigilantes, were scything their way through the Sartyans, picking apart their phalanx one soldier at a time. In the midst of them strode a man, similarly masked; It looked as though he was directing them. Char clutched at his wound, his own blood slicking his fingers, scanning the street for a path clear enough for the horses.

'Char!' someone called. 'Gods, is that you?'

Frowning, Char turned towards the voice and saw the vigilantes approaching. All were heavily armed and dressed in nondescript clothes. Their leader held a curved blade, spattered with what, presumably, was Sartyan blood. 'It is,' the man declared and he ripped off his mask.

The world's gone mad. 'Iarl Rogan?' Char said, astonished. What was he doing here? The iarl wore a face he'd never seen before: adamant, *alive*.

'I will be soon,' Rogan replied enigmatically. His eyes flickered past Char to fix on Kyndra. The Starborn self-consciously raised a hand to cover the glowing mark on her cheek. 'Ségin hoped you'd come,' he said with a tight smile, 'though Char is quite the surprise.'

'Are you Ségin's –' Kyndra stopped, shook her head. 'How do you know who I am?'

'Why don't we go and wash off this blood?' Rogan said. 'I've a proposition to put to you.'

26

Cymenza, Acre
Kyndra

When Rogan joined them in the parlour of his home deep in the iarls' affluent district, he looked a different person. An olive-skinned man in his middle years, he'd swapped his plain clothes for a light tunic with gold brocade. Clean shoes replaced his bloodstained boots. Kyndra eyed the polished table and the ordered cupboards that lined the walls behind him. There was a strange stove-like apparatus with a flat top and four circular metal plates. It carried a faint layer of dust. She guessed it might have been something powered by ambertrix, the strange energy that was once the source of Sartya's strength.

'Who is he?' she'd asked Char as they'd followed Rogan through the smoky streets. 'Do you trust him?'

'Gods, no,' Char had answered, frowning. 'I thought I knew him . . . I want to know what he's doing here, how he's involved in all of this.'

'He seemed pleased enough to see you.'

'That doesn't mean we're friends. Rogan pretends to be a

loyal imperial citizen, but he's always had one foot in the under-world.' Char paused. 'I just didn't know how deep.'

So this was Ségin's Cymenza contact. Now Kyndra sat, uncomfortable in the heat of a fire, and wondered what exactly Ségin had said about her. A fat man sweated over the flames, hanging a pail full of water to warm. 'Will there be anything more?' he asked somewhat bitterly and Rogan shook his head.

'How's the Hozener shaping up?' Char asked when the man had gone.

The iarl shrugged. 'Didn't mean to buy him. Just wanted to give Genge a hand with the bidding. How is he, by the way?'

'Dead,' Char said shortly.

Rogan's face stilled. 'I am sorry to hear it,' he said. 'We've many ken-years between us. I considered him more a friend than a business associate.'

Char grunted and his expression grew a little cooler. Kyndra wondered what he was thinking. 'Who was Genge?' she asked.

Rogan raised an eyebrow. 'Char hasn't spoken of the slave master?' He looked back at the young man.

'Wait a moment,' Nediah said, a wrinkle creasing his brow. 'How exactly do you two know each other?'

The sudden silence was uncomfortable. Char and Rogan exchanged a glance. Kyndra guessed that they'd never expected to encounter each other outside their usual dealings. Eventually Rogan said, 'My business frequently takes me to the Beaches. It's the only place one can obtain certain . . . goods.'

'By "goods" you mean slaves,' Irilin said, her face darkening.

'Among other things,' the iarl answered, holding her gaze. 'Do not be too quick to judge, young woman.'

'Are you planning on telling me what's going on?' Char said loudly in an obvious attempt to change the subject. 'We reach

Cymenza to find a full-blown riot in progress, almost get killed by Sartyans, and then I find you in the middle of it all, dressed as some vigilante of the streets.'

Rogan narrowed his eyes. 'You have an unfortunate habit of asking dangerous questions, Char. I don't doubt it'll get you killed one day.'

Kyndra glanced out of the window. The iarl's manor sat high on a hill above the city. She could see the fires that ravaged the trade district, burning bright and hot in the twilight. 'Aren't you worried the fires will spread here?' she asked.

The iarl smiled. 'They burn only what they're supposed to.'

'Did you orchestrate this?' Char demanded.

'Another dangerous question. You could say I'm one of the pieces.' Rogan studied each of them in turn. 'The players are far higher up. Cymenza is under their control now.'

'And who are these players?'

Rogan shook his head. 'Come now, Char, don't force me to kill you.'

Kait, Kyndra noticed, had been watching the exchange closely, her hands curled tight around the arms of the chair. 'Are you with the Defiant?' she asked.

The iarl barked a laugh. 'Tools, but they have their uses. Their agents in Cymenza were happy enough to start a riot. I suspect they're also happy to take the credit for ousting the Sartyans, though they couldn't have done it without my help.'

Kyndra opened her mouth, but Nediah asked the question before she could. 'How many people do you have working for you?'

'More than the Sartyans had stationed here. Cymenza has a history of kowtowing to authority and the empire grew complacent. They pull more soldiers out of the city every year.'

'The Davaratch will come down hard,' Char said. 'He'll send the Fist. Whoever your mysterious players are, they won't hold the city for long.'

'The last I heard, the Fist had suffered losses of its own.' Rogan looked at Kyndra. 'Isn't that right, Starborn?'

She felt a ripple of disquiet. 'What did Ségin tell you?'

'Some associates of mine are very keen to make your acquaintance,' Rogan said without answering, 'particularly after the uncompromising way you dealt with Hagdon's forces.'

Kyndra thrust down the memory of *Sigel*. 'That's not something I ever intended,' she said quietly.

'Intended or not, it certainly drew attention.'

'The wrong kind.'

'That depends on whether you help us,' Rogan said. 'Would you hear me out?'

'Who is "us"?'

'I can't give you names, you understand.' His face was serious. 'Not until I know you won't betray us. But we call ourselves the Republic of Acre. We aim to break up the empire, restore independence to all territories.'

'I've never heard of this Republic,' Char said suspiciously.

Rogan looked briefly irritated. 'Of course you haven't. Why do you think we still exist?' The iarl returned his gaze to Kyndra. 'We're not without power, or influence. We've agents in every major city in northern Acre, including the imperial court. We even count disaffected Sartyans among our number.'

She frowned. 'What about the Defiant? You say they're tools, but aren't their goals the same as yours?'

'The Defiant are a front,' Rogan said. 'A front we've hidden behind for many years. They were created to deflect attention away from us. Their raids on outlying garrisons, their attacks on the prison wagons in order to recruit aberrations – inflammatory tactics designed to capture and hold the interest of imperial spies.'

'There was a spy planted among the Defiant.' Kyndra felt a pang of regret as she thought of Tava. 'If they have access to Defiant secrets, how come they haven't rooted you out?'

Rogan folded his arms. 'Because only the leaders of each cell know that they work for us. And each is given a different contact. We knew Iresonté would get her claws into the Defiant. It's part of their purpose.' He smiled thinly. 'It leaves us free to work.'

Just as Kyndra was wondering what the others made of this, Nediah leaned forward. 'What does your Republic propose to offer Kyndra?'

'An alliance,' Rogan said without preamble. 'That's what you seek for Rairam, no?'

Kyndra stared at him. 'Is that what Ségin told you?'

'Amongst other things. He has a rather high opinion of you.'

'He and his people are safe, then?'

Rogan nodded and a knot inside Kyndra loosened. She'd managed to save some lives for all those she'd taken.

'And what are the terms of this alliance?' Nediah asked, green eyes sharp on Rogan's face. Kyndra watched the Wielder closely, remembering his earlier horror at the punishment meted out by the Sartyans. If there was an alliance to be made, it seemed he was predisposed to find Rogan's preferable.

'What it comes down to is this. You help us bring Sartyan rule to an end and we guarantee peace for Rairam.'

'That seems awfully convenient,' Kyndra said, though her

heart had begun to beat faster at the possibilities. 'I know nothing about you, or whether these claims of power and influence are true. Why shouldn't I make overtures to Sartya instead?'

Rogan's expression soured. 'You'd be a fool to try. War and conquest is the lifeblood of Sartya. The empire will never treat Rairam as an allied power.'

'And where does Khronosta stand in all of this?' Medavle asked suddenly.

'Ah.' Rogan sighed. 'The honest answer is – we don't know. For the moment, they seem to hate Sartya as much as we do and they've inadvertently helped us by taking out the few ambertrix technicians left in Thabarat.'

'But what do they *want*? What's their overarching goal?'

'If it's to seize power, they'll have us to contend with,' Rogan said, leaning back in his chair. 'Otherwise, I couldn't say.'

Kyndra glanced at Char and found him looking at her. Perhaps they were thinking the same – how exactly would the Kala help the Khronostians seize power? Could one man really make a difference?

'If you're open to my proposal,' Rogan said, 'I'll introduce you to some contacts of mine. We can discuss what you'll bring to the Republic –' here, his eyes flickered over the Wielders – 'and what the Republic might then do for you.'

It's better than nothing, Kyndra told herself. *You came here to make an alliance and he's offering you one*. Should she trust him? Char didn't, but then Char had history with this man – he'd thought him someone else entirely. Kyndra glanced at the others. Medavle's expression was neutral, but that light still burned behind his eyes. Kait would agree to the alliance – she'd argued vehemently in favour of the Defiant, after all. Nediah was more cautious, but Kyndra could tell he was giving Rogan's offer serious thought.

'I'll leave you to talk it over,' Rogan said, breaking into her musing. He rose. 'And I'll have refreshments sent in. Please make yourselves at home.'

'It's all a bit precipitous,' Irilin said when the iarl had gone. 'What do you think?'

'Precipitous or not, he's handed you your answer on a plate,' Kait said predictably. She was taking Rogan at his word and had propped her feet comfortably on the table in front of her. 'We could do far worse than ally with the organization behind the Defiant.'

'We don't know enough about it,' Kyndra argued. 'This Republic's an unknown quantity, even more so than Sartya. At least we've had some experience of the empire.'

'It wasn't exactly a good experience,' Nediah said. 'I know you had hopes of Hagdon. But even if the general had been willing to listen to you, he was just one man and subject to the emperor.' He sighed, loosening the ties at his neck in the heat. 'And everything we've heard about the Davaratch has been bad. He and his empire are, by all accounts, monstrous.'

'We will be involving ourselves in a war either way,' Medavle said. The temperature didn't seem to affect him. He stood with arms folded, leaning against the wall. 'If you ally with Sartya, they'll expect you to fight for them. If you ally with the Defiant, and this Republic, they'll expect you to fight for them. If you don't ally with either, you have no insurance against an invasion of Rairam.' His gaze was characteristically penetrating. 'A hard choice, but better than none at all.'

*

They discussed it for an hour until Kait – after announcing that she'd given her opinion – threw up her hands and left to get some air in the adjoining garden. A moment later, Nediah followed her. Kyndra frowned after them, feeling like she was betraying Brégenne by not saying something. *It's none of your business really*, she reminded herself. But she'd seen the way Nediah looked at Brégenne, how he blushed whenever she touched him. And Kyndra remembered Brégenne's face on the night Nediah left for the Deep – she'd wept, believing she'd never see him again.

Kyndra felt a ripple of anger at Kait. The Nerian woman had history with Nediah, she knew that, but they'd all heard their argument in Skar. Kait had left Nediah to become one of Kierik's people. She'd made her choice. What was Nediah doing then, encouraging her?

'Brégenne must have received the envoi by now,' Irilin said, as if she'd pulled the image of the Wielder right out of Kyndra's head. Her voice was very quiet. 'Gareth will have heard about Shika.'

'Yes,' Kyndra said, equally quietly.

'I wish I could talk to him,' Irilin whispered, 'but I wouldn't know what to say. What is there to say?'

'I'm sorry.' Kyndra felt utterly helpless. Shika's name kept bringing back that awful day, the wails of the wraiths, their hatred, Medavle's belief that they were remnants of the slaughtered Yadin. She thought she'd experienced terrible things in Naris, what with the tests and the Madness that destroyed Wielders' minds . . . but it was nothing compared to the brutal reality of Acre.

'My tunic needs mending,' Irilin said. Her face was carefully blank, but Kyndra suspected she was holding back tears. 'I think I'll take it outside.' While they'd been talking, Medavle had disappeared too and Kyndra was left alone with Char.

He was dipping a finger into the water that had been warmed over the fire, presumably testing the temperature. Then, with a quick glance around, he shrugged out of his shirt.

Flushing, Kyndra jumped up to go, but – 'Stay if you want,' Char said, bundling it up and dunking it in the water. 'You've seen me bleed. You know I'm all wrong.'

'You're not wrong,' she said, perching hesitantly on the edge of a table. He glanced at her and she blushed harder, wondering why she'd spoken.

'I remember –' he wrung the shirt out – 'what you said to me.'

Nediah had healed the sword slash, but blood still fanned across Char's ribs and over his stomach. He dabbed it and the shirt came away black. Kyndra knew she was staring, but she couldn't seem to stop. As the blood came off, she could see the strange shadow-shade of his skin, the taut muscles of his chest and abdomen, no doubt built up through years of training with those sticks of his.

Char glanced up, blood-stained rag in hand, and met her gaze. 'You said I wasn't human.'

Kyndra remembered the force she'd felt coiled beneath his skin. It was the second time she'd sensed it – before, Char had refused to talk about it. 'Nediah told us . . . when he healed you.'

'What else did he tell you?'

She shook her head. 'Nothing.'

Char was silent. If he asked, she would tell him what she'd sensed: a great force inside him like wings unfolding to catch wind, a rushing, unstoppable roar. But he wouldn't ask. They shared the same pride.

'There is a rage,' he said, dropping the sodden shirt. 'Sometimes it comes without warning. Every time it's stronger.' He turned to dress in the spare clothes Rogan had loaned him and Kyndra looked away.

'How long has it troubled you?'

'"Troubled me"?' He snorted. 'You make it sound like an illness.'

'It isn't?'

'Three years,' Char said. He came to lean against a table across from her. Where Kyndra suspected she'd look quite ridiculous in them, the borrowed clothes suited him. He wore a shirt rolled up to the elbows under a tunic, long and dusty as the dunes, loose trousers that narrowed at the ankle and sturdy boots. The strange sticks he used as weapons hung from scabbards attached to his belt. A plain headscarf held the hair off his forehead, trailing ends pushed back over his shoulder.

There was something exotic, even handsome about him, but then she noticed the tattoos on his forearms and wondered at the things he had seen and done. How had he found himself in such a life?

Char seemed to reach some silent decision. He pushed himself off the table and came to stand a little closer. 'I haven't said thank you,' he said awkwardly, 'for stopping it.' His yellow eyes were intense on her face.

'I didn't –' It emerged as a croak and Kyndra coughed. 'I didn't do anything.'

'That's twice you stopped it from getting free. Nothing else can.' A shadow passed over his face. 'It almost consumed me back there in the street. It's never been so strong.'

'I saw what you did to the soldier,' she said.

Char swallowed. 'It's happened before. The first time I didn't kill anyone, but today . . .'

A breeze from the open door blew hair into her eyes and Kyndra raised a hand to brush it back. Char caught her fingers and brought her hand close to his face, as if it were some strange object worthy of study. Her heart skipped; his skin still felt unnaturally warm. He turned her wrist and there was *Hagal* emblazoned across it, clearer after she'd used it on the wraiths. 'What is this one?' he asked.

She blinked, surprised by the question. '*Hagal*,' she said and then when he looked like he was going to touch it, she added, 'I wouldn't, if I were you. It's good at destroying things.'

'You've used it before,' Char said, staring at the sharp constellation. 'It's clearer than the others.' He let go of her hand, his eyes raking over her neck, her bare forearms. 'There're so many.'

'So many there's not enough of me to wear them all.'

He pointed at her cheek. 'What about that one? Why does it glow?'

Trying to push down the memories of that night, she said, '*Sigel*. I was afraid. I'm always afraid of using them and I let it get the better of me. I lost control. I only just managed to regain it in time.' She paused, said more softly, 'That's what happened with the Sartyans. The rumour's true.'

Char's face was blank. She couldn't tell what he was thinking. Probably wishing he'd never started this conversation.

'We can only ever be who we are,' he said finally and it was hesitant, as if he wasn't just speaking to her.

Kyndra met his gaze, a challenge. 'And what if I don't want to be? What if I want the same life other people are entitled to?'

'That's your choice,' Char answered with an echo of flame in his eyes. 'It's not my place to tell you who to be.' He turned away from her, went towards the far wall. Kyndra followed his gaze and found herself staring at a tapestry. It was finely woven, its colours a little faded, a complex scene of a mountain landscape, white peaks and a grey city, high in the clouds. Bright creatures roamed the foreground, their sinuous bodies turned to catch the wind.

'Ségin said the Lleu-yelin were gone,' Kyndra murmured regretfully, captivated by the images. 'No one has seen them for twenty years.'

Char was staring at the lines of the weave too, a small crease between his brows. 'I remember the Khronostians saying something about a battle with the dragons, a battle they claimed to have won.'

'The Khronostians fought the Lleu-yelin? Why?'

Char slowly shook his head. 'I don't know. They said the Lleu-yelin wouldn't trouble the world again, that they were locked in a place no one would find them.'

Kyndra tore her eyes away from the tapestry to look at him. 'How many people know that?'

'None, I'd bet. *I* didn't know, before they told me.'

'Someone must have searched for the Lleu-yelin when they first disappeared.'

'Yes,' Char agreed, 'except that the dragons' city, Magtharda, isn't easy to reach if you don't have wings.'

Kyndra still found it difficult to accept that the dragon-riders were real. If she ever met one, it would be like stepping into the pages of a story. 'So there's a possibility they're still up there?' she said.

Char shrugged. 'Maybe. But why would they just cut off all communication with the outside world?'

'Were they friends or foes of Sartya?' Kyndra asked after a moment.

'Good question. I'd say neither, but then the dragons have always been secretive.'

Kyndra turned back to the tapestry, tracing the dip and curve of sleek bodies. Each dragon had a rider, with swept-back horns and a scaled face. 'Do you think we'll ever see them again?' she asked.

Char's yellow eyes were distant. 'I hope so.'

27

Brégenne stared at Gareth. 'Mother?' she repeated.

'I promised to kill you if you ever showed your face here again,' Ümvast said. The great dark hall had filled with whispers, but her words silenced them.

'How did you recognize me?' Gareth asked in a small voice.

'No mother would fail to know her own flesh and blood.'

Gareth briefly closed his eyes; the chamber's poor light seemed to deepen the circles around them.

'Have you returned to your homeland to die, Kul'Gareth?' Ümvast said. 'You are a bag of bones. Your eyes have death in them.'

Stirred to anger, Brégenne seized Gareth's upper arm and dragged it into the air, high enough for everyone to see. She was shocked at how wasted it felt. The gauntlet seemed to draw strength from the gloom; it pulsed sickly and Gareth let out a groan, swaying on his feet.

'*This* is why he has come here,' Brégenne said. 'I haven't brought him halfway across Mariar to die.'

'And who are you?' Ümvast ignored Gareth's upthrust arm and the gauntlet, taking in Brégenne's face, her clothing. 'My son's bodyguard or his southern *whore*?'

Brégenne dropped Gareth's arm and raised her own. Silver energy crackled down it, blazed in each fingertip. 'Why don't you say that again?' she asked softly.

The tall woman's eyes widened at the blaze that filled her hall, but not with fear. 'So,' she said, 'you are one of those responsible for taking my son away.'

'I am a Wielder, yes,' Brégenne replied, the Lunar power spitting like lightning. 'But Gareth has a gift and he chose, quite wisely, to nurture it. Why should you condemn him for that?'

'Kul'Gareth's place was here,' Ümvast said, 'yet he forsook his people, turned his back on his family –' Brégenne caught the barest flicker of regret in her face – 'and wilfully discarded the duties to which he was born.' Her gaze returned to Gareth. 'For that, there can be no forgiveness.'

Before Brégenne could reply, Gareth said, 'Don't think the choice was an easy one.' He coughed and when he next spoke, his voice was a little stronger. 'But what Master Hanser showed me . . . I couldn't turn my back on that, even if it meant leaving my home.' He raised his eyes to his mother's. 'Even if it meant that I could never return.'

'And what you learned amongst the southerners,' Ümvast said slowly, 'was it worth the price?'

'It served you today,' Gareth said.

At Ümvast's frown, Kul'Das stepped forward and whispered in her ear. When she was done, she remained standing at her chieftain's side. Ümvast's eyes sharpened as they flicked between Gareth and Brégenne. 'Kul'Das informs me you fought off a pack of wyverns.'

'It's true,' said one of the warriors, who'd accompanied them into the hall. 'They drew the beasts' attention. Without their help, I doubt I'd be standing.'

'For that, you have my thanks,' Ümvast said, 'but I am still unsure of your purpose in coming here.'

Gareth straightened. 'My companion is Lady Brégenne of the Lunar,' he said formally. 'We came to speak with Ümvast, leader of the north. I had no way of knowing that a new chief had been chosen.' He paused. 'Or that it would be you.'

A tiny smile like a snake's tongue flickered at the corner of Ümvast's mouth. She nodded. 'Then speak.'

'Our quest is twofold,' Brégenne said, letting the Lunar power fade. A hushed relief swept through the hall like wind in meadow grass. 'First we want to warn you of a threat to the west.' Ümvast's face darkened and, watching her closely, Brégenne added, 'It's likely where the wyverns have come from.'

The northern chief rose, shrugging off the mantle that adorned her shoulders. Standing, she was over six feet tall. Anger kindled bright flecks in her eyes. 'My people will soon be forced to leave Stjórna. No other who has carried the title of Ümvast has ever had to do so.' She glanced at Gareth. 'My first-born shames me, abandons me, my husband is years in his grave. The Rib Wall that once sheltered this land is gone and the ice creeps southward, bringing these wyverns with it.'

'Is this why you built the camps?' Brégenne asked.

Ümvast's look was scornful, but Brégenne heard a whisper of fear in her voice. 'We are no strangers to cold or hardship, but always the forest has protected us. Now the sap freezes in the trees and shatters them. She swept a hand at her near-empty court. 'This is something we cannot fight.'

Muttering filled the hall, grim sounds of agreement. Brégenne felt an echo of that cold in her chest. She'd not considered that Acre would bring other changes with it, changes more primal, perhaps more devastating than war between humans. 'You plan to move south,' she said.

'We must, if we are to survive.'

'Where do you intend to go?'

'Where we will,' Ümvast said baldly. 'There is plain-land near our southern border. Not ideal, but better than nothing. Or we've heard tell of a rich city on the shores of the ocean. Perhaps we may settle there and become fishermen.' She flashed her teeth amidst ugly, scattered laughter.

'Those are people's homes,' Brégenne said, unable to hide her dismay. 'Their lands and livelihoods don't belong to you.'

'We will give them the chance to defend them.'

I came to seek your help, she told Ümvast silently, *to defend Rairam from the powers in Acre. Instead you'd make the promise of war a reality. You'd march on your fellow people.*

'The south is weak,' Kul'Das said and Brégenne looked up at her. The woman's fingers were clamped around her staff and one of the raven heads knocked gently against her knuckles, its beady eye seeming to wink. 'They have grown soft, let their skills rust. They'll not present a challenge.'

Brégenne narrowed her eyes. 'You are no northerner.'

'Kul'Das is a trusted friend,' Ümvast said. 'She is one of us by deed, not by blood.'

'And what great deed did she perform to earn her title?'

Kul'Das's look became one of loathing and even Brégenne was shocked at its vehemence. 'My deeds are not under discussion here,' she snapped.

'Indeed they are not,' Ümvast agreed. 'I am beginning to

wonder what is.' She looked at Brégenne. 'Why are you *really* here?'

'I came to seek your aid in the war that looks set to come,' Brégenne said, unable to rid her tone of its bitterness. 'My companions volunteered to undertake a dangerous journey into Acre—'

'Acre?' Kul'Das interrupted. 'What nonsense.'

Brégenne turned a disbelieving stare on her. 'What else caused the Rib Wall to fall? You've seen the Acrean ice fields for yourself, you've seen these creatures invading your homeland and you haven't put two and two together?'

'Wait.' Ümvast held up a hand. 'The lost world is returned?'

Brégenne reminded herself that, once upon a time, she had found the fact just as unbelievable and so she swallowed her frustration and turned a calm face to Ümvast. 'It's a long story, if you care to hear it.'

The four of them retired to a small chamber with a fire that could not keep out the cold. The stones of Ümvast's fortress felt like ice when Brégenne accidently brushed against them. Kul'Das had seated herself arrogantly in a carved, unpadded chair that made Brégenne ache just looking at it. Instead she chose the most comfortable one she could find and ignored the scorn Kul'Das sent her way.

'A story worthy of our warrior poets,' Ümvast said when Brégenne had recounted the events of the last few months. 'I thank you for it.'

Kul'Das looked sour. 'How do we know she speaks truth?'

'Why would we come all this way to lie to you?' Gareth asked, eyeing her with dislike.

'You have already said you came in search of our aid,'

Kul'Das retorted. 'No man is above stretching the truth to get what he wants.'

'Their story is not in doubt,' Ümvast said and Brégenne was gratified to see the woman's expression curdle. 'It goes a long way to explaining our own predicament.' Ümvast looked at Brégenne. 'Nevertheless, I cannot give you what you seek, Wielder.'

'Why not?' Brégenne said. 'I'm only asking you to defend your lands, your freedom. The Sartyan Empire was responsible for starting the war that ended with Rairam being separated from Acre and my companions claim that it's still a force to be reckoned with. As long as Sartya's in power, Rairam is under threat.'

'We are losing our lands already and not to this empire you speak of.'

'I understand,' Brégenne replied, 'but that doesn't mean you can take what isn't yours.' She looked Ümvast in her cold brown eyes. 'Rairam needs to stand united if it's to have any chance of resisting the empire. And the Breaking has caused enough chaos without you adding to it.'

There was silence. The fire crackled half-heartedly, as if tired of fighting the chill outside and, looking into it, Brégenne felt her own weariness. She'd started out full of purpose, determined to bring the people of Rairam together. But peace, it seemed, bred its own divisions.

'Did you not say your quest was twofold?' Ümvast said finally.

Brégenne looked up. Gareth sat bleak and pensive, staring into the fire. 'The gauntlet Gareth wears,' she said. 'He found it in Naris's archives. We keep many artefacts there that we know little to nothing about – relics of Acre mostly. There's a powerful enchantment on it that prevents its removal.' She didn't mention the terrible ability it granted Gareth, not yet. Instead she thought back to the conversation with Argat. 'On our journey here, we heard a story of two warriors from Ümvast who were searching for a pair of gauntlets, one light, the other dark. It would have been years ago, but it's our only lead. I was hoping you might know more.'

Ümvast shared a look with Kul'Das. The woman's expression was neutral now, but Brégenne had been watching her and had seen a brief surge of interest brighten her features.

'Show me, Gareth of Naris,' Ümvast ordered. When Gareth drew off his glove and lifted his right arm, the gauntlet glinted darkly in the firelight, flush with his skin and looking more like an extensive tattoo than a piece of armour. Both women leaned in to study it, while Brégenne kept a close eye on their faces.

'What think you, Kul'Das?' Ümvast asked after a while. 'Is it *his*?'

She grunted. 'Could be. The way it's melded to his skin.' She turned her blue eyes on Gareth. 'And the boy's condition bears out the stories. How long have you worn it?' she asked him.

Gareth glanced at Brégenne. 'About three months.'

'He should be dead,' Kul'Das said to Ümvast. 'If it is one of the pair, he should not have been able to withstand it more than a few days.'

'Gareth's a Wielder,' Brégenne said, thinking back to the day in the forest where he'd withered the trees. Only the Solar power had broken the influence of the gauntlet. 'It could be his ability's protecting him. The two powers are fighting each other.'

'What did you mean when you said "his"?' Gareth asked. He lowered his arm and tugged his sleeve over the gauntlet, as if he couldn't bear to look at it.

'A legend—' Kul'Das began, but Ümvast overrode her.

'Not a legend,' she said. 'A story with its roots in truth, a story of Acre,' she added with a nod to Brégenne. 'Have you heard of the Kingswold Knights?'

Brégenne blinked. Yes, she'd heard of them – they were another myth out of Acre. But something Kyndra had said came back to her, a point the young woman had made when stressing how strong the empire had been in Kierik's day. The knights were the only force capable of holding their own against the Sartyan soldiers, but they'd made a stand at a place called Kalast and suffered a ruinous defeat.

'I don't know much,' she answered, 'except that they fought the empire and lost.'

'In the days before the sundering – the Deliverance –' Ümvast clarified, 'our ancestors were numerous and held great lands, far more than we do today. Though they were all renowned warriors, one group considered themselves the elite. They accepted only the best, trained children from the age they could walk, and their prowess in battle was unmatched. Their leader and founder was a man they called Kingswold.'

Gareth was staring at his mother with the same intensity he'd reserved for the frieze on the throne-room doors.

'I do not know how he acquired them, but Kingswold had in his possession a pair of gauntlets, one symbolizing light and the other darkness. When worn together, they bestowed great power—'

'What sort of power?' Gareth interrupted, a strange light in his sunken eyes.

'That knowledge is lost,' Ümvast said and Gareth sat back with a sigh. 'When Kingswold wore the gauntlets and led his knights into battle, they were unstoppable.'

'So what happened?' Gareth asked. 'How did the empire wipe them out?'

'One of the gauntlets was lost. And Kingswold had cause to regret the safeguard built into them, for he could not wear the remaining gauntlet or utilize its power. Naturally, the knights' enemies cornered them, demanded their surrender. In his desperation, Kingswold donned the remaining gauntlet.'

A heavy silence was all about them. 'It granted Kingswold great power,' Ümvast said, 'but without the other to temper it, he lost control. Half his knights were dead before the enemy engaged. The rest were slaughtered by the empire. It's said he was laughing when they put a spear through his chest, his face alive with an unholy joy that remained upon his visage even unto death.'

'And the gauntlet?' Gareth asked in a whisper. 'Was it lost with him?'

'That I cannot say,' Ümvast replied, her brown eyes – so like Gareth's – sharp on his face. 'It could still lie in the spot where he fell, or it could have been taken by the enemy. At any rate, it is irrecoverable. If the gauntlet you wear on your wrist is indeed one of Kingswold's, it is a death sentence.' Her voice was inflectionless.

'If it's irrecoverable, why were two warriors searching for it?' Brégenne asked. 'I assume they knew the story.'

'The story of the Kingswold Knights is a powerful one,' Kul'Das said. 'The warriors you mention would not be the first to seek to reclaim the gauntlets, no matter how foolish the errand.'

Gareth went to bury his face in his hands and then snatched the right one away just before it touched his cheek. Instead, he dragged his chair nearer the fire. 'I'm always cold,' he complained.

Kul'Das squinted at his hand. 'The power of the dark gauntlet is necromantic,' she said. 'When worn with its partner, it's said it can raise the dead.'

Gareth looked at her. 'And what about when it's worn alone?'

'You're in a better position to answer than I.' Kul'Das shrugged. 'But if the story of Kingswold's demise is anything to go by, that power will turn upon the wearer.'

They all stared at Gareth, at the dark circles around his eyes, his sunken features. He looked half-dead already, Brégenne thought with a creeping despair. He couldn't hold out forever. She imagined the two powers warring inside him, draining his strength, the life in his face, and vowed she wouldn't give up. But the only thing she could think of was trying to locate Kingswold himself. 'If we could find his resting place,' she said, 'if we could find Kalast—'

'He died over five hundred years ago,' Gareth said hopelessly. 'And if Kalast was destroyed by the Sartyans, we'll probably find a new city built on its ruins. If we can find it at all.'

He was right. This was Acre: a land for which she had no maps and only the scant knowledge Kyndra and the others had supplied. A foolish errand indeed.

And what of her duties here? Brégenne asked herself. If she left, who would prepare Rairam's defence, who would make its people aware of the threat? She glanced at Ümvast, but the woman's eyes were on Gareth. It wasn't a motherly look or even a sympathetic one. It was speculative, ambitious, and Brégenne didn't know what to make of it.

'There's a chance that the light gauntlet was buried with Kingswold,' Ümvast said slowly. 'The enemy would likely have been too afraid to touch it.'

'How do we know he had a proper burial?' Kul'Das argued. 'It was a battlefield. There were hundreds of bodies. The victors might just have dug a pit and thrown them all in together.'

'Something tells me they didn't,' Ümvast said. 'The fame of Kingswold and his knights was such that they have passed into legend. No warrior, whatever their allegiance, would fail to honour such a band. It is likely he and his men were given a burial, but what kind, we can only guess.'

Kul'Das looked sceptical. She was no warrior, Brégenne guessed. Battlefield etiquette was not a subject in which either of them was versed. Perhaps Ümvast was right and there was a chance – the tiniest, most unlikely chance – that they could find the other gauntlet and save Gareth's life.

'Let's send a message to Kyndra,' Brégenne said to him. 'Perhaps she knows of Kalast and can tell us if it still exists.'

Gareth didn't say anything for a moment and the fire hissed and popped, as it fought its own battle with the cold. Finally, he dropped his eyes to his lap. 'I can't ask you to help me, Brégenne. You're needed here – Mariar needs you. What's one life compared to all the thousands that could die if war comes?' His voice was very quiet.

What he said made sense, but it opened a hollow in Brégenne's chest and she found anger there. Why did Gareth have to die for a mistake? For a power that had nothing at all to do with him? It wasn't fair.

Ümvast had that speculative look again. She tilted her head on one side so that her braid fell over her shoulder. 'If you could find the gauntlet, my son, it would bring glory to our people.'

Gareth glanced up, his eyes widening.

'I could not accompany you, of course,' Ümvast continued. 'I must lead us south. But Kul'Das shall go in my stead.'

The woman spluttered. 'You . . . you want me to go to Acre?' Her already pale face had whitened.

'Certainly,' Ümvast said. 'It is an honour you have well earned.'

Judging from her obvious chagrin, Kul'Das did not consider it an honour. Her hand strayed to the staff propped against the wall beside her and she clasped the wood tightly as if begging it to refute Ümvast's words.

'I can't let you march south, knowing what you plan,' Brégenne said. 'I left Naris with the intention of making alliances, not enemies.'

Ümvast regarded her with a steady gaze. 'If you discover that Kalast does indeed exist, I propose a pact. You and Kul'Das shall guide my son on his quest. Should you find the other gauntlet, you will return them both to Kingswold's rightful descendants. To me.' Her eyes were hungry. 'In return, I promise you every blade I can spare should war come to Mariar. We will take no land that is not ours.' Her eyes narrowed. 'But my people need a home. You *will* find us one, whether through bloodshed or accord, I care not. If I do not hear from you at the end of two months, the deal is broken and I will act as I see fit and in the best interests of my people.'

Brégenne's heart thumped painfully against her ribs. It was a dangerous promise; she'd effectively be condoning a civil war unless, by the slimmest chance, they actually found what they sought. The Trade Assembly wouldn't tolerate the northerners on any land they considered theirs. Blood would be spilled and Brégenne didn't think it would be Ümvast's. And what of their promise to Argat? She glanced at Gareth, wondering whether he was thinking the same.

'Two months hardly seems long enough to enter Acre, avoid the Sartyans and find Kalast,' she said. 'Three months.'

Ümvast nodded reluctantly. 'Three months, then. But without the gauntlets, our pact is void.'

Brégenne held out her hand to shake on it, but the fierce woman reached for the knife on her belt instead. Ümvast sliced open her own palm and then gestured at Brégenne, who grudgingly turned hers up. She didn't bother to hide her wince as her skin was slit. She clasped bloodied hands with Ümvast. The warrior woman's was large and long-fingered and made Brégenne's hand look like a child's. When it was done, she snatched it back, healed herself and wiped the blood off on her cloak.

She beckoned for Ümvast's hand. The chieftain gave it and watched her own wound close up. 'Yes,' she said, staring at her now-unmarked palm, 'you will serve.'

'She's not doing this because she cares for me.'

Brégenne glanced up from the envoi she was busy imbuing with a message. Gareth sat brooding before the fire in the rooms they'd been given for the night, staring into its yellow heart. 'She doesn't care whether *I* live or die,' he said. 'She wants the gauntlets to save her people.'

Brégenne couldn't bring herself to deny it. Gareth wasn't stupid. They'd both seen the light in Ümvast's face and the change in her attitude towards her son. Calling him her son, for starters. She'd even patted him on the shoulder and informed him that this was a chance to earn back his title.

'I take it you didn't know about your mother before this?' she said.

'My mouth falling open didn't give it away?' Gareth replied sourly. 'When I left, Ümvast was a big man with shoulders like an ox and a temper to match.'

'You said a new chieftain is chosen through a Melee, if I recall?'

'Yes.' A hint of pride touched Gareth's wasted face. 'I had no idea Mother would enter. She must have been good.'

'She said she lost her husband,' Brégenne said, watching him carefully. 'Your father?'

Gareth dismissed him with a wave. 'Died before I was born.'

They lapsed into silence for a while. 'I don't much care for Kul'Das coming with us,' Brégenne said eventually. 'I don't trust her.'

Gareth shook his head. 'Me neither. I'm surprised Ümvast keeps her around, being an outsider. We're notoriously suspicious of outsiders in the north.'

'I think she's as reluctant to come as we are to have her along,' Brégenne mused, turning the half-formed envoi in her hands. It didn't have a shape yet. Perhaps she'd make it a raven. 'And that staff she carries – is it usual here?'

'No. Ümvast – that is, the people – are warriors. They've no interest in magic or anything you can't swing a sword at. It's why Mother couldn't accept my leaving.' He dragged his gaze from the fire to look at her. 'I think you might have impressed her though.'

Brégenne snorted. 'If all it took was a little lightning—'

'Not just the lightning. She respects you. I saw it in her face.'

Brégenne didn't know how to reply to that. 'Kul'Das is no

385

warrior,' she said, retreating to the matter at hand, 'so what did she do to merit her title?'

'We could ask her.'

'I get the impression she isn't fond of me,' Brégenne said wryly.

'She's not the only one coming. We've a dozen of Ümvast's personal guard.'

'This is if we're going at all. If Kyndra says Kalast is gone . . .'

'I'm dead,' Gareth said. He looked down at the gauntlet, once more concealed beneath his glove.

'I'm sorry,' Brégenne said quietly. 'I didn't think.'

'No, you're right. If we went into Acre without anything to go on, it would be a wasted journey.' Gareth returned his gaze to her. 'You're needed here. You shouldn't put one life above thousands.'

Brégenne looked at the envoi, half-finished in her hands, and said nothing.

'A raven,' Gareth noted with a touch of humour. 'An omen of death. Thanks for the vote of confidence.'

'I thought it would get their attention,' Brégenne said apologetically. 'Kul'Das's horrible staff gave me the idea.' She turned her attention back to the envoi, wondering what else to imprint it with. The memory of Nediah's last was still with her, that feeling of Kait's presence in the weave. Although she chided herself, she couldn't help recalling the golden wolf with its bright paws on her knees. She hadn't forgotten the surge of warmth she'd felt as it faded, his presence so startlingly strong that it snatched her breath away. And though she'd had nothing like that since, she realized she'd come to expect it, she'd looked forward to it. But to find Kait there instead . . .

Her eyes prickled and, shocked at the sting of tears, Brégenne blinked them rapidly away. Gareth's life depended on her; she didn't have time to waste. If they were going into Acre, she'd likely need every ounce of skill she possessed.

So she addressed the envoi, not to Nediah, but to Kyndra. It was Kyndra who would know about Kalast and the knights, after all. Making sure to imbue it with a sense of urgency, she released it and watched it flap off through a wall.

Gareth stood up. Brégenne pretended not to see his grimace, as if even the act of standing tired him. 'How long do you think it will take to reach her?' he asked.

'I don't know, Gareth,' she said. 'But it will fly as fast as I am strong.'

'And how long do you think –' He broke off, but Brégenne thought she knew what he'd intended to say. *How long do you think I have left?*

She went to him, laid her hand on his thin arm. 'You're a Wielder of Naris,' she said, 'and a man of the north. You can do this, Gareth.'

When he met her gaze, she saw that the brown in his eyes was gradually darkening to black. 'I'm a novice,' he corrected, 'and an exile. What if I can't?'

Brégenne gave him a grim, determined smile. 'You won't be alone,' she said.

28

'Now this really *is* Calmaracian wine,' Medavle heard Kyndra say. He glanced over from his place by the open garden doors to see her holding up a clear pale vintage to the light of the candles.

Nediah smiled at her. 'Are you planning to sell me a cask?'

'That depends whether Rogan would be willing to sell *me* one.'

'We might come to an arrangement,' Rogan said, 'to celebrate our newfound understanding.'

Medavle frowned and looked out into the night. While he wasn't wholly convinced by this Republic of Acre, the others had backed Kyndra's decision to remain in Cymenza and meet with Rogan's mysterious contacts.

A pale flash caught his eye. Heart in his throat, Medavle followed it into the garden. There it was again, among the cypress trees. The evening was balmy, the sea wind blowing the smoke of the fires away from the iarl's district.

Her robes gleamed in the light streaming from the house.

Medavle blinked, but she didn't vanish. He took a few steps closer. Isla turned her face to him, tears on her cheeks.

The rational part of Medavle knew she wasn't there, but she seemed so real . . . was that the wind ruffling her hair? Surely she wasn't just an invention of his heart. He closed his eyes and –

He's running again, running through the halls of Solinaris, desperate to find her. He knows what the Starborn plans to do to his people. He's done all he can to stop him, but how many Yadin will die regardless? He doesn't even know whether binding his own life force to Kierik will work and right now he doesn't care – he must find her.

Chunks of glass litter the marble floors like the tears of a grieving god. Wielders dash past him to lend their strength to those holding the gates, but Solinaris is doomed. The empire has men to spare and flings them mercilessly at the fortress. Flaming balls smash into the walls and there aren't enough Wielders to bolster the structure. It will fall before the night is through. Whatever Kierik's greater plan, the Starborn won't stop the fortress crumbling out from under him.

'Marius,' he gasps, grabbing hold of a passing Yadin, 'have you seen Isla?'

The blond man shakes his head. 'Not since this afternoon. I have to go, Meda, I have to help Master Varen.'

He watches his brother hurry away and anger lashes his insides. Even in the midst of chaos, when all rules are broken, still the Yadin serve. Perhaps Isla is with her own Wielder, but how is he supposed to find Master Laniel in all this? Why would Isla go to her instead of to him?

There's still time, he tells himself, knowing how little is left. Still time.

He races through hall after hall, corridor after corridor, until his breath rasps and his heart pounds in his chest. The pain is nothing compared to Isla's absence. If he cannot take her out of the reach of Kierik's spell . . .

A scream draws him. It's Duela, crouching over a discarded bundle of white clothes. When she sees him, she cries his name. 'What's happening?' Her eyes are huge and fearful. 'Lukas . . .' she chokes, picking up the white cloth. 'He was here. He was right behind me.'

A dreadful cold seizes Medavle. It has begun and he hasn't found her.

'Medavle –' Duela cuts off sharply. A shadow surrounds her and there is a rushing, as of a chill, dark wind. Before his horrified eyes, she bursts into light, into nothing. Her clothes drop empty to the marble and he turns and flees.

He cannot escape the wind, but as long as he has form, he won't give up the search. Medavle rounds a corner and skids to a stop. A man stands at the end of the corridor, a little blurred, as if seen through poor glass. He has dark hair, darker eyes and an ageless face, wearied by time. It is a face Medavle knows well.

The man sees him and his expression changes. Revelation, it says, understanding . . . triumph. Medavle blinks and the man becomes his own reflection, gazing out at him from an as-yet-unbroken mirror.

'But it wasn't a reflection,' he whispered, coming back to himself. And the pale figure he'd followed into the garden wasn't Isla. The robes were grey and the form they clothed was small and hunched. He walked slowly forward, eyes fixed on the wizened shape beneath the trees. The man – or creature, for Medavle couldn't truly see its face – spread its arms wide, as in a gesture of welcome. One hand held a staff. 'You are the Yadin?' it said.

Other figures, all bandaged, melted out of the night, surrounding Medavle. 'How are you here?' he said, taking a step back. 'How did you find us?'

'Wherever the Kala walks, he seeds change,' the stooped figure said. It turned its cowled head towards the house. 'But we have a pattern on the Kala now. We will always know where he is.'

'Who are you?'

'We are the eldest who foresaw the Kala's return.' It tilted its head. 'But we did not foresee yours. You are the Yadin who came with the Starborn, yes? You asked our people for their names. You wished to meet us and we are here.'

Medavle glanced at the *du-alakat*. There were ten he could see and who knew how many he couldn't. 'I am the Yadin,' he confirmed, 'the last.' He briefly closed his eyes. 'Save for those half-things that haunt the red valley.'

The eldest clucked an unseen tongue. 'Bodiless, just memories,' it said and Medavle fought down a surge of sorrow. 'Would you see them restored to what they were?'

'You know I would,' he said harshly. 'I'd do anything to save them from that fate.'

The *du-alakat* circle tightened and Medavle's hand tensed on his flute, but he didn't draw it.

'Together,' the eldest said, 'we could do much.'

Medavle regarded it. 'You would use me as your anchor.'

'The Kala told you of our ways.' The figure seemed pleased. Amongst the folds of its cowl, Medavle caught a slow smile. 'Your long years hold such promise,' it breathed and he almost flinched from the greed he heard. 'You have no idea what we

391

could do with them. But –' it looked again towards the house – 'we need the Kala. We do not yet have the power to touch the past without him.'

'He will not come willingly,' Medavle said. 'He claims he isn't your leader.'

'He was turned against us,' the eldest replied with a hiss. 'Who knows what poison Mariana poured into his ears as he grew?'

'The Starborn will protect him.'

'We are a small people and enough precious lives have been wasted attempting to take him by force. So –' the shrivelled being turned its hooded head to look at the *du-alakat* – 'we will try another way.' As soon as the words were spoken, the Khronostians converged on Medavle. Bandaged hands closed on his arms and he flinched from the tightness of their grasp. The eldest moved closer, close enough for Medavle to look down into the cowl.

A man looked back, eyes frosted with age, his features lost in a mass of wrinkles. A withered hand reached out, gently touched Medavle's chin. 'You bear three times the years we do,' the old man whispered, 'and yet remain untouched by the ages.' The hunger was clear in his face now. 'The Kala will be made to see reason. He will help his people. And with you as an anchor . . . why, Acre may never have been sundered at all.' His sunken eyes brightened. 'The Yadin never murdered, Solinaris never conquered.' He stepped back, holding tightly to his staff. 'The empire overthrown before it ever began its war.'

Medavle could only stare, his heart pounding fiercely.

'We will unmake history,' the eldest said. 'And remake it to our liking.'

The *du-alakat* began to dance, while three others held on to

Medavle. They wove an intricate pattern, their bandaged feet soft on the garden's lush grass. A light began to spread in the wake of each, reminding Medavle of the way he'd used his own life force to bind himself to Kierik. Perhaps the Khronostians somehow derived their power through the same means; perhaps that was why it exacted such a terrible toll from their bodies.

The eldest spread his arms again. 'Come, Yadin,' he said, 'we go to Khronosta, there to await the Kala's coming.'

'They won't follow,' he replied, his eyes beginning to water from the speed of the dance. 'They won't know where to find me.'

'The Kala knows,' the eldest said. 'We will force him to come to us. He understands your potential . . . and your danger.'

Before Medavle could argue further, figures burst from the house, running towards him across the dark lawns.

'Medavle!' Kyndra cried and he imagined how the scene would look to her – him, in the grasp of the *du-alakat*, as others danced their bright pattern around them. Through a haze of light, he glimpsed her face and was surprised at the emotion he saw there. The Khronostians moved faster and he began to feel squeezed, as if two great forces were determined to trap him between them. Terror followed; he remembered those *du-alakat* faces he'd seen, the horrible price exacted by their manipulation of time. What would it do to *him*?

I'd pay any price, he thought, *if I could only see Isla smile again.*

'No!' he heard Kyndra shout and for a moment Medavle was torn, his hand on the flute at his waist. She had been his hope, but a hope for an empty vengeance. Here was a hope for life, something far more precious, a hope that cost a sacrifice, a betrayal. Medavle looked into the eyes of the eldest as the twin forces squeezed tighter and tighter. Slowly his hand uncurled from the flute and fell at his side. The light grew blinding and he knew no more.

29

Cymenza, Acre
Char

Char's eyes were patterned with after-images. In the darkness behind each blink, he could still see the glowing pattern imprisoning Medavle; he remembered the terror in the man's face. What were the Khronostians doing here? How had they tracked them so swiftly?

'*Du-alakat*,' Rogan hissed and the word brought Char out of himself and back to the now tranquil garden. '*Here*.' The iarl scowled. 'How did they get in?'

'Evading whatever lookouts you've posted wouldn't have been a problem for them,' Char said. 'Neither would bypassing locked gates and the like. They can choose where and when to appear.' He glanced at Kyndra. She seemed to be in shock, her gaze fixed on the spot where Medavle had last been.

Rogan whistled high and sharp, a sound that – in seconds – summoned nondescript figures from the house and gardens. 'Check the perimeter,' he ordered and they melted away into the twilight. 'I don't like surprises, not in my own home.'

'Why did they take him?' Kyndra said blankly, looking at Char. 'They've only ever wanted you.'

'Because through him, they have the means to remake the world.'

The voice was like the night: husky, accented, concealing. Kyndra jumped and, next to her, Irilin did too, but Char's breath caught in his throat. He knew that voice, had grown up hearing it, chastising and praising him, soothing him after a bad dream. Once, when he was very small, it had sung to him. He hadn't heard her sing for so many years.

Ma strode up the sloping hill towards him. Her kali sticks hung at her waist. Thick hair tumbled free from a headscarf. Her dark skin gleamed in the light from the house, a gold torque at her throat.

'Ma,' he whispered.

Rogan took a step forward and Char shot him an icy glare. He found himself hurrying across the grass. Part of him wanted to fall into her arms, another part remembered the terrible night he'd left Na Sung Aro and wanted to rail at her, to demand answers.

'Hello, Boy.' Ma's eyes travelled over him, as if checking him for injuries. They touched on his forearm and widened slightly at the thin scar – all that remained of the wound which had nearly killed him. 'You move swiftly,' she said. 'I almost lost your trail in the city.'

'You've been tracking me?'

'What else would I do?' Ma cast a fierce glance at the empty ground where the Khronostians had danced only minutes before. 'Son of my heart,' she said, 'they will not have you.'

Char's eyes prickled, but he blinked angrily and took a step away from her. 'Why not?' he asked, hearing his voice harden. 'You're one of them.'

'Yes,' she said simply.

He could feel the others' shock. It mirrored his own. 'You . . . you don't deny it?'

Ma walked over to Kyndra. 'You are the Starborn,' she said, gaze flicking to the glowing tattoo on Kyndra's cheek. 'Thank you for protecting my son.' She paused. 'You know not the service you've done him.'

Kyndra looked a little taken aback. 'Char mentioned you. He didn't say you were from Khronosta.'

'I have done my best to forget it.'

'You don't look Khronostian,' Kait said, sizing up the other woman. 'All the ones we've seen so far have been –' She gestured at her face.

'The *du-alakat*.' Ma shook her head. 'Not everyone born in Khronosta follows the path of the warrior.'

'*You* did,' Char said. '"The greatest of the *du-alakat*" – that's what those Khronostians claimed back in 'Aro.'

She shrugged. 'An exaggeration. I was but twelve.'

'*Twelve?* How young were you when you began training?'

'Six – that is when the first selection is made. Another selection comes at nine and the last at twelve.' Ma looked down at her gloved hands. 'Accompanying the *du-alakat* and the eldest to confront the dragons was my reward for passing. My first and last duty as a warrior of Khronosta.'

Char met Kyndra's eyes and knew she was thinking the same as he. 'So they were telling the truth,' he murmured. 'Khronosta *is* responsible for the Lleu-yelin's disappearance. Why?'

Ma's expression became guarded. 'I could not say. But when I refused to help, my people turned on me. I escaped.'

'And they let you go?' Kait asked. She stood with her arms folded, her long hair pulled over one shoulder. 'A girl who was destined to be the greatest of them? I'd have given chase.'

'They did,' Ma said. 'But I wasn't called the greatest for nothing.' She matched Kait stare for stare. 'Every skill they taught me, every trick – I used them to vanish.'

'That's when you found me,' Char put in.

Ma looked at him and then away. 'Yes, that's when I found you.'

'You've been hiding from Khronosta ever since. That's why we had to stay with Genge.'

'I am sorry, Boy. I needed a home on the move, a place where, once you proved yourself, nobody asked questions. I needed somewhere I could train you to fight against the day they found us.'

Char frowned. 'You knew they would?'

'I feared it. Every year brought rumours of more *du-alakat* murders. Their reach was growing. People began whispering the name of Khronosta. I knew it wouldn't be long before our paths crossed again.'

'Because they began searching for this Kala?'

'Yes,' she whispered.

'Ma.' Char went to her, took her gloved hands in his own. 'Please –' he was surprised to hear desperation in his voice – 'tell me I'm not their leader.'

She looked at him, her eyes sad. 'You are not.'

'But . . .' It wasn't the answer he'd expected. When the Khronostians had named him Kala back in Na Sung Aro, she'd not refuted it. 'What about the rage?' he whispered, aware of the others listening. 'What about my blood?'

Ma slowly shook her head.

'Then . . .' Char gripped her hands tighter. 'How can I convince the Khronostians?'

'There is a way,' she said softly and pulled her hands free. 'We must rescue your friend,' she said, turning to Kyndra. 'He cannot know his own importance, or what he is to the eldest.'

'What will they do to him?' Nediah asked.

'They will use him as an anchor,' Ma said. 'His life is a link to the distant past, to the time of the Conquest, to Solinaris. They will make him the first piece in their plan to topple the empire.'

'You mean they could go back that far in time?' Nediah said, incredulous. 'They could change the past?'

'They could,' Ma said. 'Your friend – they will use him to scout the past just as you would a new and unknown region. I fear they will soon have the power to touch it. We don't have long.'

'How do you know about Medavle being a Yadin?' Kyndra asked her suddenly.

'Following your trail, I overheard four *du-alakat*,' Ma replied evenly. 'You thoroughly succeeded in unnerving them, Starborn.' Her smile was thin. 'They are unused to encountering a person beyond their control.'

'Does that mean they can't harm me?'

'I would advise against complacency,' Ma said. 'With a large enough group, they may be able to trap you. Even a Starborn would be hard pressed to escape from a pocket of dead time.'

With all the talk of Khronosta, Char had almost forgotten Rogan, standing uncertainly on the edge of the group. Remembering their last meeting in Na Sung Aro, he could hardly believe *this* Rogan was the same person. He watched as the iarl approached Ma, looking a good deal less sure of himself. She gave him a pointed glance. 'Mines, Iarl Rogan? Some of your soft-footed servants look very familiar.'

Rogan pursed his lips. 'Perceptive as always, Ma. I do own mines, in fact, but they aren't staffed by slaves. Every one I've bought from Genge is given the same choice: pledge themselves to the cause I serve, or work until their debt is paid. Once it is, they go free.'

'Isn't that dangerous?' Char asked. 'Won't those you set free spread word of this Republic of yours?'

'None hear that name until they have sworn. I suspect they believe my cause the Defiant's.' Rogan frowned at him. 'By grace of the company you keep – and that's a story I have yet to hear – you were an exception. But from the things I've seen and heard tonight, it's not Sartyan interference I have to worry about.'

'We cannot delay,' Ma said to Kyndra. 'I can lead you to Khronosta, but the temple's current location is a three-week ride away, in a place called Samaya.'

'Isn't that an old Sartyan watchtower?' Rogan said. 'Abandoned, if I recall.'

Ma nodded. 'It is dangerous to leave the Yadin alone with the eldest.' Her expression darkened. 'He is mad and his madness is contagious. I would not want it to spread to your friend.'

'Why would you help us?' Kyndra asked her. She'd said little so far, but Char noticed her face tighten at the mention of madness.

'Because they are my people,' Ma answered after a moment. 'And I have been running long enough.'

'Wait,' Rogan said sharply. 'The Starborn and I have business to conclude in Cymenza. My superiors travel swiftly, but they won't arrive for another two days.'

Ma glowered at him. 'There are greater things at stake, Iarl Rogan. We must rescue the Yadin before Khronosta learns too much from him. If they find a means to change what has been without destabilizing the whole of time, you might not even have an empire to plot against.'

Rogan stared at her, his mouth slightly open. 'That's a bad thing?' he asked eventually.

'Instead of Sartya, you would have an ascendant Khronosta with all of time at their fingertips.' Ma wrapped her arms around herself, as if chilled by the thought. 'Total control. The smallest change can lead to the greatest upheaval. Think – if just one of your ancestors ceased to be or if their path strayed a little from the course it has taken, there would be no House Dukett . . . no Rogan.' Her eyes narrowed. 'They could unmake anyone.'

Rogan had paled. 'You said they didn't have the power.'

'I said they didn't have the power *yet*.'

The iarl didn't reply. He stared at the black trees, silhouetted against the rising moon. It was full dark now and the insects of the Cymenza night had begun to chirrup their shrill chorus.

Finally, Rogan sighed. 'If the threat is as great as you claim and your mission this vital, the Republic will assist. You shall have military support, supplies, whatever you need to reach Samaya swiftly. I will send the necessary messages.'

'Thank you, Rogan,' Ma said without expression. 'It would be welcome.'

'Come, let's return to the house,' the iarl beckoned them. 'I can't stand those damn cicadas.'

'You had a way to convince the Khronostians that I'm not the Kala,' Char said to Ma as he walked beside her.

'I do,' she replied heavily. 'When I am done with them, Boy, they will not hound you further.'

Char wasn't sure what to make of it. She sounded as if she meant to kill them all. Ma might be good, but she couldn't take on the whole of the *du-alakat*. He was just about to step into the parlour when a bright shape swooped down out of the night. Char cursed, ducked instinctively, but the thing soared right on over him to land on Kyndra's shoulder.

'An envoi,' she said, clearly surprised. 'Are you for me?'

It was a bird, Char realized, a raven carved as if from solid light. It hopped onto Kyndra's hand and promptly dissolved. Astonished, he watched words bubble out of the molten silver.

'It's from Brégenne. She –' Kyndra frowned as she read. 'That's odd. She wants to know about the Kingswold Knights.'

'Where is she?' Irilin and Nediah both said together.

'Ümvast, when she sent it.'

'So Gareth went home. Did she mention him?' Irilin's voice dropped. 'Did she mention Shika?'

The words faded and Kyndra shook her head. 'She said something went wrong with the last envoi. I don't think she knows.'

'Oh,' Irilin said. She swallowed. 'How is Gareth?'

'She's worried about him.'

'It's the gauntlet, isn't it?'

'Yes. They think they know what it is – part of a pair crafted over five hundred years ago by a man called Kingswold. He founded the knights.' Kyndra looked around at them all, her face framed by the dark fall of her hair. Char found himself staring at it, candlelight catching in its red strands. As if she felt his gaze, she turned to meet it and her eyes were the eyes of a

Starborn, depthless as the void. He suppressed a shiver, but he didn't look away.

'The knights were killed at Kalast,' Kyndra said, 'slaughtered in a battle with Sartya. I was –' She stopped. 'I mean, Kierik was there, but he arrived too late.' She looked down. 'Brégenne says that Kingswold's other gauntlet was lost in the battle. They need to find it.'

'Or what?' Irilin asked, anxiously twining her fingers together.

'The gauntlets are cursed so that they can't be worn separately. Brégenne thinks it's only because Gareth's a Wielder that he's still alive.'

'Who's Gareth?' Char asked.

'Our friend,' Kyndra said shortly. Her expression turned introspective. 'If the story's true, I wonder how Gareth's gauntlet ended up in Naris.'

Rogan raised a hand. 'Wait a moment. This happened in Acre?'

'A place called Kalast,' Kyndra said. 'Have you heard of it?'

Rogan grunted. 'No. Is it a city?'

'It *was* at the height of the empire – between Lycorash and Parth.'

'Lycorash was renamed Sarterion,' Rogan said, 'but most people call it by its old name out of Sartyan earshot. And I've been to Parth.'

'Kalast was about equidistant between the two,' Kyndra said, holding her hands apart. 'Is there nothing there now?'

'Yes,' Char said suddenly, his skin prickling with the thought. 'Not a city though,' he added when Kyndra turned to look at him. 'There are some ruins on the far side of the Deadwood. I heard stories about them. They're called Ben-haugr.'

Rogan frowned. 'I thought they were burial mounds,' he said, 'but I suppose there could be ruins beneath them. I wouldn't want to be the one to find out.'

'Why not?' Kyndra asked.

Char favoured her with a dark grin. 'You know in stories where they say *none who venture there ever return*? Well, in Ben-haugr's case, it's true.'

'Why would people go there, then?' Irilin said.

'Treasure,' Char suggested, 'renown, a bet . . . people aren't smart.'

Kyndra's brow furrowed. 'It could have something to do with Kingswold and the massacre of the knights. How far is it?'

'From here, I'd say a six-week journey on horseback,' Rogan said. 'Quickest way is through the Deadwood, though it's home to some unsavoury types.'

'Gareth's still in Mariar,' Irilin said despondently. 'It could take him a month to get even this far. What if he can't hold out that long?'

'Brégenne's with him,' Kyndra said. 'She'll make sure he gets there.'

'But she'll need a map, directions,' Irilin argued. 'And if this place is dangerous, she should be warned.'

'We can send an envoi just before dawn,' Nediah stepped in. 'It's tricky, but I'll teach you how. With your Lunar power letting it travel at night, it'll reach Brégenne in a few days.' Char heard his voice catch on the woman's name.

'I wish we could help them,' Irilin said, looking at Kyndra.

Before she could reply, Ma said brusquely, 'Send this envoi, if you must, but as soon as it's done, we strike out for Khronosta.'

'Khronosta,' Kyndra repeated, her eyes distant. 'Medavle

wanted me to contact them, you know. He talked about making an alliance.' She paused, took a breath. 'What if, when the time comes, he won't return with us?'

Ma's hands strayed to her kali sticks, fingers lightly touching their smooth surface. 'I will do what I must to protect this world,' she said.

30

'Thank you for coming so swiftly,' Brégenne said to Argat as they stood once more on the deck of the *Eastern Set*. 'It seems we're in your debt again. Gareth isn't up to a long journey on foot.' She lowered her voice. 'The trek south from Stjórna nearly killed him.'

Gareth slumped on some barrels nearby, his eyes hollow and staring. If it hadn't been for Ümvast's warriors, Brégenne wasn't sure they'd have made it back to the forest's edge, not with Gareth collapsing every hour. They'd been forced to leave most of the warriors behind – there wasn't room on the ship for them all – but half a dozen remained to watch over Gareth . . . or to ensure he kept his end of the bargain.

'Looks like he's on his last legs,' Yara muttered. 'What've you been doing since we dropped you off?'

Brégenne thought of the withered forest and the deathly chill in Gareth's eyes. She thought of their battle with the wyverns, the shock of their confrontation with Ümvast and the revelations about the gauntlet. 'It's been a mad few weeks,' she sighed.

'I might be inclined to accept payment in stories,' Argat said with a nod to Gareth. 'I'm thinking of writing a book.'

Yara rolled her eyes. 'To business,' she said to Brégenne. 'You might feel reassured to know that there's only one viable route into Mariar.'

'We've flown up and down the border, looking for potential crossing points,' Argat added, 'but the wasteland is as extensive as the mountains used to be. No army of reasonable size could cross unseen or with any speed.'

'That *is* reassuring,' Brégenne said. 'But to be honest, I'm amazed you haven't flown halfway across Acre by now.'

'We spent some time in Jarra,' the first mate said. 'I told the captain it would be a poor idea to fly into the unknown with anything less than a full complement of fuel.'

Brégenne gazed at the hills of broken stone beneath the airship's hull. From this height, they resembled the ridged back of a colossal beast stretched out in sleep. 'Kyndra sent me a message,' she said. 'She and her companions believe that the ruins of Kalast still exist as part of an extensive burial ground.' Brégenne strove to suppress a shudder, but she didn't quite manage it. Kyndra's description of Ben-haugr reminded her unpleasantly of the images she'd seen when she'd tried to remove the gauntlet. The enthroned king, winding passages, the ceiling pressing down like the lid of a coffin.

She shook herself. 'We just need to find some landmarks. One's a city called Parth. Kyndra says it'll be a nine-week journey on horseback.'

Yara's brow creased. 'I'd say we could more than halve that,' she said, after some swift calculation. 'But we'll be running at a reduced speed to conserve fuel—'

'And tying up at night, if possible,' Argat told her. 'I won't endanger my ship by flying blind across unfamiliar terrain.' He looked at Brégenne. 'Don't suppose you happen to have a map?'

'I have a rough one in here.' Brégenne tapped her skull.

'Much good that will do.'

'You'll have to trust me,' she said, which only caused Argat to grumble.

'How accurate is your information?' he asked suspiciously.

'It's the best we're going to get, Argat. Kyndra told me everything she knew about the knights.' That wasn't all Kyndra had told her. Brégenne glanced at Gareth. The news of Shika's death had deeply shocked her, coming so suddenly in the midst of the message about Kalast. She knew she owed Gareth the truth about his friend, but she hadn't been able to tell him. He was already so frail; she feared what it might do to him. She had so many questions about events in the red valley and such an incomplete account of Shika's death. What did they mean by saying they'd had no body to bury? If she told Gareth, he'd want to know everything, he *should* know everything.

'This is intolerable!'

Kul'Das's strident voice broke into her thoughts and Brégenne briefly closed her eyes. How she wished they'd been able to leave the woman behind. When she opened them, she saw Kul'Das tottering across the deck, her hand clapped to her mouth.

'I demand you land this . . . this *thing* right now.'

'Demand?' Argat said with a dangerous smile. 'No one demands anything of me, especially on board my own ship.'

'I am a Kul —' she began but stopped. Yara was casually toss-ing her dagger back and forth between her hands.

'You are under the captain's authority,' the first mate said. 'If you want off, the rail's right there.'

Kul'Das glanced over the side of the airship and then clearly wished she hadn't, for the hand went back over her mouth. She turned and rushed to the other rail, where they all heard her violent retching.

'That should keep her busy,' Yara announced smugly to Bré-genne. 'It took me a full six months to stop feeling ill when I first came aboard.'

Doing her best to block out the sounds of Kul'Das losing her lunch, Brégenne sighed. This was going to be a long voyage.

The first night passed without incident. Yara stilled the rear paddles and the crew scurried like rats down ropes to anchor the great ship amongst a stand of pines. They'd come to the end of the wasteland that evening. Though they were officially in Acre now, to Brégenne it didn't seem any different. *I'm travel-ling a land out of the stories,* she thought, but the rock looked like rock, the trees like trees and she couldn't help but feel it was all a bit anticlimactic.

When morning came, they sailed west. Brégenne stood at the rail, enjoying the breeze in her face and her hair flying behind her, as she studied the landscape beneath. She wasn't the only one; Argat's crew were fascinated, often glancing up from whatever chores he'd set them to gaze at the scenery. So too were the warriors from Ümvast. Though a few shared Kul'Das's distaste for flying, they were all as equally stunned at the fact that they'd passed over the westernmost mountains into a land long thought lost.

At midday they flew over a settlement and had their first glimpse of Acre's people. The town was small, built into the rocky highlands, and when the shadow of the ship slid over it like a hunting dragon, cries reached Brégenne's ears. The crew's eyes were bright, the warriors crowded at the rail like excited children, and even Gareth managed a grin. Kul'Das looked as surly as always, but she was the only one. Argat and Yara stood shoulder to shoulder at the prow and their smiles were as wide as Brégenne had ever seen them.

'We'll sail into history,' the captain declared, his leather coat slapping the wind. 'Our names will be inked for luck in the margins of every logbook.'

Buoyed by the mood, they spent the rest of the afternoon gliding along the fringes of the highlands, but enthusiasm gradually faded to nervousness as evening fell and the time came to anchor. Brégenne thought she knew why. Up in the sky, they felt as untouchable as gods. Down here, they were mortal again.

Argat finally found a spot he deemed acceptable, at the steep lip of a valley that sloped back into barren hills. The braziers were extinguished and without their constant heat, the vast balloons sagged until the ship settled to ground with a groan. They took it in turns to eat and keep watch. The air was still cold, and Brégenne was glad they'd left the snows of Ümvast behind. It was a clear night, the stars scattered like silver coins across a merchant's counting cloth, and she felt the moon in her bones. Its light was crisp and strong as it flowed through her body.

Gareth was restless. Brégenne noticed his eyes straying to the edge of the trees that marched down the high valley, until they stopped short of the airship. He was always worse when the sun set and the Solar power slept – she was certain it served as a buffer between him and the gauntlet. She watched as he wandered to the ship's rail, the moon riming his fur-trimmed cloak.

He had no shadow.

Brégenne's breath caught. The moon scored her own silhouette in sharp lines on the deck behind her, but when she looked at Gareth, there was nothing, as if he lacked substance. She glanced around. Sailors were superstitious; there'd be no telling what the crew would do if they noticed. Gareth seemed unaware, so Brégenne decided not to say anything. He still complained of feeling cold, even standing in sunlight, and each day his face was more corpse-like, his skin more waxen.

'Are you all right?' she asked cautiously, coming to lean beside him on the rail.

The look he gave her was answer enough. Brégenne tried to inject some confidence into her voice. 'We'll find it, Gareth.'

'Even if we do, my mother wants it. She wants them both. We promised the gauntlets to Argat.' His tone was expressionless.

'It's a problem I haven't figured out an answer to yet,' Brégenne admitted. She studied him closely. 'Don't say you want to keep them, Gareth? After everything you've been through?'

He was silent.

'Your mother wants them to protect her people,' Brégenne said. 'Perhaps we can convince Argat that it's a worthier cause.' She paused. 'If it were up to me, I'd say nobody should have them. They sound too powerful and too dangerous.'

'She'll do it, you know,' Gareth said. 'If she doesn't hear from us, or if we don't return with the gauntlets, she'll march on the southlands.'

'Would she really?' Brégenne asked. 'Knowing that Rairam is

itself in danger of invasion, would she weaken what strength we have?'

Gareth stared at the moonlit woods. 'You don't understand. It's a matter of honour. Whoever holds the title of Ümvast is responsible for the well-being of the north. None of Mother's predecessors have ever been driven from our ancestral home.' He sounded old to Brégenne, his voice, his choice of words, as if a lifetime had passed since he'd left Naris. 'She will do what she must to protect our people. If that means starting a war . . .' He trailed off, leaning forward over the rail to peer more closely at the treeline.

'I *knew* I saw movement,' he said, clenching his fist as if in self-rebuke. 'There –' he pointed – 'and there. We're being watched.'

Brégenne drew on her Lunar vision as she had done for so many years, but still couldn't see anything. 'Are you sure it's not just an animal?'

Gareth shook his head. 'It's people.' He glanced at his right wrist, shuddered briefly. 'I can feel them.'

'Stay here and keep watch. I'll tell Argat.'

She found the captain in his saloon. 'Gareth spotted movement among the trees,' she said as soon as she opened the door. 'He thinks we're being watched.'

Argat snapped a box shut and swiftly made it disappear. 'How many?' he asked, heading around his desk.

'I don't—'

The rest of her sentence was lost in a wild shout from above. She and Argat both ran for the deck. One of the balloons was on fire. Yara tore past Brégenne with a bucket, her teeth bared in fury. 'Get those flames out!' she bellowed, tossing her water at the fire, which hissed and spat.

As Argat added his voice to the order, Brégenne looked for Gareth. The young man had backed away from the rail, his eyes sweeping the darkness on both sides of the ship. 'It's just a distraction,' he gasped as Brégenne hurried up to him. 'They're surrounding us.'

Brégenne looked where he was pointing and saw figures creeping out of the night. One held a torch; the bowman responsible for setting the balloon alight. He wore a dented breastplate and his legs were dubiously protected by scuffed greaves. An axe – more a woodcutter's than a warrior's – hung at his side.

But the Lunar revealed other men, a whole lot of them, whose armour looked more serviceable and whose unsheathed weapons gleamed violent promises in their hands. The bowman was on the verge of sending another lit arrow into the balloon, but a man stopped him. Bandits who wanted to keep the airship intact? Brégenne wondered.

She was almost rewarded for her staring with an arrow through the neck. Brégenne seized the Lunar and a barrier sprang up at her skin, knocking the missile harmlessly aside. She saw the bowman call a warning as he pointed in her direction. Nediah had told her about 'aberrations' – Acre's name for Wielders – maybe they took her for one.

There was no sign of Kul'Das when Ümvast's warriors burst out onto the deck. 'Keep them off the ship,' Brégenne cried at them. Their leader, a woman, nodded at her and unsheathed a bow, taking careful aim in the low light. The airship's crew was still focused on the balloon, though the flames seemed to be under control now. Brégenne threw up a shield behind which the warriors could safely shoot. 'Argat!' she shouted.

The captain's face was as furious as Yara's as he took in their situation. They were badly outnumbered – there had to be a hundred men out there.

Brégenne gathered her resolve. If they wanted a fight, she'd give them a fight. Once they saw what she was capable of, they'd flee into the hills. She raised her arms, exulting in the power that burned in her veins, sending the same Lunar lightning that she'd conjured in Ümvast's hall shooting into their midst.

Smoke curled up from charred patches of earth and voices cried out in pain. Brégenne hardened her heart. Using the Lunar to harm had always seemed abominable to her, the very worst exercise of power. She clothed herself in the moon, so that she appeared a blazing, faceless figure, hoping she'd instil enough terror to send them running.

The bandits retreated. Frowning after them, Brégenne had only a moment's warning before a storm of arrows hurtled at the airship from both sides. She moved faster than she ever had, sending out a wave of light that incinerated the projectiles in mid-air. But she'd panicked and thrown too much energy into the blast. Depending how full their quivers were, she couldn't use the same technique more than half a dozen times. Perhaps a shield instead, she thought feverishly – they needed to get out of range. Could she hold a shield large enough to cover the whole ship?

Another volley of arrows came and she wasn't fast enough to destroy them all. One grazed her cheekbone and thudded into the mast behind her. The pain arrived almost instantly; she raised a hand and stared numbly at the blood on her fingers.

Their attackers shouted as they saw her falter. One of Ümvast's warriors was down, an arrow through his knee. The woman who led them raced low across the deck, using whatever she could find as cover. Her quiver was nearly empty; Brégenne watched her last two arrows streak into the dark and heard screams as they found their marks.

Gareth was standing rigid. He was staring at Brégenne, at the blood on her face, and she watched his own darken with anger. His chest rose and fell hugely, as if he struggled for breath. His thin ribs stood out with the movement.

Before her eyes, he changed. Darkness like descending night enveloped him, flowing out of the gauntlet. 'No!' she gasped and stumbled towards him. 'Gareth, fight it.'

If he heard her, he gave no sign. His eyes were black, filmed like an oil slick over clear water. Despite the still night, tattered shadows streamed off him as if he stood in a gale. He walked towards the airship's rail.

'Gareth!' she screamed, watching helplessly as he climbed over and dropped onto the bare ground below. Regardless of the danger, Brégenne rushed to the rail, still calling his name. His rash action gave their attackers pause; they eyed him uncertainly, but the young man bore no visible weapon and their hesitation didn't last long. They encircled him until Gareth was an island in a bristling sea of steel. He seemed a figure of darkness, clad in shifting ebony armour hammered out of shadow.

Gareth crouched and plunged his hands into the earth.

It was impossible, of course, the ground here was solid rock with a scant layer of dirt atop it, but Gareth's fingers sank straight through and black streams boiled up around them, flowing towards their attackers. When the first tendril licked at a man's boots, he began to scream. His companions backed away as he held out beseeching arms swiftly riddling with rot. The bones in his legs disintegrated beneath him and he toppled to the ground. Brégenne stood frozen, unable to tear her eyes from the scene. The dark power devoured the man's flesh until the only thing left was a perfect skeleton, its jaw hanging open, as if to scream still.

Their attackers broke, turning and hurling themselves into the night. When some tripped and fell in the gloom, the black bubbling streams found them too, turning flesh to rot and then bone. Gareth – or the thing that had been Gareth – straightened to watch. He was floating a little off the ground, Brégenne saw, and the black raiment continued to billow about him.

Yara was shouting orders at the panicked crew. 'Get them reinflated!' Brégenne heard her yell. 'They're not too damaged to lift us out of here.'

'Wait!' Brégenne called. 'We can't leave him.'

'I'm not having that *thing* anywhere near me,' Yara gasped, the whites of her eyes showing. It was the first time Brégenne had seen her scared. And maybe she was right. When Gareth turned to look at her, there was nothing of the young man in his face, nothing even of the living. He'd come back from the brink before, but had never been so consumed. Her heart sank. Dawn was hours away – there was no help to be had from the Solar.

Brégenne swallowed. Lunar *was* Solar, she thought. In its basic state, the energy was the same; perhaps she could use it to reach him. *I have to go down there*. Her courage wavered; a part of her desperately wanted to turn and flee. The ground around the airship was spotted white with bones and the charnel stink of decaying flesh lingered in the air.

Gareth started to drift towards them. Before her nerve failed, Brégenne hooked a leg over the ship's rail and used one of the trailing ropes to swing to earth. Yara screamed her name and she hoped the ship wouldn't just cast off without her. She couldn't spare a look, too frightened to break eye contact with Gareth.

His face was almost as skeletal as the skulls surrounding them, covered by a bare scrap of flesh, but she had to believe she could reach him; if she failed, she would die. He extended his gauntleted hand towards her, slowly splaying his fingers. Brégenne looked at that hand and she shuddered, knowing what it was capable of.

Then she seized hold of it.

The Lunar pouring into her spasmed in protest. She struggled to maintain the connection, to pull energy down from the sky to fill the space inside her. Brégenne gritted her teeth, fighting harder, dimly aware that her skin was mottling black where it touched Gareth's. Those soulless eyes widened as she stared into them, as she forced the energy down her arm and into the wasted hand she held.

Gareth let out a shriek, a high, cold wail that no human throat could make. Though it chilled Brégenne, she didn't let go, but forced more Lunar energy into him, feeling it battling with the power of the gauntlet. Slowly, slowly, the silver spread and the shadows that wrapped Gareth withdrew, shrinking from his body, curling down into the gauntlet on his arm. While his face was again familiar, it was still a death mask.

As the power that held him aloft relinquished its grip, Gareth's feet touched earth and immediately his legs crumpled, pulling Brégenne down too. She stopped the flow of Lunar energy, but she couldn't let him go, not yet, not until she was sure she had him back. His eyes were closed as she leaned over him, ear to his chest, listening hard, looking for signs of life.

There were none. Gareth was dead.

31

'You're holding it wrong.'

'I'm holding it like you showed me.'

'No, you're not. It's a stick not a sword – no sharp edges. You look like you're planning to run me through with it and, believe me, the most I'd get is a nasty bruise.'

Kyndra scowled, adjusting her grip on the kali stick. 'Better?'

'Not really,' Char told her. 'You need to angle it across your body like this.' He demonstrated with the other stick, holding it at a diagonal in front of him, left end pointing up.

Kyndra copied him.

'Good,' he said. 'Now loosen your wrist. You've got it in a death grip.'

She tried to hold it less tightly.

'I can still see the tension in your hand. You need suppleness in order to move fluidly from form to form.'

'If I loosen my grip any more, I'll drop it,' she snapped.

'It's about finding the balance. If you hold it too tightly –' he swung his own kali stick, it struck hers hard and sent it flying

418

from her hand – 'your wrist locks and you can't block in time.'
He poked her in the stomach with the end of his stick. 'Dead.'

She suppressed a growl. 'You didn't give me any warning.'

'And you think an enemy will?'

Kyndra struggled to master her frustration as she collected
her dropped kali stick. Why had she ever asked Char to teach
her in the first place? He was a terrible teacher.

Or you're a terrible learner.

She grudgingly acknowledged the truth of that. Perhaps she
just wasn't warrior material. *I didn't exactly grow up in a place
that encouraged weapons training*, she thought, picturing sleepy
Brenwym. She felt a fleeting urge to laugh: wine was her spe-
cialist knowledge, along with ale and beer and convincing people
they wanted to buy it. She'd not be fighting battles wielding
that.

Ma sat beneath a tree, watching them. Her face was closed;
they were a week out of Cymenza and still Kyndra couldn't
decide what to make of her, or of her relationship with Char.
She claimed he was like a son, but treated him much as she did
everyone else – with quiet words and distance.

It also felt strange to be on the road again without Medavle.
The Yadin could be as reticent as Ma, but Kyndra realized
they'd unconsciously looked to him to guide. She might be the
Starborn who'd led them into Acre, but it was Medavle's presence that had kept them from feeling they were moving blindly.
She remembered Ma's unveiled threat on the night he'd been
taken and shivered; Medavle couldn't know what the Khronostians were planning to do with him, surely he couldn't.

'An opponent isn't likely to wait for you to stop dreaming,'
came Char's voice and Kyndra started. Night was coming down
fast, concealing the lush valley where they had camped to await

the arrival of Rogan's promised backup. His agents were out there even now, watching for the hundred or so fighters who'd accompany them to Khronosta. She'd feel a lot better with a sizable force around her, Kyndra admitted.

She raised her stick again, angling it as Char had shown her. He nodded in approval. When he swung his kali stick, she successfully blocked it, jumping back as it came swishing in again at a different height. 'Unorthodox,' he said at her leap. 'You're supposed to be practising blocking, not dodging.'

'At least I didn't get hit,' she said and then gasped as he darted forward, swung his weapon and once again sent her stick spinning into the air.

'You're letting your guard down,' he said reprovingly, as he bent to fetch the kali stick from the ground. 'Few fights are finished in a single strike unless one of the participants is especially skilful.'

'Well, you're only letting me practise with a single weapon. Why can't I try with both?'

'Because you need to get your stance and your grip right first. Otherwise there's no point.'

Kyndra gave him a dark look and Char held up his hands, still clutching the kali sticks. 'All right. Here –' he thrust the sticks at her – 'be my guest.'

She took them, feeling how light and yet tough each one was. They'd once been polished, but were scuffed now through use. 'What wood is this?' she asked curiously.

'It's not wood. They're made from a kind of vine.'

'A *vine*?'

'Rattan,' Char clarified. 'These are the basic type. Ma has a pair of ironwood ones – much more dangerous – so she used rattan for sparring with me.'

Kyndra glanced at the woman beneath the tree and then turned the kali sticks over in her hands. 'I can't believe they'll actually turn a blade.'

'They don't splinter like wood and they're far lighter. They're built for moving quickly.'

She planted her feet in the defensive stance and raised the stick in her right hand, but she was unsure what to do with the left.

'Like this,' Char explained as he moved behind her, positioning her arms so that the right guarded her upper body, the left her lower. 'Bend your knees a little more,' he murmured in her ear and she couldn't suppress a shiver at the feel of his breath on her neck, the touch of his hands on her bare forearms, his skin feverish hot as always. His hands lingered a little longer before letting her go. She tried to ignore how hard her heart was beating.

She stole a glance at Char as he returned to stand in front of her and couldn't help noticing the strength in his arms, the contrast his hair made against his dusky skin, the coiled way he held himself, as if he never dared relax.

They stopped the practice when it grew too dark to see. *What's the point anyway*, Kyndra thought despondently, going to check on her horse. She hadn't shown much prowess at fighting and didn't have the time to learn to wield the sticks as Char did. She knew the real reason behind her request was to avoid using her powers; frightened of losing herself to the unfeeling dominion of the stars. She feared Char knew it too.

The black stallion snorted into her palm and she fed him one of the apples from her saddlebag. She'd finally decided on a name; he deserved one after what he'd been through. Alioth, she called him, which meant literally 'black horse' in Acrean. It was a word she'd learned unwittingly from Kierik – not very imaginative, but she liked the sound of it.

'Kyndra? Are you all right?'

She realized she'd buried her face in her horse's flank, trying to still the turbulence inside her. When she looked up, she saw Nediah, his green eyes serious. 'We'll get him back,' the Wielder said.

'It's not just about Medavle,' she said softly. 'I . . . everything that's happened. I feel like I've been blundering along, making mistake after mistake, and it's only you and the others who've kept things from falling apart.' When she saw him about to speak, she rushed on. 'We couldn't have gained Ségin's trust without you healing Owen. The Defiant would be dead if Medavle and Irilin hadn't helped clear that passage. *You* were the one who saw the truth about the Sartyans – I should have listened to you. I was so determined to avoid repeating the past.'

Nediah frowned. 'Where has all this come from?'

'I just . . .' Kyndra shook her head. 'I don't know why any of you ever looked to me to lead. Shika –' her voice cracked – 'is dead because of me, along with hundreds of soldiers who were only following orders. All because I don't want to be a Starborn. I don't want to be what I am.'

'Shika's death was not your fault, Kyndra.' He lightly touched her shoulder. 'And every decision you've made – I wouldn't have supported them if I didn't agree. It was an admirable goal, seeking a way to avoid war by allying with Sartya.'

'Why did you come with me, Nediah?' Kyndra asked him baldly. 'You were under no obligation to. None of you were.'

'I couldn't have let you go alone into Acre.'

'But you left Brégenne.' She looked him in the eye, seeing the familiar hardening of his face whenever anyone spoke

Brégenne's name. 'Don't pretend you don't care. I know what she means to you. We were all there when you healed her. And then you left her behind without a second glance.'

Nediah looked away. 'I know,' he whispered. He turned to face the night, putting the camp at his back. 'It was for the best, Kyndra. She doesn't want me. She said so herself.'

'That's crazy,' Kyndra said, anger stirring at how foolish they both were. 'It's quite obvious how she feels.' She glanced back at the camp where the others sat. 'Kait knows it. Why do you think she came with us instead of staying with the Nerian?'

'Kait –' Nediah broke off, a flush in his cheeks. 'If you're implying she still cares for me, you're wrong.'

'Gods.' It was a word she'd unwittingly picked up from Char. 'Are you blind? You're the only reason Kait stays. She hates Medavle because of what he did to Kierik. She hates me because Kierik would still be alive if I weren't here. And I don't imagine she cares a bit for Irilin.' Kyndra wanted to shake him. 'Why would she risk her life walking into the unknown if it weren't for you?'

Nediah stared at her and a flush rose to Kyndra's cheeks too. His love life was none of her business – surely they all had bigger things to worry about. 'Sorry,' she muttered.

'You've given me something to think about,' Nediah said a little ruefully. 'And I came to see whether *you* were all right.'

'I'm glad you're here, Nediah,' Kyndra said after a moment. 'Even though I meant what I said about Brégenne. I couldn't have made it this far without you.'

To her great surprise, he hugged her. 'None of *us* would be here without you, Kyndra. You stopped the Breaking, saved the citadel from the Madness, and you were brave enough to walk into the unknown for the sake of a world and its people.' He pulled back so that he could look down into her face. 'I don't know many eighteen-year-olds who could say the same.'

'Aren't you afraid of what I am?' she said quietly. 'Of what I could do?'

Nediah smiled at her. 'Do you want to know what Brégenne said to me the night we met in your inn? She's always had a feeling for such things.'

Kyndra remembered looking back at the two strangers, as they'd been at the time, as she left to fetch her Acrean book, seeing Brégenne whispering into Nediah's ear. It seemed so long ago, as if it had happened to someone else. She nodded.

'She said, "When we leave, the girl must come with us."' Nediah's smile faded to seriousness. '"With the power she might one day wield, she could change the world. I'd like to be there when she does."'

His look spoke of respect between equals and it brought a lump to Kyndra's throat.

'Master Nediah, Mistress Kyndra,' came a voice and they both turned. One of Rogan's scouts melted out of the darkness. 'Our people should be here in minutes.'

'Thank you,' Nediah said when Kyndra was silent. He offered her his arm and they walked back to the others. Kait gave Kyndra a glare that said she strongly suspected they'd been talking about her.

Kyndra was looking north when the first torch appeared from behind a hill. The heart of Calmaracia cut a stark contrast to the dusty wastelands they'd encountered in Baior, full of little rivers and dales. Except for the golden vineyards, it made her think of the Valleys, of her home. She watched a bit nervously as the bobbing lights came closer. There were only a handful;

just enough to see by. Clearly the Republic didn't choose to court attention.

Char got to his feet, easing the kali sticks in their scabbard. Kyndra guessed the years he'd spent in the desert had given him a healthy suspicion of anyone and everyone. Irilin came to stand beside her. 'I don't trust him,' she said quietly.

'Rogan?'

'The slaver.' Irilin stared at Char's back with burning eyes.

'He's never given us reason not to.'

'Has he ever shown any remorse for what he is? Ever offered us an explanation? How can you trust someone like that?'

Kyndra bit her lip. Char hadn't talked about his life in the Beaches at all. She'd assumed it was because he wanted to forget it. 'Perhaps he thinks it's none of our business,' she said.

'We saved him from those Khronostians. It *is* our business.'

Maybe she was right. But Irilin didn't know what Kyndra did. She didn't know about the rage Char struggled against, the violent force inside him desperate to claw free. And she didn't feel what Kyndra felt whenever she looked at Char. They were alike, both outsiders, fighting a nature they wanted to deny. Their small campfire limned his silhouette in flame. *She* would have to give in one day; perhaps Char would too. Then, whatever he was, they'd both be changed irrevocably.

Beside her, Irilin tensed, as the first of the newcomers reached the outskirts of their camp. She was a shade away from calling the Lunar and Kyndra placed a reassuring hand on her arm before moving forward to greet Rogan's people. They were plainly armoured, nothing like the distinctive blood-red mail of the Sartyans. Most of the faces she saw were grim, some were scarred; there were men and women and others so young they could barely be called either. They all had one thing in common:

425

each wore a cloak of black feathers that covered their shoulders and backs.

A man emerged out of their midst, striding right up to Kyndra. 'You must be the Starborn,' he said. He ran a hand over his shorn scalp and then held it out briskly for her to shake. 'Amon Taske. Apologies for the delay. We ran into trouble near Deliar. I'm a fool for underestimating Iresonté.'

Kyndra frowned. 'The captain of the stealth force?'

'You know of her?' Taske looked surprised. 'She's recently moved up in the world. That's one promotion I hoped never to see.'

'Promotion?'

There was a stir in the feathered ranks, as people parted to let someone through. 'Ah,' Taske said, turning, 'here's the commander. He can tell you more.'

'When did I say I'd take the job?' came a familiar voice. Kyndra's eyes widened and she exchanged a stunned glance with Irilin.

'General Hagdon,' the young woman said quietly as Hagdon walked up to them. The same black feathers adorned his shoulders and beneath the cloak, he wore scuffed armour that had seen almost as much use as it could take. His beard was untrimmed, his dark eyes harried; he seemed to have aged since Kyndra had seen him last. She stared at him, utterly at a loss for words.

'Well, shit,' Char said behind her.

32

Calmaracia, Acre
Hagdon

Once Hagdon could have laughed at their shock, but Carn's death and the death of his old life were still too raw. 'Our paths seem fated to cross,' he said to the Starborn, 'Kyndra Vale.' He looked at the young woman beside her. 'Irilin.'

Irilin blinked at hearing her name; perhaps she hadn't expected him to recall it.

'General Hagdon,' Kyndra said with a faint nod.

'Not general,' he replied a little bitterly, 'just James Hagdon. Our fortunes have somewhat reversed.'

'How?' Kyndra asked. 'What happened?'

'Apparently the emperor no longer desires my service,' Hagdon said, clasping his hands behind his back. 'He would rather have my head. I've yet to hear it from his lips, of course.'

'*General* Iresonté', Taske explained, 'took it upon herself to speak for His Majesty.'

Kyndra frowned. 'You mean he doesn't know?'

'Oh, I suspect he knows,' Hagdon said, 'and did nothing to stop it. He excused Iresonté the first time she tried to kill me.'

He studied Kyndra; she looked a little different. A tattoo glowed on her cheek and he found himself staring at it. 'You realize you were the root of the unrest. My officers demanded retribution for the deaths of so many men. Iresonté was particularly upset by the loss of her second.'

A shadow passed across Kyndra's face. 'I am sorry,' she said. 'I didn't intend for it to happen. If you'd only agreed to a truce, if Iresonté hadn't planted Tava in the Defiant—'

'The boy,' Hagdon said, rolling his injured shoulder. 'A good shot. A little more to the right and Iresonté wouldn't have had to take matters into her own hands.' He looked away. 'Carn would not have died.'

'Carn would have been her first victim,' Taske countered forcefully, gripping Hagdon's arm. 'She'd have begun by eliminating all those loyal to you. A clean slate.'

Hagdon stood looking into the night before sighing and rubbing his forehead. 'A clean slate. I suppose you're right.'

'I've offered you the same.'

'And I'm grateful, Taske. For the offer and for my life. But I've seen the way some look at me. I've had a long career with the Fist and resentments run deep.'

'We leave our old selves behind when we join the Republic,' Taske said, folding muscled arms across his chest, 'and count nearly as many Sartyans amongst our number as other folk. If we want to break the banner of the empire and give Acre back to its people, we need to show that we can work together now – or what hope is there of working together once Sartya is overthrown?'

'If only we'd found you when we first arrived in Acre,' one of Kyndra's companions said ruefully. Hagdon recognized her and the man beside her from their last encounter. She was a tall woman with almond eyes and long brown hair. She stood like a warrior; Hagdon made a note to keep her at a distance. Those eyes had an odd light in them.

Instead of the Yadin, on whose kidnapping he'd been briefed, there were two strangers, a young man and a woman, both dressed in the clothes of the desert. Kali sticks hung from their belts and the sight brought back memories of Khronosta, its great orange pillars carved with sinuous forms, the courtyard piled with Sartyan dead. Hagdon found himself tensing. 'You two,' he said. 'Tell me who you are.'

'They are my allies,' Kyndra said, stepping in. She glanced at them. 'Char and Ma Lesko. Ma is . . . familiar with the Khronostians. She's leading us to their temple.'

Hagdon sensed there was more. Ma was perhaps a bit younger than he, her dark eyes assessing him as he assessed her. If she was Khronostian, she didn't look it – at least, she didn't possess the terrible features of the *du-alakat*. Hagdon switched his gaze to the young man – he didn't look Khronostian either; neither did he look like Ma. It was hard to tell in the low light, but there was something unusual about his skin and his yellow eyes were discomfiting; they seemed to glow.

Hagdon scratched his chin, feeling the rough growth of beard he hadn't bothered to shave. He hadn't bothered over many such things in the last two weeks and could almost hear Carn's voice berating him for neglecting his appearance.

'Why would you want a Sartyan officer as your commander?' he'd said to Taske when the former commandant explained his plan.

Taske's reply was sober. 'Who better to marshal our forces against the Fist than the Fist's own general?'

429

'And you don't care about the things I have done – the people I've killed in the emperor's name?'

'We care,' Taske said softly, 'but the Republic must look to its future. Although more join every day, our numbers cannot equal the Fist's. Nor are we as well trained and equipped. Militarily, we're at a disadvantage.' He looked Hagdon in the eye. 'With odds like ours, we need the best.'

'If I was the best, I'd still be general.'

'No.' Taske's gloved hand was heavy on Hagdon's shoulder. 'Change is coming. A Starborn walks Acre once more, Rairam has returned and Khronosta – so Rogan reports – seeks the power to rewrite history. Ambertrix and the days of the empire's strength are spent.' Taske's hard face was flushed; Hagdon had never seen him so vehement. 'Either we seize the chance change offers, or we allow ourselves to be swept aside.' Taske removed his hand. 'You never struck me as a man who would tolerate being swept aside. Not by the Fist, not by the emperor.'

'Now might be the time to discuss our plans,' a voice said, bringing Hagdon back to the present. The man standing beside the almond-eyed woman held out his hand. 'I'm Nediah,' he said, 'and this is Kait. You already know that we're Wielders.' There was a hint of reticence in the way he said it that brought the spectre of Tava to hover between them. 'If you are leading this mission to Khronosta, you should be aware that we can only use our abilities during daylight.'

Hagdon gave a cool nod, despite the fact that his insides were tying themselves in knots. He still dreamed of the last mission he'd led to Khronosta – the shock of Iresonté's treachery, the horror of stumbling over hundreds of his own dead, the face of the *du-alakat* woman, all wrong, lying among the splinters of the gate. The whole foreign beauty of the temple with its orange stone and carvings . . . beautiful, yes, but terrible – he'd felt the unnaturalness of the place in his blood.

'You have seen it,' the woman called Ma said. Her gaze was sharp, knowing. 'You have seen Khronosta.'

Hagdon frowned. 'How do you know?'

'It is written in your face.'

'I led a raid,' he admitted, 'several weeks ago. It was a disaster.'

Ma nodded as if it could never have been otherwise. 'Brave,' she said, 'to take the fight to them, but foolish too. The temple is their ground and will be well warded.' She turned to gaze west. 'We should not venture inside it. I do not know what power the stone holds.'

Familiar with the Khronostians. 'It sounds as if you're more than familiar,' Hagdon said suspiciously.

'I was raised there.'

'You –' For a moment he could only gape at her. 'You're one of them?'

'I was,' Ma said softly. She wore elbow-length gloves and fiddled with them as she spoke. 'Long ago. But I . . . disagreed with the eldest and he frightened me. He had dark ambitions. The power of the Khronostians is not supposed to be used to bend the world to their will.' Her eyes held a light that was somehow both dangerous and sad. 'I left my people. Now I fear the power the eldest has gathered in the years I've been gone.'

'How do you propose to rescue Medavle?' the Wielder called Nediah asked. 'If these *du-alakat* are stronger in the temple, how will we lure them out to fight?'

Ma glanced at the young man standing beside her. 'With something they desperately want.'

'But you said I wasn't the Kala,' Char protested.

'They do not know that.' She touched his face. 'Their belief blinds them.'

Hagdon remembered the Khronostian Iresonté had dragged into his tent, bruised and bleeding. Hadn't he mentioned something about a 'Kala'? '*What* aren't you?' he asked the young man.

'Their leader,' Char said bitterly. 'Prophesied to return to them.' He ran a hand through the ashen tangle of his hair. 'They seem convinced.'

Hagdon scratched at his beard again; it would have to go. Was this what Iresonté had meant by leverage? 'Iresonté is searching for you,' he said to Char. 'She had a Khronostian prisoner who told her about the Kala.' A prickle ran down his neck. 'She also claimed to have Khronosta's next location. It could be we'll have company.'

'Perfect,' Irilin muttered. Hagdon glanced at her, abashed now he remembered their fight. But she'd been a different being then, all ice and silver, her blond hair full of moonlight. He looked quickly away.

'I will deal with Iresonté.' Kyndra had been quiet until now, Hagdon realized. For a moment, her eyes were frighteningly empty. 'If it comes to it,' she added and expression returned to her face. Hagdon recognized the look; he'd worn it often enough on the eve of battle, part fear, part resolution. Despite the fact that she wasn't his enemy, he remembered the reports of the night he'd been shot – the graphic descriptions of fire and ruin – and didn't feel entirely reassured.

33

Kyndra had to admit she felt better with the feathered body of the Republic around her. They rode west, scouts ranging ahead of them, a great murder of crows, ears always to the ground, listening for signs of Iresonté. After an uneventful ten days, the land began to change, the hills growing steeper, more mountainous, the pale green of the vineyards darkening to a poisonous kind of emerald. A dark stain appeared on the southern horizon.

'The Lotys Jungle,' Hagdon said when she pointed it out. 'It was one of our – I mean, Sartya's – first territories to fall.' He glanced down at his horse's reins in his lap. 'The lotys people are the only ones who can live there. Almost everything's out to kill you.'

'They're barely people from what I've heard,' Char said. 'They've lived there so long, they're almost part-forest themselves.'

'So they have no contact with the outside world?' Kyndra asked him.

'They do trade for some things,' Char answered. 'The jungle's the only place where you can grow lotys stems. That drug basically built Na Sung Aro.'

'What does it do?'

'It's a hallucinogen.' Char flashed sharp teeth at her. 'Only the most expensive ithum parlours can provide it, as it's so rare and valuable.'

'And so illegal,' Hagdon added. 'If the mysha hadn't overrun the Beaches, the emperor would have torn down Na Sung Aro years ago.'

'No doubt,' Char said. 'I for one wouldn't miss it. But why risk lives for a wasteland on the edge of the world?'

'My thoughts exactly,' Hagdon agreed. Kyndra caught him eyeing Char's tattooed arms. If he knew Char had been a slaver, he didn't say anything.

'Did you try it?' Kyndra asked.

Char shook his head. 'Chewing the stems leaves you a drooling wreck for hours. Total surrender,' he added softly.

Kyndra heard what he really meant. He needed to be in control, never letting his guard down for a moment in case the force he called the rage rose up to claim him. He was looking at her, his eyes secret. Her face felt hot; she pulled her gaze away, but she sensed he still watched her.

'Tell me about the emperor,' she said to distract herself. 'And ambertrix.'

'The emperor,' Hagdon said expressionlessly. He seemed to draw into himself. 'He's a man who inherited a dying empire. He's a man who carries the weight of history on his shoulders.'

'It sounds like you're defending him,' Irilin said with a frown.

Hagdon glanced at her. 'Once I thought I understood the

reason why he is as he is – trying desperately to hold a bust seam together, to strengthen his grip on lands long held by his ancestors. I couldn't like him, couldn't admire him, but I respected him.' He looked away from her. 'My respect died the day he killed my nephew. I had given years to the Fist, to the cause. I'd sworn oaths of fealty, taken countless lives. It meant nothing to him. My family is one of the oldest in Sartya. The empire's in my blood –'

Hagdon stopped abruptly, as if shocked by the torrent of his own words.

'Sorry about your nephew,' Irilin muttered.

Hagdon briefly closed his eyes. When he opened them, he said, 'He and Paasa, my sister, they were the price I paid for my loyalty.'

None of them asked what had happened to his sister; it was clear Hagdon didn't want to speak of her. 'What about amber-trix?' Kyndra asked, hoping to nudge the conversation away from Hagdon's family. 'Surely *you* know what it is and where it comes from?'

To her consternation, the ex-general shook his head. 'Only the emperor knows and his technicians in Thabarat College – where they study ambertrix. Its very nature is a secret passed verbally from one emperor to the next. It isn't written any-where.'

'Isn't that dangerous?' Nediah said. Riding on Kyndra's other side, he was leaning over, his eyes bright with interest. She remembered how fascinated he'd been when they'd found the rusted contraption outside the Baioran village. 'What if the emperor is assassinated, or someone infiltrates this Thabarat?'

'Thabarat is well protected. So much so that the building's set to destroy itself should it become compromised.'

Nediah shook his head. 'Why go to such extremes to keep it secret?'

'I have a theory,' Hagdon said to him. 'If ambertrix wasn't developed in Thabarat, but was instead being supplied by an outside source, how else would the original Davaratch have stopped others from approaching the same source? He constructed a veritable fortress of a secret around it.'

'If so, what deal did he strike with the source?'

Hagdon shrugged. 'It's only speculation.'

Thoughts of ambertrix and the empire kept Kyndra occupied most of the afternoon. It wasn't until evening fell and Ma said that they would likely reach the site of Khronosta tomorrow that the nervous dread she'd tried to suppress came crawling back. When they made camp, she again found herself seeking solitude – it was a habit she indulged more and more frequently. Whenever she was around the others, she felt their eyes upon her, judging, perhaps remembering the terrible things she'd done as *Sigel*. What if it happened again tomorrow? What if she gave in to the star, let it usurp her will? She might not be able to regain control this time.

Stop fighting them, a voice whispered. Kyndra didn't know whether it belonged to the stars or to her own subconscious. If she stopped fighting, it would be a different kind of surrender – she would take the stars into herself; she would become a true Starborn. *Sigel* would not be able to use her again.

But she wouldn't be Kyndra any more.

'There you are.'

She whirled around, heart jumping in her chest, to see Char coming towards her, kali sticks in hand. 'You scared the life out of me.'

'You look perfectly alive to me,' he said, grinning. He proffered the sticks. 'I thought you might like a lesson – take your mind off tomorrow?'

'What's the point?' she said. 'I'm hopeless and you know it. I've just been fooling myself.'

Char was silent. The gentle rushing of water reached Kyndra and she turned to follow it to the bank of a stream, clear and pebbly, flowing out of the crowded foliage that hid the crest of the hill. She made a cup of her hand and scooped some up. It was cold and tasted of leaves.

A twig crunched behind her and she turned. Char was leaning against the bole of a tree. They looked at each other. 'You know what I am,' Kyndra said quietly. '*I* know what I am. I should stop pretending.'

Char stooped to pick up a stone, began tossing it from hand to hand. 'It's hard to stop,' he murmured, 'when the truth is waiting for you.'

Kyndra didn't reply. She watched the leap of fading sun in the water.

'I've done . . . awful things,' Char said and Kyndra had to look at him. One of his hands was clenched around the stone. 'I could have chosen not to, but I'm a coward. I had power. They didn't. It was easier just to go on, to look the other way.'

'You're not a slaver any more.'

Char hurled the pebble at the stream. It splashed, settled. 'Only because of Khronosta,' he said savagely. '*Du-alakat* came and I ran. I left Ma behind.' His voice dropped. 'I left her behind, the only person I ever cared about.'

'You were injured though,' Kyndra said, 'your arm—'

He moved fast, caught her wrist. 'Don't make excuses for me. I've made enough for myself.'

They were standing very close. Kyndra could smell the sharp scent of the grass they'd crushed beneath their feet, the mineral rush of the stream. She could feel the unusual heat coming from Char's body as if a fire burned inside him. His hand was still around her wrist. 'Why did you follow me?' she whispered.

He kissed her. It wasn't a gentle kiss, but rough, hungry, and it made Kyndra's heart pound. When he drew back, she felt light-headed, her legs wanted to tremble beneath her. 'I'm sorry,' he said, letting her go, looking away. His breathing sounded as ragged as her own. 'That was stupid.'

'Why?'

He met her eyes. 'Because –' He made a sound in his throat, almost a growl, and pulled her back to him. His hand against her cheek was hot; she slid her own up to his shoulders, holding him tighter. When she kissed him back, only a very small part wondered whether it was a good idea. The rest of her wanted to *feel*. He was everything the stars were not – all passion and motion. His lips touched her neck, sent a ripple of hot and cold through her and she found her hands slipping under his tunic. When she pressed her palms to his chest, he groaned and pulled her down with him. They knelt amidst the trees. Kyndra let him lift the hem of her shirt and it was a sweet shock to feel his hands on her bare skin. He breathed her name. When he brought his lips back to hers and kissed them, they were full of intent.

'Well,' a voice said. 'Right.'

They sprang apart, Kyndra furiously tugging her shirt down. She stumbled to her feet and saw Kait watching her. The woman's expression was even colder than usual.

'How long have you been there?' Kyndra demanded.

'I'm no voyeur,' Kait replied coolly. 'I merely came to find you. The others seem to value your opinion.' Her eyes flickered over Char. 'But I see you have more important things to attend to.'

'Mind your own business,' he said, his yellow eyes guarded.

'I will,' Kait answered, 'if *she* minds hers.'

Kyndra scowled. 'What's that supposed to mean?'

All Kait's casualness dropped away. Her look was so hostile that Kyndra almost took a step back. 'It means,' she said, 'that you keep your poison to yourself. You want to turn him against me. What did you tell him?'

'This is about Nediah?' Kyndra shook her head. 'He's old enough to make his own decisions, Kait.'

'He listens to you,' she snarled. 'He trusts you. *What* did you say about me?'

'I told him the truth.'

'The truth?'

'I told him Brégenne loves him,' Kyndra said and Kait flinched. 'I told him he shouldn't have left her.'

Except for the high spots of colour in Kait's cheeks, her face was very pale. 'Brégenne,' she said. 'It's *always* Brégenne. She's not the only one who –' Kait stopped speaking abruptly. She turned her back.

'I told him that too,' Kyndra said quietly.

'I should have let the *akan* kill you,' Kait's voice sounded choked. 'I saved you because Anohin believed you would help Kierik. Instead you killed him and stole his power. And for what? You are a coward. You will never achieve even a shred of the greatness he possessed.'

Without looking back, she walked away and the woodland dusk swallowed her. Kyndra closed her eyes, trying to ignore Kait's accusation, but it too closely echoed her own thoughts.

She felt a touch on her arm. 'I don't pretend to understand what she meant,' Char said softly, 'but she is wrong.'

'She isn't,' Kyndra replied. 'I didn't kill Kierik, but I am a coward. I don't want to be like him.'

'Then don't be,' Char said. He took his hand away. 'You have a choice.'

She looked at him; his eyes glowed slightly in the twilight. 'Do I? Then . . . what about you?'

'I don't know,' he said. 'Tomorrow comes first.'

Tomorrow they'd reach Khronosta. Tomorrow they'd have to face the *du-alakat*, who still believed Char their Kala, who intended to use Medavle to change what shouldn't be changed. Tomorrow she would have to call on the stars, or risk losing them both. Kyndra turned as the smoke from the campfire reached them through the trees. 'Yes,' she said. 'Tomorrow comes first.'

34

The sun was rising.

All night Brégenne had sat beside Gareth's lifeless body, the first hours spent in desperation, trying every form of healing she knew. Exhaustion came in the later hours as the moon set and nothing had worked. Gareth lay on a blanket on the deck of the *Eastern Set*, thin and sunken, his flesh cooling. Brégenne's eyes stung, the skin beneath them puffy from crying.

The ship was ghosting high above the treetops, the crew silent about their work. Ümvast's warriors stood at a respectful distance.

'I'm sorry,' came a whisper and Brégenne felt Yara's hand on her shoulder. It brought a fresh wave of tears. She couldn't believe Gareth was gone, after everything they'd been through, and when they were finally on their way to finding the means to save him.

As if to mock their loss, the sky was a clear blue, the day warming. Birds sang and Acre lay tranquil below the hull.

441

Brégenne couldn't bear their joyful song, not this morning, not when Gareth wasn't there to hear it.

'Not that I want the damned thing any more,' Argat murmured, his eyes on Gareth, 'but shouldn't the gauntlet come off now he's . . . ?'

Brégenne frowned. Argat was right. The gauntlet had taken all it could from Gareth – he didn't have any life left to give. She peered at his arm, but the metal was still fastened tightly, melded to his skin.

She stepped away from the body, dragged a weary hand across her eyes. Her throat was raw from weeping and her knees hurt from her long vigil. There was nothing else to be done here. She should sleep, but it would only be postponing the inevitable decisions she'd have to make.

Kul'Das had kept her distance during the night, but now that the sun was up, she walked across the deck to their small group, staff in hand, to look down at Gareth.

'I'm sorry,' Brégenne said to her, too exhausted to feel her usual distaste for the woman. It seemed petty, with Gareth laid out at their feet. 'I tried everything I know.'

Kul'Das simply nodded. She seemed in two minds about something; her eyes moved from Gareth to the sky and back again. Then she crouched and touched the tip of her staff to Gareth's chest. The raven heads lolled in grotesque sympathy.

'What are you doing?' Brégenne asked, startled.

Kul'Das ignored her. She closed her blue eyes and her hand tightened its grip on the wood. They waited, but nothing happened.

'Kul'Das,' Brégenne said, reaching for the woman's shoulder. 'Let him be.'

Just before her fingers touched cloth, the staff sparked into life, golden light shimmering along its length. Solar light.

'You're a Wielder.' Brégenne couldn't help it, so shocked was she to hear the familiar roar of Solar energy. 'Why didn't you tell me?'

Kul'Das's eyes remained on Gareth. 'Don't be foolish,' she said. 'It is the power of the staff.'

'No it's not,' Brégenne said. 'It's *you*. The staff's just a piece of wood.'

'This was given me by a powerful shaman,' the woman said, still not looking at Brégenne. 'I earned the right to bear it.'

'I bet it doesn't work at night though.'

'Because it is a sun staff. My mentor had a moon staff, but he claimed this would suit me better.'

'Mentor?' Brégenne was too tired for this. Here was a Wielder, right under her nose, and she hadn't noticed. A corona now surrounded Gareth's body, limning his wasted flesh in gold. She caught her breath, as dark tendrils began to worm their way through the light, dimming it, fusing the gold and the black into a murky shroud which sank into Gareth's skin, leaving it sickly.

Gareth opened his eyes.

As one, they recoiled. His eyes were black, deep-set and shining. A suggestion of the ebony armour wreathed his limbs, but Brégenne could see Gareth's clothes beneath as it shifted phantasmagorically around him. Kul'Das's hand trembled on her staff. 'Kul'Gareth?' she said in a small voice.

There was no recognition in Gareth's face as he looked at her, as he looked at all of them. Brégenne held his gaze, though it raised the hairs on the back of her neck and she longed to glance away. He opened his mouth, spoiling the air with the stench of the tomb. 'Where is Serjo?' he said, his voice grating and unfamiliar. 'Where is my brother?'

'Gareth,' Brégenne said after a moment, 'do you know me? Do you know where you are?'

The black eyes gazed at her blankly. 'Serjo,' he said again. 'I didn't kill you, my brother. You know that. You know me. I wouldn't kill you.'

'Please, Gareth,' Brégenne said, bending nearer despite the reek that hung about him. 'You must remember. You are a Wielder. You were born in Ümvast and lived at Naris. You know me – it's Brégenne. We set out to—'

'Brégenne?' The black eyes blinked. 'I . . . don't . . .'

'Stay with me, Gareth.' She took his hand and almost dropped it again when she felt how cold and stiff it was. Gareth looked down at it, face corpse-pale.

'What's happened to me?' he whispered. He raised his other hand, fingers twitching as he struggled to open it. His skin was waxen and the hand's movement jerky. His hair had grown since they'd left Naris; now new strands of white started from his temples, streaking the brown like fingers of frost.

'We thought you were dead,' Brégenne said, as she helped him sit up.

Gareth pressed a hand to his chest. 'My heart,' he whispered.

Brégenne forced down trepidation, laying her hand beside his, flat to his chest. The flesh beneath his tunic was cold and still.

'No,' Gareth said, panic starting up in his face. 'It's a mistake.' He glanced at the gauntlet with its overlay of shadowy armour. 'You said you'd get it off, Brégenne.'

She flinched. It wasn't at his reproach – there was none – but at the bald fact that she'd failed.

She was unprepared for Gareth's lunge. He snatched the knife from her belt and, in one smooth motion, plunged it into his thigh. Yara and Argat had thrown themselves towards him, perhaps thinking he meant to stab Brégenne, but Gareth ignored them. He stared at the knife in his leg, at the lack of blood pumping out of the wound. 'I don't feel anything,' he whispered.

'Gareth –' Brégenne began, but he'd already wrenched the blade from his flesh. Although beads of blood rolled sluggishly down the metal, the injury wasn't really bleeding at all. Before he could plunge it into his chest, she caught his hand, held it tightly. 'Stop it, Gareth. Harming yourself does no one any good.'

The knife fell from Gareth's grip to clatter on the deck. 'What *am* I?' he asked, despair thick in his voice. 'If I am not dead, why doesn't my heart beat?'

There was that strange duality again, as if another presence overlay Gareth's own. Had his link to the Solar revived him, Brégenne wondered? Alone, it could not have brought him back from the dead. It seemed the gauntlet wasn't finished with Gareth.

'I don't know,' she said, 'but we're going to find the gauntlet's partner and make you well again.'

'I don't *feel* anything,' Gareth repeated.

A shiver went through them all. Brégenne could tell Argat and Yara shared her unease. Just being near Gareth raised hairs all over her body. Kul'Das, however, was gazing at him smugly. She twitched her staff and the raven heads jostled each other for space. 'Now that you've seen the staff's power for yourselves,' she said, 'I hope I'll be shown a little more respect while on board this infernal vessel.'

'*You*,' Brégenne said, rounding on her. 'What gave you the right to keep your abilities secret? Does Ümvast know of them?'

The indignation ran off Kul'Das's lips like water. 'No,' she said quietly.

Brégenne eyed her. 'I wouldn't count on that. Ümvast isn't someone to choose arbitrarily. She selected you to accompany Gareth because she knows you are—'

'Responsible,' Kul'Das finished. 'Ümvast trusts me with her son's life.'

'She knows, Kul'Das.'

The woman turned away. 'Impossible. Ümvast scorns magic.' She darted a glance at Gareth. 'She exiled her only son because of it.'

'We don't call it magic,' Brégenne said after a moment. 'There are natural energies present in this world and we can harness them – it's that simple.' She paused to look at Gareth too. 'Thank you for whatever you did,' she said, putting aside her instinctive dislike. 'I think it was the touch of another Solar that reminded him who he is. You brought him back.'

Kul'Das lowered her voice. 'I don't believe he came back alone,' she said.

The airship's crew was skittish. Brégenne noticed it over the next few days, as Gareth recovered his strength. Perhaps not *his* strength, she thought, as she watched him sweep across the deck. Sometimes he walked with the confidence of an older man and those were the times he muttered and mourned for the brother called Serjo. The crew had the superstitious nature common to sailors; unsurprisingly, a dead man walking their decks rattled them to the point where their casual singing ceased and their work grew slapdash.

She couldn't blame them. Gareth's skin had the mottling of a corpse's and he pulled his hood about his face whenever he was himself enough to remember it. The smell that clung about him didn't help. When they travelled during daytime, the wind blew it away, but at night, the stench returned like an open plague pit, and Brégenne feared it was only a matter of time before Argat's crew refused to sail further with Gareth aboard.

Argat realized it too. On the seventh evening since they'd crossed into Acre, with the lights of a city flecking the western horizon, he took Brégenne aside. 'The crew are restless,' he said. 'They've started calling him as that woman does. Kul'Gareth. They think he's some kind of necromancer.'

'It's true he's . . . not always Gareth,' Brégenne said. 'I can't pretend he's safe to be around.' She looked Argat squarely in the eye. 'You've been more than a help to us both, Argat. I know it's not just because of our deal.'

The captain grunted.

'Whatever else he is,' Brégenne continued, 'Gareth's a man of his word. He promised you the gauntlets. Putting us off the ship won't change that.'

Argat angled his body into the wind. His knuckles were white on the ship's rail. 'I don't want the cursed things any more.'

Brégenne couldn't blame him. 'In that case,' she said, 'if you would fly us as far as the forest, we'll be able to follow Kyndra's directions on foot. Ben-haugr lies on the far side.'

Argat regarded her. 'From the little you've told me, this forest doesn't sound too hospitable. Didn't I hear you call it the Deadwood?'

'Yes,' she conceded wryly. 'But I am not defenceless.'

'I don't doubt your abilities when the sun sets,' Argat said, 'but what about in the daytime? Even though you claim she's like yourself, the Kul'Das woman seems of little use. And my gut tells me you can't trust the boy.'

'We'll travel by night, then,' she said reluctantly, 'and hope that Gareth's still himself by the time we reach Ben-haugr.'

'And if he isn't?'

She felt a chill in her blood at the question.

'Brégenne,' Argat said and she looked at him – it was the first time he'd actually used her name, 'have you the strength to do it, if it comes to it?'

She didn't ask him what he meant. She knew well enough. 'Gareth's not lost to us.'

'Yet,' the captain added with a glance at the figure that stood at the prow of the airship. Brégenne followed his gaze and watched the black armour coalesce around Gareth so that his face was all but hidden.

'Yet,' she agreed.

35

Khronosta, Acre
Medavle

The inside of Khronosta was like nothing he'd ever seen. White sand covered the floors, carefully raked into mandalas morning and night by shaven-headed children, who looked at him with eyes that belonged on beings far older. Even Medavle, who had seen five centuries of life, felt discomfited by their stares.

They'd taken away his flute. It was the first time he'd been without it since forging it from metal and magic. *It's only a tool*, he reminded himself. The flute merely augmented the power he already possessed. But it was part of him, something he'd borne through rage and terror and grief. He missed its familiar weight at his hip.

He brushed a hand along the porous orange stone. It felt warm to the touch, not unlike the pocked skin of some animal. Great bricks of it formed the temple, neatly mortared, climbing towards the central dome. The space directly beneath was called the mandala chamber – where the Khronostians danced their way into the past. He was forbidden to go there.

Pain stabbed his forehead and Medavle suppressed a groan.

Whatever they'd done to him, he could feel it in his flesh, a twisting serpent that burrowed in him, rooting through all the long years of his life. It was the eldest's will – he'd extract it soon, in order to read Medavle like a chronicle. He wanted to find the best point to enter the past, the safest point, which would not destabilize the future. They'd explained little to him, claiming that no non-Khronostian could grasp the concept of time as they saw it. Their arrogance reminded him of the high Wielders of old, those who would have condemned him for loving Isla.

I do this for you, he thought as the pain reached a crescendo. He dropped to his knees, images from his past racing before his eyes. In them, he followed a dark path through a forest, moss slippery beneath his feet, tangled branches catching his white robes. He was consumed with the need for vengeance, with hate for the Starborn who had taken his people . . . who had taken Isla. Water ran over basalt rocks, a crow cawed high above him, and his echoing scream silenced the wood.

He was back, looking at the orange floor, the grains of sand rough beneath his palms. When he raised his head, he saw a child gazing at him reproachfully; he'd fallen into one of the mandalas. Medavle got to his feet, aching, feverish. Was this what humans meant by illness? He had never suffered such a thing. It felt as if his head were stuffed with wool.

'We were right, Yadin,' came a hissing voice. 'The Kala comes for you.'

The eldest stood behind him, flanked by two *du-alakat*. Inside the temple, they had no need to hide and Medavle found himself staring at the terrifying collage of their faces, old and young and dreadfully sad. 'They're here?' he asked, his heart beginning to beat faster. 'The Starborn too?'

The eldest nodded. Medavle didn't know what to think. Kyndra had come, but was it to rescue a kidnapped friend or to eliminate a threat? She'd heard of anchors – she must have realized what the Khronostians could do with him. 'Come, Yadin,' the eldest said, 'we will go to welcome the Kala. It is with his power that you will change your story.' To Medavle's surprise, the eldest handed him his flute.

The *du-alakat* formed up around them both – thirty warriors trained in the art of manipulating time. Kyndra wouldn't be able to stop them from taking Char, not as she was, not when she spent half her energy fighting herself. Medavle knew why she did; he respected her for it but at the same time he thought it foolish. He looked at the walls of the temple, carved with symbols augmenting the Khronostians' power. He looked at the *du-alakat*, fixing their bandages in place. Behind his eyes, the memory of a past Medavle crouched in a forest, his body wracked by sobs.

They passed into the outer ring. Wooden gates, new and only half-decorated, opened on a wooded clearing. Yellow trees listed like ships in a high wind, rattling their dry leaves. A watchtower lay in ruins to his right, built on a slight rise. Now its stones had tumbled down into the clearing, as if a giant fist had simply scattered them. Strange glass orbs glinted beneath the afternoon sun, some still affixed to fallen walls, others half-submerged in the grass.

Medavle caught movement. Figures approached from both sides, sliding between the tight-clustered trees. His eyes widened when he recognized the bloody armour of Sartya. The other force were armoured too, black feathers adorning their shoulders. A breeze swept the clearing, making the feathered cloaks flutter as if they were indeed wings. Beside him, on the steps of the temple, the eldest waited in silence.

The two forces stopped, facing each other. He spotted Kyndra standing beside Char and a dark-skinned woman Medavle didn't know. The soldiers in the feathered cloaks were ranged around them. Was this the Republic? A man stepped out of the ranks and Medavle caught his breath in surprise when he recognized General Hagdon. A Sartyan from the opposing force mirrored Hagdon's movement, face concealed behind a helm, carnelian-coloured cloak tossed by the wind. When the figure raised its hands and removed the helm, Medavle saw a raven-haired woman. Her lips twisted into a sneer as she regarded Hagdon.

'Have you forsaken civilized society to become a barbarian?' she called. 'How the mighty general falls.'

'You wasted no time stepping into my shoes, Iresonté,' Hagdon replied. He loosened his sword in its sheath. 'I am not surprised to find you here.'

'Very clever to use some of my own stealth force against me.' Iresonté's eyes flickered over those behind Hagdon. 'It is a shame they will not live to serve you longer.'

'Enough.' The ranks of Sartyans parted to let five people through, four armoured, the fifth an old, robed man. Medavle found his gaze drawn to the figure in the centre. He was tall, bald and one-armed. The fat that padded his bones only made him more imposing. His red plate seemed grafted on, straps lengthened to accommodate his bulk and his greaves looked like little islands of metal surrounded by fleshy straits. As the man and his guards drew nearer, Medavle made out his face, deceptively soft. But his black eyes had no mercy in them. They were the eyes he remembered from the days of Kierik – the eyes of the first emperor, Davaratch.

Hagdon's face had paled, his hand visibly tightening on the hilt of his sword. The emperor's gaze moved from the former general to the temple where Medavle stood surrounded by *du-alakat*. There was a hunger in his face, a triumph. 'Khronosta,' he said.

'Your Imperial Majesty,' the eldest replied, his mocking voice somehow filling the clearing. 'We had planned to take the fight to you. Yet you come to us.' His shrunken lips twitched. 'If you seek death, death will find you.' He signalled the *du-alakat* and the warriors began to fan out.

'Wait.'

The old man who'd accompanied the emperor stepped forward and Medavle was disturbed to find himself the object of his gaze. 'You,' the stranger said in a cracked voice. Uncaring of the *du-alakat*, he hobbled towards Medavle, his squint deepening the creases in his face. Slowly, he extended a hand and splayed it and Medavle felt something he hadn't felt in centuries: the urge to obey. When his knees began to fold, he railed at them, but they refused to straighten. He found himself bowed on the steps of the temple. The terrible compulsion bent his elbows too, pressed his stomach into the ground. Above him, the eldest hissed something.

It was the old Yadin duress, the sole province of the high Wielders of Solinaris, of those who'd created the Yadin. But the high Wielders were long dead. Terror washed through him; the old man could order him to tear out his own heart and Medavle would do it. 'Who . . . are you?' he croaked.

'Shune!' came a shout and Medavle was able to move again. The old man turned to regard the Davaratch. 'What are you doing?' the emperor demanded, a dangerous note in his voice. 'Do you know this man?'

'I know *what* he is,' Shune said, 'but not how he came to be here.' He looked back at Medavle. 'I thought your kind were dead.'

'I thought yours were too.'

The old man paled with sudden fear. 'Be silent,' he snapped and Medavle found himself unable to speak.

'You dare issue orders in my presence?' the emperor said. 'As usual, you forget your place.'

The old man's fear spoke louder than words. Whatever he'd told the emperor about himself, it wasn't the truth. Medavle fought harder against the compulsion sealing his lips shut. He'd been a free man for five hundred years; he wouldn't serve again. 'Wielder,' he managed to say, Shune's compulsion like a rope around his neck.

'I told you to be silent!' the old man shrieked, but the word had been heard, at least by Kyndra. She was staring at Shune and there was something distant in her eyes – the look she wore when Kierik's memories spoke to her.

'Traitor,' she said in a tone unlike her own. 'It was *you* who betrayed the citadel.'

Shune looked at her and whatever he saw made him stagger back.

'You ignored my warnings, Realdon Shune,' she said implacably, as if Kierik really were speaking through her. 'You turned the Sentheon against me.'

The old man found his voice at last. 'You are not Kierik.'

The distance abruptly left Kyndra's eyes. 'No,' she agreed faintly. 'Kierik is dead.'

'Beware, Majesty,' Shune said, whirling. 'She is Starborn.'

The wind strengthened in the darkening sky, blowing in the vanguard of a storm. The sound of it in the leaves was a snake's rattle.

'We don't need to fight,' Kyndra said loudly, though her voice held a tremor. 'We've come for Medavle.' She looked from him to the eldest, her eyes guarded. 'Let him go.'

'Go then, Yadin, if you will.'

Medavle glanced at the eldest, felt the Khronostian's will in his flesh, rifling through the memories he'd carried across the years. He closed his eyes as one of Isla arose – another fleeting time when he'd held her in his arms. They'd kissed and laughed, having lost themselves in the white corridors. The danger had become part of it; every snatched moment could have been their last. His arms had felt empty when she wasn't in them. Five hundred years of emptiness.

Medavle opened his eyes. Kyndra was staring at him; he could see the realization beginning to dawn in her face. 'Why?' she asked quietly.

'Because they can go back and save her,' he said, hearing his voice catch. 'They can save Isla.'

36

'No,' the old man said. 'You will stop this, Yadin. I *forbid* it.'

'Shune,' the emperor barked. 'Explain yourself.'

'Do you recall what I told you of anchors, Majesty?' Shune's eyes did not leave Medavle. 'If they use the Yadin, the last five centuries are at their fingertips. They could unravel the empire.'

'Worse,' Ma said, coming forward. 'They could unravel the fabric of this world.'

'We wondered whether we would see you, Mariana.' The eldest spread his grey arms, welcoming. 'Won't you return to us – in the hour of our ascension?'

'You are mad as well as blind.' Ma's fists clenched around her kali sticks. 'What happened to the people I left? Gentle nomads who used my knowledge to preserve this –' She stopped speaking abruptly.

'Everything you learned, you learned from us,' the eldest said. 'Yet you turned your knowledge against us. You used it to hide the Kala.'

'Yes,' she whispered, looking down.

456

A whistle ripped through the clearing like the cry of a hunting hawk. Char had just enough time to see the woman called Iresonté lower her hand from her mouth before people stepped out of the air to seize his arms. They wore the armour of the stealth force. Four heavy cloaks lay discarded at their feet, blue light rippling over the material.

'Ambertrix cloaks,' Hagdon warned. 'There may be more hiding among us.'

The blue light flickered and died, leaving the imbued cloaks no more than garments. Char couldn't stop looking at them. For a moment it had seemed as if the rage would awaken, but the feeling was somehow outside him; it had lived in the bluish light. Then he felt a blade against his throat and all thoughts of the rage sharpened to terror.

'One move,' Iresonté said to the eldest, 'and your Kala dies.'

The hand holding the blade to Char's throat pressed harder and he felt a trickle run down his skin. His captor drew in a breath at the sight of his blood, but the knife remained where it was.

'No!' Ma cried at the same time as the eldest. She drew her weapons. Behind him, Char felt a surge of heat and thought of the Wielders and Kyndra, but he couldn't turn his head to look.

'One move,' Iresonté repeated.

Ma stood torn; Char knew what she was thinking. Even *she* couldn't reach him before the blade flashed across his throat. And even if she could, she wouldn't risk it. He felt helpless as he met her eyes. *You said I wasn't the Kala.*

'Leave him,' Ma shouted. 'He is not the one you seek.'

'Why would you protect him otherwise?' Char heard fear in the eldest's voice – the ancient man had never sounded so human. Was the Kala really worth so much to Khronosta?

'I protected him from *you*,' Ma said, 'when you imprisoned his people. He was just an infant, separated from his mother. You would have killed him.'

Char couldn't speak, not with the knife pressed so closely against his throat. He stared at Ma. The story about finding him abandoned on a road – another lie?

Horrified realization was dawning on the eldest's wizened face. 'Pah –' he spat – 'you rescued one? You *knew* what they were. You knew they supplied Sartya with its greatest weapon.'

A sound came from off to Char's left, as the emperor walked into his line of sight. A sword burned in his single hand, rippling with the same blue light as the stealth-force cloaks. Again Char felt the lure of the rage; he could sense it in the sword, in the flames that licked along its keen edge. The Davaratch looked from Char to Ma to the eldest. 'If he is not the Kala, who is he?'

'Forgive me, Boy,' Ma said, her proud face anguished. 'I was too afraid. I'd hidden for too many years. When they showed up in the Beaches, I thought they'd found out about you. Instead . . . they believed you the Kala.' She bent her head. 'I let them believe it. It was safer that way.'

The tension was palpable. Ma was the focus of all eyes. It began to rain and for a moment all that could be heard was the *plink* of drops on drawn weapons. Ma walked a little way towards the Khronostians and then she stopped and threw down her kali sticks.

Pulse pounding in his throat, Char watched her unlace her bracers. They joined the sticks on the ground. Then she began to peel off the gloves he had never once seen her without. Ma flung them down and held up her hands so all could see.

Intricate mandalas, white on brown skin, twined up her

wrists. In the centre of each palm was a snake biting its tail. Char watched in horror as it came alive, surging in and out of her flesh as if it were water. '*I* am your Kala,' Ma said. 'I am Khronos.'

As one, the *du-alakat* fell to their knees, but not the eldest. 'It can't be,' he said, expression changing from shock to disgust. 'We have spent blood in our search for you – the blood of your people. And you betrayed us.'

'You *betrayed* yourselves,' Ma said. 'I . . . died.' There was a remembered terror in her face. 'I died to share my knowledge with you. You turned it to darkness. When I was born again, you raised me in violence, you made me forget myself and now we both bear the marks of it.'

Some of the *du-alakat* touched their bandaged bodies; one cried out. 'You left us at the mercy of Sartya,' the eldest said. 'We saw evil in its rule. The ways of peace and enlightenment you taught us could not take root in such a world.' His hand tightened visibly on his staff. 'It had to be cleansed.'

The blade disappeared from Char's throat. The woman who'd held it slumped on the earth, a throwing knife buried in her neck. Ma held another two in her hands, ready to hurl – she'd used the distraction to free him.

'Kill her,' the emperor said and the Sartyans converged on Ma. Char watched his eyes sweep over the soldiers of the Republic, gathered behind Hagdon. 'Kill them all.'

Iresonté whistled again and more stealth force stepped out of the air, right in the middle of Hagdon's forces. They dropped their ambertrix cloaks, drew their daggers, and a dozen soldiers were down before Hagdon could begin to shout a warning.

A swarm of red-armoured Sartyans surrounded Ma, and the *du-alakat* came to meet them. Char had no time to dwell on her

459

revelations or what they meant – he found himself facing the remaining members of the stealth force who'd first captured him – two men and a woman, he thought. Black masks concealed much of their faces. He drew his kali sticks, a pair of ironwood ones Ma had given him only this morning. Three on one. He didn't like the odds, not against stealth-force.

The men darted at him, one from each side. They attacked with assassin's tools, stilettos, the metal slightly discoloured at the edge – poisoned, Char realized with dismay. The odds against him lengthened. He parried one blade and just managed to twist his body aside before the second scored his shoulder. The tip snagged in the fabric of his shirt, tearing it. They didn't wait for him to recover, but moved in to flank him; Char turned a circle, trying to keep them in sight. Rain slicked the smooth sticks in his hands. Unlike his opponents, he was hoodless; water dripped into his eyes.

There was a flash and Kait appeared behind the woman. She thrust with a flaming scimitar and Char watched it burst from the woman's chest. She cried out. Kait kicked her, pulled her blade free, whirling to face one of the men who'd been stalking Char. His odds improved, Char grinned. Spinning a kali stick in his hand, he lashed out, managed to catch the man across his forearm. Bone cracked, his opponent hissed and even Char was surprised. Ma had not been lying about the ironwood.

Kait's blades half cauterized the wounds they made. Even the rain couldn't dampen the stink of burned flesh. She was gradually whittling her opponent down; Char glimpsed a dozen gashes in his light armour. He parried a blow from his own adversary, slipping from form to form, as Ma had taught him. Offence, defence, offence, offence – his strikes grew faster and he knew the man was barely keeping up. Char found an opening and he took it, jabbing the end of his kali stick at the man's throat in the same move Ma had used on him so many weeks ago.

His opponent choked, automatically clapping a hand to his injured neck. Char brought the other stick up fast, knocked the poisoned blade aside, sent it spinning through the air. Then he cracked the man's skull and the stealth-force agent crumpled.

He turned to help Kait and saw everything in a tableau, as if events were unfolding with agonizing slowness. The Wielder's teeth were bared in a snarl of triumph, her opponent sprawled at her feet. The dropped stiletto had landed near the woman Kait had stabbed; she reached for it and − in a last surge of strength − slashed it across Kait's knee.

It was a weak blow, just a scratch, and even as Char watched, the stealth-force woman fell back dead. Kait looked down at her knee, the grin sliding off her lips. Her scimitars hissed and faded, as if extinguished by the rain. She put out a hand to steady herself, but there was nothing to hold on to and she collapsed beside the dead woman.

'Kait!'

Char could hear Nediah fighting his way through the melee to reach her. Kait's breathing was laboured, her face very pale. 'Aberration,' came a voice and a Sartyan made for Kait, sword naked in his hand. Char threw himself at the Sartyan, caught the stroke as it fell and, with a flick of his wrist, disarmed him. The loss of his sword only stalled the man for a moment. He drew a pair of daggers from his belt . . . and a hand axe whistled past Char's nose to take the soldier in the head. Char cursed and turned in time to see Hagdon give him a nod as he plunged back into the fight.

'Kait.' Nediah dropped down beside her. What with the

fighting and the rain, the ground was swiftly turning to mud; it coated Char's boots. 'I'll cover you,' he said to Nediah as the Wielder knelt over Kait, his hands glowing.

The sky thundered and the rain grew heavier, throwing a curtain over the scene. Char looked for Kyndra and couldn't find her. Sartyan bodies lay beside those of the Republic, comrades in death, if not in life. The battlefield was a patchwork of red and black, punctuated by grey figures. The *du-alakat* scythed through the Sartyans, wind pulling their bandages loose, revealing the odd hand or face. Although the emperor had the greater numbers, he was pressed on both sides, caught between the *du-alakat* and the Republic. Char could see him fighting not far away, that blue ambertrix blade drawing lines of fire in the air.

'Nediah,' Kait murmured.

'Hush.'

'I'm . . . glad you found me . . . before –'

'You're not going to die,' Nediah said.

'You would know,' Kait breathed and she fainted.

Char stared at her. 'Is she going to be all right?'

'I hope so,' the Wielder said. 'I think I found all the poison in time.' He made a disgusted gesture at the stiletto and it shattered.

'Have you seen Kyndra?'

Nediah gave him a searching look and Char belatedly realized how fearful he sounded. *Worried about a Starborn*, he chided himself, but he was. In a battle, even the slightest hesitation could mean disaster. And Kyndra had hesitated before. Despite the death and dying around him, a memory of her lips on his returned to him in a rush and his insides twisted, as he scanned the battlefield and failed to find her.

Nediah bent to pick Kait up. 'I'll weave her a shield and come back.'

Char was searching through the ranks of the Republic, trying to spot Kyndra's red hair amongst all the black-feathered cloaks. The clash of metal on metal filled his ears and the rain ran into his face. He wiped his eyes clear, looked again.

Nediah straightened, Kait's limp form in his arms. His face blanched. 'Char!' he cried.

Char began to turn, but found he couldn't. Something was stopping him and he looked down. A full foot of steel protruded from his chest, blue light flashing and flaring about it. Bemused, he blinked at it, wondering how it came to be there. The light hummed through his body. He glanced up . . . and saw Kyndra. Life had a cruel sense of humour. She was staring at him, wearing the horror he knew he ought to feel.

Someone shoved him; the metal disappeared from his chest in a gush of black blood. As Char fell to his knees, he heard an exclamation and managed to turn his head. The ruler of Sartya stood above him, studying his sword . . . which was now only a sword, its blue energy gone. Char could have told him where – he felt the ambertrix inside him. It *was* the rage, the same force he'd held off for three years. He raised a hand to his face, watching as his skin rippled and began to tear. Through his fingers, he saw Kyndra and, as the rage flung him into a dark place of pain, the last thing he knew was regret.

37

Samaya, Acre
Kyndra

She couldn't concentrate, couldn't find the door in her mind. It was there, she sensed it, but so was her fear and the fear was stronger. She saw the emperor looming behind Char, saw Nediah's mouth shape a warning, but he was too late. *She* was too late. The terrible weapon tore through Char's flesh, blue light arcing over his skin.

The sight wrenched a scream from her. Grief and rage – at the battle, at the emperor, at her own weakness. She thought of Shika's little cairn, she saw Kait unconscious in Nediah's arms. Irilin had a bloody gash down one cheek; Hagdon fought to keep the stealth force away from her. Medavle was lost among the *du-alakat*. He should be here fighting at her side.

The soldiers of the Republic weren't as skilled as the Sartyans. Too many feathered mantles lay among the dead. They were *her* people now and she couldn't allow them to die here. She *wouldn't*. The woman who called herself Ma held off the *du-alakat* almost singlehandedly – they evaded her blows, but none raised a hand against her. She was working her way closer to the steps of the temple.

The emperor pulled his sword free. Even from this distance, Kyndra could see his consternation at the lack of ambertrix flames coating the blade. He looked up and their eyes met. She saw cruelty in his face, a cold lack of emotion that she recognized. Had it always been there? she wondered. Was it the burden of leadership that had made the emperor who he was? *We become who we must*, she thought . . . or maybe Kierik did, thinking through her. The possibility no longer made her shiver.

I can't lead them. Not like this. Not as I am. If she'd embraced her heritage sooner, none of these lives would have been lost. Kyndra looked at the temple. Khronosta couldn't be allowed to use Medavle. If they changed the past, what would happen to Rairam – to her world and its people? There were ways to deal with an invading army, but the terrifying possibilities that could result if history were reversed . . . everyone she knew, her family, her friends, might cease to exist. And she owed her own existence to Kierik's downfall, to Medavle's plan. If he chose to undo that, she would never have been born at all.

She steeled herself. *Yeras*, she commanded and the star hearkened to her call. *Isa*. Others listened too, as if they sensed her resolve strengthening. Rairam was part of Acre now, Kyndra thought, and she was the only Starborn to watch over it. She gazed at her friends, at Char kneeling on the ground, black blood staining the front of his shirt. There was no choice to be made. Not really. Just an inevitability to accept, as the stars had always known. They banished the last of her fear, as she took hold of *Yeras* and *Isa*, the bridges over the void.

Their exultation found its way onto her lips, curving in a euphoric smile. She had a fleeting mental glimpse of the dark door before it blew apart, black shards dissolving in light. The last barrier vanished, taking the fabric of all that was *Kyndra* with it.

She, it, they – all were one now. The force of the stars was catastrophic. The joining could have destroyed everything in a league's radius, but she drew it back. Controlled it. There were people here whose lives must be preserved, people on whom the future of Acre relied. She knew that much: she'd given up her humanity for their sake.

Now that meant so little. In a moment past, she'd considered it a sacrifice, but how was *this* a sacrifice? She was a being of light and void. The sheer power in her veins made her laugh aloud. She was one with the sky, with the stars – their names were hers now. She could speak with the tongue of *Austri*, or strike with the fist of *Sigel*. It wasn't like the time she let the star take her over. Now *she* was in control, avatar of them all, separate and together, bound into one form.

See, they told her triumphantly, *see*.

The joining had burned away her clothes. When she looked down at herself, she saw a figure of darkness and stars, a cut-out of the night sky. White suns blazed in her eyes and through that blinding light, everything looked different. Irilin's slim form shone silver, Nediah's bright gold, Kait's a little dimmer. Another blaze of Solar gold surrounded the old man, Realdon Shune, and there were other glows too, even among the Sartyans, although she could tell their abilities were unrealized. It was Char, however, who held her attention. A gale appeared to whip around him, shot through with the blue of ambertrix.

The emperor and his guards were backing away from Char's hunched figure. So were the soldiers of the Republic. The change he'd resisted for so long had finally caught up with him, seemingly kindled by the emperor's ambertrix blade. A hot wind rose, sweeping the rain aside. It tossed cloaks, tangled hair; it came with a roar like fire, dragging Char to his feet. His dark face was twisted in pain. He grew taller as he stood there, his limbs lengthening, a pattern of diamonds appearing on his skin, as if scored by an invisible blade. There came a shocking crack and Char screamed, ridges springing up along the length of his spine. Cloth ripped as the same sharp ridges sprouted from his calves and the backs of his arms. His ash-coloured hair grew longer and wilder, his cheekbones and jaw more pointed.

Char stood panting. Seven feet tall, his clothes barely covered him now, shredded by his new flesh. He flexed a clawed hand, turned to the nearest Sartyan and seized him by the neck, lifting him high until his feet dangled. The claws pierced the soldier's armour and the man screamed. Char smashed him into the ground and turned to find another victim.

There was no shortage. The *du-alakat* were advancing on him, determination in their readied weapons. They spread out to surround Char, who lifted bloodstained claws. His feet were clawed too, sharp spurs having burst through the leather of his ruined boots. The first *du-alakat* darted in, landing a blow on Char's shoulder. He roared and spun around, but the warrior was long gone. The blows became a flurry as the Khronostians called on their power. They were too many and too swift for Char to keep up; even scaled as it was, blood began to appear on his new skin.

Kyndra seized *Raad* and in the next moment she was there beside him. She held up a hand and a shield shimmered into being. Those *du-alakat* caught outside spread out to surround it, searching for any weaknesses. While she still had the element of surprise, Kyndra grabbed one of the three warriors inside the shield and *Sigel* boiled the blood in his veins.

After one shocked glance at her, Char seized another warrior and used his claws to tear out his throat. The third warrior gazed at the remains of his companions and threw down his weapons. Kyndra bound him with *Thurn*. There had been enough killing.

'Kyndra?' Char asked and she realized she still appeared as a star-studded shadow. She exerted her will and resumed the form he would recognize. She glanced down at herself, a little rueful. The stars could do many things, but creating clothes out of nothing was not one of them. She wrapped herself in a shifting robe of smoke and starlight.

'I thought you looked fine as you were,' Char said, grinning despite the blood that streaked him.

'I came to tell you your name.'

He sobered. 'It will change me again, won't it?'

'Yes.' Kyndra studied him, seeing the wind and the blue as a vortex that tumbled inside him. 'Will you hear it?'

Char glanced at the invisible shield, which muted all sound except their voices. 'You found yours,' he commented.

'Mine was there all along. Your name is buried.' She tilted her head. 'We can leave it that way.'

Char swallowed. The black slits of his eyes were far more pronounced now. He stared out at the chaotic world beyond her shield. 'It seems it's a day for names.'

Kyndra followed his gaze and saw Khronos – Ma, as she called herself – stalking towards them across the field of the dead. Her kali sticks dripped blood and her eyes were fixed on Char and on those *du-alakat* who surrounded him. The emperor was shouting soundlessly.

'So?' Kyndra asked. 'Will you hear it?'

Char studied her face. Whatever he saw there made him close his eyes. 'Tell me,' he whispered.

'Your true name,' she said, 'is Orkaan.'

He opened his mouth to reply, but whatever he wanted to say was swallowed in a scream. Kyndra dissolved the barrier and herself, reappearing some distance away. A great sheet of blue light blasted out of Char, knocking the *du-alakat* off their feet. She watched impassively as he began to writhe, his agony a palpable thing. His new skin burst, the ridges on his back grew larger and sharper, his shoulders swelling as the bones beneath them cracked and expanded once more. Char's scream grew hoarse, deepening into a roar. His arms lengthened and his spine curved until he fell forward onto his hands. The claws became talons, the same wicked hooks sprouting on his feet. His neck grew sinuous and great wings unfolded on his back. Only his colour remained the same, a dusky black.

He was beautiful, Kyndra thought. The Lleu-yelin had always been beautiful.

Orkaan reared onto his hind legs and roared. The force that emerged from his throat was blue and Kyndra had the answer she'd long sought – the secret power of the Lleu-yelin and of the empire's might: ambertrix. So simple, she thought, chastened. Even Kierik had not guessed at the link between the two.

The dragon's roar cut through the storm. In the silence on the other side, Kyndra heard chanting. Beyond the open gates of Khronosta, the courtyard was full of people: adults and children alike, some with shaven heads, each dressed in grey robes. An elderly woman stood in the centre and Kyndra realized that none of the positioning was random. The Khronostians' bodies formed a complex mandala, a web of light stretching between them.

'*Du-alakat!*' the eldest cried. His wizened hand was clamped tightly around Medavle's wrist and his deep-set eyes were on Kyndra. The warriors disengaged in a blur, retreating to the steps of the temple, taking up positions in the courtyard.

'Leave the Yadin,' Ma said. She raised her fists, showing the serpents in her palms. 'Eldest, do not do this.'

'If you have the power to stop us, use it.'

Ma turned her gaze on the temple, on the human mandala. She spread her hands. The light linking each person pulsed and dimmed. Cries of distress reached them, though none of the Khronostians broke from their positions. Sweat stood out on Ma's forehead and although Kyndra could not see how she was doing it, she guessed she was holding the temple fast in this place and time. The eldest's face paled. He let go of Medavle and raised his right hand. The glow in the courtyard grew brighter and a metallic scent filled the air.

Kyndra seized *Raad* again, appearing on the steps of the temple, which were fast becoming insubstantial. Before she could strike the eldest, a staff swung, knocking her arm aside. 'I am glad they returned my flute to me,' Medavle said as they faced each other. 'It helped me against the last Starborn I fought.'

'Barely fought,' Kyndra corrected. 'You laid a trap and Kierik was foolish enough to walk into it.' She girded herself in *Tyr*, raised a hand to push the staff aside, but Medavle swung it and sent her stumbling back with a blast of energy.

'You are not so experienced as he,' the Yadin said, 'and I have lived far longer.'

'If you opposed him, why choose the same path?' Kyndra

gritted her teeth, privately shocked at Medavle's strength. 'He created Mariar to start afresh instead of trying to mend the damage the empire had done. Changing the past, starting over – you're just like him.'

'I am *nothing* like him,' Medavle hissed. He spun the staff and Kyndra had to use a shield to block it. 'The last five hundred years were a mistake. They should never have been.'

'You don't care about the world. You're doing this for the woman you loved. For Isla.'

Medavle's face contorted at the name. 'What would a Starborn know of love?'

'More than you suspect,' Kyndra said quietly, 'and less than I should.' She grabbed hold of the staff and *Sigel*; the star's white heat melted the metal and Medavle yelled as it ran over his hand.

She became aware of a tugging, as if two forces were pulling her opposite ways. She could see the earth through the stone steps beneath her feet before everything faded to grey. In the next instant, arms were around her and she was somewhere else, being squeezed through a space that seemed both infinitesimal and utterly vast. Then the wooded clearing reappeared around her and Ma let her go. 'Caught you,' she panted and fell exhausted to her knees. 'They have become so strong.'

The temple was gone, Medavle and the eldest with it. The twisted remnants of a flute lay behind on the earth. Kyndra looked around. Although only fifty or so remained to fight, the Republic had rallied behind the dragon, pressing the Sartyans back into the trees. Orkaan tumbled soldiers with every blue-veined breath, swinging his horned head to catch those trying to flank him. The Davaratch was staring at him with greedy eyes.

'Stop!'

The emperor's voice had a power of its own. Orkaan came to a halt, claws restlessly gouging chunks out of the earth. 'Hagdon,' the Davaratch shouted, 'call off your dragon. There's no need for this.'

'I am not *his*.'

Orkaan's voice arrived like thunder, seeming to echo both inside and outside Kyndra's head. Hagdon stepped out from behind the dragon, the dark feathers of his cloak rippling in the wind. As he passed by him, Amon Taske hissed something, perhaps a warning. Blood covered the ex-general; Kyndra couldn't guess how much of it was his own.

'I misjudged you, Hagdon,' the Davaratch said calmly. 'I won't ask you to reconsider – you're too proud. But circumstances have changed. We both came here to fight Khronosta.' His eyes flickered to Kyndra. 'We both failed.'

Hagdon was silent.

'With the Lleu-yelin, we have a chance to strike back. Come to Thabarat, Hagdon. We will resupply the military, recharge our weapons.' The Davaratch lifted and dropped the once-glowing sword in its scabbard. 'When Khronosta strikes again, we will be ready.'

'You fool,' Ma said. She pushed herself to her feet. 'They do not need to strike again. They know I will not aid them.' She looked at Kyndra. 'The eldest will burn up as many of my people as he needs to gather the power to travel back in time. And we have no anchor to follow him.'

'You have me,' said a cracked voice.

It was a miracle the old man had survived the fighting. But then, Kyndra thought, he couldn't be without his tricks. Realdon Shune shuffled up to stand just behind the emperor. He had changed almost beyond recognition since his last meeting with Kierik in Solinaris. Then he had been young and self-satisfied, arrogant enough to stand up to a Starborn. Now the years rounded his shoulders and his skin was brown with liver spots. Only his eyes were the same; they still smouldered, still challenged.

'How did you come to be here?' she asked him.

'The Solar,' Shune said, 'though the ability to wield it has almost left me. I pour it all into extending my years.'

'Why?'

'Why not?' he croaked. 'I have no wish to die.'

Kyndra shook her head. 'But why spend your life serving the empire?'

'Sartya was Acre's future,' he said. 'At the time, I saw good in it.' His sharp eyes flickered to the Davaratch and Kyndra could not read the expression in them. When her only reply was a nod, Shune's brow creased. 'You are not like your predecessor. He was a slave to his ambition. Nothing else – no one else – mattered to him.'

'Don't judge Kierik too harshly,' Kyndra found herself saying. She looked beyond Orkaan's folded wing and saw Kait, conscious again, leaning against Nediah. She met the other woman's eyes. 'His choices cost him everything.'

'So,' the Davaratch said, 'it seems we have something to bargain with after all. I offer you the services of my relator. You offer me the services of your dragon. We have a common enemy.'

'We do,' Hagdon said and he drew his sword.

The glow around Shune was weak with evening approaching, but it was there. He met Hagdon's eyes over the emperor's shoulder and something passed between them.

The Davaratch's face paled when he reached for his weapon and found he couldn't move. 'Guards!' he screamed, but no help came. Abruptly, Kyndra realized that all of the soldiers surrounding him wore the black masks of the stealth force. They looked to their left, to a woman who stood in the shadows beneath the trees. Then they slowly backed away.

The Davaratch watched them wide-eyed before returning his gaze to Hagdon. 'I will give—'

The sentence ended in a gasp as Hagdon plunged his sword into the emperor's chest. The large man slumped, held up like a grotesque puppet by Shune's power. Cries rang out from the Republic and their Sartyan captives both, a mingling of shock, of triumph.

'Nothing you can give will bring them back,' Hagdon said and pulled his sword free.

The glow about Shune faded, dropping the emperor to earth. 'Paasa,' Kyndra heard Hagdon whisper, 'Tristan.'

She could have stopped it. She had seen Hagdon's intent in his face. But despite the chaos this would sow, she thought of everything she'd learned about Sartya; she thought of the trials laid out before them all, and was glad she hadn't.

Hagdon calmly wiped his blade on the emperor's mantle and sheathed it. He glanced again at Realdon Shune and the old man nodded.

'I should thank you, Hagdon.'

The voice came from the treeline. Iresonté stood there, a blue-limned cloak over one arm. The woman's chill eyes gazed at the corpse of the Sartyan emperor and she smiled. Shadows resolved into figures, masked and in black. Those stealth force who had abandoned the emperor went to join them.

'You let him die,' Hagdon said tonelessly. 'Why?'

'It was time,' Iresonté replied, dismissive, as if they weren't speaking of the ruler of all Sartya. Her eyes flickered towards Kyndra. 'Everything is changing.'

'You think the Fist will follow *you*?' Hagdon looked at his own clenched hand. 'You may have the loyalty of the stealth force, but the army supported your insurrection only because they believed it the will of the emperor.'

Iresonté gestured. Along the line, the stealth force donned their cloaks and vanished one by one. How had she come by these resources, Kyndra wondered, when ambertrix was so scarce?

'Play with your rebellion,' the dark-haired woman said. 'When we meet again, it will be for the last time.' She swung the cloak around her shoulders and was gone.

'I wish they'd never invented those,' Taske murmured.

38

Samaya, Acre
Hagdon

The storm was easing, wind dying to a fitful breeze. Without it, the stench of the slaughtered rose up around them. Blood had collected in a fallen shield, its lip of beaten metal holding the liquid like a grisly cup. Hagdon gazed at it a moment longer before looking up. 'Drop your weapons,' he said to the surviving Sartyans, corralled amidst the ranks of the Republic. How strange to think of them as Sartyans and not as his men. Their eyes moved from the dragon to the Starborn and they complied. Kyndra was certainly striking, Hagdon thought, clad in a robe that wasn't quite smoke and wasn't quite water, her every tattoo aglow.

His eyes returned to the emperor's body. There was a buzzing in his ears – perhaps it was the others speaking, or the sound of his thoughts fighting to escape. Sartya's ruler looked small in death. Everyone did. But he'd imagined the Davaratch would be different. This was the man he'd built his life around, whom he'd pledged to protect. In the end, he was just another corpse at Hagdon's feet.

He turned, walked away; he had to put some distance between himself and the life he had taken. His throat felt tight, a knot of words he could never say.

'Hagdon –' a voice began.

'Give him a moment,' someone else said and Hagdon wanted to laugh. As if he needed a moment to come to terms with the death of his nephew's killer. As if a moment could ever be enough.

He didn't know how long he'd been staring into the feature-less dusk before a question roused him. 'What will you do now?'

It was a woman's voice. For a wild, hopeless second, he thought it was Paasa, his sister. Instead, Irilin stood there. There was blood in her pale hair, staining her cheek. 'You're hurt,' he said.

'I'd probably be dead if it wasn't for you. I came to thank you. Besides,' she added, gesturing at him, 'you look a lot worse.'

She was right. Gore coated his armour, matted the feathers of his cloak. Some of the blood was his and a dozen new wounds smarted impatiently, awaiting attention. 'I don't know how to heal,' Irilin said, 'or I'd offer.'

Hagdon was glad she didn't; he still carried the deep-seated suspicion of aberrations common to all Sartyans. Just one of the opinions he'd probably have to revise, he thought, in the days to come.

'What will you do now?' Irilin asked again.

Hagdon glanced at the remaining soldiers of the Republic. 'Take up Taske's offer, I suppose. Someone needs to put Acre back together.' But the truth was he had nothing left. No ruler to serve, no army to lead, no family to protect.

'I'm sure Kyndra would welcome your help.'

There was an edge to her voice that Hagdon couldn't decipher. 'And what of you?' he said.

Irilin was silent for a few moments. 'I lost a friend to Acre. I'm afraid I'll lose another.' She paused, met his eyes. 'He's on his way to a place called Ben-haugr.'

'I know of it,' Hagdon said tightly. 'It's not somewhere I'd venture, had I a choice.'

'Why not?'

'It's a ruin, a hill of the dead. That's what Ben-haugr translates to in old Acrean. There is a . . . power there that keeps others away.' He could tell by the hardening of her face that his warning would go unheeded.

'It's Gareth's only hope,' Irilin said. 'I can't lose him as well.'

'I will talk to Taske. If our road leads north, perhaps we may accompany you.'

She frowned. 'Why would you risk your Republic's lives to help someone you don't even know?'

'Your friend is like you? A Wielder?' When she nodded, he said, 'Then his aid would be invaluable. Without the emperor, the Fist is the only power capable of holding Sartya together. If the army were to follow Iresonté . . .' Hagdon folded his arms. 'Kyndra's alliance with the Republic is a powerful one – one I doubt Iresonté will challenge directly. Instead, she'll work to divide our strength.'

'How?'

'There's always Rairam.' He watched her closely. 'Are you saying Kyndra wouldn't defend her homeland?'

Irilin shook her head. 'If the Khronostians succeed, Iresonté won't have an army to march into Rairam. Can't she see that?'

'Perhaps she underestimates the threat, or is blinded by her position. Once you've tasted power, it's hard to let it go.'

He could feel her eyes on him, too sharp, too knowing, and he looked away. 'In any case,' he said, studying the night as it crept stealthily through the forest, 'we need a plan to gather additional allies, a base to work from. Iresonté will spread news of the emperor's death, she'll rally Sartya against the Starborn, against me.' The words wearied him; Acre was balanced on a knifepoint, poised to slip over the edge into chaos. 'We will have to answer her.'

'You will lead us?' Irilin said, forcing Hagdon's eyes back to hers. She regarded him narrowly, her face silvered by the sheen of the moon. It made her seem older, stranger, a creature from a world he knew nothing about.

'I'm a murderer,' he said, 'and now an oathbreaker. Do Sartya's enemies want such a man to lead them?'

Irilin said nothing, pale in the light of her magic. She looked sad and determined. Hagdon wished he had her confidence. He pulled off his gauntlet. Beneath the mail, his palm was red; blood had found a way inside and collected under his nails. After a moment, he held out his hand to her. 'Might we start again?'

Standing in a field of corpses wasn't the best prelude to friendship, but Irilin clasped his bloodied hand and shook it, her grip firm. 'Yes,' she said. 'I think we might.'

Brenwym, Rairam
The Starborn

Brenwym. It was as Jhren had said: after the Breaking, there was nothing left of her home. She barely recognized the familiar streets she'd played in as a child. Only the hills and the mountains and the river remained the same. Otherwise all was skeletal, a ghost town, the struts of burned-out houses pointing accusing fingers at the sky.

But the southern edge of town was a different story. There her people worked at the calm, steady pace of those well-used to labour. Fresh-sawn logs were stacked in piles near bundles of straw ready for thatching. Strangers walked among them, wearing the plaid tunics of the northern Dales and the bright shirts common in Dremaryn. They worked as diligently as the survivors of the Breaking, as if Brenwym were their home too.

Less than a wisp of starlight, Kyndra watched them. They must have been toiling through the summer, for some buildings were already complete and she could see figures moving about inside. Brenwym wouldn't be as large as before and it certainly wouldn't be the same, but it *would* be here. Once, she'd have felt comforted by the thought.

She summoned *Raad*, remounted, and rode through the town. Today the star's power took the form of a great horse with eyes of shadow and sun. She kept a hold on *Fas* too, cloaking herself. So far, channelling three stars was her limit, though she knew Kierik had woven dozens simultaneously when he separated Rairam from Acre.

Finally, she found the two she was searching for. They wore heavy gloves and overalls smudged with dirt. Jarand was holding a plank steady while Reena sawed through it. The end thumped to the ground and Reena lowered the saw, wiping away sweat with her free hand.

Kyndra went closer; she wanted to see their faces. Making sure *Fas* concealed her, she came to rest a few steps from them, watching as Jarand handed Reena a mug. They were flushed with exertion, but they looked well, unchanged save for a weary cast to her mother's eyes.

She wasn't sure why she'd come here, following some instinct from the time she'd been only Kyndra. But that same instinct made her stretch out a transparent hand, no heavier than light, leaving her fingers to hover inches from her mother's cheek. For just a moment she kept them there, reaching.

A cloud blocked the sun and Kyndra let her hand fall. Reena shivered. She put her mug down on the workbench and looked around, her gaze passing right through Kyndra.

'What is it?' Jarand asked.

'I . . .' Reena's eyes swept the smoke-stained cobbles of the town, the people labouring to rebuild it. 'Nothing. I was thinking . . . I just thought it was her. Somehow I thought it was her.'

Jarand put down his own mug and went to enfold her in his

arms. 'Reena,' he whispered and his words were near-stolen by the wind. 'It won't help, this constant searching, it will wear you out.'

'I can't help it,' Reena said and tears slid down her cheeks. 'I think of her all the time, every minute. Sometimes I think I'll turn around and see her there. I don't even know if she's . . . if she's alive or dead.'

'Shhh,' Jarand murmured, stroking her hair. He kissed her forehead, kissed a tear from her cheek. 'She's alive, of course she's alive. She's a smart girl, Reena. And she said she'd come back. She gave us her promise.'

'What's a promise?' Reena spoke into Jarand's shoulder, her voice choked. 'She's so young, never been away from home. There's so much I should have said to her, that I wish I could say to her.'

Kyndra watched as her mother began to sob, her body shaking, tears soaking Jarand's shirt. He held her, murmuring words too low to make out and stroking the red hair that tangled around her face. All it would take was a relaxing of will and Reena and Jarand would be able to see her.

But they wouldn't see their daughter. They would see a Starborn, a sovereign being of power and ice. They wouldn't recognize her. How then could she reveal herself, knowing it meant telling them that the daughter they loved was gone? Let them believe her alive and unchanged just a little longer.

We can only ever be who we are.

The Starborn drew a breath. She turned away, putting Brenwym at her back. Far to the west, beyond the curve of the world, the sun was rising in the Heartland.